A ROYAL FLUSH

Libbie Richman

iUniverse, Inc.
Bloomington

A Royal Flush

This is a work of fiction. All of the characters, names, incidents, organizations, and dialogue in this novel are either the products of the author's imagination or are used fictitiously.

iUniverse books may be ordered through booksellers or by contacting:

iUniverse
1663 Liberty Drive
Bloomington, IN 47403
www.iuniverse.com
1-800-Authors (1-800-288-4677)

ISBN: 978-1-4759-4195-1 (sc)
ISBN: 978-1-4759-4194-4 (hc)
ISBN: 978-1-4759-4193-7 (e)

Library of Congress Control Number: 2012913912

Printed in the United States of America

iUniverse rev. date: 8/27/2012

This book is dedicated, in loving memory, to my devoted parents, Henry and Rachel Fox, Holocaust survivors, who dedicated themselves to preserving the memory of the millions who perished.

I miss you.
Libbie

CHAPTER 1

She felt delusional. She couldn't focus. Her mind kept wandering. She knew she was exhausted, but why was it so hard to concentrate? The driver in the limo had just said something about pulling over to let a fire engine go by. She felt anxious. She had been fine until today.

Lisa examined the book in her hand, and closed her eyes, remembering the last time she was in California, more than two years ago. She fell in love with superstar Yale Frye, and he with her. She never got over him, but returned home from L.A. to make a final effort to save her stagnant marriage. A marriage, that if nothing else, had given her two marvelous sons.

Leaving Yale Frye was one of the most difficult things she ever did. However, she was smart enough to realize if she walked away from the marriage, and her two teenage boys, without trying to salvage the relationship, she would leave with permanent doubts and guilt.

Her love affair with Yale was brief, by comparison, to the years of history with her husband. But Yale had given her, in their short time together, a sense of herself—her essence, and the realization that the life she had been leading, was not nearly enough to sustain her for the rest of her life. Yale had made her feel alive, really alive, and special in a way no one ever had before.

She was afraid of change and never denied it. But she was more afraid of her life meaning less, and being much less than she knew it could. She wasn't sure if it was stupidity or bravery that finally forced her hand. She asked Ronnie for a divorce.

Ronnie tried to talk her out of it. He was in love with her, and worse, very afraid of being alone and letting go of the dependency which he misinterpreted for bonding.

Traumatized for the last two years, it was only now that she was coming to terms with the realization that pain was often the price for change.

Her meeting with superstar Yale Frye was a consequence of her intervention when a member of a radical organization attempted to shoot him during a concert performance. Yale wasn't injured, however Lisa was shot during the struggle with the assailant holding the pistol. Her hospitalization led to her first meeting with the singer.

The following weeks, after the assassination attempt on Yale, Lisa had the opportunity to get to know him. When he took her to his Beverly Hills estate to recuperate, they fell in love.

Yale had never been the classic celebrity. He was not arrogant or egotistical. He was not selfish or self absorbed. And he was not a snob, like many who made it big.

Yale was charming, warm, sensitive, and gifted. He could grab and hold an audience as few other entertainers of his caliber. He had been able to sustain success in the competitive entertainment arena for over two decades without diminishing in popularity.

Lisa was lost in thought, in the back of the limo, on the way to her final book signing session, when the driver, a young man in his early twenties, commented, "Ms. Klein, I'd like to say, I really liked your book, "Run—Don't Walk." I recognized you from the picture on the back of the jacket. Although, I thought you'd be taller for some reason."

"Thank you," Lisa answered. "I'm glad you liked it. It's my first novel, you know. I still can't believe it's been on the best seller lists two months."

Lisa put her head back against the leather interior, closing her eyes again, proud that someone she'd never met before would take the time to tell her they liked her book. It meant a lot. It was what finally gave her independence, and a new meaningful identity. She finally believed in herself.

It had taken the last two years of hell and confusion to get her to this point. It had taken hard work, tears, frustration, pain, anger and determination. The voyage had been agonizing. The obstacles at times felt insurmountable. But she did it. She proved she could stand on her own, and she had something worthwhile to offer. The most difficult part was handling the guilt she felt in hurting and disrupting, so many lives in order to make a new life for herself. It was so hard admitting she'd inflicted pain as a result of her desperate need to be her own person.

When Lisa left the arms of Yale Frye to return to her husband and sons, Marc and Steve, it was their needs which forced her to return to her role of wife and mother. Guilt convinced her she had no alternative. Ronnie had given her an ultimatum. She was pushed into giving him a date when she'd be returning from L.A., back to where he felt she belonged. Her two sons were also constant reminders of her obligations and responsibilities.

Less than a month back in Canton Ohio, after leaving Yale Frye, she was convinced she couldn't go on living a charade any longer. She felt suffocated. She resented being stifled by other people's demands.

Any attempt on Ronnie's behalf to bring romance back into their lives ended in frustration for both of them. Ultimately, they chose to live as "friends," avoiding intimacy, hoping they could somehow rebuild, what was a failing relationship. They didn't quarrel, nor did they broach topics which could cause a disquieting atmosphere to the congeniality they maintained. They simply drifted further and further apart, until she couldn't live in the state of silent avoidance any longer.

As the limo hit a bump in the road now, Lisa's insides also reacted while she reflected on the turbulence which had dominated her from the time she first filed for divorce, to the time she moved out of her home. With terror, she left a safe life. A life of familiar things and sacred moments. What hurt so badly was that she cared about Ronnie, just not in the way he wanted. She loved her sons, but eventually they would go on to make lives for themselves. She needed to have a chance to find happiness for herself, and discover if it was something real and attainable, not just an illusion. Lisa knew if she didn't try when she was approaching forty, there would never be a right time.

Lisa was acutely aware she often acted on impulse. Therefore, she was careful not to make irreversible changes in her life without a great deal of deliberation and consideration. She was accustomed to her coexistence with Ronnie being less of a marriage than either of them wanted, but she was unable to live with the pretense that—"you made your bed, now lie in it". For a long time she had accepted her mundane existence without anger, but the taste of "honey" Yale Frye had placed on her dry palate evoked a new desire to rebel against the conventional-going nowhere lifestyle she hated.

It wasn't all her fault. And it wasn't all Ronnie's. Both had taken too much for granted, moving through the years with nonchalance and complacency, instead of attempting to keep the fires burning. Life was a pattern, and the style had become old. Desire to please became a chore. Nights were filled with isolation. Both felt lonely.

She and Ronnie had married at a young age. They were teenagers escaping the restrictions imposed by their parents. They ran away together, and played house, so as not to have to follow other people's directives. Lisa was more mature than Ronnie. She always had been. Therefore, she assumed the role of controller in their relationship. She handled the majority of responsibility, from the finances to the planned weekend get together with friends. She handled the meals, the shopping, and her job. Lisa maintained the nurturing, supportive role for more than two decades. It was only the last few years when she admitted she was sick of it. She was miserable and filled with resentment.

Ronnie liked their life. He couldn't comprehend why Lisa craved change. He was happy with the way things were, and pleased he had someone to take care of him, never feeling a need for deviance. He eventually blamed Lisa's affair with Yale Frye for the ruination of their marriage. He was willing to forgive Lisa for her brief affair, since he wasn't, and never had been, a very sexual person. He wanted a life with Lisa. He wanted them to stay together. He wanted them just to try a little harder to please each other. For a while Ronnie would bring her gifts, show more attention, and fake sexual desire to try and save their relationship. Lisa knew it was an effort—an honest one—but it was Ronnie trying to do what he thought Lisa might want, not Ronnie being honest with himself.

There was nothing harder than always being on guard; being afraid of doing something the other might not approve of, and trying to save what couldn't be saved. The effort was draining, and left a trail of anger. Ronnie became sacrificial…Lisa felt guilty…Ronnie promised to change…Lisa didn't want him to change who he was for her. It was a sad, hopeless situation. There was no remedy. Both knew it, but only Lisa would admit it. Finally, she became the antagonist, asking out of the relationship.

After Ronnie capitulated, seeing he had no choice, the hardest thing for both of them was explaining to their boys that they were separating and parting permanently. They were getting divorced. Lisa, again, was designated to relate the situation to Marc and Steve.

It was near the end of dinner, on a rare night when they ate together as a family, when Lisa stated, "Boys, don't leave the table for a minute. I need to tell you something very important."

"Oh, oh," Marc voiced. "This sounds like an—I mean business talk."

"Marc, Steve, there is no easy way to say this. Dad and I are splitting up. We're getting divorced. We've discussed it. We aren't happy together anymore, so we are going to start separate lives."

"Boys," Ronnie said, his eyes filled with tears, "Mom is not happy. I'm agreeing, that's all. I don't want the divorce. I love mom. But she said she wants her freedom, and I'm too tired to keep fighting her. She's leaving us."

"Thanks Ronnie. I'm glad you put things in 'perspective' for our sons. Well boys, dad is right. I want my freedom from him, and our marriage. I am, and always will be, your mom. I'll be there for you any way I can. Always! We love you as we always have, and that will never change. We will just love you from separate houses."

The boys sat silently, unable to comprehend they were no longer going to be a family. She wanted to leave them. She wanted freedom. Dad said so. They must have been a real burden. "Mom," Steve said sharply, "I'm living here, in this house, with dad. I'm not going to live with you."

"Me either," Marc said, looking at his mother's dry eyes, while his fathers were overflowing. "You know mom, I think you're a spoiled 'Jap', who never appreciated dad anyway. He doesn't need you. He'll have us."

"I'm sorry boys. I love you. I always will. I realize that you can't understand all of this. I hope you know I'm always going to be your mom—"

"Sure!" Marc shouted, "You'll be a mom, when you feel like it; when you aren't busy being "free". Sorry, we kept you from being somewhere else. Well, if you want freedom, go ahead. But I thought you liked being our mom."

"I do, Marc. I love being your mom. I love being Steve's mom. I just can't be dad's wife anymore." What she almost said, was that she couldn't be dad's "mom" anymore, since that would have been more accurate. Brutal. But true. And Lisa didn't want to stoop to that.

"Well Marc," Steve said, "You were right about women. They're never happy."

"Stop it!" Lisa shouted. "I've been here all of your lives—for all of you, including dad. Don't judge me!"

"I hate you! I hate you!" Steve screamed, bursting into tears, and running from the table.

"Mom," Marc asked, with tears rolling down his face, "Maybe we can all try harder, so you'll be happy? Maybe we can do something so you'll change your mind? Maybe—"

"No, Marc. I'm sorry. I can't change my mind—"

"Bullshit!" Marc yelled. "You can change your mind! You just don't want to! You don't care enough about us—I hate you, too! You're selfish!" He, too, ran from the table.

"Well, I guess the boys want to stay here with you, Ronnie. It seems I've been elected to be the one to move out."

"Not if you change your mind, Lisa."

"I'll pack and be out by the end of the week, Ronnie. Thanks for 'helping' me tell the boys." She couldn't keep the sarcasm from her tone.

"Get fucked, bitch! You know, I've tried and tried and tried! Right now, even I hate you!" He, too, left the table. Lisa sat there, alone, surrounded by the dirty dishes, and leftover food she'd prepared earlier. Calmly, an hour later, she went and packed a suitcase, leaving the dinner dishes on the table, and left the house. She checked into a cheap motel, and spent the next five days looking for an apartment. When she checked out of the motel and handed her credit card to the cashier, she was told her card was not valid. Ronnie had closed their account. When she went to the bank, their joint savings account had been depleted leaving a five-dollar balance.

"Well, so much for friendly divorces," She had said to herself, as she drove her car to the apartment she'd rented. In the middle of that night she went to the house and took Ronnie's new car from the driveway. The next day she sold the car, in a neighborhood where crime was high, to a stranger, for twice what had been in their savings account. She then took a cab to her apartment and waited ten days in the ugly, cheaply, furnished brownstone before going to her house to get some of her belongings. When her key wouldn't open the doors, she realized Ronnie changed the locks. She broke a window, took a ladder from behind the garage, climbed in, and called an attorney for immediate help. He said, by law she shouldn't have broken in. He advised her to leave. She decided differently. She called a moving company that would be there within the hour.

When Ronnie came home and saw the moving van, he threatened to call the police. "Go ahead, asshole. It'll be the first thing you've ever done on your own!" He slapped her across the face. It was the first time he'd ever hit her in all the years they'd been together. "So Ronnie—this is what happens when love dies? Anything else you want to do, Ronnie? Go ahead. Well, Ronnie, why don't you go down the list of things I never appreciated? The things I took for granted—go ahead—if it makes it easier for you. It doesn't matter, Ronnie—I've lost my boys because of you! You love me so much that you sat at the table—not only watching me lose them—but helping me lose them. You are a schmuck, Ronnie. I despise you! Now—get the hell away from me! I'm only taking what's mine. My attorney will be in touch about the rest."

"You bitch! You dumb bitch! You don't know how good you had it!"

"Right, Ronnie! So good, I couldn't stay! Ronnie, get away from me, before I lose it."

"Well, that's nothing new for you—you sick bitch!"

"You should know—you're responsible for making me sick—you pathetic excuse for a man—who can't even get it up without playing with himself!"

"Go to hell, Lisa!"

"I've been in Hell—living with you! Don't you get it? I'm trying to get out!"

"Stop—Stop—" Marc and Steve yelled, watching the scene from the driveway. Lisa didn't know how long they had been there. She looked at her boys, and cried for the first time. "I'm sorry boys. Forgive me. Maybe, one day you'll understand."

She got in the car, and had the moving van follow her to the low-income apartment she was renting.

Ronnie didn't bother following her. He knew, then, it was over—really over for them—permanently.

CHAPTER 2

"Ms. Klein, are you alright?" The limo driver inquired as he waited for the red light to change. She had been lost in remembering, unaware tears were rolling down her face.

"Yes. I'm fine. Just nervous. My first book tour. Don't mind me."

Lisa put her head against the window and watched the morning rush hour traffic, feeling the weight of loss as she remembered how close she and her boys were until she left Ronnie. She missed the way they would confide in her, tease her, worry about her, and most of all—adore her. She wasn't sure if the lack of breakfast caused the sudden queasiness in her gut or the vividness of recollections she couldn't dispel.

She had lost the special relationship with Marc and Steve when she chose to fulfill herself outside of her confining marriage. A lousy tradeoff, losing what mattered most, to gain what matters most. There was no denying everything in life has a price. Maybe one day her sons would understand that everything is not black and white. Maybe, they'd realize how hard it was for her to leave the security of marriage, a spouse, a nice standard of living, friends, her home, her safe haven, and opt for freedom of soul and spirit. It had cost her the love of her sons, financial stability, a year of doubt, fear, agony, and apprehension. A year of struggling to survive monetarily, and working hours on her writing each night, to pursue a dream, her dream. A year of macaroni and cheese, and parents who called her 'crazy'. A year of sons who wrote short notes from school, once a month, and saw her only twice during that first year, for a short visit, unwilling to forgive her for breaking up their home.

How ironic it was that twelve months from the time she'd left her home, and received her final decree, granting her the divorce—the paper that officially stated she was no longer married—was the same day she received an invitation in the mail to attend the marriage of Ronald Klein to Sue Blum. How ironic, that Ronnie found a new life for himself almost immediately, and someone new to take care of him. And she, who wanted the divorce, was isolated and the one left with nothing. That first year was hell. But she had survived. But, even now, with a best seller under her belt she couldn't let go of the pain.

Ronnie had been fair after the initial shock was over. He'd kept her on his Blue Cross until the divorce was final, knowing she needed medical coverage. He sent her the monthly checks for her portion of the net worth of their assets, which helped ease some of her burden, and he called once a month to see how she was. They were civil. Six months later, Ronnie started dating Sue Blum. He'd told her, and she was genuinely glad for him. He tried to be nice. He even sent a plant for her 40th birthday. But Lisa knew she'd never be able to forgive him for the way she was made out to be the enemy when she had told the boys they were splitting up. She remained polite and pleasant, realizing Ronnie was just too stupid to understand how hard he had made life for her. He never was in touch with her feelings; or his own for that matter. And now when they talked she was void of any feelings. She saw him only occasionally, for a specific reason, like the boys' birthdays. But, now, she was the outsider. When conversations got going, she'd usually leave early, to go home and sleep. Then when Ronnie asked her to come to the house for Thanksgiving dinner, after marrying Sue Blum, and he was, again, happy and in love, she went for lack of anything else to do. Actually, she was hoping she could recapture something of her former relationship with Marc and Steve. The dinner had been good. Ronnie remarked often what a good cook Sue was. She asked the boys about school. They said they were doing fine. She tried getting closer, and asked if they were dating anyone special. They said, "not really" in unison, when Sue said, "Come on guys; tell the truth." It was only when her two sons looked at Sue Blum and said harmoniously, "Not now, mom," directing their remarks to Sue, that she snapped. Lisa recalled, now, how she had stood up, looked at her boys, and shouted, "I'm your mother! I'm not dead yet, even if that's what you wish. So, as long as

I'm alive, have the fucking courtesy not to call anyone else mom—and if you can't do that—at least in front of me—don't call me—don't write—don't visit, and don't ever see me again!" With that Lisa left the table shaking. Her final remarks were directed at her ex-husband. As she looked Ronnie in the face, she said, "I can't believe you hate me this much."

She had left the house; the house that had been her home for more than half her life, and drove to a bar downtown; something she'd never done before. She got drunk and sick. She passed out, then began screaming uncontrollably after regaining consciousness. The kicker was, when the paramedics took her to the hospital, and asked if there was someone they could call, she had no one, not one fucking person, for them to call. She signed herself out after a few hours in the emergency room, and went back to her apartment by cab. When she stepped out of the cab, Ronnie and the boys were there, waiting for her. She told them to go to hell, before fainting on the sidewalk.

That night, six months ago, was a turning point. The boys and Ronnie took care of her for a week. By the end of the week they all had re-established a basic relationship. They could communicate again, and accept the changes they had been battling against. It would never be like it was before. But it was something. It was the start of some understanding without all the bitterness. It was making the best out of what was, and letting go of what never would be again. They tried to be more considerate of each other. It wasn't what she wanted. She was okay about being civil with Ronnie, but still resented his actions which attributed to her separation from her sons. And she wasn't comfortable about being friends with her sons. She was their mother, not their friend. But for the moment it would suffice; it would have to. Lisa knew they all needed more time to heal. She didn't push for more than the boys were able to give. It hurt to accept meager distributions of affection from the two boys who had given her life purpose for the last sixteen years. But something was better than nothing. She needed her boys in her life.

Ronnie and the boys had cleaned her apartment. They cooked for her. They helped her back on her feet. Then at the end of a week of nurturing, when she was going from her dismal bedroom to the kitchen, she overheard her boys talking. Ronnie was at work. The boys were putting a dinner together for her.

"Steve, did you notice how empty the cupboards are. There is hardly any food, just a lot of boxes of macaroni and cheese. Mom always kept lots of food at home. Do you think she's hurting for money?"

"Marc, I think she fucked up. She left dad, and both of us. Now she's living in this hole. I think she's got a screw loose, or something."

"Do you think dad would have taken her back, Steve?"

"Probably. I'm not so sure he really loves Sue. I think he married her to show mom he doesn't have to be alone. Sue is weird anyway. She talks baby talk to dad, and thinks it's cute. I think it's nauseating."

"I thought you liked her, Steve?"

"She's okay. I just think she's weird."

"I don't like her that much. But since dad does, I act like I do."

"Why, Marc?"

"'Cause I feel sorry for dad. He was like a lost puppy after mom left. At least, now, he has someone who cares about him."

"Marc, why do you think mom stopped caring about him?"

"Who knows? Maybe she cared, but just got bored. You know how dad is—work, eat, sleep; work, eat, sleep."

"I think dad should give mom money instead of buying Sue all that jewelry and stuff. Look how mom is living. Did you notice how messy this place was when we got here? That's just not like mom."

"Steve, mom never got presents from dad like Sue does, did she?"

"I don't know. But, I think, we should tell dad that mom is really broke. Look in this cupboard. There is only one box of cereal in it."

Lisa went back to bed. She felt sudden determination she hadn't felt in a long time. She didn't want pity. She didn't want their help. She had to prove to her boys that she was capable. She wanted them to see her as a successful person. She had to focus on building a new life. She had to accomplish something meaningful, not just for herself, but to regain the respect of her sons.

She declined Ronnie's check for five hundred dollars in front of her boys that night. She asked them to keep in touch, but to give her some space to work on her book. She said, she wanted to be ready with a manuscript by the beginning of the year. She kissed them goodbye that night, determined to make them proud of the woman they now felt so sorry for. She worked days as a telephone operator, and nights on her book. By January she had a manuscript to mail. She had saved a little money by eating cheaply and spending little. After hocking some old jewelry for cash, she took her money and sought out a literary agent to help sell her manuscript.

In eight weeks the book was sold, and now she had a novel on the New York Times bestseller list. She had agreed to promote the book, and her attorney estimated she could be financially secure by the end of the year since a lucrative sale of her novel for film rights was also in negotiation.

She had succeeded in her efforts. She was going to buy expensive watches for her sons to show them how their 'poor' mother prevailed; despite all the odds against her. She wouldn't have to be pitied by them anymore. She had attained her goal. She was triumphant!

When she got out of the limo in front of the bookstore she wondered if she should call Yale to say she was in town. It had been two years since she'd last seen him, but he had never been out of her heart in all that time.

"Welcome to L.A., Ms. Klein," the proprietor of the store greeted her cheerfully. "We have your table set up right here."

"Thanks. It's nice to be back," she responded, feeling suddenly as cheerful as the day was bright. With an irrepressible smile she noticed the line of people gathering outside the store.

CHAPTER 3

Ben Shinsky, Lisa's literary agent, had mapped out a three-month tour for the promotion of Lisa's novel, with autograph sessions, interviews and public appearances. She started the tour on the east coast and was concluding the signing sessions on the west coast. Ben told her he had offers for movie rights, but was holding out for a more lucrative offer. Lisa was new to the literary field, therefore allowed Ben to handle most of the intricate business details. She had felt confident in his abilities from their first meeting, when he called her from New York to ask her what she expected from her first novel.

She said to Ben, during their first telephone conversation, when he sounded patronizing, "Look, I don't need to be a Hemingway. It's enough I'm Lisa Klein. If you don't like the manuscript, please return it. I'll find someone who will appreciate its merits."

"I asked what you expected, I didn't say that I don't like it, Lisa."

"Well, Mr. Shinsky, I expect to make a lot of money, and get my name known. Then maybe I'll try to write like Hemingway. Right now, all I want is a chance to prove myself."

"Ms. Klein," he replied, "if I send you a plane ticket, how soon can you come to New York so we can talk business?"

"Well, Mr. Shinsky, if you call the airline and find out when the next flight is, I'll be on it."

They signed a contract four days later. He took time from his busy schedule to show her New York himself. Watching her very closely, Ben concluded she was capable of selling herself, and her book, with a little guidance. He introduced her to Jean Roth, an expert in advertising and marketing, and asked Lisa to stay in New York for two more weeks. He wanted her to work with Jean. Lisa quit her job with one long distance call, and stayed in New York with the one suitcase she'd arrived with.

Jean Roth became a fast friend, mentor, and ear for Lisa, who needed someone. Lisa worked hard to make herself appear confident, poised, witty, and a marketable commodity. She had her hair lightened, lost fifteen pounds in three weeks, learned how to sign her name quickly, how to smile even when distressed, and how to create an illusion that would make her name and face memorable. Jean taught her how to be an actress in just weeks, and gave her the reassurance no one else ever had. Jean was honest and giving. She showed understanding, and most of all was never judgmental. She gave Lisa what she needed most, and had for a long time, total and unconditional support. The initial two-week stay in New York evolved into two months. When Lisa returned to her shabby apartment, in Canton, she came back with a fifty thousand-dollar advance from the publishing house, and four new suitcases of clothes for a book tour. Jean was going to get her started on the tour and planned to accompany her. Jean stayed with Lisa on the east coast and assisted for part of the Midwest. When Lisa was scheduled to leave for Colorado, Jean said, "Honey, I showed you where your wings are, and how to use them. Now fly!"

"Jean, I'm scared. I can't—"

"No, Lisa, 'can't' is not a word we ever use. Remember?"

"Lisa—FLY! You can and you will. I've arranged hotels, limos, and an aid to meet you at each stop. The game is yours; now play to win. Call me whenever you want, to tell me how great you feel, and how proud of yourself you are."

Lisa left for Colorado alone. She built confidence as she went, and a gratitude to Jean, she knew she'd never be able to repay. When she arrived in Colorado, a limo was waiting with her name in the front dash glass. A young woman, Joyce, greeted her at the car. Joyce directed the porter to load her luggage. Joyce accompanied Lisa to the hotel, gave her a key to her suite, a package of papers, and indicated she'd meet her at the bookstore in the morning, for the signing session. Then she left. Inside the packet was a list of arrangements for Lisa, mapping out the next twenty-four hours, until she was to leave for her next destination. At the bottom of the last piece of paper Jean had written, "Celebrities are made, not born. Head tall. Shoulders back. Pretty smile, and positive attitude—Go!"

A porter led her to the suite. At three she was dressed, as designated on the outlined itinerary, and welcomed a local columnist for an interview. At five, dinner was brought to her room. At seven, a limo took her to a local fundraising event, where she mingled for two hours. At ten, the limo brought her back to the hotel for the night. At seven, the next morning, she had one cup of coffee, a banana, and showered. At eight, the hotel management sent a hair stylist and cosmetologist to her suite as prearranged. At nine, she dressed, and by ten was ready to leave. By eleven, she was at the bookstore, warmly thanking everyone for coming, and signed books for three hours. By five, she was ready to check out of the hotel and leave for the flight to the next destination. This routine continued with little modification. In some cities Lisa stayed an extra day to attend a special function. Otherwise, she followed the schedule.

Now she was in L.A. The final leg of her tour. She had asked to stay at the Oak Plaza Hotel, where she once shared a romantic night with Yale Frye. And here, in L.A., she was scheduled to appear on The Myra Sullivan show, the highest rated TV talk show, promoting her book. The last time she was in California she had appeared on Myra Sullivan's talk show, with Yale, to explain the events surrounding the attempted assassination during his concert tour.

She forced her thoughts back to the present. She sat at the table readied for her. In half an hour they would open the doors to the line forming outside the store. She unbuckled her attaché case, pulling out a large envelope, containing newspaper clippings she continuously saved. She put the ones about her novel aside, and glanced through the articles about Yale she had been accumulating for the last two years. She thought about how close they once were; how interwoven their bodies and souls had become in a short period of time. She wondered if he thought about her as often as she thought about him. It was doubtful, considering there wasn't a day since she'd left Yale she didn't think about him.

Lisa remembered, after she returned to Canton, how hard it had been to resume her old life style; to be an appendage to everyone else's life. She had so many obligations she couldn't neglect. Her efforts to put Yale out of her mind were impossible. Her longing for him was so intense that seven days after leaving him, when she was alone, she called him. She told him how much she missed him. She asked him how it was going on his new concert tour. He'd said, he was able to overcome his fear of crowds and was getting wonderful reviews. He said, it felt good to be busy and discovered he was stronger than he realized. He told her he was taking the show to Europe after he concluded the tour in the states. Then he inquired if she had gone back to work. She lied and said yes, not wanting to tell him she barely left her room because of the depression she couldn't shake since she'd left him.

He told her he was writing new material and hardly had a spare minute. Then he said it would be best for them not to call each other. If they had to let go of each other it would be easier for both of them if they put it behind them. He suggested they just remember a special time that ended. She had said she agreed, but only called this time to say she missed him, adding the decision to go home was the hardest thing she'd ever done. He'd told her everyone had choices, and everyone had to live with the consequences of their decisions. She wished him well, sending along her love to his mother, after inquiring if Ruth was well. Yale said, he'd pass on her love and told her to be happy. When she got off the phone she went to bed, staying there for five days, praying she would die. She told Ronnie she had a virus. It was only when her parents called from the resort in New York, where they were vacationing, to say they were coming to visit her and the boys that she forced herself out of bed. The visit with her parents proved to be a good diversion from her self-pity. She was kept occupied so she didn't dwell on her perpetual unhappiness. Her folks stayed three weeks. After they left to return to their home in Florida, she was busy getting the boys outfitted for school. Eventually, she resumed a routine and stopped torturing herself about what might have been. The hardest times were at night, when dreams so vivid about Yale woke and plagued her so she couldn't go back to sleep. Finally, she couldn't stand it and bought sleeping pills that were sold over-the-counter. When one pill didn't work anymore, she went to two. When two pills weren't enough she took three, until Ronnie discovered what she was doing and called her psychiatrist. She went back into therapy. Dr. Bruce, her "shrink," was the only person she trusted enough to confide in. It took her months to resume normal activity and finally admit she had to attempt to find what it would take to make her a happier person.

Now, as she looked at the newspaper clippings in her hand, she thought Yale apparently had been able to adjust to life without her much easier than she thought he would. Maybe she was the ultimate fool, thinking he would long for her, as much as she did him, after they separated.

The first clipping she reread was from a gossip column, published only a month after she'd returned to Ronnie, in Canton, over two years ago.

> *"Yale Frye, has successfully returned to the place*
> *he belongs—the stage. Now that the radical group*
> *which planned to assassinate the superstar has been*
> *eliminated, and justice has prevailed; Yale is completing*
> *his concert tour.*
> *Yale is performing to sell out audiences.*
> *Yale indicated he was glad to be back on*
> *tour. And if you haven't seen his show yet; don't*
> *miss it! Mr. Frye—Welcome back."*

Lisa flipped through the clippings reading several of the familiar sentences again, as she had done so often, over the last two years:

> *"Yale Frye hosts and performs at AIDS Benefit*
> *in New York tonight, hoping to raise over a*
> *million dollars to help in financing programs*
> *dedicated to AIDS research."*

> *"Yale Frye attends New Orleans Jazz Festival*
> *with long time friend Marissa Myers."*

> *"Yale Frye attends Liza Minelli opening performance*
> *at Radio City Music Hall."*

"Yale Frye and Marissa Myers were seen dining at Tavern on the Green last night, alone, holding hands."

"Marissa Myers' divorce is final. Has Yale Frye been waiting for Marissa to be single again, before asking her to marry him?"

"Yale Frye attends wedding of business associate Philip Dodd. Is Yale getting ideas for a wedding of his own?"

"Yale Frye cancels performance in Denver, Colorado due to intestinal flu. Plans to reschedule the concert dates are indefinite."

"Yale Frye seen shopping at Cartier's. Could he be buying a diamond engagement ring for a special lady?"

"Yale Frye organizes benefit concert in Las Vegas for AIDS research. All monies to be allocated for people without medical insurance, to insure they receive medical assistance, and treatment when needed."

"Marissa Myers and her seven year old son, Josh, attend Disneyland Day of Doing, with Yale Frye. They join several other celebrities in giving a special day to hundreds of handicapped children."

"Yale Frye to appear on David Letterman's show Friday."

"Yale Frye attends tribute to Miles Davis with long time girlfriend Marissa Myers."

"Yale concludes U.S. tour of his latest show in San Francisco."

"Yale Frye to write the musical score for a Neil Simon play."

Lisa put the clippings back in the envelope thinking about her conversation with the clerk of the Oak Plaza Hotel. She had asked if she could change her room from the suite she was registered for, to room 1232, remembering the night in Yale arms, in room 1232, when she started to unravel the man beneath the image. The clerk had indicated it was a smaller room. She replied that it didn't matter. She had wanted the room for sentimental reasons. He switched her to room 1232 and asked if she'd like anything else. She had responded negatively, while actually thinking—"Yes. But I'm not sure he'd still be interested."

CHAPTER 4

The smog had lifted, but the air was heavy, and you knew it was going to be a bitch to be outside for long. The state still had a water shortage and the usually green grounds were dry and dull this hot August day.

Yale sat in his leather recliner in the spacious den of his Beverly Hills home reading the newspaper. He was up early and at his piano working before seven, but felt uninspired. After three hours of composing absolutely nothing, he showered and dressed. He looked through the mail his personal assistant, David, had dropped off the previous day. After making a couple of necessary calls he picked up the morning paper.

He was reading the sports section when his houseman, Victor, buzzed him on the intercom to let him know his mother was on the phone. Yale had instructed Victor earlier he didn't want to be disturbed and turned off the telephones in his bedroom, and in the den. Victor, however, had been with Yale long enough to know that when Yale said he didn't want to talk to anyone it didn't include his mother.

"Hi Ma, what's up? I thought you were scheduled to be at the hospital today." Ruth did volunteer work at Sinai Hospital two days a week, helping care for children afflicted with AIDS.

"I was there for a couple of hours, but my shoulder was throbbing from the arthritis so badly, I left early. I'm very stiff today. It's probably the weather."

"Ma, did you take your Celebrex?"

"Yeh, yeh. It doesn't help much. Yale did you read the paper today?"

"I just sat down with it a few minutes ago. Why?"

"Turn to page 4E, and hold on a minute; someone is on the other line."

Yale turned to page 4E, realizing why his mother had called. "At Bordins Book Store, on University Drive, Lisa Klein will be signing her best selling novel, "Run, Don't Walk" from noon to 3 P.M.. Ms. Klein is completing her autograph signing sessions here in Los Angeles today. She will appear on the Myra Sullivan show tomorrow. Lisa Klein has not been in Los Angeles for over two years, when she was here recuperating at the estate of Yale Frye, after intervening in an assassination attempt on mega star Yale Frye's life in Canton, Ohio. Her first novel has sold more than 3 million copies, and it has been verified, she has received several offers for screen rights to her novel. Lisa Klein is currently working on a second book, due to be released in time for the Christmas holidays. Her current best seller has been on top of the fictional sales charts for two months—and for good reason. If you haven't read, "Run, Don't Walk" yet, put it on your must read list. Lisa Klein's novel will open your eyes and touch your heart."

"Yale, are you there? Did you see the article?"

"Yeh Ma, I saw. I'm glad for her. She deserves good things to happen to her."

"So, Yale, are you going to get in touch with her?"

"I don't know. Maybe she would prefer not to see me."

"Maybe Yale. And maybe not. Well, I gotta go. I'm meeting Agnes for a quick lunch and to pick up the toys for the kids at the hospital she purchased. I'll talk to you later, Yale."

"Okay Ma. Have a good day. Don't overdue. I love you."

"I love you too. Bye, honey."

Yale looked at his watch. Since it was almost noon, he figured Lisa was probably at the bookstore by now. He wanted to see her, but was afraid. He knew she had divorced Ronnie from a magazine article he'd read when her book first came out, and had wondered why she never contacted him after her divorce. Maybe there was someone else in her life. He mulled over several possibilities until he glanced at his watch again and realized it was two o'clock.

On impulse, Yale got into his car and drove to his offices. He got David and asked him to drive his car. At ten to three they arrived at

Bordins Book Store. He sat in the car with David for forty-five minutes, waiting for the cutoff for the signing session. When there were only a few people remaining he stepped out of the car.

"How many people did you see inside, David?"

"Looked like about fifteen left. Want me to check again in a few minutes?"

"No. It's okay. Come on. Just remain nearby."

"It's okay Yale. You'll be able to get near her without being hassled."

"Maybe I should forget it, David?"

"Want me to ask if she'll come out to the car, Yale?"

"No. Thanks. Fuck it. Come on. If I don't see her, I'll regret it, and I know it."

They walked into the store. There were ten people still in the line to see her, in addition to the store employees, security people, and curiosity seekers. He was spotted immediately, although he wore his 'shades' and a sports cap, but casually purchased a copy of her book and got at the end of the line. He kept his head down, pretending to be engrossed in an excerpt from the book. She hadn't seen him yet, but he couldn't keep from peeking up at her. She looked wonderful. Her hair wasn't permed anymore, but worn in a soft bouncy bob. It was lighter than he remembered, but still auburn. She had lost weight. She looked sexy, yet sophisticated, in her Givenchy navy suit and red silk blouse. She was smiling warmly as she chatted. Her skin was tanned and glowing. Tiny beads of perspiration forced her bangs to cling to her forehead.

She wore no jewelry, other than a watch, and she appeared confident and poised. He observed that her nails were long and manicured as she handed a book to a young man. There were five people in front of him. His stomach was gurgling since he hadn't eaten all day. His palms were unusually moist. She looked up and spotted him.

He took his sunglasses off as he reached the signing table and said, "Once you stood in line for my autograph. Now, I'm standing in line for yours, Lisa."

"I'm sure this line was much shorter than the ones you always attract, Yale."

"I don't know about that. How are you, Lisa?"

"Tired. And sore from sitting," she said, smiling up at him with her almond shaped hazel eyes. "It was nice of you to come, Yale. Thank you."

"Would you have called me if I hadn't?"

"I'm not sure. I wanted to. But I don't know if I would have."

"How long are you in L.A. for?"

"I have to go to San Francisco for a benefit the day after tomorrow. Then I'm done touring."

"Are you free for dinner tonight? I'd like to talk to you before you have to leave."

"Are you asking me for a date, Yale?"

"Yes, I guess I am. Do you have other plans?"

"No. I have no other plans. And, yes, I'd love to have dinner with you."

"Where are you staying, Lisa? I'll call to see what time is good for you."

"I'm at the Oak Plaza, Yale. Room 1232."

He looked into her eyes feeling relief. He leaned over and kissed her cheek. "Can I pick you up at seven?"

"What should I wear?"

"The terry robe that hangs inside the bathroom would be fine."

"Be there at six and you've got a deal, Yale."

He laughed with her, and said he'd see her later as some store employees approached. He turned to leave when she called out to him, "Yale, don't you want your book signed?"

"Sure, I do. But I'll give you time to think about what you want to write."

"I'm a slow thinker, Yale."

"I'm in no hurry, Lisa."

Yale left with David. He dropped David off back at the office, then hurried home to change before going to see Lisa. He asked David to call the florist they frequently used and order three dozen red roses. He indicated he'd pick them up, so he could hand deliver them to Lisa himself. When he arrived home, Victor related Marissa called twice and left a number where she could be reached. She had told Victor there was an emergency. He and Marissa Myers were only an "item" in newsprint.

In truth, they were the best of friends, and nothing more. He helped her through her ugly divorce, and she had helped him with the loss of Lisa two years ago. He became Marissa's shoulder, and she his. Marissa's son, Josh, loved him and Yale enjoyed spoiling Josh. They were very close, like family, to one another. Yale had slept with Marissa only once a long time ago, when he was drunk and she was stoned. It was after a party they had attended together. Neither had dates that night, if he recalled correctly. They were both lonely, depressed, and had needed to feel the closeness of another body. When Yale had taken Marissa home that night, she'd asked him to stay. Somehow, they wound up in bed releasing pent up emotions. They didn't talk about it afterwards, and resumed their relationship as best friends, knowing that particular night was just a purging for both of them. Neither wanted to change the relationship they already shared. The only other sex they may have had was party sex when they were young and dumb.

Yale took the message slip from Victor and dialed the number on it. She answered the phone on the first ring.

"Marissa, it's Yale. What's wrong?"

"Yale, I'm at Pam's house. My house was set on fire. Yale, Josh is missing." She was crying into the receiver. "Tony said he'd get even with me for ruining his life when we got divorced, but I didn't think he'd do something like this. I told you that the judge said Tony had to complete his rehabilitation program, for substance abuse, before they would grant him visitation rights with Josh. Yale, I called the police when Josh didn't come home after school." She was sobbing and becoming incoherent. "They just called me back. An officer said, a friend of Josh's said that Josh went with his dad, and didn't get on the bus after school. The police checked if Tony was still in the rehab program. They said, he stopped coming to the meetings two weeks ago." She was speaking rapidly and nearly shrieking.

"Yale, I drove around looking for Josh. Then, when I went back to the house, the fire department was still putting out the blaze that they said originated in my bedroom. My housekeeper was still standing outside, Yale, crying. She said, something had broken upstairs that sounded like glass, and when she went upstairs to see what it was, my bedroom was on fire! Oh God…I'm worried about Josh. Yale, what if

Tony leaves the country with him? What if they don't find him? I don't know what to do. Yale, I don't even have my house to wait in if Josh tries to call. There is too much smoke damage. I won't even be able to go home." She became more hysterical, and Marissa was not prone to over reacting. By nature, she was a calm and collected person. But Josh was her life. Tony had become violent prior to their divorce, which was precipitated by his cocaine addiction. It had cost Tony his job, his friends, and his money. Marissa stayed strong through the divorce so her son would be spared as much hurt as possible. She had unsuccessfully tried to help Tony, but finally filed for divorce when Tony broke her arm during a violent argument.

"Calm down, Marissa. What did the police tell you to do?"

"To wait, Yale. To wait. Oh God. I can't just sit here, Yale. I just can't."

"I'll come get you, Marissa. We'll go to the police station and see what else we can do. Maybe you can give them names of places or people Tony might go to. Okay? We can call a private investigator to help find Josh. Give me the address. I'll come get you."

"Yale, I don't have a home. I don't have Josh. I don't have shit!"

She was sobbing as Yale heard someone in the background trying to calm her down.

"Marissa, now is not the time to fall apart. Keep it together. Tell me where you are. I'll come get you. We'll get Josh back. You'll stay here until your house is repaired. Marissa, where are you?"

She gave him the address. "I can drive over Yale. Don't come to get me."

"I don't want you driving."

"I want my fucking car, Yale. It's about all I have right now."

"Marissa, put Pam on the phone."

"Hello. This is Pam. Do you know how to get here?"

"Yes. Pam, can you follow me back to my place with Marissa's car, so at least she knows she has her car?"

"I'll have to wake my baby, but I can—"

"Never mind. I'll be there in twenty minutes with my houseman. He can drive Marissa's car back here. Let me tell Marissa, okay?" Marissa got on the line.

He hung up and left with Victor immediately for Pam's house, completely forgetting he was supposed to be at the Oak Plaza Hotel with Lisa.

When Yale and Victor arrived at Pam's house, two squad cars were there. They were told they had some leads, and asked if Marissa could give them some additional information and recent photos of Josh and Tony. By the time Marissa was done answering all the questions and escorted to her office, where she had some recent photos of Josh and Tony, it was after eight. Yale and Marissa didn't get to Yale's house until close to nine. Once inside the house, Yale remembered he was supposed to have been at the hotel with Lisa earlier. He went to the phone to check his messages, figuring Lisa probably tried to reach him. He noticed that he and Victor had left in such a hurry, they had forgotten to turn on the answering machine. Victor had been in all day, so there had been no need to have it turned on.

Yale got a comforter for Marissa, while Victor brought her some hot tea. Yale dialed the Oak Plaza and asked for room 1232. There was no answer. He called back wondering if he had the wrong room number. He asked the clerk for Lisa Klein's room.

The desk clerk said Lisa Klein checked out of the hotel an hour ago. He inquired if she left a forwarding number. The clerk stated one was not left.

Yale asked if she had left a message for him, by any chance.

"No sir. Ms. Klein left no messages. The only thing she said prior to leaving the hotel, Mr. Frye, was that she made a mistake. She stated, she should have taken the suite originally reserved for her. That room 1232 was not as she remembered it."

"Anything else?" Yale asked.

"No sir. Only that she left behind a purchased copy of her novel in her room. It's not signed, but there's a receipt in it from Bordins Book Store, with today's date on it."

"Thanks," Yale said, putting down the phone. He felt like the wind had been knocked out of him. He walked back to Marissa, sitting next to her. She took his hand with tears streaming down her face.

"Oh, Yale. Why can't things ever go smoothly?"

"I don't know, Marissa. I wish I knew. Sincerely, I do"

CHAPTER 5

Lisa left her last book signing session, at Bordins Bookstore, euphoric and proud. She had established herself as a successful writer, and the turnout across the country went beyond any expectations she might have fathomed. On top of it all, Yale had come to see her today, obviously interested in renewing a relationship.

Her heart had started racing when she first observed him standing at the end of the line, holding her novel, waiting patiently to approach her. It was the best culmination to her tour. She was overjoyed at his interest and the ease with which they were able to converse. When he looked at her, she felt sure he still loved her. The chemistry was there. The magic was there. She was sure of it.

Yale looked fabulous. When his sparkling blue eyes looked into hers, she instantly felt the old familiar longing for him return with ineffable force. He looked younger than his forty-two years, wearing faded jeans and a blue Polo shirt. He carried his six-foot frame well, with broad shoulders and a lean torso. He appeared a little thinner than when she'd last seen him, but that was a typical illusion for men who had such long legs. There were a few lines around his smiling eyes, which only gave his face more character.

It was almost five when she returned to room 1232 of the Oak Plaza Hotel and hurriedly showered. She put on the terry robe, freshly hanging on a hook in the bathroom, to be ready when Yale arrived. She touched up her makeup and put on a generous amount of Obsession, but left herself naked beneath the white robe. She hadn't bothered unpacking, when she arrived, knowing she had to be in San Francisco in two days. She just shoved the suitcases, still full, under the bed. She ordered a bottle of wine, and a tray of fresh vegetables, from room service and sat to await his arrival, which would be momentary, since it was already after the six o'clock hour they'd agreed upon. She remembered Yale hated being late for anything.

When the knock on the door occurred minutes later, she went to greet Yale with a smile and a kiss, only to be disappointed that it was merely room service. When Yale had not arrived by seven she called his house to see if there was a misunderstanding, but there was no answer, and the answering machine wasn't on. She considered the idea he may have changed his telephone number if he was receiving repeated unwanted calls and maybe forgot to tell her. She hadn't thought to ask if his phone number was the same when she saw him earlier.

At seven-thirty she called his mothers number. She had wanted to say hello to Ruth anyway, and perhaps she knew where he was. When the answering machine took the call, Lisa hung up without leaving a message.

Close to eight her phone rang. Lisa picked it up after the first ring, anxious to hear Yale's voice. Instead, it was Jean calling from New York to congratulate her on completing a successful signing tour, advising her the book was holding at the top of the New York Times best seller list. She told Jean she was expecting Yale any minute and she'd fill her in on everything else the next morning.

"I'm happy for you, Lisa. I know how important he has been to your life. I'm really happy he came to your signing session today."

Lisa got off the phone, grateful she had someone as special as Jean for a friend. Most of Lisa's close friends in Canton had let their friendships diminish after she and Ronnie had split up. She had accepted it as a natural course of events, feeling couples want to get together with other couples, not with a "third wheel" tagging along. She wasn't bitter, but disappointed in a few people, when they didn't even bother returning her calls. She felt hurt that they found it so easy to let go of relationships Lisa thought had more substance. There were many lonely days, and nights, before she met Jean. She had desperately needed a friend to confide her feelings to, and she didn't have anyone until she met Jean.

At eight-twenty the phone rang again. This time it was the executive producer for the Myra Sullivan television show, calling to ask if they could reschedule her appearance for Friday. Apparently, Myra Sullivan's grandmother died suddenly, and they were going to be showing pre-recorded shows until Myra returned, Thursday evening. Lisa agreed after they offered to pick up all additional expenses through Friday for her. She mentioned she had to be in San Francisco, for The City of Hope Fundraiser on Wednesday, but would return to L.A. that night.

"What a coincidence Lisa," Frank Lee, the executive producer said. "I'm flying out in an hour for the same function, and will be coming back Wednesday, as well. Where are you staying, Lisa?"

"The Bay Plaza, where the event is being held. I've never been to San Francisco, so I thought I'd play it safe."

Well, Lisa, I'm at the Bay Plaza too, and I know San Francisco like the back of my hand. I lived there for three years. How about flying out with me, and I'll show you the city myself. We can even stay until Thursday if you fall in love with the city like most people who visit do."

"Well, Frank, I can be ready in fifteen minutes. Sounds great. Thanks."

"Good. I'll pull in front of the hotel in fifteen minutes. And if you wear something a little dressy, I'll take you for a late night supper at a great club when we get there."

"Sounds wonderful. Frank my hotel reservations in San Francisco aren't until Wednesday. Do you think I'll have a problem?"

"Of course not. I have a five room penthouse suite."

"Then we're in business. See you in a few. Thanks Frank."

"My pleasure. Bye."

Lisa was dressed and in the lobby, checking out, fifteen minutes later. She had to fight to maintain her composure, when she left the room, having been stood up by Yale. She looked at room 1232 feeling sad and hurt. She looked at a Warhol painting on one of the lobby walls as she followed the porter with her bags outside. She thought to herself, "Andy Warhol, if what you once were supposed to have said is true—"that everyone has fifteen minutes of glory in their lifetime" I hope I didn't sleep through mine."

She had to force a smile as Frank Lee got out of a limo to greet her.

Frank Lee was a very wealthy and powerful man. He was extremely bright and confident. He owned several radio stations across the country, and was part of a conglomerate which owned several major nationwide hotels. He was in his late fifties, and had been divorced from his third wife for close to four years. Frank Lee was tall, and a big man. His six foot, and two hundred ten pounds of muscle, either elicited a sense of security or was intimidating. He smoked a pipe filled with a sweet cherry scented tobacco. He was originally from Brooklyn. He talked a lot, laughed easily, and had a passion for fun, people, adventure, and excitement. He was aggressive, energetic and loyal to those he cared about. His first wife had died during childbirth, and his first and only son was stillborn. It was said, he never completely recovered from the loss, and that it had changed him from a stable reclusive man to an endless wanderer. His motto was quoted in articles—"Live while you can, because there won't be another today".

Frank owned homes in England, France and Switzerland. He was known to throw lavish parties, which lasted days, and included the most celebrated people in the entertainment industry and political arena. Frank liked to gamble and frequented Las Vegas often, even if only for a day. He owned his own airplane, yacht, and a private island off the Southern coast of Florida, complete with a lavish estate, several houses, an apartment complex, a tobacco factory, and one hundred factory employees. He also employed another twenty domestic workers to keep his island estate running smoothly year round.

It was on impulse he'd asked Lisa to join him, feeling the need for a new face and fresh company. He read voraciously and had enjoyed her first novel. He was curious about this woman. His longtime friend, Ben Shinsky, had signed her to a five-year contract even though he had only known her for a few days. Ben was a good judge of people, and had told him months ago about signing Lisa Klein, expressing confidentially, "This broad is going places. She's hungry, and she's full of fire."

As Frank got out of the black limo to greet Lisa he thought Ben forgot to tell him the lady was a 'knock out' as well.

"Hi, Lisa. Frank Lee—escort to fun—at your service. You look lovely," he added; smiling with a pipe dangling from his mouth. Her taupe chiffon wrap dress was feminine; without a lot of frill. She got into the limo, laughing, as he bowed to her, holding out a dozen long stemmed red roses, wrapped in clear cellophane, with a big bow across the bundle. He climbed into the limo, sitting across from her, watching her smell the flowers. "Thank you, Frank. This is very nice, but I better tell you up front, if you expect anything more than 'fun' company, I should dodge now."

"I don't expect, Lisa. If I want it. I buy it." As the limo pulled away from the curb he said, with obvious arrogance, "So honey, do you often go to strange cities with people you don't know?"

"Well, Frank, I do when I've been stood up by someone that was the essence of life to me; and when I feel I've been fucked over enough."

"Well, Lisa—Frank—doesn't fuck over—unless he's been fucked over. And Frank doesn't try to fuck anything that isn't interested. So, now that we know each other a little better, are you game for 'fun' or are you going to have your 'fun' playing little 'miss innocent' games?"

"I don't play games, Frank. Now, try and show me I'm capable of having 'fun' if you're such an expert. I honestly don't know what the definition of 'fun' is, and I'm not sure I'd understand the meaning, if it was explained to me."

"That's because it's not definable, honey. It's experienced. Hold on, Lisa. I'll introduce you to my best friend—'fun'."

Frank looked into Lisa's eyes and saw the same suffering he'd been practicing burying for many years, so that now it was no longer visible and rarely surfaced from the depths. He noticed she wore no jewelry, except a watch, and wondered if she was a gold digger, like so many of the women he knew. Halfway to his private jet, after making some small talk, he took out an 18-carat gold cigarette case from a leather briefcase, noticing she smoked heavily. "Here, honey. I like pretty things, so I buy a lot of extra crap. This cigarette case is a little nicer than yours. Have a present on Frankie."

"Ooh, pretty. How much did you pay for it, Frankie? It looks very expensive. It must have cost a pretty penny."

"Not much for someone with a lot. A lot for someone with little."

"So, how much, rich boy? Impress me."

He pulled out a receipt which displayed the price—twelve hundred.

He watched her face. "I think you overpaid, but what the hell, it's pretty." She opened her purse, wrote out a check for $1200, then handed it to him. "Thanks, Frank. I deserve to treat myself a little better. Now, I won't have to go shopping for one. I don't owe you tax, do I? I don't think there's tax on a resale. Or am I wrong?"

"No, Lisa. No tax on a resale." He put her check in his briefcase. He watched her transfer her cigarettes to the gold case, one by one. "It's nice to be able to buy expensive things isn't it?"

"Yes, Frank," she said, her voice trembling, as she closed the gold case, squeezing it shut. She looked up at him with pained eyes. "It beats the shit out of eating macaroni and cheese everyday. But, somehow, it doesn't make me as happy as I thought it once would."

"Maybe, you bought the wrong thing to make you happy, Lisa."

"Frank, I can't buy what would make me happy. But, I guess I haven't learned how to acquire what would make me happy. So, I'll accept lobster, over macaroni and cheese, while I try to figure it out."

"I'm sorry, Lisa."

"For what, Frankie? For testing me—tempting me—baiting me—playing games with me? Or because I haven't been able to secure something that might make me happy?" She couldn't help sounding bitter and sarcastic.

"All of it, Lisa. I'm sorry for all of the things you mentioned, and for some you probably can't talk about, honey."

"Go ahead, Frank—tell me you've been there now, so I'll pretend it makes me feel better. Go ahead. Go on, Frank. Show, the dumb broad, how you've learned, and how wise you've become—and then tell me it'll be a bad memory one day. Go on, Frank. Go on. I'm waiting."

"I can't, Lisa. I can't tell you lies." The limo stopped and the door was held open for them.

"Frank, I think I'll pass and go back. I'm sorry. This was a bad idea."

"Come on, Lisa. Let's do the best we can. We both know there are times you can't go back, even if you want to, so let's move forward and see what happens next."

Reluctantly, she took his hand and got into the airplane. She didn't know what was ahead of her, but prayed it would be better than what she just left behind. Her heart ached that Yale had stood her up. It hurt that he hadn't even bothered to call with some excuse. She was quiet on the short flight, and Frank didn't invade her cataclysmic state.

It was midnight when Lisa and Frank landed in San Francisco.

CHAPTER 6

At two in the morning Lisa was eating poached salmon, escargot, and Beluga Caviar, listening to an alto sax that made her cry and gave her new appreciation for jazz. She had consumed six glasses of expensive wine when Frank said to the wine steward to bring her some black coffee, and hold the wine. He introduced her to several people, but she forgot their names almost immediately. It was four AM when they arrived at the Bay Plaza.

Lisa watched as person after person kissed up to him, while he was acting casual and unpretentious, and assumed he liked preferential treatment. When they entered the suite Lisa gasped. It was enormous and luxurious. There was a pool in the suite, with a fountain in the pool that kept changing colors. There was a lot of bric a brac, including bronze Egyptian sculptures and hand painted European vases. The traditional furniture was tasteful with earth tones dominating. The wall decorations included original works by Chagall and Renoir, as well as less conventional paintings such as an abstract oil and acrylic by American artist Caio Fonseca. A black ceramic tiled terrace overlooked the bay, with a breathtaking panoramic view. "Well Frankie, this is one hell of a room," she said, still inebriated, moving slowly around the room as she looked at everything. "I think I'm tired. Where should I go?"

He opened a door to a bedroom with a canopied bed and satin sheets. It was a huge room, beautifully furnished and very French Provincial. "Well, I guess this will do. Thanks" she said, as she plopped down on the bed fully clothed, passing out.

In the morning, she looked around and vaguely remembered the room, but had no idea why she was in her bra and panties and hadn't put on a nightshirt.

She went to the bathroom and laughed at its opulence. Gold faucets. A black porcelain toilet and sink, and mirrors everywhere. She found her pill container and was taking out her morning medication when she said, "Entrée," to the knock on the bedroom door. Frank came in wearing a silk smoking jacket, over silk pajamas, and a pipe in the corner of his mouth. He was about to ask her how she felt when he saw her gathering pills that lay spilled on top of the bed.

"I don't do drugs Lisa, and either does anyone who wants to be in my company."

"Good Frank. I like a man with principles. Now Frank, this pink one is for panic and anxiety, which I take three times daily; this maroon one is Premerin—a hormone pill—I take one Monday through Friday, stop for the weekends like my gynecologist directed after my hysterectomy. This blue one is a vitamin with iron, since I've had problems with anemia, on and off, for a couple of years; and you know what—fuck it—they're not working anyway," and she threw a container across the room watching as several pills fell on the carpeting. Now we have this bottle of blue pills Frank, but I—"

"Stop it, Lisa. I'm sorry. Now, pick up your pills, come out, and have some breakfast. There's a lot I want to show you today. Dress comfortably with good walking shoes." He turned and walked out of the room.

She came out in the crested terry hotel robe and sat down at the dining room table. He had ordered a lot of food. She picked up her juice, took her pills, and poured herself a cup of coffee from the sterling silver carafe. "Coffee, Frank?"

"Yes. Thanks Lisa."

"I usually only have one cup of coffee in the morning. I only drink decaf the rest of the time," she offered, making small talk.

He got up, went to the phone, and ordered up a pot of decaf, asking, "anything else you'd like, Lisa?"

"Yes. A hot fudge sundae with lots of whipped cream and no nuts."

"With or without the cherry on top?"

"With, please."

"With the pot of decaf coffee, would you also send up two hot fudge sundaes with lots of whipped cream and cherries on top? Make one with sprinkled nuts on top, the other without nuts please." He put down the phone, looked at her smiling, "Sounded good. Maybe, I'm due for a change."

After 'pigging out' they got ready and met in the central sitting room. He was in a designer, cashmere, aqua sweater, khaki Armani slacks and beige Bally loafers. He had a gold chain around his neck, a huge diamond ring on his right hand, and a Rolex watch on his left wrist. He, definitely, looked ready for a photo session with GQ. She was in jeans, with a red t-shirt, covered by a simple brown flecked blazer, and a pair of comfortable platforms that Jean had insisted she bring. She had her hair pulled back with a scarf, and her jewelry consisted of the watch she'd been wearing every day since the tour began. Even with Jean's help she was no match to his haute couture.

"Wait ten minutes, Frank. I'll change real fast. I guess, casual is different to you than it is to me." She was embarrassed, and he felt stupid for not being more sensitive to what casual might mean to her.

"No, don't change. You're fine. Let's go."

"You sure, Frank?"

"Yes, I'm sure. Just pull off that scarf around your hair. I like the way it looks loose."

"Sure." She pulled off the scarf, shook her head, and they left. He was amazed at her lack of vanity. She was who she was and made no pretext at being anything other than herself. He liked that. He liked her. She was her own person.

They had a wonderful day. Frank couldn't remember having so much fun showing the sights of a city to someone, He took her to the Asian Art Museum in Golden Gate Park, Chinatown, which covers about sixteen square blocks, and introduced her to sushi at Fisherman's Wharf. He laughed when she made faces trying the raw fish delicacies at Alioto's and finally said, "I give up," when they left the restaurant and Lisa asked if there was a McDonalds nearby. One minute she was like a little girl asking question after question, the next she was adult, very intense and philosophical. She was enthusiastic and open to new experiences. She laughed at his jokes sincerely, and told him to loosen up when he became impatient about something. She didn't agree with everything he said, and was willing to challenge him on issues she felt differently about. When they got in the limo to return to the hotel, she asked if he knew where she could purchase two expensive classy watches for her boys which could be engraved expeditiously. He took her to a jewelry store in Ghirardelli Square he was familiar with and asked the owner, Bill, to give the lady a good deal. She found two gold encased Movado watches, with a single diamond on the black faces, and asked if she could have something inscribed on each. Frank stood beside her when she asked to engrave-"there has never been a time I didn't love you". Bill said it was too lengthy. After a moment of careful consideration she said, "How about, "Time does not diminish love".

"I can fit that on them. I'll have them ready by tomorrow afternoon."

"Oh, great! I'll pay you now and come back then. Thank you."

"Bill, Lisa is my guest. Can you have them brought to the Bay Plaza for her?"

"Sure, Frank. Do you want them tonight?"

"That would be good."

"I'll take care of it. Anything else I can show you, Lisa?"

"No, thank you. You've been very helpful. I appreciate it."

"I think your boys will like the watches. Sounds like you're a special mother."

"No. I just have special sons. Thanks again. Bye."

They got back into the limo and Frank asked, "Can I buy you a special watch for a special day, Lisa?"

"No Frank, but you can buy me a hot dog, with ketchup, and lots of onions, from that vendor on the corner."

"You drive a hard bargain, Lisa."

"Yes, I know Frank. I've lost a lot as a result," she replied seriously in response.

"Well, don't feel sorry for yourself. At least you have two sons. I have no family. Not one living relative."

"I don't have my sons, Frank. I lost them. Now, I'm trying to get back a little of what I've lost. I had a husband Frank, for over twenty years, whose life style suffocated me. I was too weak to look for change. But I took a big risk and divorced him. And now that I'm free, I'm no better off. I had friends, Frank. They stopped accepting my calls when I became single. Now I'm their adversary, no longer their friend. And I have parents, Frank, who think I've ruined my life. They remind me, every time I talk to them, how stupid I was to leave such a good, fine husband. Such a good father. Such a good provider."

Would you do it again, if you had the choice now, knowing what it's cost you?"

"Yes, Frank. I was dying then. Now I'm only hurting. But I'm going to fight the suffering and learn how to live. I'm just sorry for the pain I've caused others in the interim."

"What about your pain, Lisa?"

"I'm used to my pain. It's become a friend in a way. As long as I can feel, even if it's pain, I know I'm alive. I'm afraid of not being able to feel anything, Frank. Then I'm really dead, or I might as well be."

They ate hot dogs in the limo on the drive back to the hotel. She marveled at the limo's ability to climb what seemed to be ninety-degree hills and not careen down the opposite side. Twice Lisa took her napkin and wiped mustard off Frank's cheek casually. She mentioned interest in seeing Alcatraz while they were in San Francisco, and he said, "Another time". He suggested the symphony and she wrinkled her nose adding, "boring".

Back in the suite Frank watched Lisa take her afternoon medication. She came and sat next to him on one of the sofas, kicking off her shoes, and putting her feet up on an ottoman.

"Lisa, your feet are red and puffy. Do they hurt?"

"I'm used to it. One of the pills causes water retention. I brought a couple rings with me, but one day they're tight, the next loose, so I just don't bother putting them on. Don't worry; I'm fine. They're just a little swollen from all the walking we did today."

"Put them on my lap, Lisa. I'll massage them for you."

She put her legs on his lap, and as he rubbed her feet and legs she fell asleep. He relaxed, kicking his shoes off too, putting his legs up on the ottoman. The telephone woke them two hours later.

Frank got off the phone after a brief conversation. He related that Myra Sullivan was taking a few extra days off and they'd like to reschedule her appearance for September, if that was okay."

"Did you tell people I was traveling with you, Frank?"

"No. I told them we're attending the same function. Why? Are you ashamed to be here with me?"

"No, Frank. I just don't want any publicity that could affect people close to me. Everyone is not as open minded as the people in California are."

"That's bullshit, Lisa. This is a daily occurrence in every state. Guy meets gal and they either make it or they don't. Most people don't really give a damn what anyone else says or thinks. I certainly don't."

"I'm not most people, Frank. I need the respect of my sons. I lost it once and don't want to jeopardize it further with publicity."

"Lisa, live your own life. When your kids grow up they'll see the world differently. They're young now, and probably very idealistic."

"How many kids have you raised that you're such an expert?" she asked tartly, knowing he had no children of his own.

"Don't hit below the belt, Lisa. I don't like it."

"Then stop deciding for me, what I should and shouldn't do, or how I should feel, act, or live my life. I'm me. And I can't react the way you do. I don't expect you to react any other way than you do. Don't try to manipulate me, Frank, because then you're hitting below my belt—and I don't like that!"

She was a little spitfire. She let you know just how she felt. She was different from most of the women with whom he surrounded himself. They would kiss his ass, just to be near him, because they knew if they were seen with Frank Lee they were among the 'special' people invited to exclusive parties.

He used and got used. Usually he didn't care, as long as he was having 'fun'.

"Get dressed, Lisa. We'll go to China Town for dinner. I know a great place you'll like."

"What are you wearing, Frank? A suit and tie?"

"No. A sweater and slacks. We can change again later and stop at the benefit for a while."

"Okay. Sounds good." She smiled at him, as she rose to go and change.

They went to their separate bedrooms. Lisa was in the adjoining bathroom to her room when she knocked her cologne bottle on the floor. She cut her hand while picking up the pieces of shattered glass. The terry robe was now dotted with blood. She rinsed her hand, applying pressure with a washcloth to the cut, but it felt like there was glass in the wound. She walked to Frank's room, pressing against the cut with her other hand, and called to him. When Frank didn't answer, she pushed the door open, calling out to him again. She heard water in the bathroom being turned off, and a second later he came out naked, except for a plastic bag attached to the side of his abdomen. He obviously had undergone colon surgery.

"Don't you knock? Get out of here! God damn it! What, the fuck, is the matter with you?"

"Sorry". Blood was dripping on the carpeting as she left the room. He noticed the blood as soon as he regained his composure, then quickly pulled on a robe and went to her room. She was in the bathroom, wrapping a clean towel around her hand.

"What happened, Lisa?"

"I dropped the cologne bottle and cut myself picking up the glass from the floor."

"Why didn't you just call housekeeping? Let me look at it."

"Gee, I'm really dumb. I forgot I was with Mr. Mega Bucks. I tried to clean up my own mess. How stupid can I get? Well, I've learned something new today." She stomped to the phone and dialed. "This is Ms. Klein, the very famous author that's shacking up with your real rich patron, Frank Lee. It seems I broke a bottle of cologne and cut my hand. Could you send housekeeping to clean up the mess, and get me a fucking doctor, to remove the glass, from my fucking hand, and why, don't you send up a new, fucking, bottle of "Obsession" while you're at it." She listened for a minute then said, "thank you," and put down the phone. She sat down and started laughing. "They said, right away, Miss."

"Lisa, can I take a look at your hand now?"

"Not unless you have M.D. at the end of your name."

"Lisa, you are a pain in the ass. Someone should have taught you ladies don't cuss like that. You should have been spanked years ago."

"I never said I was a lady, Frank. Don't make assumptions."

He answered the door. The hotel doctor removed a large sliver of glass from Lisa's hand, and gave her a tetanus shot. Housekeeping cleaned up the bathroom, and a clerk brought up a new bottle of Obsession. She insisted she was fine and still wanted to go to China Town. She said, she just had to make one quick call first.

Marc was in his second year at the University of Michigan, and Steve was in his freshman year. They both had picked a school away from home, wanting to taste independence. They were sharing an old house off campus with two other boys. She had a strong need to say hello, missing them deeply, and impulsively decided to call.

"Hi Steve, it's mom. How are you?"

"Fine. And you?"

"I'm okay. How's your brother?"

"Fine."

"So, I'm done with the tour. I'll probably be going home soon. When will you guys be going home? I know school just started, but I'd like to see you both."

"Not for a while. We'll let you know."

"Maybe I could come to the University, and we could visit, and go to dinner or something?"

"We're kind of busy now. How about in a month or so?"

"Okay. I understand. Do you need anything?"

"No."

"Well, tell your brother I'm on the phone and let me say hello."

"He's out, but I'll tell him you called. I gotta go now."

"Okay. I love you. Bye, Steve."

"Bye."

She got off the phone fighting back the tears. "Okay Frank, let's have some 'fun'."

He took her arm without commenting on the hurt she was enduring. When they got in the limo she looked at him, "I'm sorry I barged in on you upstairs, Frank. I just don't always know the rules of a game, and when I finally learn the rules, someone changes the game." He didn't comment, just held her hand.

"Does 'fun' make pain go away, Frank?"

"No. It's just a diversion. But it beats the shit out of one alternative."

Which is?"

"Suffering."

CHAPTER 7

By morning Marissa was incoherent and frantic. Pacing outside Yale's house, she swore she would kill her ex-husband if anything happened to Josh. She had slept very little. She sat next to the telephone with Yale all night; only dozing occasionally in his arms, when exhaustion ruled and she allowed herself to become submissive to Yale's gentle consoling.

Yale's mother, Ruth, came over and stayed at Yale's estate, too, attempting to give Marissa additional reassurance and comfort. However, by the third day, Yale had to have a doctor come to the house and sedate Marissa, so she would get some rest, since they still hadn't gotten Josh back, and the police still hadn't located Tony.

Marissa's house had sustained a considerable amount of damage from the fire. Yale persuaded Marissa to stay at his place indefinitely, until the house was repaired. They hired private detectives, and offered a large cash reward to anyone with information regarding the whereabouts of Josh. Marissa made public television appeals for the safe return of her son, and Josh's picture was in every newspaper across the country. Because Marissa was a famous entertainer, the media gave her dilemma excessive coverage, often referring to the constant support she was receiving from her companion, and love interest of the last two years, Yale Frye.

It was a nearly a week after Lisa had left Los Angeles when she turned on the television for the first time in the suite at the Bay Plaza Hotel. She heard a newscaster state that the police were still investigating the disappearance and suspected kidnapping of Joshua Myers, son of singer Marissa Myers, long time girlfriend of superstar Yale Frye. The television was also airing an appeal by Marissa, begging for the safe return of her child. It was then that Frank came out of his bedroom suite, looking at the plea on the screen.

Frank and Lisa had been partying all week. This was the first they'd heard about the disappearance.

"I hope her kid is okay and he turns up soon. Marissa is a fragile lady. She'd be a mess if something happened to her son."

"Do you know her well, Frank?"

"I've known Marissa since she was a back up vocalist, long before she made it big in the business. She's a decent person and a fine performer. When I met her, she wasn't quite as thin, had a long nose, not the cute little one she has now. But she fought long and hard for public recognition. She had no family to speak of, plus a drug problem when she was still married to Tony Jenson. She got help; he didn't. They split up and she pulled it together, while Tony got worse. His drug habit used up all his money. He lost his foreign car dealerships, and hit bottom. About a year ago, Marissa went to court to keep Tony from having visitation rights with Josh until he went through a rehab program. I heard he hadn't completed the rehabilitation program and started using drugs again. A social worker from the rehab center publicly stated that Tony swore to get even with Marissa for keeping his son away from him."

Frank looked at Lisa, waiting to see if she was going to ask if he knew about Marissa's relationship with Yale Frye, but she didn't ask anything. "Josh has Marissa's last name because she had the child before she married Tony," he continued.

Spending the past seven days together, Frank and Lisa had gotten to know each other well. They not only had 'fun' but they opened up, feeling comfortable and safe with each other. Lisa confided to Frank about her affair with Yale Frye over two years ago, and her love for him. She talked about her divorce, her sons, and the lonely isolated life she'd been living for the last couple of years.

Frank told Lisa about the only woman he truly loved and how she never wanted children but agreed to have a child for him, only to die along with the infant during childbirth. He told Lisa about the divorce four years ago from his third wife, and how he found her in his bed with another woman when he came home from a business trip earlier than was expected. He told Lisa he was an executive producer for 'fun', and liked being around people all the time because he couldn't stand being alone. He told her he was diagnosed with a malignancy two years ago, when he had the colostomy. No one knew, since he'd taken care of it abroad. He admitted that psychologically he hadn't been able to adjust, although they caught the cancer in time, and he hadn't slept with a woman since the surgery, afraid of letting anyone see the bag. He talked to Lisa bout losing his parents, who were originally from Hungary. He related he was only twelve when he came home from school, one day, to find that his parents were killed in a gas explosion which demolished the tenement they called home. Frank said, he'd sworn at the time, that he was going to work until he had so much money he'd never want for anything. He related he had been placed in a foster home, where he was physically abused after his parents were killed, and that he finally ran away at the age of sixteen. He then took a job in a steel mill, went to school at night, lived in a rented room, and saved every cent until he could buy into the steel company. He married the owner's daughter, his beloved first wife, inherited the prosperous mill a couple of years later. By the time he was twenty-eight he owned four steel mills and his net worth was in the millions. Many wise investments brought him more wealth. Soon he started mixing with important people so he could become even richer and more important. He confided, he thought power and money were synonymous with happiness. He was thirty-five when he lost his wife and baby, after ten years of marriage. After the tragedy he became a different person.

He admitted, although he didn't believe in God, he felt sad that when he would die he wouldn't have anyone to say Kaddish for him. His eyes had been misty then, and moist the previous night when he said his billions could buy everything except real love, a family, and good health. He would be sixty in a week.

"Well honey, it's our last day here. Anything special you want to see or do before we leave, Lisa?"

"Yes. Let's lay in bed all day and not get dressed. We can have room service bring up hot fudge sundaes, and look through a stack of magazines that have no real social value—just pretty pictures."

"Party-pooper," he accused. "Why look at pictures? You don't buy yourself anything anyway."

"I don't have to. I just like knowing I can if I want to."

"Do you have to go home, Lisa? Come with me to Las Vegas for a few days instead."

Before she could answer, the phone rang. Frank handed her the phone. "It's your son Marc, Lisa."

It was the first time one of her boys had called since she'd been on tour. She became alarmed. "Hi Marc, what's wrong?"

"Nothing, mom. Just sitting here with Steve. We have a four-day weekend next week—no classes Thursday or Friday—so we thought we'd see what you were doing. Maybe we can celebrate that your book has been number one for such a long time, or something, if you're not busy."

Tears streamed down Lisa's face. "I'm not busy. Anything you'd like to do, or were you planning on going to Canton?"

"No. We don't want to go home. Dad and Sue fight a lot. Steve and I are kind of down and bummed out."

"Why are you guys bummed out?"

"Because we feel like we have no real home." Marc started to cry.

"Don't cry, honey. I'm sorry you feel you have no real home. I'm sorry I made changes that hurt you." Lisa reached for Frank's hand, trembling and unsure she could keep talking. "Hold on a minute, honey." She put the phone down, covering the mouthpiece, unable to stop the sobs. Frank took the phone from her lap.

"Marc? Hi, this is Frank Lee, a good friend of your moms, even if I am an old fart. I was just trying to talk your mom into going to Las Vegas, for a few days, instead of going to Canton. But you know what, Lake Tahoe is prettier. I'd like the opportunity to meet you boys. Would you and Steve consider a little trip? You know, in Tahoe you could even gamble a little although you're under age. I have some connections. How about it? I can send my plane for the two of you. I'll pick up the whole tab and we can have some fun."

"How can we gamble if we're under age?" Marc asked, skeptical about his mom's choice of friends.

"Because, I'm a partial owner of one of the hotels. So, what do you say? Or would you rather have your mom to yourself and just let, poor, old, lonely me, go off somewhere all by myself?"

"Hold on." Marc and Steve talked a minute in disbelief. "Okay, if it's okay with mom," Marc said into the receiver."

"Well, I'll let you ask her. Hold on, Marc."

Lisa, Frank, and the boys arranged to meet in Tahoe, the following week. Lisa and Frank were going to go straight to Tahoe after checking out of the Bay Plaza. Frank was sending a limo for the boys; and then they would fly to Tahoe Wednesday night. They were going to spend four days together. Lisa couldn't stop crying. An hour after talking to her sons, flowers were sent to Lisa at the suite she was sharing with Frank. Attached was a note: "Thanks for the great watches, mom. Looking forward to having a good 'Time' together. We love you, Marc and Steve."

Even Frank got misty-eyed when he read the card that arrived with the bouquet of flowers. They sat on the sofa leafing through magazines a little later when Lisa put her head down on Franks lap. They still hadn't dressed. It was relaxing just sitting together with the radio on, looking at the pictures in the magazines, eating truffles and potato chips.

He stroked her hair, after she put her head on his lap, and said, "I forgot I could have a good time like this; being with someone who makes me feel good, and doesn't make demands."

He felt a strong desire for her. He'd been able to keep it in check until now, but his longing was taking hold of his body. He didn't want to alter what had been really nice so far. He stopped touching her hair. When she moved her head, purring for more, she felt his hardness. She pretended not to notice, and said, "Do it some more. It feels nice." He started stroking her hair again, feeling his desire mount. He was about to ask her to let him up; when she moved her head against his groin, and turned on her back. He looked at her, knowing she could feel his hunger. She opened her robe exposing her breasts. He took his hands and ran them over her gently, watching her nipples harden. He pushed himself to the side a little and said, "Lisa, it's been a long time. Why don't we just go to The Square and walk?"

"I don't want to." She turned so she was on her left side, still on his lap, and started touching the insides of his thighs. She saw his bulge, and felt the tension in his legs as he fought against his desire. She moved her hand inside the opening of his pajama bottoms and grabbed his penis firmly. She heard him groan.

"Lisa, are you changing the rules of the game?"

"Frank, I don't play games, and I'm not following rules anymore. Loosen up and have a good time." She bent, putting his hard penis in her mouth. She felt him relax and sucked deeply, while her other hand moved over his thighs. He started jerking, his passion building, and was moaning as his body urged for more of the same.

"Lisa, stop. Stop." He pushed her head away, breathing hard, bridled and consumed by desire.

"No Frank. Let me hear how you feel when you have 'fun' this way." She stroked his shaft as he arched, holding back. "Don't fight it, Frank. Feel." He kept his body tensed, afraid to let go; unable to keep fighting his need, not wanting to be out of control, not wanting to show how vulnerable he could be. She bent, running her lips and tongue over him. He pulled away again, and the bag attached to his body came loose and fell off while the contents spilled on the sofa.

"Enough!" he shouted; trying to push away, feeling humiliation and anger, coupled with frustration.

"No Frank. Not enough. She pushed him back against the sofa, and started stroking the penis that was losing its erection. He looked at her as she looked up at him. "You have a nice penis, Frank. I bet it's throbbing, isn't it? I bet you feel that sensation inside that makes you want to come. She kept stroking. He was hard again, and tensing as she rubbed him. "Frank, if you don't come soon, I'm going to have to rub myself instead of you. I want my turn. She bent, sucking vigorously, as he started groaning louder and thrusting upwards, forgetting his inhibitions, until he was beyond control. She pulled her head away quickly as he cried out, climaxing. He pulled her up to him fiercely kissing her with the passion he'd kept under lock and key. He put his hand between her legs and stroked her masterfully until she came. She put her head on his chest afterwards, stating, "Frank, that was good. Can we do it again later?"

"I think I've ruined the sofa, Lisa."

She laughed. "So what? Buy another one. Take me to bed. I want to be with you, Frank."

"I have to put a fresh bag on. Give me a few minutes."

"Okay."

He came to get her a few minutes later, figuring he'd clean up after she was in the bed, and found she'd already cleaned up, and placed a towel over the wet area. He went to her bedroom and knocked.

"Come in Frank."

He opened the door. She was beneath the sheets. She held out a lit pipe for him, and lifted the sheet for him to climb beneath. She moved her naked body against his. "Make me feel safe, Frank."

They stayed in bed the rest of the day, exploring each other's minds and bodies, feeling good. Really good. She was cradled in his arms, when he whispered, "I'm old enough to be your father."

"Yup, you are. And I'm wise enough not to give a damn."

"I'm going to marry you, Lisa. I'm going to take care of you forever."

"Not until you ask my father for my hand. I'm old fashioned."

"What if he says no; thinks I'm too old, or doesn't like me?"

I guess you'll have to make sure that doesn't happen."

"What if your boys hate me?"

"Then they're not as smart as I believe they are."

"I want to make love again, Lisa."

"So do I, Frank. He moved over her. This time they took it slow, and he whispered to her afterwards, "I'm going to love you until all your sorrow is forgotten, Lisa. I'll love you enough for both of us; so don't ever feel guilty about your feelings for Yale Frye. Just take what I'm going to give to you Lisa. That'll be enough for me."

She stayed close as he held her with quiet understanding and tenderness. "It's okay, honey. Everybody has something in their life that won't go away or stop hurting." She fell asleep cradled in his arms, holding on to him. Her face was wet from tears.

CHAPTER 8

On the way to the jet, Lisa sat in the limo going through her list of things to do, which she had started compiling while having her morning coffee. Frank had been on the phone for a long time before they checked out. It occurred to Lisa, when she heard his business conversations in the background, she hadn't planned for anything beyond her book signing tour. At the top of her list she put the word "RELOCATE". She didn't want to stay in Canton, and really had nothing to keep her there. Her boys were out of state, at college, for the majority of the year, most of her friendships had ceased to exist, and the last two years left scars which would forever remain ugly reminders of Canton.

The problem was Lisa didn't know where she wanted to live, and this change like others wouldn't come easily. Frank had just finished a phone conversation, grabbed the paper on the seat of the limo and stared at Lisa.

"Here's a story about Yale and Marissa's efforts to find her son in the paper. It seems the police found Tony's car abandoned right here in San Francisco. But there's nothing regarding why he might have come here. Do you want to see this? It's on the front page."

"No thanks. Frank, are we stopping at the hospital to get your supplies soon? I need a bathroom."

"It's just a mile from here. Want to stop in the restaurant at the next corner?"

"No. I'll wait."

"Lisa, I want your hand looked at too. As long as we're stopping, let's make sure that cut is healing properly."

"My hand is fine. It's my arm, from the tetanus shot, that's sore."

"I'll have you looked at by a friend of mine and a brilliant doctor. His name is Harvey Stone. He's very involved in AIDS research, and has gone to Washington several times to fight for more federal funding. You'll like him. He's a young fellow in his early forties."

"I like older men, Frank. They're experienced. And they're smarter."

"Don't stop. I need all the encouragement I can get." He leaned over and kissed her tenderly.

Lisa walked with Frank to a private office in the hospital, and was introduced to Harvey Stone. Frank and Harvey hugged warmly. Doctor Stone said to Lisa proudly, "Without this guy, the research department of this hospital would not exist. He is responsible for raising over five million dollars for us in the last few years. And that's not counting the checks he's slipped me from his own pocket, to help someone he's heard needs assistance. How are you feeling Frank? You look pretty good."

"Not bad for an old geezer. I'm going to Tahoe and needed a few things, so I stopped by. There's no medical reason for my visit, but I'd like you to look at Lisa's hand while we're here. She cut it a few days ago. It still looks discolored and swollen."

"Why don't we go into an examining room down the hall for a few minutes then? I want to check your pressure while you're here, Frank. Last time, if I recall, it was a little high." They walked into the hallway, and Lisa asked where they'd be, as she opened the door to a rest room. Dr. Stone pointed to a room. She said she'd be there in a minute.

Lisa came out of a stall and was washing her hands when she saw a small child hiding behind a large metal receptacle in the corner of the ladies room.

She slowly approached the child. "Are you lost, because I can help you if you are?"

"I'm supposed to stay here and hide," he said, looking at Lisa with tears in his eyes.

"Who said so?"

"My dad. He's going to take me home soon. He promised."

"What's your name?"

"I'm not supposed to talk to strangers. I just want my mom."

"My name is Lisa. Want me to call your mom?"

"Okay. Will you do it now?"

"Yes. Do you know the phone number?"

"I know the buttons to push."

"What's your mom's name? I can look up her phone number. Okay?"

"Marissa Myers."

Lisa gasped. "I'm going to help you. Don't be scared. But I have to call my friends to help me. Okay?"

"My dad will get mad at me. I have to hide. He said so."

"It's okay. Don't be afraid. I'll make sure no one hurts you. I promise." She opened the door and grabbed a passing orderly by the arm. "This is an emergency. Go down to the third door on the left and get Dr. Harvey Stone and Mr. Frank Lee—Fast!"

He stood and looked at her. She yelled, "Now! Hurry."

Frank and Harvey Stone rushed in seconds later. "Lisa, what's wrong?" Frank asked in alarm even before he was through the door.

"It's okay, Frank. I met a young fellow here," she pointed to the child, "and I said I would help him, so his dad doesn't get mad at him for not hiding like he was supposed to, until his dad comes back. His moms name, Frank, is Marissa Myers, and he knows he's not supposed to talk to strangers, but knows which buttons to push on the telephone to call home. We can help him, right Frank? Right, Dr. Stone?"

"Sure we can. Young man, how about coming out and we'll go to a phone?" Frank stepped forward extending a hand. "You know, I know your mom. She's at Yale Frye's house, and I know she would like to talk to you."

"I can't. I can't. My dad will be mad at me." He started crying. When Frank moved closer, the boy started screaming, "No. No. Go away." Dr. Stone approached taking the boys swinging hands, and said, "Listen to me. We're going to help you. Don't be afraid." The screaming intensified, as the child became terrified and confused.

"Stop it, Josh. That's your name. Right? I read it in a newspaper." Lisa was on the floor next to him. "Josh, it's okay," she said firmly. He grabbed her and cried, "Get my mom. Get my mom." He was clinging to Lisa when several staff people who had heard the screams shoved the door open. The commotion frightened the child even further.

"Out. Out of here now," Dr. Stone directed, holding up a hand. Everyone backed out. Lisa remained on the floor, holding the sobbing child, "We'll call your mom. Don't be afraid, okay?" He was calming down, holding tightly to her.

He was completely confused. She put him on her lap, sitting on the floor, and he leaned, trembling, against her listlessly. "Josh, where did your dad go?"

"To get some medicine, of course. That's why I have to wait here. So no one will see. 'Cause kids aren't allowed to go where they put the medicine."

Frank leaned toward Harvey Stone, whispering, "This is the Myer's boy from L.A. His father is a junkie. Have you seen the articles?"

"Yes, Frank. I'm going to call for assistance. Stay here with Lisa and the boy. I'll be right back. I've already signaled my pager. It won't take long." Harvey Stone moved toward the door looking at the trembling child and Lisa.

"See you later Dr. Stone. I'm going to stay here with Josh for a little while, until we're ready to call his mom. Right, Josh?"

"Okay. But I'm not going out now, so my dad won't get mad. We'll wait 'til he gets his medicine, and then you'll tell him you know my mom. Right?"

"That's right. We'll just wait here, and no one will be mad at you. Okay?" Lisa put her arms tighter around Josh's shaking body. "You're okay, honey. Put your head back down against me and we'll rest for a few minutes. I won't let anyone hurt you. I promise. Cross my heart." Josh put his head on Lisa's chest. She stroked his arm reassuringly while Dr. Stone left the rest room to call the police, and alert hospital security of the situation.

"Tell him to go away too." Josh said to Lisa, referring to Frank.

"He's my friend. My best friend. He won't do anything bad. He'll help us, 'cause he even has a real airplane, so maybe he can take us to your mom after we call her in a little while, okay?"

"Does he fly the airplane?"

"No. A pilot does that. But it's real neat. It has couches and a TV on it."

"A TV on the airplane?"

"Yup. You'll see later. Are you cold or hungry?"

"Yes, but I'm scared, my dad's gonna be mad, too. He was yelling at me, and he hurt my arm. He was holding it too hard. Then when I said I wanted to go to mom, he called mom bad words."

"Maybe it was because he needed medicine, and was feeling sick. You know how sometimes we act funny 'cause we feel sick and stuff. Did that ever happen to you?"

"Yeh. I broke a glass with water in it once, 'cause I pushed it on the floor when I was sick." Lisa was still stroking Josh's arm gently. He was quieting, but still trembling. "Frank, could you see if you can find a blanket. Josh and I are cold."

"I'm thirsty too," The little voice added.

Frank left to get a blanket and soda. Meanwhile Josh fell asleep with his head on Lisa's chest. Frank returned quickly and put the blanket over Josh, the can of soda next to him, and asked Lisa if she was okay; as she sat on the cold tiled floor holding the child.

Harvey Stone returned. Within minutes the hospital was being thoroughly searched. Josh's dad was found dead. His body was discovered in a laundry room on the basement floor of the hospital. He had an empty morphine bottle in his left hand. A registered nurse was found, bound and gagged, in the room with him. The nurse related she was leaving for home around two in the morning, after extra hours of assisting in the understaffed ER, and with a knife pushed against her back, was forced to go back into the hospital. She was told a grenade would be detonated if she didn't get a bottle of morphine in three minutes flat. She said, she didn't want anyone else hurt, so she did it, and had been locked and bound in the laundry room since then.

The police came for Josh. They conveyed the sequence of events to Frank and Dr. Stone, just outside the lady's room of the hospital, while the child slept on Lisa's lap in the rest room. They wanted to talk to Josh, then get him home. One of the officers went with Frank and Dr. Stone to the bathroom. They bent waking Josh against Lisa's protestations. She said, they would frighten him unnecessarily. When Josh opened his eyes and saw the police uniforms, and the additional people nearby, he grabbed Lisa's blouse so hard it tore, and a button flew off. "It's okay,

Josh. It's okay. We're going to call your mom now." One of the officers reached to pick Josh up. He became hysterical, clinging to Lisa.

Frank intervened quickly, outraged at the insensitivity of the officer. "Get away from the boy or I'll make sure today is the last day you wear that uniform!"

"Who are you, buddy?" the officer snapped back at Frank.

"The child's guardian," a woman behind them said. "I'm head of Juvenile Services, for the F.B.I. I have jurisdiction here."

"Hi, Frank," she said, extending a hand.

"Hi, Martha. Lisa's friend here, Josh Myers, wants to call his mom."

"I think that's a good idea." The officers backed away. Josh kept a grip on Lisa's blouse shaking. Lisa held him against her. He had just wet his pants, which only added to his distressed state. "Josh, want to go with Lisa to call mom now?"

He looked at Lisa incapable of knowing what to do. He was puzzled, embarrassed, and afraid. He didn't say anything.

"Martha, I spilled stuff all over Josh and me. We need some dry clothes, and a few minutes alone before we call his mom. Okay?"

"Sure, that's fine. Doctor, could someone get Lisa and Josh some of those neat outfits, like the doctors wear, and a glass of milk and some cookies for Josh?" Harvey Stone sent a nurse for the items as Josh watched silently. He looked at Lisa for comfort and reassurance. She pulled the blanket around them, so he'd know she was keeping his secret. He put his head on her chest and relaxed a little. Lisa remembered from raising Marc and Steve how embarrassed they were at that age whenever they had an "accident".

Martha looked into Lisa's eyes, as she spoke to Josh, communicating that her help was important. "Josh, I have to tell you something. Your dad is not going to come back. He got sick and he didn't go to a doctor when he was supposed to."

"Where is he?" Josh asked, his head on Lisa. Martha continued, "Your dad didn't do what he should have, to get better, so now he is not able to be here". Josh didn't move, or cry, or say anything. "Josh, do you understand?" Martha went on, waiting for a reaction from the child.

Josh looked up at Lisa asking, "My dad is dead, like my dog Shultzy, when he got runned over by a car, isn't he?"

Lisa stroked the little face, unable to control the tears. "Yes, honey. You won't be able to be with your dad, just like Shultzy. But you'll be able to remember stuff about when you had fun with your dad, like you remember fun you had with Shultzy."

"Lisa, I got a new dog when Shultzy went to God. His name is Buster. Maybe my mom will get me a new dad, who won't hurt my arm, or maybe, Uncle Yale will want to be my new dad?"

"Maybe. But first we can call mommy and tell her you're coming home, okay?"

"Will you take me? And we can go in your friend's airplane. And if you want to, I'll show you Buster."

"Can I come too, Josh?" Martha asked. "I'd like to see Buster too, if you let me. You know, I have a dog too. Her name is Kitten."

Josh laughed for the first time. "That's funny. You named a dog— Kitten."

"Yes, I did. And if I get a cat I might name it—Dog." Josh laughed again. He looked up at Lisa with his big brown eyes and dimples showing. Lisa hugged him.

Lisa and Josh put on ill fitting scrubs with the hospital name embossed on them. They then went with Martha to meet everyone else waiting in Dr. Harvey Stone's office. Josh stayed next to Lisa. He wouldn't let go of her hand. He kept looking up at her for reassurance. Lisa stated several times that everything was going to be okay, inspiring confidence in the bewildered child. He was convinced she was his friend. Lisa's down-to-earth realistic way of explaining things he questioned resulted in ultimate trust.

Once inside the office, Lisa heard Frank talking to Marissa on the telephone, reiterating Josh was fine to the hysterical mother, as everyone else heard the conversation over Dr. Stone's speakerphone. "He's here. Marissa—hold on. Josh, your mom's on the phone. Talk to her into the speaker here, honey."

"Josh. Josh, it's mom. Josh are you there?" Marissa cried at the other end.

"I'm here mom. I'm wearing doctor clothes, but they don't fit so good. I'm coming home now. Right, Lisa?"

"Right, Josh." There were no dry eyes in the room.

"Mom, I'll be there pretty soon. Why is everyone crying? Lisa, why are you crying? I told you, I'm going to show you Buster."

"Josh, I asked Frank to bring you to Yale's house. We're staying with Yale for a while. Buster is here, too," Marissa's voice said from the speakerphone.

"I'm bringing Lisa, too. I said she could see Buster. Okay, mom?"

"Sure Josh. I'd like to meet Lisa. Can I talk to her a minute?"

"Lisa talk to my mom, okay? She's upset, too." Lisa looked at Frank unsure she could talk. "Go on Lisa—say hi to my mom."

"Hi-Josh's mom. This is Lisa."

"Her name is Marissa—Lisa," Josh added innocently.

"Thanks Josh. Hi Marissa. You've got a good-looking young fellow here. He's been real brave. He didn't talk to strangers, except me. But that was okay 'cause I promised to help him, and he could tell I wasn't lying. Right Josh?"

"Yeah mom, and I didn't go with anyone, except now, when Lisa told me dad went to God, like Shultzy did. Then I went with Lisa to call you—but you were already talking to Lisa's friend Frank, so I didn't push the buttons myself."

"You're a very good boy, Josh. I'm very proud of you." Marissa was sobbing, "Does anything hurt, Josh?"

"Just my shoulder, where dad was holding me too hard. But I didn't cry 'cause I saw dad was sick and acting weird. Lisa said, when you get sick sometimes you get funny and do stuff like when I broke my fire engine. Lisa one time spilled water and broke a glass from being sick, too."

"Marissa, Josh is fine. He said nothing else hurts. Dr. Stone will look at his shoulder before we leave here. He had a glass of milk and we're going to get a pizza to take on the plane. He has no other bruises, and—"

"I'm only letting the doctor look at my shoulder after he looks at yours—'cause yours is sore too, remember?"

"Right, Josh," Lisa said. "We made a deal."

"Mom, where is Uncle Yale if you're at his house?"

"I'm here Josh. I miss you." Lisa's heart started racing, hearing Yale's voice. The painful memories evoked fresh tears.

"Yale, wait till you meet Lisa—she's real nice. But she's a little bit messy right now," He looked at Lisa, "and she's crying again, but I don't know why. Probably cause she's a girl person, like mom."

I know Lisa very well, Josh. I'm looking forward to seeing her again." Lisa couldn't talk to him.

Frank, let's get Josh checked, okay?" She started to back out of the room, needing a minute to pull herself together. Josh noticed and got upset.

"I gotta go now, Uncle Yale. Lisa, stay here. I don't want to talk anymore—"Lisa, don't go away from me. Lisa." Josh started to cry, and she went to him immediately.

"Marissa, it's been a rough day. We'll see you soon and talk then. Okay? I'd like to get Josh out of here, and get him home to you."

"Lisa, thank you. I—oh God—thank you. Thank you."

"Mom, don't cry. I'll be home pretty soon."

"Okay Josh."

"Bye, mom."

"I'll be waiting, Josh. Bye. I love you. Lisa, Lisa—"

"Marissa, it's Frank. Lisa is going with Josh now. I'll call you after we're done here so you'll have a better idea of what time we should arrive." Lisa had taken Josh's hand after Frank whispered something to Harvey Stone, and the Doctor led them to another room. "Marissa," Frank stated flatly, "Martha Harper from the Juvenile Division of the FBI is accompanying us. She said Josh is doing extremely well. Please calm yourself, and we'll be back in touch soon."

"Thank God he's all right. That's all that matters to me, Frank. You'll call back soon then?"

"Yes, Marissa."

Frank spoke to Marissa six times over the next two hours. Martha spoke to her as well.

It took over two hours in the hospital for Josh to be completely examined, as mandated by Martha Harper, in accordance with the law. Harvey Stone examined Frank while Lisa went with Josh to have Josh's shoulder x-rayed. Josh only cooperated when Lisa was beside him. By the time they boarded Frank's plane, she was completely exhausted. Lisa and Josh fell asleep shortly after taking off, both in hospital garb, covered with grease stains from pizza. They slept all the way to LA, and Josh went back to sleep on Lisa's lap during the limo ride to Yale's estate. Frank had arranged escorted security for all of them until they could reunite Josh with his mother.

They reached the familiar gates to Yale's estate near dusk. Lisa was tense as the limo drove, the two miles, from the entrance gate to Yale's sprawling multi level domain. She wasn't innocent or naive anymore, and she wasn't as awed by the beautiful estate with lush landscaped surroundings as she had been two years ago when Yale brought her here to recuperate. As the vehicle halted, Lisa felt a lifetime had passed since she had been Yale's lover in this house.

Marissa came running out. Yale, his mother Ruth, Victor, and David Ross, Yale's assistant, followed close behind. Frank got out of the limo, and opened his arms to sobbing Marissa.

"It's okay. Honey, he's fine. He's asleep on Lisa's lap. Go and sit by him, so he wakes to your face." Marissa got in the car. Frank had the driver open all the windows and doors so there would be more air circulating. Marissa stroked Josh's face gently, as she cried, "Josh, it's mommy. You're home now." She repeated the words a few times, until he opened his eyes.

"Hi mom," he said, climbing on her lap. She held him, sobbing and rocking with her child in her arms. Everyone cried with relief. It was minutes before anyone moved. Frank helped Marissa and Josh out of the limo. Martha got out on the other side. Frank leaned toward Lisa, extending his hand, and she held his hand tightly as she slid out of the car. Her legs were rubbery. Frank caught her as she stumbled. "Are you okay, Lisa?"

"Once I get feeling back in my legs I will be," she laughed.

"Sit down and let me rub them. You're wobbling." She sat on the edge of the seat. Frank bent massaging her calves. "Go on in. I'll be in, with Lisa, in a minute."

"Lisa, did I hurt your legs?" Josh asked, coming back to her, pushing himself away from his mother's arms.

"No, honey. I'm fine. You didn't do anything—my feet just fell asleep, I guess. Go in with mom, Josh. I'll be there in a few minutes, okay?"

"No. I'll wait for you." He came up beside Frank and started rubbing her legs too.

"Josh, I'm okay. Thank you. Come on. We'll go in." She tried to stand, but her legs were shaky, and she grabbed Frank's arm.

"Lisa, sit down. Please," Martha Harper stated sternly. "Josh, go on in the house with your mother. Lisa will be in later."

"No! No! I don't want to. I'm staying with Lisa!" he yelled at Martha.

"Marissa, take Josh in the house with you, please. Josh, Lisa will be in soon. Go with mommy, please." Josh grabbed Lisa, and started crying. "Come on Lisa. Get up." Lisa started to move, when Martha said quite loudly, "No Lisa."

Josh let go of Lisa. Go with your mother. Now, please." She walked over to Lisa, as everyone watched, and put her hand possessively on Lisa's shoulder. Josh stood there crying. Marissa went to him and bent down, "Come on, Josh". He turned and pushed his mother's hand away screaming, "No. No." He tried to hug Lisa. Martha told her not to move. "Josh, can you tell me why you don't want to go in the house with your mom, and leave Lisa out here?" He was crying even harder now.

"Josh, it's mommy. Come in the house with me."

"Josh, did you hear?" Martha asked. "Lisa will be in very soon."

He kept on crying, pulling on Lisa's hands, while Martha told her to sit still, until she bent her head crying. "Josh, why don't you want to leave Lisa?" Martha asked again. "Why, Josh?"

He grabbed his pants and pee'd all over himself. "Why Josh—why don't you want to leave Lisa?"

"Cause—cause—cause she's gonna go to God like Shultzy and dad," he screamed, still sobbing.

"Oh God. No Josh. I'm not going to God for a long time. Josh, I'm fine." She was crying and tried to move toward him.

"Lisa, please. He has to separate and see you're telling the truth. Sit still, and tell him to go in," Martha whispered to her. "Be firm."

"Josh, listen to me, right now!" He stopped, responding to the tone of her voice. "I haven't lied to you before. And I'm telling you the truth now. I'm not going to God now—"

"Then get up," he begged, "Come on."

"Josh, I'm not ready to get up. I want you to go with your mom, right now. I'll be in soon. I promise. Now Josh—go with your mom—please!"

He stood looking at her, afraid. Her tears continued falling as she sat, wanting to hold him and tell him it was okay, knowing she had to do this. "I'll be in soon, Josh." Lisa reiterated, more softly; then waited.

"Okay. I'll wait for you inside, so I can show you Buster." He turned, took his mom's hand and looked back once before going into the house. Lisa sat with her head bent.

"Thank you Lisa," Martha said. "From observing you with Josh all day, I know how hard this was for you. Can I do anything?"

She looked up a Martha with a tear streaked face. "Yes, Martha—go away!"

"Okay Lisa, I deserve that," Martha replied. "We're going in now. You wait about ten minutes, then come in, please. You have to come in alone, and go to Josh first. Tell him you're there, that you didn't lie, and you didn't go to God—got it? Lisa,—"

"I heard you, Martha."

"Mr. Frye, do you want to give Lisa directions to the room please."

"The den," Yale said.

"Mr. Frye, would you—"

"I know the way, Martha."

"Okay Lisa. The door will be open."

"No Martha. The door is not open—doors for me have never been 'open'—just slightly ajar. Go on. Please."

They left Lisa sitting on the edge of the limo seat. Frank whispered, before joining the others, "I'll open all the doors in the world for you, Lisa. I swear I will."

She lit a cigarette and paced around outside after her legs felt steadier, knowing all the open gateways in the world wouldn't matter to her; since the only one she really wanted was not unlocked anymore;

not since she left and closed it behind her two years ago, to try and save a marriage that failed anyway.

She waited the ten minutes and walked to the entrance. The brass knob felt cold in her hand as she pulled the heavy door open to enter the house.

CHAPTER 9

Yale watched as Lisa walked into his den, approached Josh, bent to his level, looked him directly in the eyes and said, "I'm here Josh, just like I promised I would be. I'm fine and I'm not going to God. Thank you for waiting here for me."

"Do your feet still hurt?"

"No. They feel much better now."

"Want to see Buster? He's outside now; back here. Come on, I'll show you." She followed Josh to the big glass sliding doors that covered an entire wall of the den. She remembered the day Yale had closed all the blinds and made love to her on that very carpeting, in that very room, with daylight peaking beneath the blinds, as her body arched to his. She walked outside with Josh and looked at the familiar Olympic size pool where she and Yale had played. She felt bereft for all she gave up.

Buster was a black Standard Poodle that almost knocked Lisa down with his welcome. He was playful and good with Josh, who hung onto him, although Buster wanted to be left alone. He came when Josh called him, and showed off, like most well-trained animals did on command. Josh gave Lisa a Frisbee to toss to Buster. He started laughing really hard when he saw what a lousy tosser she was. Everyone came out to see what was going on.

"Try again Lisa. But do it straighter this time." Lisa tossed the Frisbee. It curved, hitting Frank on his ass.

"Oops. Sorry Frank," she laughed. Josh was giggling so robustly it became contagious. Frank picked up the Frisbee and tossed it to Josh, who caught it, one handed, and tossed it to Yale. Yale tossed it back to Josh, but Buster intercepted and ran away with the Frisbee. They went back into the house, since the bugs were biting. Josh and Lisa sat on the floor eating the M&M's Victor had put out. Marissa joined them stroking her son's face lovingly. Josh started talking about going away with his dad, and how his dad wouldn't let him call or come home. He explained, they stayed in motels and his dad yelled a lot. He mentioned that he drank out of a bottle a lot, and would throw up a lot, too. The scenario was ugly and frightening. Josh comprehended enough to know his dad was sick, but being seven saved him from realizations far more agonizing for Marissa as the story unraveled. Josh stopped talking for a minute, looked at his mother and asked, "Are you crying because dad went to God, mom?"

Marissa didn't know how to answer. She didn't want to lie to Josh. She was so emotional from the hell she'd been living for the last seven days, not knowing where Josh was, or if she'd ever get him back. She grabbed Lisa's hand, needing to thank her for ending the nightmare, and helping Josh get home safely. "Oh God. Oh God." Marissa sobbed, reliving the past week of horror and agony.

Lisa moved closer and held Marissa, sharing the pain, knowing as one mother to another, the torture Marissa must have experienced. "It's over. It's over, Marissa," Lisa said, letting herself be held onto, and allowing Marissa to release what she could not contain. Josh was quiet as he watched his mom cry in Lisa's arms. Lisa answered for Marissa. "Josh, your dad was sick, really sick; so it's okay he went to Heaven and God. I think your mom was sad when your dad didn't tell her where he took you. She's glad your home now. Back with her where you belong."

"I'm not sad dad went to God, Lisa. I'm not—I'm not," Josh screeched, finally admitting what he was feeling.

"Come here, Josh. It's okay, honey, to feel like that." Marissa put out a hand, and Josh came over. "I'm glad dad is dead," he admitted. "I'm not sad. He hurt you once. I saw. He hurt me too," he cried. Marissa pulled Josh against her. "God. Oh Josh. Josh—I love you."

Lisa lent comfort until they calmed. She looked at both of them. "It's over. It's okay. Come on Marissa. Why don't you take Josh and get some rest?" Lisa stood, and helped them up. "Josh, I'll be going in a little while. I'm glad I got to know you and your mom. Maybe, one day, when I'm back in LA again we can visit, or go to a movie or something. Okay?"

"Where do you live, Lisa? I can come over tomorrow," Josh suggested.

"I live in a different city, pretty far from here. I'm going on a vacation tomorrow, so I'll be away for a while. But when I come back to L.A. I'll call you. Okay?"

"Do you want to come to my birthday party, Lisa? You don't have to buy a present if you don't want to."

"When is your birthday, Josh?" Lisa asked, watching his eyes fill with tears. He looked up at his mom with new tears falling, and Marissa picked him up, letting him cry on her shoulder.

"He just had a birthday two weeks ago Lisa," Marissa answered. "He knows it's a long time until his next birthday. He won't be seeing you for a while, so he's inviting you now—that's all." Marissa walked to a bedroom carrying Josh, while Lisa stood motionless feeling like a knife had pierced her heart.

"You did the right thing Lisa," Martha offered. "You did what you knew you had to. You've been remarkable all day."

She turned, looked at Martha and said calmly, "I always do what I have to Martha. Don't patronize me. Please. I don't like it." She walked away, "Excuse me. I need a bathroom. I'm going to be sick."

Lisa came out of the bathroom pale and weak. Yale and Frank were waiting for her in the hallway, "Are you all right, Lisa?"

"Compared to what, Frank?"

"Want to lie down, Lisa?"

"No. Thanks Yale. I'm going out for some air. I'll be back—I need a minute."

"I'll go with you," Frank said, concern showing on his face.

"No. Please—just give me a minute. Please." She looked at him, turned and walked away. She felt weak, tired, drained. She stopped in Yale's kitchen for some water before going out the front door.

"How are you, Victor," she asked, smiling at Yale's houseman, "It's been a long time!"

"I'm old, but doing fine, Miss Lisa. I'm glad to see you again. You sure wrote a good book."

"You read it, Victor?" She asked surprised.

"I bought it the first week it came out, Miss Lisa. Yale bought several copies of that first book of yours, too. He liked it, and so did Miss Ruth."

"I'm glad. Can I have a little water, Victor? My mouth is dry."

"There are all those different kinds of juices Yale keeps in the fridge. Want some juice instead?"

"No. Water is fine. Thanks." She took the glass from Victor and patted his hand. "You look good, Victor. It's nice to see you again."

She stepped outside for a breath of air but the mosquitoes were vicious and forced her back into the house. She walked back to the den unaware the intercom was on throughout the house. She sat down next to Frank and Josh came running in, clean and bathed, wearing Ninja Turtle pajamas. He smelled good to Lisa, as he climbed on her lap and hugged her. He gave her a kiss on the cheek. "Good night. I'm going to sleep. Mom is taking me to see Godzilla tomorrow, so I gotta rest, 'cause it's a long trip."

Yale was standing beside Marissa when she said, "Godzilla is a major attraction in the San Diego Zoo."

"Yeh. He's real big. Uncle Yale said I could take pictures. He's gonna help me."

"That's great. Have a good time, Josh." He climbed off her lap and stood in front of Frank, "I like your plane. It's neat. Do your kids like it—I bet they go on it a lot?"

"I don't have children, Josh. I'm glad you liked it. We'll have to do it again sometime." He climbed on Frank's lap and kissed his cheek. "I'm inviting you to my next birthday party, too." He climbed off, ran to Marissa and she walked him to bed. Lisa watched Frank's face, noticing his left eye twitching, like it had whenever he had been uncomfortable during their week together. She watched him feel his pocket, looking for his pipe. She opened her purse, and handed him his pipe and a pouch of Cherry blend tobacco. He looked at her with unspoken appreciation. Marissa and Yale returned after tucking Josh in, sitting down next to each other, across from Lisa and Frank, asking simultaneously, "Anyone want a drink?"

"Not me," Lisa answered. "Yale, I need to make a couple of quick calls. Mind if I use your kitchen phone?"

"No, of course not. Use any phone you want, Lisa."

"Thanks. I'll be right back." She got up, still in her dirtied hospital garb, and Frank noticed her arm had goose bumps.

"Are you cold Lisa?" Frank asked.

"Yup—and tired. Can we go soon?"

"Yes, right after your calls, if you want." She walked to the kitchen, taking her cluttered purse with her, and took out her address book. She called Jean in New York. The answering machine went on. After the message Lisa said, "Jean, pick up the phone. It's Lisa. Jean, unless you're getting laid, you better pick up the phone, because you won't here from me for another week, and it's only one in the morning in New York so I know your—"

"Lisa? Where, the hell, are you? I've been calling Ben every hour to see if he's heard from you. You were on the news. You'll probably be in all the newspapers by tomorrow. I am nuts from you—what the hell happened—I've been—"

"Hold on. Breather time, Jean. Inhale and exhale. And just listen. I'm at Yale's house, in Beverly Hills. We brought Marissa's child back here to her. I've been in San Francisco since Monday night. I'm leaving for Lake Tahoe for a week. My extra bags are coming to your place Wednesday night. I hope you don't mind."

"Okay Lisa. From the beginning. You got off the telephone with me last Monday night when you were waiting for Yale to arrive. So I take it the heat was still there—"

"No Jean. Yale never showed or called. Frank Lee called after I talked to you, to cancel out Myra Sullivan's show. He was leaving that night to attend the same San Francisco fundraiser I was going to on Wednesday, s-o-oo-o when Yale stood me up, I accepted Frank's offer to go to 'Frisco with him that night instead. He came for me, and showed me The City, for a week, like you would not believe."

"Lisa, Frank is, like, in the 'Top Ten' of rich, known, influential and powerful. He's friends with Ben. And honey, Frank can fix it so you never have to look at macaroni and cheese for the rest of your life.

Shit—he could buy the manufacturers out, and make it an extinct item. So, tell me where you stayed and if he hit on you."

"The Bay Plaza, and none of your business."

"What's with Tahoe and your bags?"

"Frank asked me to go, and then invited my boys when they surprised me with a call."

"So—You're not shit, or on their shit list anymore for leaving Ronnie? They understand?"

"No Jean. I'm still shit—I stink a little less because I showed them I could survive. Actually, I'm buying them back."

"How—you said, Frank asked them to Tahoe?"

"Yeh, after I sent them fancy watches and called. They admitted what I suspected. That Ronnie and Sue fight all the time. They don't want to go there. Don't say a word Jean. I had to—I need them to forgive me for fucking up their happy home. I'm willing to pay if I have to—every cent I have—and maybe, one day I won't have to buy the love I want from them anymore. Maybe, one day they'll be able to forgive me and understand."

"So, is Frank a good lay? You know he dumped his last wife after finding her in bed with another broad. Can't say I blame him."

"He dumped her for fooling around while married to him, not because it was with another woman."

"What's the difference, Lisa?"

"Cheating matters—choosing with whom doesn't, Jean. I'm not interested in bullshit or gossip anyway."

"Well, Lisa, even if you're just seen around with Frank, and get a little PR out of it, you can gain status—not to mention a sable coat for every day of the week."

"I'm going to move from Canton to somewhere warm, so I won't need sable. And if you talk, we're through as friends—forever. I want no PR—sable—or anything else from Frank. Got it?"

"Okay. Okay. I hear you. You're stupid, but I hear you. What's wrong with letting someone make things easier for you, especially after two years of macaroni and cheese, living in a dump, medical bills up the ass, no husband, kids who fuck you over, folks that turn on you, friends that stop calling, working two jobs to become a writer, and selling every piece of jewelry—except a gold Koala Bear pin, to get yourself to New York to get published? Sorry, Lisa, I love you. But you are dumb if you pass up a way to make your life easier—God knows you've earned it."

"I'm not a whore, and I won't prostitute myself for anyone. I made it this far alone, and I can still look in the mirror, Jean. That's enough."

"Well Lisa, at least you write good enough so you can eat steak now. Maybe you'll join the real world one day. We got another offer for the screen rights to the novel from Turner, for five hundred thousand. Maybe Ben can talk you into a few photos with Frank, so you can triple the take on the screen rights anyway."

"Sell for five hundred thousand tomorrow, Jean. I don't—"

"Hold on, Lisa. We're not selling now. This was an opening bid. Now we negotiate a while, then—"

"No Jean. I want to sell now, and my contract gives me the right—"

"Fuck you, Lisa. Ben and I are busting our asses. You don't sell for opening bid. I'll lose over twenty-five grand, honey, and so will Ben. Don't be in such a hurry—"

"Sell tomorrow, Jean. Sell and take an extra twenty-five thousand for you and for Ben—I'll sign for it—or I don't renew the contract at the end of the year, even if I have to eat shit instead of macaroni and cheese!"

"Why Lisa? What, the fuck, is your problem? We've been on your side—I don't get it."

"Pay attention, Jean. Numero uno—by tomorrow night I will be a headline because—a) I located Marissa Myer's child and b) because I'm with Frank. Therefore—c) you can ask for more money because of who I'm with or what I did. Sell tomorrow, Jean. Let me keep my self-respect—for God's sake Jean—it's the only thing—the only fucking thing I have left. Don't cash in on me, and don't ask me to sell out now." She started crying into the receiver.

"Okay Lisa. Chill. I'll sell tomorrow. We'll make it up with the next book, or something. God Lisa, how many weeks of touring did you do to sell the book, only to end up with so much less than you can get now? What about Yale, Lisa? Has he said why he didn't show or call?"

"No. And I'm not asking. It's history, Jean. What do you think of the outline for "Regrets"?

"It's good. Can you have a draft by December? I want a quick hit now, to follow the success of the first book. A second best seller will give you the security you want, and it can establish you as more than being a one book 'flash'."

"I think so. I'll push for it, Jean. Maybe I can have a basic manuscript by then."

"It's okay, honey. You've pushed enough, and for too long. Don't bust ass. It'll be months before the paperback is out on this one. You'll be carried for a while. Just a draft is fine. Are you over him, Lisa?"

"Some things you never get over, Jean. You just go on or get buried. I'm going on, and I'm going to have 'fun'. A lesson I've learned from Mister Frank Lee."

"Where are you going to live now, Lisa? How about New York? I could start looking for a place for you? You said, you don't want to stay in Canton?"

"No. Not New York. I'll see. It depends."

"Depends on what, Lisa?"

"Where Frank wants to live after we're married. Good Bye Jean. I'll be in touch." Lisa abruptly hung up. She couldn't help smiling as she pictured the expression Jean must have had on her face at that very moment.

Chapter 10

Lisa was searching through her purse for her apartment manager's business card after getting off the phone with Jean. She wanted to send a telegram, advising that she was sending the rent check out the next day, having forgotten about it for the last two weeks. She had the main telephone number in her address book, but not his apartment number. As she was rummaging through her wallet, Frank walked into the kitchen.

"Lisa, your phone conversations are not private. The intercom has been left on at my request. I was worried about you and Martha felt you suffered a great deal of duress today. She was also concerned about ramifications. You're very noble honey, but call Jean back and let her handle the sale of your screen rights in a more profitable manner. I won't interfere in the sale. You deserve to earn the full potential, despite being with me, or because of headlines. You'll have to be aware Lisa, I am frequently a newspaper item, and you're going to be one if we are together, like it or not. I am not reclusive, as you know. Are you able to accept that kind of life with all the invasions of privacy you'd incur?"

"I don't know, Frank, what I can or cannot handle. I'm not calling Jean back. It's my decision to make. Not yours. So, stay out of it. I'm not noble Frank. I'm honest. That's all. Also, if we marry, I want a prenuptial agreement drawn up. What's mine is mine. What's yours is yours. If I need anything, I'll ask for it. But I don't give a damn about acquisitions. I didn't know what you had when I met you, and I still don't give a shit. If you want to wear Cashmere, be my guest. Just don't try to doll me up or make me over. I'm not a purchase or possession, Frank."

"Lisa, I have fallen in love with you, so I'll accept your terms. I know you're not in love with me and, perhaps, that prevents you from accepting what I could give you. I hope, with time, you'll learn to trust me more, even fall in love with me. Perhaps you'll let me teach you that you can overcome pain, and that acquisitions can create options with which you might not otherwise be able to indulge yourself. Jean is right. You don't live in the real world. You're very idealistic."

"This is who I am, Frank."

"What is it you really need, Lisa? You say doors have never been open for you—just slit. I can open doors if you let me."

"Thanks Frank, but right now even if the doors were open wide I'd be too afraid to walk through them. Just take care of me. Protect me, Frank. I need to feel safe and sheltered before I can feel anything else. In turn, I'll teach you how to have 'fun' without buying it, chasing after it, and clinging to the notion that's the only way you can have it. Fair enough, Frank?"

"It'll do for starters, Lisa. Listen, I have to leave for an hour. I'll come back for you and we'll stay in L.A. overnight. You finish your business here. We'll leave for Tahoe in the morning."

"My business here is finished, Frank. I can make my other calls from somewhere else."

"Stop trying to run away Lisa. It doesn't work. Talk to Yale. I'll be back in an hour. When I come back, you can let me know how many rooms to reserve in Lake Tahoe."

"I must not mean very much to you, for you to take this kind of chance, Frank."

"Oh honey, you mean so much that I'm willing to take risks, and chance you'll want to remain with me. You mean so much, Lisa, that I'm also putting your happiness first. I'll protect you, Lisa, if that's what you really want. But under my wing, not by allowing you to hide, or by keeping you locked in a cage. Who else do you have to call at this time of night anyway?"

"I want to send a wire to my boys, my folks, and my landlord."

"You can do that from the hotel later. Go back in there. I'll be back in an hour, Lisa. I suggest you talk to Yale. We both know there is unfinished business between the two of you which needs to be resolved."

"What hotel? Don't you have a home here, Frank?"

"Yes, I have a home here. I don't want to stay there tonight. I'll be back." He walked out leaving her sitting there. "Come on Martha," she heard him say. "I'll drop you off. I have to go out your way anyway." She got up, left the kitchen, and passed Martha in the hallway adjacent to the den.

"It was nice meeting you, Lisa. I hope the days to follow will be good ones for you. I'm glad Josh was found by someone as sensitive to other people as you are. Good night."

"Bye," was all Lisa said, walking into the den, her eyes avoiding Yale's. She walked over to Ruth and sat next to her.

"You look good, Ruth. I've thought of you so often," Lisa began. She reached for Ruth's hand, remembering the strong, sensitive woman, who lived for her only son; yet had been a friend to Lisa when she needed her. Dear Ruth, who raised her son alone, with very little money, but with an abundance of love. Understanding Ruth, who shared in the suffering of those she cared about, and spoke with wisdom, truthfulness and intelligence, never being judgmental.

"You look tired and worn out, Lisa. Life can be a bitch sometimes, huh?"

"I've got strong survival instincts, Ruth. I've had to develop them—or sink."

"Thank you for the birthday cards, and the holiday cards, Lisa. I would have liked to reciprocate, but you never wrote a return address on the envelopes, and you have an unlisted number. I almost called Ronnie, a few times, to get your address. Then I thought better of it."

"I called you last week, Ruth. The day of the book signing session here. Your answering machine was on, with the cute—"I'll call you when I can talk. I'm busy, or out for a walk"—I just decided not to leave a message and hung up. I regretted it afterwards."

"Maybe, you should follow your first instincts more often. It might give you less to regret later."

"You know I had to leave when I did, Ruth. You've raised a son. Would you have done differently?"

"How long has your divorce been final, Lisa? An article, I read, said over a year."

"Articles I read, Ruth, stated you were going to have a daughter-in-law soon."

"You shouldn't always believe what you read, Lisa, without checking out the facts. I called Myra Sullivan to verify how long you've been divorced, after I read the clipping. Did you try to verify what you read, Lisa?"

"I thought I'd get it straight from the horse's mouth, Ruth—but my phone never rang, and I got tired of waiting."

"That was one night, Lisa. What about the entire year before then? Why didn't you try to get it from the horse's mouth before last week?"

"Because I was busy, trying to figure out who the hell I was, Ruth?"

"Have you figured it out, Lisa?"

"Yes, Ruth. I'm a survivor. I can stand on my own, make it on my own, and live on my own."

"Is that why you're marrying Frank, for protection and sheltering? "I said, I could do it all on my own. I didn't say I wanted to. Now that I know I'm capable, Ruth, I don't have to prove shit to anyone anymore, and I can let someone take care of me for a change. I'm tired. The fight was hard. I just don't want to carry the ball anymore."

"What about happiness, Lisa? Did you find that, too?"

"Ruth, that's a word for fairytales. I don't read fiction anymore."

"So you write it instead, Lisa?"

"Stop, Ruth. Don't try to break down my barriers. I'm not strong enough to keep rebuilding."

"But that's what a survivor has to do, Lisa. Maybe, you're not a survivor. Maybe, you're throwing in the towel, honey." Lisa crumbled. Ruth took her in her arms, letting her hold onto her. "I've had no one for so long, Ruth. No one but myself."

Yale came over to her. "Either have I, Lisa. No one that mattered. Don't run away again, Lisa. I still love you."

She went to his arms. The others left the room. "Hold me, Yale. Don't let go—God—don't let go." He kissed her, feeling like it was only yesterday when she was his. He whispered gently, "I told you once before, I would hold you until you told me to let go. I still feel that way, Lisa, but I'm hoping you won't ever want me to let go again."

"Yale, I tried. I swear to God, I really tried to let go of you, to work hard at saving my marriage. But it was no use. I was so utterly miserable I finally had to leave. Then, when I told my boys, Ronnie announced it was me who was walking out, making me the heavy. I haven't had the same rapport with Marc and Steve since. This weekend is the first time, in two years, they are voluntarily coming to be with me. Oh Yale, it's been awful."

"Lisa, I was picking up Marissa when I was supposed to be coming to see you at the hotel. All hell broke out very suddenly. She was hysterical. Tony set fire to her house, besides kidnapping Josh, and it was very late by the time I called the hotel. They said, you'd checked out. I had my hands full trying to keep Marissa together, Lisa. I'm sorry I didn't reach you before you checked out. I know what you must have thought."

"I don't know what I would have done if Frank hadn't been there for me this past week. I had finished the signing tour. I really didn't want to go back to Canton. He made me feel alive. He took me places I've never seen, with new experiences I've never encountered. He understood my desolation better than I did. He knew how to bring me back to life. He's a remarkable person Yale, with or without his money or name. With or without his reputation or power. I'll always be grateful to him for being there when I needed someone so desperately. I'm going to Tahoe with him and seeing my sons, Yale. I have to do this. I need you to understand. Frank knows I'm not in love with him. He accepts it. But I love his kindness, his goodness, and how he took over with my boys when they called so we could arrange a special reunion. I'll explain that I can't marry him there. But I need to go, Yale. He's a very special person."

"I understand, Lisa. I'll be here when you come back. I'm not going anywhere. I've prayed for this moment for two years. I can wait a few more days." He put his mouth on hers and she clutched him to her, opening her mouth to his probing tongue, feeling a rush of excitement in her body she'd almost forgotten existed. She clung to him, and he to her, feeling the fire spread. "I don't want to wait to be with you a few more days, Lisa." He ran his hands inside her thighs. "I want you now. God, I've waited long enough, Lisa." He kissed her again, his mouth locked on hers, his hands running over her body. "I need you now.

Lisa, I need you now." He stood up, pulling her to her feet, and led her outside. He walked her to his music studio behind the house. It was a glass structure surrounded by huge looming trees. She didn't protest, needing to feel his body merge with hers as much as he did. He didn't turn on the lights but guided her to a sofa against one wall. With the full moon shining, he wrapped her in his embrace, and they explored each others body hungrily. "Oh Lisa, I love you. I love you so." He pulled her pants down while she fumbled with his belt lamely, until he helped her. She groped for him eagerly. He moaned as she guided him inside of her, screaming her name over and over, as she moved beneath him. Thrusting and meeting each push was urgent. She held onto him feeling powerless, and unable to resist the release her body was demanding. She arched as he penetrated deeply again, knowing they were both rising to the point of no return. She arched again, squeezing her thighs tightly together, yelling as she climaxed; holding him tightly as his body jerked and filled her with his semen. She ran her hands over his body, up and down his back, feeling his penis still throbbing deep inside of her. She didn't want to move. He covered her face with kisses. He pushed his tongue back into her mouth ardently.

"I'll never love anyone like I do you, Yale. I'm only whole with you. I ask, only, that you let me love you. I'll never ask God for anything more, as long as I have you."

"We belong together, Lisa. We always will." He was hard inside of her again. She began to move. "More, Yale. I want more." He obliged, gladly, until they shared ecstasy again.

Frank was in the den with Ruth, David, and Marissa, when Yale and Lisa returned from the studio. Frank had a pipe in his mouth. A large box was next to him on the oversized sofa. Lisa's eyes remained averted when he asked if she had a preference in which hotel they stay. He sensed there was a change imminent in his relationship with her.

"Anywhere but the Oak Plaza, will be fine Frank. Are you ready to go? You must be tired, Frank."

"Yes. Here Lisa. Why don't you change first? He handed her the box. She removed the top, and withdrew a silk slack outfit, noticing several other items in the box, including a sparkling diamond watch. He took out the gold and diamond Piaget watch. "I'm sick, to death, of that ugly watch you've been wearing everyday, so I chose one I'd prefer to see you wear. And since you refuse to buy anything for yourself, but continually mail gifts to others, I took the liberty to ensure you would arrive, in Tahoe, in something other than what you're wearing now."

"Frank, you're a royal pain. And I do mean "Royal". I'm too tired to change. So Ruth, or Marissa, if you have a long jacket, or sweater I can put over what I've got on, I'd like to borrow it, in order to prevent Frank from entering a posh Beverly Hills Hotel with such an apparition. Thank you, Frank, for your gifts. I'll attempt to appear neat and respectable in the morning, before we leave for Tahoe—Your Highness."

"Your gratitude is overwhelming Lisa, and your defiance recurrent, but I appeal to you to remove those garments before I vomit."

"Okay, already. I'll take them off." Ruth handed her a long red coat sweater that was on the sofa, while Frank held out the silk slack suit. "I said, I'd take this off. But I'm not getting dressed all over again. I'm too tired." With a twinkle in her eye, she took off the top with the hospital insignia on it, and put on Ruth's sweater. She then pulled the bottoms of the hospital garb off, and stood in front of him in the sweater, with only her bra underneath and worn sneakers on her feet. "I'm ready now, Frank. Let's go."

He stepped back, looked at her, laughing. "Not exactly what I had in mind, Lisa. But cute. You are incorrigible. Someone should have spanked you years ago."

"They did, Frank. And it didn't help. Come on, I want a hot fudge sundae." He picked up the box and they walked to the front door. As he was saying goodbye to everyone, she removed her bra sneakily, and when he turned around she handed it to him. "Come on, Frank. I'll show you how to get a suite without a cent."

"Lisa, you wouldn't. Lisa—"

They all laughed as she got into the limo, followed by Frank, with the box and Lisa's bra in his hands.

As the limo pulled away, Ruth said jokingly, "I expected her to remove her panties next".

Yale turned to Ruth laughing. "She couldn't. They're on the floor in the studio."

CHAPTER 11

Before leaving with Lisa for Lake Tahoe, Frank reserved two adjoining suites. He sensed this was going to be a farewell trip with him, and that Lisa was having a difficult time broaching the subject. He wanted to make it easier for her, but couldn't help feeling he was going to be giving up something monumental and delayed talking to her. He occupied the casino for hours at a time, as a diversionary tactic, to avoid the inevitable. He loved her spontaneity, sensitivity, and sense of humor. She made him feel younger than his sixty years, although lately he was exceedingly tired. She was playful, fun to be with, and the first woman since his first wife, Maria, that he could confide in and trust, without feeling doubtful of ulterior motives. Lisa radiated warmth with every person she encountered. She was unpretentious and beautiful. He wanted her to be happy. And if Yale would give her life the joy she craved and unquestionably deserved, after the painful years she'd sustained, he was willing to give her up so she could fulfill herself emotionally. She did not care about wealth or extravagances, only for some sense of security. She constantly fought his attempts to buy her anything.

Her sons would be arriving that evening, and she excitedly dragged him to stores on the main level of the hotel to pick out a few special garments for them. He helped her select shirts, sweaters, shorts, and swimwear. He refused to allow her to pay for the articles, promising he'd create a public scene and embarrass her. She told him she'd like to watch him make a spectacle of himself, so he changed tactics, reminding her it was his idea to bring her sons to Tahoe, and he wanted the pleasure of indulging them this one time. She finally succumbed to his charm and even accepted a sequined evening gown he declared was designed specifically for her.

They went back to their suite; followed by sales clerks, carrying all their purchases, when she said, surprising him, "Stay in the room, Frank. You can gamble later. I want you to myself for a while before the boys arrive."

"Something on your mind you want to talk about, Lisa?" he asked, feeling she finally mustered up the courage to speak openly with him.

"Actually Frank Lee, I just want to climb in bed with you. I need to be held. I'm nervous about the impending arrival of the boys. I need you to make me feel it's going to be all right."

"My pleasure, madam. Your room or mine?"

"The room doesn't matter, Frank. Just the person I'm with."

They entered the suite, and after she laid out the purchases for her boys in the adjoining suite, she came back and curled up beside Frank on the sofa. He put his arms around her, kissing her cheek tenderly. She snuggled close to him and found herself crying minutes later, not completely certain why. She felt safe with Frank, but knew she had to tell him she couldn't marry him. She wanted his friendship. She valued his opinions and judgments, but it was Yale who possessed her. She wanted to spend the rest of her life with Yale.

Lisa knew Frank would understand. He wanted her to be happy. She valued the way he treated her, and was aware she was going to hurt someone very special. She hated hurting anyone, and felt awful having to tell him of her decision. She let him hold her, feeling the abrupt shift of positions as he tried to hide his arousal. She knew Frank was aware the change in her mood when they left Yale's estate was an indication she had resolved issues between herself and Yale, yet he gave her time without pressing for answers. She felt a tenderness for Frank. A respect which was immeasurable. He had a tremendous capacity for objectivity, always remaining candid, and reasonable. It was imperative she cause as little hurt as possible to this generous, noble man.

Spontaneously and decisively Frank spouted, "Lisa, life is too short for us to be prisoners by commitments which are confining or restrictive. You are not under lock and key to anyone or anything. Allow yourself the opportunity to enjoy the rest of your life. You're a special lady. Right now, I sense, you are afraid of acting on your needs, and worrying about others again instead of yourself. Honey, you've done that long enough. Take what you want, Lisa, before it's gone."

She snuggled closer, understanding he was trying to make it easier for her. He squirmed again not wanting to expose his desire for her. She rested; letting him rub her arm, quiet, feeling safe next to him. She was about to speak when she glanced up, and saw tears on his face. His eyes were closed. She moved closer, rubbing his chest. "Don't make it more difficult than it has to be, Lisa."

"Shut up, Frank, and make love to me." She moved her hand down, finding the stiffness beneath his pants.

"Get up, Lisa!" He commanded. "I want a drink. You know I'm human, and completely in love with you. But don't give me what you want to give to another. She rolled over on top of him. "Make love to me, Frank. I've got enough love in me for more than one person."

"I don't fuck whores!" he shouted, shoving her away and onto the floor. "I also don't accept sympathy fucks!" He got up and stormed into his bedroom, feeling the pain of losing her today would be easier than dragging it out.

She stormed in, and furiously came up to him, slapping him across the face. "You better watch who you call a whore, you bastard!" He pushed her down on the bed and pinned her hands down. "Who the hell are you to slap me? Whore!" He leaned over, then forced his mouth on hers. He grabbed her breasts, unleashing raging hunger. She slapped him again. "I'm no one's whore—no one's!"

He tore the clothes from her, opened his pants, coming down on her with force. "I love you—damn you! I love you!" He pushed hard inside of her, groaning, as she locked herself around him. "I love you. I love you, Lisa."

"I know. Forget love for now, you bastard, and fuck this whore." She pushed hard against his penetration repeatedly. "Fuck me harder Frank, or can't you?" she teased, scratching his back with her long nails, while tightening around him, listening to him pant and moan, as he pushed again and again, until he exploded with a scream. He was slowing and looked at her with misty eyes, "I love you, Lisa. Enough to let you go."

"Shut up Frank. Just hold me." They eventually fell asleep, totally spent, in Frank's room. He was still sleeping when Lisa woke and went to bathe, to ready herself for Marc and Steve's arrival.

She was in white slacks and red tube top when Frank walked in naked. Her hair was in a ponytail, with straggling strands, and she had applied fresh makeup. She wore the Piaget watch he had bought her. Her cleavage was provocative as she bent to adjust the straps of her sandals.

"You look like crap, Frank. Get going—my boys will be here soon. If I didn't know better Frank, I'd think you were getting a hard on again. But at your age, I'm sure it's a piss on. Right?"

He looked at her cleavage again; then appraised her as she stood up. She put her hands on her hips smiling at him seductively.

Suddenly, someone knocked on the door. "Who's there?" Lisa asked.

"Ms. Klein, your sons are in the lobby. Your phone is off the hook so I couldn't call as you requested. Shall I bring them up now?"

"No. I'll be down in a minute. Have them wait."

"Very well. Sorry to disturb you."

"Why are you having them wait downstairs, Lisa?"

"Because I'm not done here. Come back here, Frank. I want you." He moved closer, kissing her, "Later honey. You've waited a long time for them. I know what this means to you."

Fine, Frank. "Get showered and dressed. I want you to meet my boys." She kissed his cheek. "Meet me downstairs, okay?"

Lisa got in the elevator, wondering if perhaps she was a whore, provoking Frank and baiting him into sex. She knew he wanted her and she had accommodated his needs. It was not for money, love, or "a sympathy fuck" as he had put it. But she didn't hunger for him as he did for her. She knew it and so did he. She wondered if she screwed him to get rid of guilt; knowing she had to tell him she couldn't marry him but did care for him, and if that was indicative of being a whore or some form of prostitution. She felt it really wasn't significant, considering he did mean a lot to her. She just chose to express herself in a way that affirmed her feelings for him. She was still pondering over whether she should or shouldn't have been with Frank, when she spotted Marc and Steve in the lobby.

"Hi guys," she said enthusiastically. "I've missed you a lot." She hugged them, and was a little disappointed they were casual in greeting her, but didn't show it, asking, "How was the flight, boys?"

"Fine, fine," they both answered, staring at her curiously, until she asked, "Something wrong?"

"You look different," Steve said. "Did you lose weight on purpose, and how come your hair is sorta reddish?"

"Yes. This is the new me. I've lost weight and got myself a different look. Do you like it?"

"Does it matter?" Steve asked tartly; then looked at his brother.

She wasn't going to let them spoil things, right out of the chute, or get upset. But the remark hurt. "Come on, I'll show you your rooms, and if you're hungry we can grab a bite."

"Can we eat first?" Marc asked. "Then Steve and I can hang out and look around."

"Sure," she answered, remaining cool. "That's fine."

"What's fine?" Frank asked, putting his hand on her shoulder, as he walked up behind her.

"That they eat before going to the rooms. Boys meet Frank Lee. Frank, my sons, Marc and Steve."

They shook hands. When Frank saw the boys look at each other, he remarked casually, "I suppose you expected someone younger. I should have told you I was an old fart, but a decent one."

"Don't believe him boys—he's not decent. He's outrageous; full of himself and going through a second adolescence—or is it your third?" she teased.

"Thanks, Lisa. So much for good first impressions."

"Peter," he called to the manager, who immediately came over, "Make sure Marc and Steve have free reign, carte blanche, and bill it all to their mother," he laughed, squeezing Lisa's shoulder. "Just see they're taken care of, Peter," he then stated more seriously.

"Yes sir. I'll take care of it."

"Thanks. Come on. Let's eat dinner, fellows. I'm starved." He led the way through the casino, shaking several hands, and stopped a pit boss, asking for a stack of chips along the way. "What's your game guys? I'm a blackjack junkie myself."

"I like blackjack and poker," Marc said. "So do I," Steve added.

"Well, I'll give you a quick rundown on house rules. House draws on 16 and has to stand on 17; just like Vegas. Push on a tie, and one and a half on blackjack. The tables start at five bucks. Lots of luck. "Here," he said, as he handed them each a stack of chips, "See if you can double these."

They walked into a huge, lavish restaurant, and followed Frank to a table. It wasn't until they were seated that the boys noticed he'd given them each twenty, one-hundred dollar, chips. Frank watched them exchange looks. Frank ordered for Lisa and himself. He let the guys order for themselves. He asked for a bottle of wine and asked, "Lisa, is it okay for the guys to have a drink?"

"Yes Frank. Indulge them. I'm not saying shit; you're hopeless."

"Oh goodie, guys, what'll it be?," he asked in mocking good humor.

After Cherries Jubilee they hit the game tables and all walked away winners, with Lisa tripling her money. They passed a roulette table on the way to the cashier and Frank asked her, "Do you still feel lucky?"

"I'm taking my money and running," she answered.

"Chicken Shit," he said, putting down five one hundred dollar chips on number ten and losing. "I never did like roulette."

Lisa took five of her one hundred dollar chips and put them on number nine. She won. It paid thirty-six to one odds. "That's how to play, putz."

"Wow, mom! You're hot tonight." Steve said.

"She's hot every night," Frank said, pinching her ass.

"Behave yourself Frank," she said smacking his hand.

He took out a card and handed it to Marc, "Here, you and Steve go check out the action. Just show this card wherever you go and you'll be taken care of. They went into the lobby where Frank flagged Peter over again. "Is my limo in front, Peter?"

"Yes, Mr. Lee."

"Good. Show the boys the car and tell Al to take them wherever they want to go."

"Yes sir."

"Have fun, guys. We'd go, but your mom is tired. She's yawned twice in the last ten minutes. See you in the morning."

"Thanks, Frank, er Mr. Lee," Marc said.

"Frank—is fine. Bye." They shook his hand and kissed Lisa before rushing out the doors.

When Frank got up at six to pee, he went to another room so he wouldn't wake Lisa. He called downstairs to see when the boys got back. He laughed when told they hadn't returned yet. He went back to the bed, sleeping until nine, which was unusual for him. Lisa was already showered and dressed, sitting and talking to her boys, when he appeared in shorts and Ralph Lauren cotton shirt.

"I've ordered breakfast, Frank. There's some mail for you, too. I told them to bring it up with the paper."

"Thanks, Lisa. So fellas, do you have any money left?"

They bragged about their amazing luck and thanked him for the room and clothes. The day flew by, and so did the next, as they laughed, ate, swam, gambled, saw a couple of shows, indulging themselves with everything but sleep. Saturday, Frank took them to another great local restaurant for dinner, and during desert pulled Lisa's hair out of the scarf she had it tied back with. "I like your hair loose," he said matter of factly, and just as casually he handed each of the boys a box. Inside, they each found a gold ring with their initials set in diamonds. "You can have the rings sized here in the hotel. I hope when you look at the rings, guys, occasionally you'll remember this weekend. I've had a great time. I'm glad I got to meet you. Thanks for sharing some time with an old man." Lisa swallowed hard at his soliloquy.

"We are having a ball. Thanks a lot Frank. I hope we see you again sometime. You're more fun than a lot of our friends, right Steve?"

"Yeh, and I like your hair loose, too, mom. Frank, thanks for everything. You don't have to, but if you want, you could visit us with mom, sometime. This trip has been incredible."

"I'm glad you had a good time." He took out another box handing it to Lisa. "This is for you, for being you." He kissed her cheek. Inside was a gold key with "Lisa" inscribed across it.

"Is this the key to your heart, Frank?"

"No honey; you don't need a key for that—my heart has always been unlocked to you. To be specific, the key is to a Mercedes Convertible. You tell me where to have it shipped. Just promise me you'll drive it with the windows open, the top down, and your hair loose. That's how I want to picture you in it."

"You guys sound like you're not going to see each other again," Marc said, perceptively.

"I travel a lot and your mom is getting ready to write her next book, so it might be a while. Well, are we ready to go? I have to make some business arrangements, so if you boys want the limo, and Lisa, if you'd like to go with them, I'll catch up with you later."

"No, Frank, I'd like to stay here with you. The boys can meet us for breakfast in the morning." He patted her hand. "So, what color is my Mercedes, Frank?" she asked, looking at the key.

"Gold. It's covered in gold, Lisa."

Once inside the suite, Lisa went to put a lounger on in her room. Frank went to his bedroom to make a few calls. She was hanging up her cocktail dress when the phone rang. When it rang a second time, she reached to answer it, figuring Frank was busy, or in the bathroom. She was about to hang up, when she heard Frank say, "Hi Harvey," and stayed on the line realizing it was Dr. Harvey Stone, and it must be a call related to their finding Josh last week in San Francisco.

"It's bad news, Frank," She heard Harvey Stone say, and her heart started racing.

"Say it, like it is, Harvey. All of it".

"The cancer is back. Your tests show it's in your liver. It's inoperable. We can start chemo right away, Frank."

"Forget it, Harvey. How long do you figure?"

"A year, Frank. Maybe, a little longer. Maybe, less. You suspected it, didn't you?"

"At my age, you know that if your body complains it's for a reason. I was hoping I was wrong, or that it wouldn't be too bad. I drew a bad hand, Harvey. I just don't know if I have a good poker face. Keep a lid on this, Harvey. I'll call when I need you."

"Frank, I'm sorry. God, I wish—"

"I know, Harvey. Bye." Frank heard Harvey hang up and a click that confirmed Lisa had been listening in. He thought he had heard her pick up the phone a second after him, and was upset that she'd heard. It wasn't that he cared so much that she listened in on his conversation, as much as it was that he didn't want her final memory of him—of their time together—to end with her knowledge that he'd be dead in a year or less.

She sat on the bed shattered. How could this be? Frank was vital, full of life, active—God almighty, how could this be? A Billionaire—but it didn't matter. No amount of money could alter this. Inoperable Cancer. No family—no children—Dear God; he was going to die. Generous, giving, Frank. Unselfish Frank. Lonely Frank. How could she pretend and act normal? Maybe, she should tell him she knew and go to him this minute when he might need to hold someone. What to do? Jesus. How could this happen? Maybe, he should get another opinion? Maybe, he could try experimental drugs to buy time? Should she suggest it? Don't cry, Lisa. Fuck! Be strong, Lisa. Frank needs you, Lisa. Oh God, I can't pretend. How do I not cry in front of him? This can't be. There must be something that could be done?

"Lisa, are you coming out? Lisa? Hey Lisa, I feel like a hot fudge sundae. Want one?"

"Yeh, I'll be right there. Lots of whipped cream, Frank."

"I know—and no nuts, right?"

"Not on my sundae, Frank. I like my nuts elsewhere." She came out in the lounger and smiled at him. "And where, prey tell, do you like your whipped cream?"

"I'll show you, honey. I'll definitely show you."

Frank made a couple of calls after ordering room service. By the time he was off the phone, the sundaes had been delivered to the suite. Neither really wanted to eat. Lisa noticed Frank's left eye twitch, which always indicated when he was unnerved. She took a glob of the whipped cream off a sundae and put it in her hand, "Well Frank, where do you want it?" she asked, batting her lashes coquettishly.

"Trite, Lisa. I'm into originality. Can't you come up with something more creative?"

"Sure, putz," she said, flinging her full hand at him, covering his clothes with whipped cream. "I'm sick of how fucking neat you always are. If you can tell me how to wear my hair, I can tell you—or rather show you—what I think."

"Oh…is that so?" he said, putting whipped cream with nuts, from his sundae, in his hand, approaching her menacingly, "I don't even like that your hair is auburn. I wonder how you'd look with white hair," he added, dropping the handful of whipped cream on her head and rubbing it around. He stepped back and laughed, "You know, you still look sexy".

She picked up her sundae, with whipped cream from her head dripping down her face, and with a gleam in her eyes looked devilishly at him. She put her finger in the sundae, digging out some hot fudge, "and how, sweetie, would you look with a little brown added to your all white hair?"

He grabbed her hand, "Oh no, you don't. You vixen. I like my hair just the way it is," and pushed her hand, so the fudge landed on her face instead.

"Well, Mr. Clean, you still look too neat," she said, taking the glass dish with the remainder of the sundae in it, half melted by now, and quickly poured it on him.

"You little bitch," he said, as she giggled, watching the ice cream run down his pants. He went and picked up his sundae. Lisa started running away when someone knocked on the door.

"Answer the door, Frank," she yelled, while he continued chasing her with the sundae in his hand.

"Help! Help! Damsel in distress," she shouted out, hiding behind the dining room table, so he couldn't reach her.

"Mom, it's us—mom; what's wrong?"

"Well, open the door, putz. We can't alarm the boys—can we?"

"Just wait, Lisa. I'm not through with you," he said, walking to the door with the sundae in his hand, his clothes covered, as she giggled girlishly.

The boys walked in carrying bags, looked at them, and burst out laughing. "See, Steve, and you thought they'd be asleep already."

"What's wrong, mom?" Steve kidded, "did they send up the wrong flavor?"

She approached her sons laughing, thinking she was safe now, "I don't actually know. I didn't get to taste it."

Frank didn't waste a second, pouring the sundae on her head, as she screamed; the cold pouring down her face. "Well, taste it, honey. Is it the right flavor?"

The boys and Frank roared. "You play dirty, Frank. You are going to pay—You definitely are going to pay for this!"

"It'll be worth it," he laughed. "Gee Lisa, you look good enough to eat."

"I'm not touching that line, Frank," she laughed, picking up a bunch of napkins to wipe her face.

"They are sick—I think they've lost it," Marc said, looking at his brother.

They all laughed. "So fellas, anything I can offer you?" Frank asked. "How about a sundae?"

"I'll pass, thanks," Marc said.

"Ditto," Steve added quickly. "Here Frank. We got you a little something." Steve held out the bag to him.

"I hope it's a box of multicolored, ribbed Trojans. I've always wanted to screw in Technicolor."

The boys roared, while Lisa said, "I told you he hasn't grown up yet! The man is a pervert!"

Frank pulled a box out of the bag, opened it, and took out a beautiful ivory carved pipe, that he knew was expensive. He was so touched by their gift he was unable to make light of it. "Uh—this is nice, uh—very, very, nice." He was moved, and it showed.

"We wanted you to have something to remind you of us, and this trip too," Steve added. "We thought of this."

"We never bought a pipe before. I hope you don't have one like this one, or you can exchange it," Marc said, noticing Frank looked like he was going to cry.

Lisa was proud of her sons, and the genuine token of appreciation they'd shown Frank. She was near tears herself as she looked at Frank. "Well, light up. Get your tobacco, Frank." She knew he needed a minute away. He came back, eyes averted, pipe in his mouth, trying to regain his composure. As he inhaled on the pipe, Lisa said seriously, "Well,

I'm glad you're here, guys. I have something important to ask you." The kidding was over as Lisa continued, "Could the two of you fly to Florida next Friday night? You see, I'm going to Florida from here, and I'm introducing Frank to grandma and grandpa—before Frank and I are married next Sunday. It would mean a lot to me if you could be there for our wedding. A week for the arrangements should be enough time, don't you think, Frank? I don't want anything elaborate." She looked at Frank who didn't try to hide his emotions now. "You sure, Lisa? You sure that you want to be with an old fart?"

"I don't want to be with an old fart, Frank. I want to be with you. I want to be your wife—if you buy me vitamins, so I can keep up with you. Also, promise you won't buy any colored Trojans. I'm not into Technicolor organs."

"Marc. Steve. Can I marry your old lady, and let her try to force me to grow up?" Frank asked, his eyes wet, reaching for Lisa's hand.

"I think you should marry her and not grow up. What do you think, Steve?"

"I think we should buy them a box of colored Trojans for a wedding gift, Marc. Maybe, mom will discover she's into a variety of things after all."

"Well Frank, I think you should ship my Mercedes to your island, off the Florida coast, where we can be married. Boys, maybe tomorrow we can talk about the rest of the plans. Right now, Mr. Frank Lee is going to wash my hair and tuck me in. Kiss me good night, fellas."

They kissed her and surprised Frank again, by kissing him too. She walked them to the door and came back to where Frank was seated, "Well, are you going to take me to bed or not?" He looked at her, unable to speak, his heart full. She took his hand and he pulled her to him, putting his arms around her waist. She stood in front of him while he buried his face against her stomach and cried. She stood, stroking his head, letting him sob. Her own tears fell as she accepted that, once again, she was doing what she had to.

Frank gave her life meaning when she needed it most. Maybe she could do something to brighten his life when he needed it most.

"Lisa," he whispered.

"Sh. It's what I want, Frank. I want to be with you—Sincerely, I do."

CHAPTER 12

Lisa was pissed that she had slept late on their last day in Tahoe and everybody was evidently downstairs already. She rushed to get ready and went down to the main floor in search of Frank and her boys. With a sense of relief that she wouldn't have to look for long, she approached Frank who was talking to Steve in the main lobby.

"I am definitely getting lazy. I can't remember when I've slept this late. Have you two been up long?"

"No Lisa," Frank answered, kissing her, "I just came down half an hour ago, but your sons on the other hand, pulled an all nighter. They'll probably sleep through the first day of classes when they return to school.

"Where's Marc?"

"Winning at blackjack, last time we checked," Frank explained. "How about some brunch?"

"Okay. Sounds good."

"Well, I'll meet you, when I get back."

"Where are you off to, Steve?" Lisa probed. "Meet someone?"

"No. Frank needs these dropped at the post office, and I was going to check out a store next door anyway, so I'll just be a few minutes. I guess Frank knows Yale Frye too, mom, he said waving an envelope."

She looked at Frank knowingly, "Steve, give Frank back the letters. We'll handle it. I want to get out for a bit."

"It's okay, mom."

"Now Steve—Please," she said sharply, looking at the confusion on her son's face.

"It's okay, Steve." Frank took the letters, "go check out the store, take the limo, and we'll meet you when you get back. And track Marc down, if you don't mind, so he'll know where we'll be."

"Sure. See ya." Steve left realizing something he didn't know about was going on, and his mother's tone suggested she was serious.

"Okay Frank, what's in the letter? An explanation perhaps of what is going on?"

"Lisa, I love you. I think it only fair to you and to Yale—"

"Shut the fuck up, you fool," she raged. "This is my life Frank Lee, and I decide who I want to share it with. If you have any qualms about me wanting to be with you, say so now, and I'll walk. This has nothing to do with Yale, and I resent your attempt to make any kind of explanation to him. If we're not going to have honesty between us, then there is no us!"

"Lisa, I just don't want you to be cheated because—"

"Cheated? You dumb putz—I'm not being cheated of anything, Frank. I'm getting someone to watch over me, and that's what I need most now."

"Maybe, you're ending up with someone you'll have to watch over instead, Lisa. We know—"

"We both know," she cut in, "that we're good for each other. That we have a great time together, and we care for one another. By my standards, I think we have a lot."

His eyes misted as he extended the letter to her outstretched hand. She took the envelope, tearing it in half. "What's the other one, Frank?"

"To my attorney. A letter for a nuptial agreement."

"Okay. A prenuptial agreement, I told you before, I want. Anything else you haven't been candid about, Frank? I need to know now, before we're married."

"Yes, honey, one thing."

"What's that, Frank?"

"I lied when I said I only like fucking. I like sucking too."

"Well, go upstairs Frank, and drop your drawers."

He took her hand and they walked toward the elevators. She took the torn letter he was going to mail to Yale and tossed it in the wastebasket next to the elevator.

The boys agreed, before leaving, to meet them in Florida next Friday evening. Lisa called her parents to advise them she was arriving with her fiancé in the afternoon, and then she and Frank spent the evening alone making plans. She condescended to his request for a quiet ceremony, but lavish reception aboard his ship after he said, "It's not every day I get married. And who knows if we'll have time for a lot of parties while traveling to all the places I want to show you." She understood his need, and his fear that there may not be as many parties in his future as he might have liked.

She climbed in bed beside him, and let him cradle her. She was quiet thinking how ironic life was. He held her. "Lisa, I don't want to live being a burden to anyone. When the time comes I ask you to leave me, and not see me again, I want your promise that you'll do as I ask."

"Sorry, Frank. I'm here to stay, until there's no one to stay for. And I expect the same in return. This is not negotiable. Now stop talking, and make me feel good. I need to feel loved, Frank."

What if your folks don't like me?"

"Oh well."

"You'd still marry me, Lisa?"

"Yes."

"What if you didn't overhear my conversation with Dr. Stone, Lisa? Would you still have decided to marry me? Be as honest with me Lisa, as you asked me to be with you."

"You know Frank, if I had decided not to, I probably would have regretted it the rest of my life. I've never felt this safe before. Frank, I never fully realized how much I needed it. I'm tired of trying to act tougher than I am, and I'm sick of having to deny how badly I need sheltering."

"That doesn't answer my question, Lisa."

"It's the only honest answer I can give you, Frank."

He turned, moving his hand between her thighs, exploring, touching, massaging, until he was consumed by desire. He moved over her and penetrated. She accommodated him, pretending pleasure, and for the first time with Frank faked an orgasm. It wasn't until he was asleep that she left the bed, to go to the bathroom in the other bedroom; lock the door and cry.

They arrived in Florida early the following afternoon. They were met by blazing heat from the crimson sun, and blatant scrutinization from Lisa's parents. Harry and Rose Newman were full of questions as they sat having lunch in the small dining room of the Newman's condominium in Fort Lauderdale. Lisa was getting annoyed at the third degree Frank was being put through. Like it really mattered where his parents were originally from, or how much of an education he'd had. She was squirming in her chair, feeling resentment that, again, there was such a lack of sensitivity to her feelings, and flagrant disregard of what might make her happy. The focus, instead, was placed on a nonsensical, analytical evaluation of what they felt was pertinent data. She wanted to scream that she was an adult. That it would be nice if they showed enthusiasm that she found someone she wanted to marry rather than inquiring about bullshit, which eventually would result in unwarranted judgments, and dogmatic suppositions.

"Rose," Frank said, with charm and good breeding, "You and your husband raised a wonderful woman. I hope I can give Lisa happiness, and she can give me the same. I know, I'm much older than you probably expected, but we are good for each other and fill needs for one another. I love your daughter. I'll never do anything to hurt her. I'd like it, if you and Harry could help us arrange the wedding and reception. Of course, include as many of your friends as you'd like. I'll arrange for their accommodations, transportation, and everything else. Could the two of you, perhaps, come with us to see my home and ship? I'd appreciate your opinions, and if you think it's a good place for the wedding to take place?"

"I didn't know you had a place in Florida," Rose interjected, with curiosity, "Where is it?"

"An island off the southern coast. Do you have time to see it today?"

"You live on an island? Must get lonely there?"

"It will be a lot less lonely with Lisa there beside me. It's a good place for her to write her next book, too."

"Yes. She made nice money from the first book. I hope she's made wise investments, too. Huh, Lisa?" Her father inquired, worrying about her financial stability, and unaware of Frank's wealth, since Lisa made him promise not to reveal his financial stature until they got to know him.

"I did okay, Pa. I'll be making nice money for the film rights, too."

"Good. Frank, are you retiring soon, from working for a living, and going to enjoy being a senior citizen. What did you say you operated—a coffee bean factory?" Rose asked, trying to elicit more information obliquely.

"No. I'm not ready to retire yet. I'll show you the factory if you have time to see it? Come on, I have a car downstairs. Let's spend the day at my place and have dinner together."

"Okay," Rose said, "I'll change. We'll come down in a few minutes. Lisa, why don't you fix your make up a little? You don't even have lipstick on."

"We got up early, Ma. I didn't bother with makeup. We'll be downstairs, waiting outside for you. I want to walk around a little."

Once outside, Lisa lit into Frank. "So, you have to show them you're loaded to impress them, don't you? Why? It was important to me, Frank, that they accept you for who you are, not the fancy trappings. Can't you understand that? I'm really pissed. Why do you have to buy approval, Frank? It's crap and I hate it."

"Relax Lisa. Money is my ice breaker, and at my age it comes in handy. They'll get to know me a lot faster, and a lot better, when they don't feel you're making a mistake."

"It's my life Frank! Stop kissing up to—"

"Here we are," Rose said, "I took sweaters in case it's windy on the boat. I took a Dramamine, too."

They drove to the ship and even Lisa was overwhelmed by the enormity of the vessel, with the sixty plus staff, and opulent luxury. Frank gave them a tour of the five decks, with an air of causality, remarking he wished he had more free time to enjoy the ship, adding he and Lisa would try to be in the area for longer periods in the coming year.

Lisa was quiet for the rest of the afternoon, keeping her hand in Frank's every time he reached for her. She listened to him describe the years of work it took to complete the island estate to specifications, and develop the factory into a profitable enterprise, without resorting to paying substandard wages to the many Cubans who escaped and sought shelter on his island. He introduced Lisa, and her parents, to several of the people who maintained the island and factory in his absence. It was evident Frank was admired and respected by his staff, the locals, and employees. His easy manner was infectious. By dinnertime, even Lisa's parents were relaxed in his company. Frank convinced Harry and Rose to stay the night, sending members from his staff to obtain the items they requested from the mainland. One night led to another, and Harry and Rose didn't end up returning to their own condo for three days. By the time they disembarked, in Florida, they were sure Lisa had chosen a fine man for a husband. Rose even kissed Frank goodbye, remarking it was going to be a beautiful wedding and they were glad they lived to see their only child so happy, and finally have from life what she wanted.

"Rose, you and Harry raised a special girl who wouldn't be the person she is today, if you hadn't set the proper foundation. I'm fortunate to have Lisa in my life. I'll do my best to make her happy."

"Frank," Rose replied, "I think you're going to make a fine son-in-law, but do me one favor—don't call me "mom" in public. I, sometimes, lie about my age."

"Okay, Rose. But you don't have to lie about your age. You and Lisa could pass for sisters."

Lisa watched her mother's face beam; happy they were accepting her decision now, so there would be less strain to deal with. Frank had known all the right buttons to push; all the right answers to every question asked. Only Lisa was less sure about answers to questions and spent time each day finding someplace private where she could succumb to the feelings of doubt, frustration, and confusion, without being observed.

On Friday, Lisa and Frank boarded the ship for Miami to have Sabbath dinner with her parents. Marc and Steve arrived as had been planned. The party and wedding plans were being handled. Lisa opted for a beige silk dress with matching cape, and a silk wide brimmed hat, with a short veil. The next two days were hectic with last minute arrangements. It wasn't until Sunday afternoon, aboard ship, when she was changing into her wedding dress that Lisa had one moment of panic, where she felt like running away. She had to admit to herself, as she appraised herself in the mirror, before leaving her suite to take her vows, that she was afraid, really afraid, she was doing something that would alter the rest of her life. She loved Frank, but wasn't in love with him, and wasn't sure it was what she really wanted to do. She was also afraid of watching this vital man, she was promising to share her life with, decay before her eyes; uncertain she could handle watching him deteriorate from illness. She knew brides often had last minute thoughts if what they were doing was right. Her stomach fluttered as the knock on the door indicated it was time for her to come out. As she walked toward Frank and the Rabbi, walking between her parents, with her arms wrapped in theirs, she prayed silently to God for guidance and courage. When the Rabbi pronounced them husband and wife, Frank broke the traditional glass and kissed her. His lips tasted the salt of her tears, and Lisa knew for the rest of her life his words of that moment would stay with her. "Lisa," he softly whispered, "thank you for becoming my wife. Now, I won't be afraid when by death we do part. Today you have made it possible for me to know when I have to face the end, I don't leave this life having been alone."

"Frank, I married you so I, too, don't have to be alone. Don't stop fighting because I am by your side—fight harder, knowing I need you and have no one else to take care of me. If you love me, Frank. Fight to stay alive." She wiped a tear from his cheek and placed her lips on his again.

"Lisa, I'll try to make you happy, any way I can."

"Show me how to live, and that I'm worth living for, Frank. Show me life. Show me yourself."

"For as long as I can, Lisa. I'll try, honey. But, Lisa, you have to promise me one thing; you have to promise when I ask you to leave me, you will."

"No, Frank. I will never leave you. Never. Not of my own free will—and if you don't fight to stay beside me Frank, I will hate you until the moment I die. I need you, Frank, as much as you need me."

"Lisa—"

"Frank, I'm ready for my honeymoon. How soon can we leave?"

"Shortly. After we cut the cake, Lisa. So, are you really ready, now, Mrs. Lee?"

"Ready? Ready for what?"

"To live—really live, Mrs. Lee."

"Yes, Mister Lee, if you'll teach me. Keep in mind, however, I'm a slow learner."

"I love you, Mrs. Lee."

"Prove it, Frank—I need you to prove it. Don't disappoint me. Live for and with me. Stay beside me."

"I'll try, Lisa. I'll try. Sincerely—I will."

CHAPTER 13

Marissa had taken Josh to Hawaii, for a holiday, with a close girlfriend of hers, Julie, and Julie's son who was the same age as Josh. Victor had the day off, so Yale was alone in the kitchen of his home when he unfolded the morning newspaper. He screamed, "No-o-o," "No-o-," so thunderously that the words bounced off the walls, after reading the front-page caption: **Billionaire Frank Lee Weds Writer Lisa Klein.** He looked at the photograph below the byline, showing the newlyweds cutting the wedding cake aboard Frank's ship, off Florida's southern coast. Yale read the article describing the lavish party, following the simple matrimonial ceremony; pierced by pain so intense he wasn't sure he'd be able to control his wretched cries of agony. He stared at the picture, unable to believe what he was seeing; unable to accept that once again he had lost Lisa to someone else. He sat at the table dazed for a long time. He sat glued to the chair, transfixed, until Ruth approached him, putting her hands on his shoulders tenderly.

He hadn't heard his mother come in, nor did he hear the phone ringing earlier. He only heard the sound of his heart pounding so fiercely, he felt, surely, he would soon die of a stroke or heart attack.

"Yale, there's got to be more to this than we are aware of. Yale, we both know Lisa too well to believe she is capable of hurting someone she cares about intentionally. Yale, things aren't always what they appear to be. Yale, do you hear me?"

"Ma, I don't ever want her name mentioned again. I lost. It's as simple as that. Ma, I—"

"Yale, don't do this. I shared your pain when Lisa left to go back to her husband. We both knew then if her children were not so important to her—"

"Stop! Stop it, Ma! No more! Her children? What happened anyway? She got divorced and, from what I gather, lost them anyway. She made a choice then and she's made one now—and both times I lost. Ma, I don't want to talk about it."

"Yale, maybe—"

"Ma, go home, please! I have things to do."

"Yale, let's go out for—"

"Ma, I need to be alone."

"Yale, you never shut me out. Yale—"

"Ma, go home, now. Please!"

Ruth looked at her only sons face with the realization that he was going through a radical transformation. There was more than pain in Yale's eyes. There was anger, bitterness, and a veil of isolation he was self imposing. She prayed he would mourn and grieve, as he should, then go on with his life, as he did when he was forced to say farewell to Lisa two years ago. But when he jerked away from her embrace before she left, she knew that Yale was putting up new barriers. Her heart ached for her son.

"Yale, I'll be home all day. Call me later, okay?"

He didn't answer. Ruth realized he wasn't going to say anything. She was afraid for her son as she walked out of the house and went home. She called Yale three times later that day, but got the recording on the answering machine. When she tried again before going to bed she heard a new recording stating: "At the customers request, this number is no longer in service." Ruth dialed again to make sure she hadn't dialed in error then cried herself to sleep when she understood Yale was shutting out the world.

Ruth expected to find Yale disparaged when she arrived at his place the next morning. She had decided, on the drive over, she wouldn't bring up Lisa's name unless he did, and give him time to accept the shock. What she wasn't prepared for was finding Yale packing suitcases, with the help of Victor, dressed and readying himself for a trip. He greeted her casually, with, "Hi, Ma" and kissed her cheek. "I'm going to New York. David will be meeting me there soon. There's a play—a musical, I've been interested in doing for a long time, but wasn't sure I wanted to be tied to one endeavor for an indefinite amount of time. I've decided to take a shot at it. I'll be gone a while. I'd like you to tell Marissa—when she gets back—she can stay here, with Josh, for as long as she needs, and I'll be in touch."

"Yale, want some company? I haven't been to New York in ages. I could help—"

"No. I'm going alone. David will commute between here and the apartment I'm leasing, as needed. If you need anything, call the office—"

"What? What are you saying? You're not giving me a phone number, in New York, where I can call you?"

"No. David will be the only one with my number. In case of an emergency."

"What's going on, Yale? I have to go through David—your assistant—to get to you? Why are you punishing me for what Lisa—?"

"Shut up, Ma! When you can speak without bringing up her name, let David know, and I'll see if I feel like talking."

"Yale, be reasonable. This is not like you. Since when does your mother get treated like an outsider? Since when do you tell me to shut up? Since when do you—"

"Since—now! Get a life, Ma! Get a life that's not an appendage to mine!"

"Yale, I know you're upset, but I don't have to take abuse because of—"

"Ma, back off! Go have some coffee, or something—I'm busy, and I'm in a hurry."

"In a hurry for what, Yale? In a hurry to run away from your pain? It doesn't work, honey—"

"Ma, stop! Go have some coffee or go home—I'm not interested in your views, or anyone else's!"

Ruth stood still, watching her son take things out of his closet, not saying a word. David came in a few minutes later. Yale was as rude and abrupt with David as he had been with her. She was stunned by his behavior, and didn't know how to respond in order to bridge this gap he was creating. Yale gave Victor a few instructions, ordered his luggage be taken outside, and walked past her to the kitchen like she didn't exist. She followed him to the kitchen and watched him put keys on the kitchen table. He looked her directly in the eyes for the first time since she'd arrived. Flatly he said, "The keys to everything you need are here. David will keep you posted on anything you need to know, and—"

"No, Yale." Ruth snapped back, opening her purse on the kitchen table. "Here are the keys to your house, gate, safe deposit box, office, and cars. I will be changing my phone number, too. No one will have my number either. If you want to reach me—WRITE. I won't be here to tell Marissa anything—so make other arrangements. And when my son wants a mother—He'll know where to find her." She was livid and hurt. This was not Yale, and she didn't like the stranger before her.

"Yale, have a good trip." She turned to leave, hoping he would call out to her before she left, but he didn't. She had her hand on the doorknob, and had to choke back a sob, before she yelled, loud enough for him to hear, "Good luck, Yale."

He didn't respond. Ruth got in her car and went home. She stopped in front of her door, picking up the morning paper. As it unfolded in her hand she read the caption above the picture of Lisa and Frank Lee: **"Wealthy Magnate Proclaims—I Have Never Been Happier."**

Ruth took the paper inside with her, and threw it in the trash container beneath the kitchen sink. She laid down on her bed, stared at the cold white ceiling, bawling: "And I—Have Never Been More Miserable".

CHAPTER 14

For the first three months as Mrs. Lee, Frank exposed Lisa to a life she thought was only possible in a fairytale. Even as a writer, she never imagined how it might feel to be a Goddess. He showered her with lavish gifts, expensive jewelry, and an abundance of love. He took her to places she'd only read about before, and anticipated everything that might make her happy—then provided it. He had her sons flown to meet them several times to surprise Lisa, and formed a close bond with them himself. He bought Marc and Steve new Corvettes, without consulting Lisa, and laughed when she tried to scold him for spoiling them. He flew Rose and Harry to Paris to surprise Lisa, and when her parents returned home to Florida had a Rolls Royce delivered to their condo with a telegram that read: **Lisa says, you both hate driving—stop—So don't drive any more—stop—You now own a Rolls Royce and I have employed a full time chauffeur for your convenience—stop—If you want a different color it's too bad, because I'm too busy keeping up with Lisa to exchange the vehicle—stop—Thanks for sharing your daughter with me—stop—I love her.**

Wherever they were, Frank had fresh cut flowers delivered to Lisa every day. He introduced her to haute couture and fine dining—but made sure she was also served a hot fudge sundae everyday, as a private joke between them, commemorating their first meeting. He taught her about fashion and art. She had a scrapbook she was filling with all the photos and articles about them that frequently appeared in newspapers and magazines. He introduced her to the powerful and influential, then laughed when she mimicked someone who put on airs. Every night when they got into bed, before going to sleep, he stroked her hair, and said, "Mrs. Lee, I sincerely thank you for this day."

It was the morning of their three-month anniversary when Frank said casually, "You know, I've had enough of Monte Carlo. A few days here is plenty. I'm homesick. What do you say to going to the island? We'll invite the folks and take a breather."

Lisa looked up from a magazine she'd been flipping through, and just as casually said, "Nope. I don't want to go to the island just yet. I want to go to San Francisco first."

"I can't fool you, Lisa. Can I?"

"Nope."

They left for San Francisco the same day, and checked into the suite at the Bay Plaza they first shared over four months ago. Lisa called Dr. Harvey Stone while Frank was in the bathroom; then off handedly remarked, "Harvey will be here in an hour, honey. Can we order up then, or are you hungry now?"

"The only thing I'm hungry for, now, is you, Lisa. Do we have time for a "Quickie"?"

"Nope."

"What? No time, or just not in the mood?"

"Oh—I'm in the mood. But I'm not the "Quickie" type. I like it slow and long. Think you can accommodate me?"

"Hell, I can outlast you anytime."

"Prove it, big boy," she said, taking off her clothes seductively.

He watched her undress, feeling that familiar urge in his loins. He took off his clothes and came up behind her. She felt his erection against her back, as he kissed the nape of her neck and ran his hands over her body. He cupped her breasts in his hands and she slithered against him. She was moving slowly when she realized he'd lost his erection. She pretended not to notice and started moving her hands over his thighs.

"Lets go to bed, Frank."

"No, Lisa. I think we both know I wouldn't be able to do much now. Let's order up, okay?" He started to back away when she grabbed his hand. "Don't play games with me, Lisa. No pretending, okay?"

"No games, Frank. No pretending. Take me to bed, please. If you can't—you can't, But I can. Make me feel good, Frank. Kiss me all over. Touch me all over—please."

She took his hand leading him into the bedroom. She tossed the spread on the floor, lying down on her back. He had no erection. He laid down next to her and started stroking her. She spread her legs, guiding his hand between her legs. "Stroke there, Frank."

He still wasn't getting hard, and his frustration was causing him to rub her roughly. When she pulled away a little and he realized he'd been a little too rough he stopped abruptly, apologizing.

"Never mind, Frank. I know how to make myself feel good." He took it as an insult, and was getting off the bed when she called him back quickly, "No Frank. Don't go. I can make myself feel good a lot better when someone's watching. Come here. Please." He sat back down, watching as she put her hands between her legs and started moving. She rotated her hips, making soft purring sounds. She rubbed her clitoris, so he could see, moaning as she rhythmically moved. "I'm getting real wet, Frank. I'm all tingly. It feels so good." She looked and noticed his erection had returned, but didn't want to be forceful.

"Frank, rub your dick—stroke yourself, while I stroke myself—I want to watch you do it."

"I want to be inside you, Lisa." He was losing some stiffness as he spoke.

"No. Frank, rub yourself, now—I want to see—Frank, I'm getting close. Stroke your dick, for me, so I can watch you do it when I come. Frank, stroke it hard."

He stated rubbing his shaft. He stroked the front and back hard and quickly as he watched Lisa writhe on the bed making herself feel good. He was hard. And he was close.

"I'm going to come, Frank. I can feel it. Oh Frank, it feels good. Oh Frank, I'm going to come. Rub yourself, Frank. I want to see your hard cock while I'm coming. Oh Frank—Now—Now—Now—." She climaxed and watched as Frank came seconds later, the semen shooting from him.

He laid down next to her, and took her hand in his, "I love you." He didn't say more—there was no need to.

She knew what he was feeling, and said jokingly, "Sure Frank, you just had to prove you could last longer. Okay—so you win this time—big deal."

"I won the day I met you, Lisa."

She turned and snuggled in his arms, "So did I, Frank. I won, too. I want to stay a winner, Frank. Promise me, I won't be a loser ever again."

She felt his lips caress her shoulder as he whispered, "I love you, Mrs. Lee."

Lisa feigned to still be sleeping when Frank left the bed and let Harvey Stone in. He had closed the bedroom door, so she was very careful when she opened it not to be heard. She stood with an ear to the crack in the door listening.

"So Frank, how much of a weight loss have you noticed in the last month?"

"Just a few pounds, Harvey. My lady has a lot more energy than I do. It's not easy for an old fart, like me, to keep up with her."

"When did the fatigue become noticeable?"

"The first time I went to bed with Lisa."

"Any problems in bed with her recently?"

"Yes, Harvey. She hogs the blanket all the time."

Lisa knew Frank didn't want to deal with his illness. He had been quiet in the jet. He had even suggested before leaving that she go to the island and he'd meet her there if a few days. She vehemently refused, but wondered if he felt stripped of some pride because he felt so vulnerable currently. She hadn't noticed any changes. Could he have been pretending to feel better than he did just to show her a good time? He must have felt or noticed something significant to suggest leaving Monte Carlo, which he professed was one of his favorite spots in the world.

"Frank, where is Lisa now? I haven't seen the bride since the wedding. She sure looked gorgeous that day."

"She's sleeping. I think I made a mistake, Harvey. I shouldn't have married her."

"It's not going well, Frank?"

"That's the problem. It's perfect, Harvey—not just going well. She's incredible. She's smart. She's beautiful. She's giving. She's impish and she's sophisticated. She's devoted. She's loyal. She's loving—and—and—and—I'm so in love with her, I don't want her to see me die—bit by bit—before her eyes. It was selfish of me to marry her. I don't want her to witness it. I don't want to leave her with any unpleasant memories. Can you help me die quickly?"

"Frank, what atypical symptoms have you been experiencing?"

"Fatigue. Loss of appetite. Less sex drive. Most of all depression—caused by the fact that I found real love just when I'm about to lose my life."

"Will you check into the hospital for a few days, Frank? I want to run some tests and get a clearer picture of where we stand."

"No, Harvey. We both know we might prolong this a little while longer with treatment, but we can't change the inevitable. I want to die now so Lisa will only have good memories of our time together."

She couldn't believe what she was hearing. She was unable to control her fury. She stormed out of the bedroom with only a sheet around her. She marched toward Frank and Dr. Stone.

"You bastard!" she shouted. "You lying, bastard! I want a divorce. I'm getting dressed—getting out of here—and filing for a divorce in Nevada. You don't love me, Frank—you love yourself! You're afraid to share completely. You liar! "Fun" is what you know—but as for being a husband—you stink! Well, I got a honeymoon out of the deal—I guess I should be grateful. You fuck—how dare you profess love for me—you don't know what love is…You…"

"Enough, Lisa."

"No, Frank—It's not enough. I want more than a honeymoon! I want you—in sickness and in health! Doctor Stone, if Frank doesn't check into the hospital, and do everything in his power to stay alive—I will commit suicide. You are my witness to what I am saying. If Frank doesn't love me, enough, to fight for more time with me then I don't want to live anymore. He wants to die now—well so do I!"

"Lisa, I don't want you to go through hell. Lisa—"

"Shut up, Frank. You are a liar. You just told me, in bed, you won the day you met me. And now you're throwing in a winning hand. You call yourself a gambler, Frank? I call you a loser. You should play out the hand, Frank—a royal straight flush—I would have a memory of a win to remember—."

"Maybe, my hand is only "a pair," and I want you to have a Royal Straight."

"Frank, if you don't play the hand out—I walk away without even a pair."

He looked at her with tears streaming down his face. "You know Lisa, I don't think anyone has ever cared this much about me."

"Then it's their loss, Frank. She climbed on his lap and let him hold onto her.

"Harvey, what time should we be at the hospital?" She asked.

"Anytime. I'll be there before seven."

"We'll need the VIP suite, Harvey. I'm checking in with Frank. I don't trust him around any cute nurses alone. I have to keep an eye on him. He's got a way with the ladies you know."

"Frank, are you still a flirt?"

"Flirting is about all I do well these days, Harvey."

"I don't know about that, Frank. Just an hour ago you were able—"

"Never mind, Lisa. Anyway, it wasn't quite the same."

"I have no complaints, Frank. Do you?"

"Yes, Lisa—one. That it took me my lifetime to find you."

They ordered dinner up to the suite. Before Harvey left he said to Frank, "You better fight to hold onto her or I'm going to try to steal her away from you."

Frank and Lisa went to bed early. Frank held her for a long time. He wanted to make love to her, but knew his body wouldn't cooperate.

At eight, the following morning, Frank and Lisa checked into the hospital under assumed names. It only took three days of testing for Harvey to conclusively determine that Frank's health was deteriorating. The prognosis was bad. Frank was slightly jaundiced and his blood count was lower. Lisa persuaded Frank to try the experimental drug Harvey suggested, but Frank developed horrendous side affects in less than a week and ordered Harvey to discontinue administering the medication.

"Two weeks of this place is enough for me, Frank. How about going home?"

Frank looked at Lisa's red eyes, and smiled at his little trooper, knowing Harvey had talked to her earlier, and explained there was nothing else they could do.

As Frank and Lisa were leaving the hospital, Frank asked Harvey for a word with him alone. When the two men said good-bye, Lisa noticed Harvey Stone was visibly shaken. It wasn't until they were aboard the airplane that Frank related to Lisa he was giving Harvey his place in England. It was the first place Frank had taken Lisa at the start of their honeymoon; four months ago.

"Harvey loves England," he stated. "I suggested he turn one wing of the house into a research lab." Lisa didn't say anything, just looked out of the little window at the clouds that were below them. "The truth is, Lisa," he continued after a moment, "I don't want you to have a place that would be a reminder of our honeymoon. I'm also going to leave the estate in Switzerland, to a close friend, with the understanding it be turned into a home for orphaned children. I want you to promise me one thing Lisa, and I won't ask anything else of you, or bring this up again; promise me you will always move forward and not look back. I need to know when I'm forced to leave you that you will make a new life for yourself right away. I was selfish in marrying you, honey. But I can't lie, and say I'm sorry—because I'm not. You've shown me beauty in a way I didn't know it existed—please Lisa—please; promise me you will not grieve for what is over. That you will make the kind of life for yourself I wish I could stay and give you."

"You know I believe in honesty, Frank. Therefore, I can't make that kind of promise. You know, too, that I loved your specialness when I married you, but that I wasn't in love with you. But life is strange, Frank. I've fallen in love with you. And for the first time in my life I am safe, even though I knew you were ill when we married. No Frank—I can't promise you I won't look back—because by looking back, Frank—I'll get the strength I'm going to need to move forward. But I promise you, Frank, I will go forward. I love you enough to want you to know you gave me more than yourself—you taught me the meaning of character and real courage."

"They sat, hand in hand, quietly the remainder of the flight. When they arrived on the island Frank suggested she call and invite her parents to come for a visit. "No, Frank. Not now. I don't want to share myself with anyone but you right now." She took him to bed, clinging to him all night.

It was five weeks after they took up residence on the island when Lisa and Frank had their first major quarrel since they'd met. He came storming out of their bedroom, to the terrace where she was having coffee, sitting in a wicker chair while looking at the ocean, when he yelled, "Why, the hell, did you let me sleep this late? It's almost noon. I told you yesterday I wanted to go to the factory this morning."

"So you'll go a little later. Big deal."

"Maybe, it is a big deal. I don't have time to waste, like you—who does nothing but sit on her ass all day."

"So set an alarm, putz. I'm not going to wake you when your body might require more rest."

"Fine. Why don't you just bury me now—it doesn't matter where I lie anyway—in a box or out of one—I'm rotting either way!"

"Stop it, Frank. So you slept late. Don't get excited."

"Excited? No, I can't do that either. Of course—it may be hazardous to my health!"

"Frank, why are you pissed at me? Okay—tomorrow I'll wake you—all right? Are you happy now?"

"No! I'm not happy now! You know what Lisa; I think you should take another bedroom in the house. I don't want us to share this one anymore. I'm sick of worrying about waking you if I'm restless, and sick of having no privacy when I want some." He turned and walked away.

She sat pondering over what had just transpired; realizing she was going to have to make some changes around the house or Frank was going to give up. He was not restless—he slept soundly. He never craved privacy before—but he was never impotent before. Obviously, this was his way to avoid sexual encounters which resulted in feelings of inadequacy and frustration.

He returned to the terrace dressed, with a pipe in the corner of his mouth. "I'm going out. Don't wait lunch." He didn't apologize. He didn't ask her to join him. And he didn't kiss her good bye. She didn't know where he was going, but the factory wasn't the truth because it was Sunday and no one would be there.

Lisa got dressed and she got busy. She called her parents and told them they should pack for an extended vacation, inviting them to the island. She called her boys and arranged for them to arrive for a visit on Friday, and when they said they could stay ten days because of a school break, she was delighted. She went downstairs and gathered the household staff together. She told them all, as Mrs. Lee, she was going to make some changes and started with immediate instructions. She ordered flowers to be cut and placed in the house—fresh, every day. She made a list of foods that Frank liked from all over the world, to be ordered and delivered to the island expeditiously.

She instructed the cooks to plan a Sabbath dinner, every Friday night, at six o'clock, until further notice. She called Frank's top man, at his home, and told him to report in the morning with all the details regarding the factory Frank should be aware of. And to report to Frank every evening, until further notice, of the factories daily productivity, problems, and any recommendations he might have. She asked for the phone book of Frank's friends and got the names of the stores he frequented in Florida for his clothes, tobacco, wines and food. She asked that the house be maintained more meticulously, with the linens changed daily. She asked that the room temperature be kept at seventy-two degrees, at all times, and breakfast be served on their bedroom terrace every morning at eight. All guests were to be served brunch at ten in the dining room, and another freezer ordered and fully stocked. She made several calls acquainting herself, by phone, with store managers who were familiar with what her husband purchased from each of them, and ordered him some new attire. She located a masseuse and cosmetologist, on a recommendation from a director of a health spa in Miami, and employed them—on a trial basis—by telephone. They were to arrive, and begin employment in one week. She asked for one room to be furnished with a desk, sofa, computer, and writing material for her, with a sign made for the door to read: Author At Work—Do Not Disturb, Unless You Are Carrying A Hot Fudge Sundae. And the last thing she did was call Harvey Stone, advising him what had transpired in the morning.

"You're a smart lady, Lisa. I think what you're doing will be good for Frank. I really do."

"Good. Thanks Harvey. I needed reassurance. Anything else I might try, Harvey? Any suggestions?"

"Lisa, well—"

"What, Harvey? Is there something I should know?"

"Let me break a confidence, Lisa. Frank called me a few hours ago—I don't know from where—but he was asking me if he was going to remain impotent for the duration—as a result of the illness, or was it due to his frame of mind."

"Well? What did you tell him?"

"The truth, Lisa. I told him anxiety could perpetuate difficulty regarding sexual performance, and his illness, at this stage, was not the primary cause for any dysfunction."

"What are you saying, Harvey? I don't turn him on enough?"

"Lisa, what I'm saying, and what I told him, was he may require additional stimuli right now."

"What was his reply? Harvey—talk to me!"

"Lisa, he said he was going to find a hooker. Maybe, then, he could get it up. Do you understand? He loves you so much he doesn't want to feel like a failure with you, he—"

"Harvey, can you do something for me?"

"Anything."

"Harvey, get me a carton of x-rated things—movies—vibrators—sexy lingerie—sex toys—you know what to get, and ship it to me C.O.D. right away. Can you do that?"

"Yes, Lisa. I'll make a call and get you what you want, but it might not—"

"Don't worry about it. I know it might not help, but I want to try—I—I don't want to have my husband feel he's letting me down or needs a hooker. I'll know when to give up trying, Harvey."

"Okay, Lisa. Listen—"

"Harvey, you didn't talk to me today, okay? Call in a week to say "hello". I'll stay in touch."

"Bye, Lisa."

"Thanks Harvey."

Lisa had been off the phone with Harvey only five minutes when

Frank called. It was already after seven. "Don't wait dinner" was how he started their conversation.

"Oh Frank, I'm glad you finally called. Where are you?"

"Miami. I took the ship across. I don't know when I'll—"

"Oh good—Miami. Listen, I need a favor. I invited my folks to stay for a while. I was going to ask you if you'd send the ship, but since you're there already—can I call them, now, and you can escort them back here for me. I think they'd be more comfortable with you aboard anyway."

"Sure, Lisa. What made you call—did you—"?

"No, Frank. I didn't tell them anything, and don't get me in trouble—I lied and said we just arrived. I miss them, Frank, that's all. I miss my boys, too."

"So call them and see if they can get away for a few days."

"Oh—I'm glad you said that—because I already did." She giggled into the receiver. "I better tell you Frank Lee, I decided to do a few things around the house. You keep complaining I never ask for anything—so now, Mr. Lee, you are in trouble."

"What did you do, Lisa?" He was getting a kick out of the giggling he heard coming from her.

"I'll tell you when you get here. Go pick up my folks, okay? I'll call them to say you're on the way."

"Okay. See you in a bit." She giggled again. "Lisa, what else—"

"Bye, Frank. See you soon." She hung up, waiting two minutes, then called the operator to say she got disconnected from an emergency call from the mainland before she could get the telephone number. A special operator traced the call back and gave Lisa the number where her last call came from. Lisa dialed the number. A sexy voice answered, "Heavenly's, May I be of assistance?"

"I'm hoping you won't have to be," Lisa said, as she replaced the receiver.

CHAPTER 15

For the next three months life was filled with laughter and happiness for Frank, due to Lisa's ingenuity and virtuosity. She was adept at anticipating Frank's needs, and was irrestrainable in making sure his days were enjoyable and fruitful. She showered him with affection. She entertained him, and asked his assistance in reviewing her new novel—chapter by chapter. She was his link to life. She restricted his activities when he showed fatigue, and cajoled him into more activity when he showed signs of depression. He learned how to have fun by relaxing with his wife on his lap and listening to her infinite ideas on how she was going to improve the world. He laughed at her lingo and outbursts of anger when he effectively challenged one of her philosophical ideas.

Her parents visited often, and the boys bonded with him to such a degree that more than once they accidentally called him dad—and Frank loved it. Friends came for dinners or lunches, but the morning breakfasts on the terrace belonged to Frank and Lisa alone.

They had a solid relationship. Lisa was unwavering in making Frank want to live, believing he would live as long as he could if she remained steadfast in proving life was worth hoarding. She made love to him in lingerie ordered out of x-rated catalogs, and when that wasn't enough, invented games to arouse him. She unselfishly relinquished sleeping next to him when he had a restless night, feigning to be up writing her novel all night, so his dignity would not be threatened.

It was their ten-month wedding anniversary day. She was in the sunlit room, she had transformed into her office, pretending to be working on her novel when Frank walked in carrying a small gift-wrapped box.

"Okay Frank, what did you buy me this week? You know, if you keep this up you may have to get a job one day."

"This is a different gift. You rarely wear the jewelry, so no more diamonds for you. Open it." She noticed he was pale today, and had winced as he excused himself to go to the bathroom when her father was asking him something at lunch earlier. They were having a party aboard the ship that night for over a hundred people. It had been Frank's idea. He wanted to celebrate their ten-month anniversary with extravagance. She started to unwrap the box, carefully, when he yelled at her sharply, "For God's sake, Lisa. Tear the fucking paper off already." She remained calm and tore the package open. Inside was a gold key with "Home" engraved across it. "Okay Frank, I give up." She tried to appear cheerful but he knew he had spoiled the moment with his outburst.

"It's a key to your new home. I'm selling the island and the factory. I've had an offer I can't refuse. We're going to California."

"What?"

"I've decided we need a change, Lisa. The ship is all I'm keeping. But it'll be in the Pacific Ocean by next week. Surprise!"

"What's going on, Frank? You love it here. I love it here. Why do you want—Frank? Are you worse? Oh God! I understand. I love San Francisco. Frank, I'm sorry I wasn't more enthusiastic—you caught me off guard—that's all. I can be ready whenever you are—we can cancel this dumb party now—"

She was rambling. She was scared. She knew she was overreacting but couldn't help it.

"No Lisa—you've got it all wrong. I feel the same, baby. The party is on, and our new home isn't in San Francisco. It's in Beverly Hills. I have a wonderful estate there. I miss it. I miss the action in California. I'm bored here. Do you mind, Lisa? I'm tired of vegetating here. Let's make a change. Okay?"

"Alright Frank. You're telling the truth, right? No secrets? You promised."

"The truth is, I want you to learn to trust me, Lisa. With this key you are the owner of one hell of a place. I hope you'll like it. It's the only place of mine you haven't seen yet. I'm sure you'll find it magnificent, and feel it's where you belong. It's very contemporary, surrounded by lush landscaping that's as pretty as the grounds here are. You'll see."

"When do you want us to leave here, Frank?"

"How about next week? You know what, Lisa? Let's have another party there. There are a lot of people I haven't seen in a long time. We'll have a "Welcome Home" party. What do you say?"

"Okay Frank. It sounds like fun."

"Good. I'll start the ball rolling then. Don't you have a present for me, Lisa? It is our ten-month wedding anniversary, you know?"

"What do you want that I could possibly give you, honey?"

"Simple, Lisa. Your promise that the clouds covering the brightness of your eyes, now, will pass. And as you face the new dawn, in California, it will be with eyes that sparkle like stars." He kissed her and left the room.

During their party that night she pulled Harvey Stone aside. He had visited several times in the past few months and each time said, convincingly, Frank's condition was stable. Tonight she was frightened and told him so.

"Lisa, Frank said he's holding his own. He looks no different than he did a few weeks ago, and he hasn't called me with any complaints. He told me you're moving to California. I'll come down from San Francisco as soon as you're there and check him out again then. Okay?"

"Have you noticed anything significant recently, Lisa? Any specific changes?"

"He winced at lunch today and looks a little pale."

"Lisa, cancer of the liver doesn't get better—only worse. Actually, he appears to be doing better than I anticipated he might by now. I'm sure that's due to your devotion and strength. Don't fret, Lisa. I'll examine Frank next week."

"Thanks, Harvey. I'm just—"

"There you are, Lisa. You're ignoring our other guests. Harvey, are you flirting with my wife?"

"No Frank. Actually she's worried about you. Anything we should discuss, Frank?"

"No. No. I'm okay. Come on, I'm racing the speedboats. You want to see if you can outrun me, or are you chickenshit?"

Harvey lost the race with Frank, as well as seven others who challenged him.

The following morning, during brunch, Frank told Harvey, Rose, Harry, and Lisa's boys about their relocation plans. "California is home for me. I've been lazy long enough. Will the four of you join us there next week? I want to show off."

"Frank's had an offer for the island and factory he can't refuse, so we'll be leaving here right away," Lisa added, without the ability to disguise some emotion.

"It's not a bad idea," Rose said. "Lisa, you're getting fat again, sitting around here all the time. You don't look so good lately."

"Thanks Ma. That's just what I needed to hear." She got up from the table and went outside. Frank found her sulking an hour later. He thought her sadness was still because her mother had insulted her, until he noticed a newspaper beside her, with a caption that glared: **"Yale Frye's Broadway Show Flops".** She tried, unsuccessfully, to conceal her feelings with light heartedness when Frank said, "Too bad about Yale's show. I heard he lost a bundle."

"Money's not everything, Frank. I'm sure failing hurt Yale more than the money he invested in the show."

"You're probably right. I've learned money isn't everything myself, Lisa. Self-esteem wears no price tag. Fix yourself up, Lisa. We're leaving for the ship in an hour. Our guests are expecting us." Frank always had everyone he invited for a party put up at a hotel afterwards. The following day, he'd appear to say good-bye, with a memento for each person.

When they arrived in the private room of the hotel, sometime later, bidding farewell to their guests, Frank made an announcement that he and Lisa would be in California by next week, and they were all invited to join them for a celebration there. Lisa didn't even remove her sunglasses when she said good-bye to her boys, or her parents, for fear they would leave feeling badly if they saw the conspicuous puffiness her make up couldn't conceal. She felt relief when she was finally home alone, and could let her defenses down, in a tub, behind locked doors, where no one could observe her. She was unaware Frank had heard her anguished sobs when he put his ear against the door. He knew she was constantly putting an effort into disguising her feelings for his benefit, but he knew her too well to be fooled by the transparency her heart could not mask from him. She came into their bedroom spirited and playful a little later. "Boy Frank, I finally have you to myself. I'm not sure how I'm going to like living in California. You may be too busy to have enough time for me. At least here I don't have a lot of outside interferences when I don't want them."

"It's called isolation, Lisa. It's a poor substitute for living. You think by escaping from the real world you can rid yourself of distress or fear? It doesn't work, sweetheart. I can vouch for that. Come here. I want to hold you."

She snuggled against him while he caressed her tenderly. "I need you, Frank. I need what we have."

"Honey, you belong in California now. No kidding. Don't cheat yourself. Life is too short."

"Sometimes I get so scared, Frank. Keep me safe, Frank."

"I can't, Lisa. And I don't want to. You have too much to give. I want you to flourish. Prosperity doesn't even mean anything to you. You need to blossom like spring flowers, and thrive like the ocean does from rain." He made love to her, holding her afterwards until she fell asleep in his arms.

When Lisa woke the following morning there was a note on the nightstand from Frank. **"Don't be angry, sweetheart. But I've gone to the estate, in Beverly Hills, so I can have it just as I want you to see it for the first time. It was important to me. I've concluded the details regarding the island, and would like you to meet me here next Saturday. I'll call later—don't be angry."**

I love you, Frank

At first she was alarmed that he was hiding something from her, but decided not to over react and wait for his call. Early in the afternoon, true to his word, Frank called.

"No, Frank. I'm not angry, but I don't understand. Why couldn't you handle everything, by phone, from here? What exactly do you have to do that requires you to be there?"

"I'm not telling, Lisa. You'll see when you fly out with your folks on Saturday."

"Can't I come earlier? I don't want—" He cut her off.

"No. Please Lisa, this is the way I want it. Now, listen. I'll be busy, so I won't call all the time—" Now it was her turn to cut him off.

"Hey, you're hiding something, aren't you? You never wanted to be away from me in all the months we've been together. And, now, you're not going to call all the time—suddenly. I don't like this, Frank. I'm flying out today."

"Okay, Lisa—go ahead and spoil it. I want to do something that's important enough to me to be away from you for the next five days and you have to start up. Alright Lisa, I guess you can't let me—"

"Okay. Okay. I'll wait until Saturday, putz,—but it better be good if I have to be here without you for five days. What's the number there Frank, so I can call and leave messages for you—like—I miss you, schmuck—sincerely, your wife?"

"That's one of the reasons I said I wouldn't be calling a lot. I have to have the phone connected. I was getting nonsense calls according to the security company guarding the house, so I'm going to order a new unpublished number later today." Frank despised cell phones and never carried one with him. "Anyway Lisa, I'll be in and out. I have other business out here I have to take care of. Listen, sweetheart, I'm late for an appointment now. I promise to call whenever I can. Now, say goodbye."

"Bye, putz. I hope you have a hard-on waiting for me when I get there. I liked last night, and I want more."

"Go ahead. Make me feel sorry I left, Lisa. Thanks a lot. Here I am trying to do something special—"

"Okay Frank—you win."

"I know, Lisa. I got a Royal Straight Flush. Bye."

Frank didn't call again until the next morning. He apologized for not calling her the night before with a joke, saying he was busy getting laid by a starlet. He said, the phone would be connected by the end of the day, and his plans were going so well she might be able to come out on Friday. He related the ship would be docked by Friday, too, and he still had a lot to arrange before the party, Saturday night.

"Lisa, I want you to go through the house there, and if there's anything you want, have it packed before you leave." He suggested she put her writing materials together, and order whatever she wanted from Florida shipped before she left as well. He said he would call her later with the phone number, ending the conversation with, "I'm in love with you, Mrs. Lisa Lee. Bye."

Frank didn't call her back with the new phone number Tuesday night. She was frantic when she hadn't heard from him by Wednesday night. She tried to get the new listing from the operator, but was told it was disconnected at the customer's request. She argued with the operator that she was Mrs. Lee, and her husband said a new number would be available by today. She got nowhere. When she hadn't heard from Frank by noon on Thursday, plus all the calls to places and people he knew in L.A. proved fruitless, she became alarmed and placed a call to Harvey Stone, in San Francisco. She was told he was in surgery, and they'd relate her message, as soon as he was free. She realized San Francisco was on Pacific Time, but was formidably upset as each hour passed without a return call. When the phone finally rang, Lisa was so perturbed when she heard her mothers voice, she was rude. She abruptly ended the conversation on a sour note.

In San Francisco, Harvey Stone was on his way to his private office, after a long surgical procedure, when he was stopped by the personnel director of the hospital with an envelope that had arrived for him, earlier, marked: Urgent and Personal. He took the envelope to his office, removing the contents. Inside were two letters in sealed envelopes. One was addressed to him. The other to Lisa. Both had Frank's name, in the upper left corner, with no forwarding address. Harvey opened the letter addressed to him and read:

Dear Harvey,
I am not one to ask favors, and wouldn't now if there was an alternative. The disease has reached the stage that impedes the quality of my life as I choose to live it. The most difficult part, however, is not the daily pain I make an effort to conceal, but the knowledge that I married Lisa knowing our life together would be limited. I have done

my wife a great injustice by taking selfishly what I needed for myself without regard to any long-term consequences for her.

I was completely aware Lisa was in love with Yale Frye when she married me. But so giving is Lisa that she could not fathom the thought of me living out my days alone. I took advantage of her vulnerability and soft heartedness. I should be ashamed of my actions, but I am not. She brought to my life more than I would have believed possible, and as a result I leave this world grateful rather than full of remorse.

My favors are the following: First and foremost, I ask that you be there for Lisa through the transitory period she will incur due to my demise. She is like a petal on a flower and I don't want the petal to fall. Never, in all the days we shared, did she make one demand of me, or complain about the altercations I often provoked when fear would grip my heart. I know she has come to love me, and was finding solace in our love—but Harvey, she deserves so much more than taking care of an old sick man, and giving up a chance to be the passionate person she is. Her preoccupation has become the preservation of Frank Lee. It is with total presence of mind that I am taking the bridle into my own hands. Please, help Lisa adjust to the circumstances.

The second favor, Harvey, is my request that you destroy any evidence of my illness. I would like to be remembered as one who lived life to the fullest and left life by accident—an untimely accident. I have suppressed the pain for as long as I can. I will rest in peace, Harvey, if I know Lisa is living life with greed, gusto, and enthusiasm, and that I need not suffer any longer.

My final request, Harvey, is that you destroy this letter.

Thank you my friend. Frank

Harvey picked up the phone and called Frank's island estate. Lisa picked up the telephone on the first ring. "Hi, Lisa. It's Harvey. Is Frank busy?" He didn't waste time with amenities.

"Who knows?" she shrieked. "The jerk left me a note that he was going to California, Monday morning, to fix up his estate and surprise me. I haven't heard from him since Tuesday night. That's why I called you."

"Oh. I didn't know you called. I just got out of surgery. He hasn't called since Tuesday night, you said?"

"No. And I thought he might be keeping something from me—even though he said he wasn't. I've been trying to get the new telephone number, but the operator says there's no listing— and the old number is disconnected. I've called the network—Myra Sullivan, and everyone I can think of—"

"Calm down, Lisa. What did he say Tuesday night—what were the plans?"

"For me to stay here and fly out with my folks on Saturday. Then he said, that his plans were going smoothly and I might be able to come out Friday when I protested—and now I can't locate him. I'm going to ream him a new asshole for this. I don't want surprises—I hate surprises! I can't believe he hasn't even called—I'm so angry—."

"Lisa, calm down. Listen, it's already Thursday afternoon. Why don't you arrange to fly out in the morning with your parents? I'll reschedule my roster here, and meet you at the airport. We'll go to Frank's estate and surprise him. Okay?"

"Do you think something could be wrong, Harvey? Maybe I should call some hospitals or—"

"No Lisa. If Frank needed medical attention, he would have contacted me. I'm sure of it. Just pull yourself together then advise me what time you'll be arriving. If I hear from Frank, or you do—we'll touch base, okay?"

"Harvey, when I get my hands on him, I'm going to—"

"Lisa, did he say anything about what he was doing, or where he might be going Tuesday night when you spoke to him?"

"No Harvey. Just for me to let him do this—that it was important to him—and the party plans—"

"What party plans—"?

"On the ship Saturday night. Remember, he invited everyone—"

"Lisa, when was the ship supposed to arrive?"

"Oh, Harvey—that's it. Today. The ship was arriving today. Maybe that's where he is—He is going to get it, if some fucking party plans are more important than calling me—"

"Lisa, I've got to go. I'm being paged. Call me with your arrival time—page me. I'll drive to L.A. tonight, and see if the ship is docked yet. If I find anything out, I'll call you."

"Thanks Harvey. Meanwhile, I'll try to reach the ship, too. He is going to be so sorry—"

"Lisa, I'll get back to you soon."

"Okay. Thanks Harvey. Bye."

Harvey was certain after reading the letter, and talking to Lisa, that Frank would have disconnected communications to the ship by now. He called the airline and was on a flight to L.A. in less than three hours. His fear, as the limo headed to Frank's Beverly Hills estate, was that he may be too late.

Frank's estate was dark. The security guard related, "Mr. Lee hasn't been here in two days, sir."

Harvey made several calls until he was able to determine and confirm the ships whereabouts. Lisa, who had chartered a private plane for a red eye flight, paged him. He arranged to meet her at the airport, six a.m., Pacific Time, the following morning. Neither had heard from Frank. It was almost midnight when Harvey reached the pier where Frank's ship was docked, and observed a crowd of people and several squad cars. He approached the populated area and heard an officer convey to a reporter, "We don't know anything else, right now. All we know, at this time, is an unidentified individual took a speedboat out—presumably from Mr. Lee's ship, and the speedboat was noticed twenty miles from the vessel, unoccupied. Someone reported a body floating a mile from the speedboat. We are in the process of recovering the body from the water now."

"Do you have any idea who the individual might be?" A reporter inquired.

"Not at this time. We have no further information."

But Harvey knew. He didn't need to wait around. He knew he was too late.

CHAPTER 16

Although there were several times before Frank's funeral when Lisa wanted to scream… "No! It wasn't an accident"…She didn't.

The police report and consequent headlines across the nation all reported: **"FRANK LEE DIES BY ACCIDENTAL DROWNING".**

She was on her way to the chapel with Harvey Stone when she spoke for the first time, since collapsing Friday, after her greatest fear was confirmed. Frank was dead. Harvey had her admitted to a hospital, with exhaustion as the diagnosis, after she identified Frank's body. She was Frank's next of kin—his only kin. She had to answer question after question, to so many people, after identifying Frank that eventually everything became a blur. She fainted. When she came to she was in the hospital.

Lisa wouldn't see her parents when they arrived, nor did she communicate with her sons when they came to her side on Saturday.

It was only now, in the black limousine, with Harvey that she asked "How much more time do you think I could have had with Frank?"

Her soft quivering voice tore at his heart as he honestly answered, "Not long, Lisa".

"The coroners report—after the autopsy—will it reveal—" She couldn't continue.

"As far as the public is concerned, Frank's death was an accident, Lisa. An unfortunate accident."

"It was always so important to Frank that no one know he was ill. Even when I first got to know him, he—". She stopped speaking again, and swallowed hard.

"Frank was a very proud man, Lisa. Do you want the letter he sent that's addressed to you now, Lisa?"

"No."

They arrived at the chapel in silence. Harvey had taken care of everything after he was informed Frank's attorney listed him as Frank's executor, the previous day. Prior to stepping out of the limo at the chapel, Harvey took Lisa's hand. "Lisa, the instructions can be altered. I don't know why Frank wanted the Shiva period of mourning aboard the ship."

"No. It's alright, Harvey. I don't want to change anything. It doesn't matter where I stay—I'm alone now, regardless."

Lisa was completely unresponsive as people extended their sympathy to her in the funeral chapel. She sat numbly through the eulogies. Then like a mannequin, she was escorted to the hearse for the procession to the cemetery. She sat, composed, under the canopy until the Rabbi asked for those who would recite Kaddish to come closer. The traditional ten Jewish men needed to make up the minion for the service by Jewish law, now had hundreds of men moving close to the casket for prayer. Lisa fell apart as her father and two sons led the service in Hebrew. Lisa sobbed as her dad, with a hand on each of his grandson's shoulders, recited the final words of farewell to the man they had come to love. Frank left this world having had a family.

Lisa wandered around the ship aimlessly after the burial. She couldn't stay in any one area. People continuously approached, trying to console, comfort, or comment as to how tragic the whole thing was. All she wanted was to be left alone. Finally, she went to the master suite aboard the vessel, which she had frequently shared with Frank when they wanted a private interlude on the ocean. She opened the closet to get an extra pillow for the bed and noticed only her apparel hung on the hangers. There was nothing of Frank's in the closet. She immediately went to the built in chest of drawers that spanned an entire wall. There, too, all of Frank's things had been removed. She laid down on the bed, holding a pillow against her, and screamed, "It won't work, Frank. Removing your things won't help me accept this. You lied, Frank. You lied to me—you bastard! You said, you'd stay with me as long as you could. Oh God, Frank—why did you leave me? Why did you do this? You didn't keep your promise. Oh God. Oh God." She hugged the pillow to her, rocking on the bed, when Harvey walked in without knocking.

"I thought I locked the door. Go away. I don't want to talk or see anyone right now."

"You did lock the door, Lisa. I got the spare key. There are a lot of people asking about you. Your kids are worried about you, and your parents are very upset. Why don't you come out of here—even if it's for a little while?"

"Maybe later."

"Okay Lisa." Harvey turned to go, then turned back and removed the envelope Frank had left for her from his jacket pocket. "Here, this is yours. I don't want to carry it around anymore. It might get lost." He put the envelope down and left the room. She left the envelope on the bed where Harvey had placed it; turned on her stomach and went to sleep.

It was nightfall when Lisa emerged and walked toward the room that had been Frank's library aboard the ship. It was late. The wind was still warm. She opened the door to the library, anxious to see something familiar of Frank's, and there sitting in Frank's library was her father. He was holding a pipe in his hand, staring at it. He didn't look up, just said, "You know, Frank always looked right with a pipe. Don't you think so?"

"Yes, Pa. He did."

"I had a feeling, Lisa, when you married Frank, that you both knew you weren't going to have a long time together. Was it a feeling, Lisa, or more than a father's intuition?"

She walked over to her father and sat down on the floor, putting her head against his leg. "We knew our time was limited from the beginning, Pa. But somewhere along the way, I convinced myself I could make it otherwise."

Her father stroked her hair gently, "Lisa, you really are a survivor. I should know—it takes one to recognize another. I survived the Holocaust, and went on making a new life for myself. And you know, honey, my life, for the last forty years, has been pretty damn good. Lisa, this is your Holocaust. You can pick up the pieces, too."

"What for, Pa? I don't have your strength. I wish I did."

"You've got more strength than you're aware of, Lisa. Or you wouldn't have been able to marry Frank, knowing he was dying. Now your obligation is to honor his memory, by making the best possible life for yourself without him." She sat and let her father stroke her hair. Her tears were endless.

"I don't want a life without Frank. I want to die. I can't believe he left me. I can't—"

"Lisa, I didn't want to go on after the war—when everything I cherished was gone—but, I'm glad I did. I wouldn't have had you— your mother—so much; so much."

"How does a person go on, Pa? I don't even know how to start."

"By walking from today into tomorrow—a minute—an hour—a day at a time. Until it becomes easier. And Lisa, it will become easier. Trust me. I know."

"Why, Pa? So I can learn to feel about something else that can, and probably will, just end up causing me grief in the end?"

"No Lisa. I went on to live a happy life, to honor the memory of those I lost—all those that didn't get to live, by no choice of their own. It's my way of paying tribute to their memory. Do you have enough loving memories of Frank to want to honor him that way?"

She sat silently, absorbing her father's words. He, still gently, stroked her hair, feeling her sorrow and loss. It was a long time before either of them spoke. Eventually, she whispered, "I'm scared, Pa. I don't think I've ever been this scared."

"I know, Lisa. I know. You know, honey, once I was in hiding from Nazi soldiers with my best friend. We had a loaf of bread and a little bit of sugar in a bag to share. During the night, I woke up and found my best friend, who I had saved from death previously, sneak a piece of bread he had hidden in his pants, and eat it himself without sharing it with me. He looked at me, and made a quick excuse about how weak he was, and started to apologize. He said I could have the other heal of bread and sugar for myself, in a feeble attempt to rectify the situation. You know what I told him, Lisa?"

"What?"

"That he was weak of heart more than weak of body. I gave him the last heel of bread and sugar. Before I left him, I said, I shared everything with him because I wanted to. I told him it was not a sacrifice on my part, but a gesture of love. You did the same thing. Didn't you, Lisa? You stayed and gave Frank love because you wanted to—not as a sacrificial act."

"Yes—but what does this have to do with anything. What are you saying?"

"I lived. I survived the worst—that's all. I was blessed. My friend didn't. There are blessings waiting for you, yet, too. You just have to have faith that even from the hardest of times—you will survive. Come on, Lisa, I'll walk you to your cabin. I'm talking too much."

Before she entered her cabin, she kissed her father asking, "You really believe I have blessings in my future, don't you, Pa? You really believe in people, don't you, Pa? In spite of everything?"

"Yes, Lisa. And I want to live long enough to witness your blessings." He handed her Frank's pipe that was still in his hand. "You were a blessing to Frank, you know. He knew it, and you should remember it. Goodnight Lisa."

He turned and walked away. She went into her cabin and picked up the envelope Harvey Stone had left with her earlier. It took several minutes before she could muster the courage to open the sealed letter and read Frank's final message to her.

"My Sweet Lisa,

I thought this was going to be the most difficult note I would ever have to write—but somehow it's not. In my sixty years of life I have never been as happy as I have been sharing this last year with you. I learned from you. You taught me that a person can achieve success without financial wealth, if they are willing to look beyond the trappings that so often disguise the true and more valuable aspects of life. You made me feel alive, Lisa—really alive—like a year of sobriety after decades in a dense fog.

I am not angry that my life is over. I am not bitter, nor do I feel cheated—and all because of you.

We both knew, from the beginning, our time together was limited, but what I didn't know was how much you would come to

love me, and how fortunate I'd be. You gave me a home—a family—two boys, that if I'd had sons of my own—I couldn't love more. You gave me passion, honesty, loyalty, and a new interpretation to the word "fun". I leave with a true appreciation for life.

In the past few weeks I was agitated, since the symptoms of my illness did not permit me to disguise the pain, adequately, to spare you from noticing—but, then, you know me too well. You know, as well as I, that I am not a person easily discouraged, and can be stubborn and strong willed beyond reason. However, I am begging you to grant me a final wish... TO LET GO. I have to. So do you.

As our time together comes to a close, I hope you will love me enough to move forward, and make a new life for yourself without looking back at the end. My final prayer is for the sparrow who sought shelter under my wing, and instead taught me how to fly, will spread her wings and soar.

Honor my memory, Lisa, by being happy.

I have never loved anyone more selfishly or more SINCERELY..............Frank.

Lisa sat clutching Frank's farewell letter until the dawn filtered into the cabin. Unable to sleep, she eventually put the letter in her purse, lit a cigarette, and walked to the top deck of the ship to wait for the sun to rise. She grabbed a blanket off a chaise along the way, and was on the top step when she spotted Harvey, standing at the far end of the highest point of the vessel, looking at the horizon through Frank's telescope. He was caught off guard when she approached asking, "You couldn't sleep either?" He jumped; then quickly attempted to compose himself and brush away the tears on his cheeks. Lisa put a hand on his arm and softly said, "I'm sorry, Harvey. I know, you and Frank were close. I can't seem to share my pain or be empathetic to others who are feeling the loss."

"Don't apologize, Lisa. Everyone expresses sorrow differently. A portion of my sadness is combined with guilt and responsibility. Frank did so much for me, and when I wanted so desperately to be able to help him—I was powerless. I'm sure he must have told you when I was an intern and forcibly considering general practice because of huge debts, he developed a scholarship fund, and insured I was the first recipient. Word had reached him that an oncology student would have to go into general practice without pursuing a specialty because of financial difficulties."

"No, Harvey. Frank related, a young, gifted, medical student was almost forced to give up his dream because he couldn't find enough hours in the day to work, study, and care for his ailing mother, all at the same time. Frank said, you were brilliant and it would have been a great loss to cancer research if you had not had the opportunity to serve in a capacity so well suited to you. Frank was on target when it came to people, Harvey. You received the scholarship because you deserved it. Humanity benefited with a gifted physician. And Frank got a remarkable friend."

Harvey reached for her hand, and together they watched a new day emerge.

When the traditional Shiva period was over, Frank's attorney, Howard Fixler, asked Lisa if he could assemble the people listed on the legal document for the reading of the will. Frank had even prearranged the final distribution of his assets so Lisa wouldn't attempt to delay the process by objecting, or explaining that she wasn't ready to deal with the will yet. A document was also presented to her indicating Frank had sold the ship. A conglomerate was taking possession of the vessel the following week. It was to become a floating hotel.

Mr. Fixler implemented the assemblage of persons. Those required to be present listened intently as Howard Fixler pontificated that Frank Lee, of sound mind, bequeaths his island off the Coast of Florida to be developed into a private learning facility for immigrants from other lands, and essentially train unskilled persons in a trade under the supervision of Ted Boren, his business associate, and board of director of the Lee Coffee Bean Factory. All profits are to be distributed to various organizations whose primary function is to assist in establishing permanent residences to those without a home and/or country. Frank asked that Rose and Harry Newman be designated the directors, overseeing the completion of the—Lee Foundation For a New Life— and in return be the new proprietors of his island estate, for as long as they live, with a yearly allowance of one million dollars for their time and effort.

In addition to the house in England, Frank bequeathed fifty million dollars to Harvey Stone, to assist him in setting up a new research laboratory for Aids research. The disbursement of allocated monies shall be left to the discretion of Harvey Stone.

Frank had also left trust funds for Marc and Steve, with distribution dates to be determined by his wife, Lisa Lee, per her decision as to dates of dispensation. The amount of the trusts is not to be disclosed to Marc and Steve until they graduate college, or is deemed otherwise by Lisa Lee.

Several other generous gifts were bequeathed to friends. Howard Fixler concluded the reading of the will with—"and finally, I leave the bulk of my assets, worth more than several billion dollars, in monetary value, to my beloved wife, Lisa Lee. A gift completely worthless in providing happiness to any person who has the wisdom to know what it is that makes life truly valuable." Howard Fixler, then, extended a small packet to Lisa, stating, Frank had this packet delivered to him several days prior to his death. Lisa opened the seal. She withdrew a gold and diamond charm. The charm was a poker hand. The ACE, KING, QUEEN, JACK and TEN of HEARTS. Engraved on the back was— "I WON. FRANK."

CHAPTER 17

Theoretically, Lisa was one of the wealthiest women in the country. When she kissed her boys goodbye, and said her farewells to her parents and Harvey, she was in the position to go where, and do whatever her heart desired. An inner strength prevailed. Although, the challenge was frightening, Lisa ultimately decided to go to her new home—the Beverly Hills estate Frank had left her. She went alone by choice. She needed some space, and time, to deliberate what to do next, knowing if she allowed herself to remain in a vacuum, she might never find the strength to persevere.

She had spoken to Harvey prior to her decision. He concurred, that although the transition would be easier if she had support and assistance from people close to her, it would only delay facing the difficult moment when reality clobbered her. She was going to have to make a new life for herself; independently.

As the limo approached the tall gates surrounding the acreage of her new residence, she removed the gold key Frank had given her, with "HOME" engraved upon it. Closing her purse, she muttered to herself, "Okay Frank, let's see this place you wanted to have ready for me. Let's see the house you wanted prepared perfectly before I arrived."

The security guard was in front of the looming gateway to the entrance. He introduced himself as Mac Evans, handing Lisa a remote control to the iron gates. "I guess my job is over now. Mr. Lee said, I was to stay until you arrived with your gold key. Then I was to give you this remote and leave. Here's my card, miss. If you need my services again, I hope you'll call. The directions to set your own gate code are on the back."

"Thank you" was all Lisa could say. The limo drove along a winding road, until it reached a mansion of white brick with cathedral windows. All her belongings from the island estate and ship were scheduled to arrive later in the day. She stepped from the limo and told the driver she wouldn't need him anymore that day when she spotted the gold Mercedes convertible Frank had bought her. It was parked, in the circular driveway, in front of the main house.

Lisa put the key in the lock and entered the mammoth structure which was now going to be her new home. She anticipated seeing beautifully furnished rooms, knowing from past experience; Frank liked to surround himself lavishly, expensively, and tastefully.

When Lisa entered she was surprised alright. Frank had removed all the furniture in every room of the house. All thirty rooms were empty. There were no window treatments, no carpeting. Nothing. The only exception was a singular, king-size mattress in the center of the master bedroom. The house was completely naked. She wandered from room to room, looking for something familiar of Frank's, but couldn't locate anything that Frank had left behind. Her mouth was dry. She walked to the kitchen for some water. She opened cupboard after cupboard, unable to even find a glass. She turned on the faucet and laughed, "Thanks Frank. At least I have running water." She didn't even have a chair in the kitchen to sit on. Finally she sat down on the floor and yelled, "You son of a bitch! It won't work, Frank. I can't erase what we had together in a flash. Damn you, Frank Lee! Damn you, for being so easy to love! Damn you, for leaving me! Damn you—Oh God. Help me."

Lisa sat on the cold marble kitchen floor until her sobs subsided. She stood up, and removed a tranquilizer from her purse. She put her mouth under the kitchen faucet to take the pill. "Well, Frank, I guess the first thing I have to do is get some staples." She opened the double doors to the stainless steel refrigerator and freezer casually, expecting they, too, would be bare. Her heart skipped several beats when she saw a hot fudge sundae, solitarily, in the freezer. She took out the sundae, which was topped with lots of whipped cream, a cherry, and no nuts. Attached to the bottom of the glass dish was a note: **Make it your home, Lisa. Not a mausoleum. Memories don't fade when we start anew—they are** only put in a special place. I don't expect you to forget. But I expect you to go on. Get going! Frank

She sat back down on the floor and ate the sundae with her fingers. "You putz!" She said to herself. "You could have, at least, left me a spoon for my sundae."

CHAPTER 18

Thunder and lightning woke Lisa from a sound sleep in the middle of the night. The repairman had said he wouldn't be able to get the motor for the air-conditioning system until today, so this hot, humid, June night left her feeling cantankerous, and restless. After an hour of tossing in frustration she got out of bed.

By the time Belle arrived from her quarters at six, Lisa had already consumed an entire carafe of coffee, as well as half a box of chocolate chip cookies.

"Belle, I'm going to need you to verify the serviceman will be here today to fix the air conditioning. Will you make a note to call him at eight, please? This heat is unbearable."

Belle was hired two weeks after Lisa moved into the house, when she answered Lisa's personal ad for an "on premises, full time, do everything, responsible, discreet housekeeper—needed for immediate position." Lisa liked Belle immediately. She was direct and smart. She didn't need to be told what to do, and had a keen sense for reading peoples moods and knowing when to take the initiative on issues that Lisa didn't want to deal with. She was making a fresh pot of decaffeinated coffee, with her back to Lisa, when she replied, "I already took care of it, Miss Lisa. I put an emergency call in to Mr. Fibbs, before I walked over, and told him to be here with the motor by nine or he didn't have to bother 'cause we'd find someone else. He'll be here soon."

"Thanks, Belle. If this rain keeps up, they'll probably call to put off delivering the dining room furniture today, too.

"No. They're coming. I called Mr. Larsen's answering service and told them, even if they have to pitch a tent, we want the furniture today.

He picked up on the call, and said, he was going to personally inspect each piece and have it here before noon."

"Thanks, Belle. Boy, do I feel bitchy today. I know you've only been with me a couple of months, but I feel like you know me."

"I do, Miss Lisa. And I like what I know. Now, I'm going to start your bath water. Then I'll tell that lazy ass chauffeur you won't fire—'cause he needs the money for his tuition—to bring the Cadillac in front by nine, so you won't be late for your ten o'clock appointment with the dentist."

"You know, Belle, the tooth feels fine right now—"

"Never you mind. Here, take your medication and I'll start the water in the tub now. Wouldn't hurt you none to do a little shopping on Rodeo Drive today, if you ask me—which you didn't—but, at least you wouldn't have to be here when the delivery people come. Anyway, you've been rushing every which way for weeks now ordering things for this house."

"Well, it's shaping up nicely, don't you think?"

"Yes, Missy. You sure got good taste. I like the black and white theme you decided on. But if you don't slow up, you're gonna end up covered by a white sheet, in the black earth, to match this house."

Lisa couldn't help laughing at Belle's analogy, but was aware this young Afro-American, who had lost her husband and only child in a car accident, was right. "Okay, Belle. You win. Pick out slacks, a top, and comfortable walking shoes—I'm going shopping."

Lisa's mouth was still frozen from the Novocain when she walked into Giorgio's and collided with Marissa Myers a few hours later.

"Lisa. Hi. How are you? It's been a long time."

"Hi, Marissa. I'm fine, and yes, it has been a long time. How's Josh?"

"Wonderful, as usual. Do you have a minute? He's outside, in the car with my driver? School's out and he leaves for overnight camp in a couple of weeks. I managed to persuade him to go shopping today for some clothes. It's not his favorite thing to do, but I bribed him, with my word of honor, that he could pick out his own clothes. Please; I know he'd love to see you."

"Sure. I'd love to see him, too."

Lisa followed Marissa out to the car and was warmly embraced by Josh, who leaped out of the backseat when he spotted them approaching. "Lisa, you're back. You said, you'd see me when you came back here."

Lisa hugged Josh hard. "Wow! You got so much taller since last year I hardly recognize you. I hear you're going to an overnight camp. That's terrific. I bet you're excited."

"Sort of, I guess. I just wish Buster could go too. He got bigger too, Lisa."

"Well, maybe they should invent a dog camp so you could both be away someplace special at the same time."

"That's silly, Lisa. Dogs couldn't go to camp 'cause they'd just do nothin'."

"Yeh, you're probably right."

"So, Lisa, now that you're back do you wanna come to my birthday party with your friend Frank? Remember, I invited you when you were here?"

"Josh," Marissa interjected, "I think Lisa is probably busy since she just got back to town."

"Are you busy, Lisa? You said we could get together when you came back. You said—"

"Josh," Marissa tried again to intervene feeling uncomfortable and uneasy that her son might open fresh wounds unknowingly. "We have to get to that shopping. Why don't we let Lisa get in touch with us when she has some time—"

Josh interrupted, so he wouldn't be put off, "Lisa, don't you have time to come to my party with Frank? Are you going away again? If you don't come to my party, I'll be at camp, and you won't get to see me then."

Lisa put a hand on Marissa's arm. "It's okay," she said softly. "Josh, Frank can't be at your party. But I'd love to come. When is it?"

"Tomorrow. It's for lunch. We're having hot dogs and hamburgers. And you know what kind of cake mom ordered me?"

"What kind?"

"A space ship cake, with ice cream in the middle. It's neat. You'll see. My friend Billy had one, and mom said I could have one, too."

"Wow! That does sound special. "What time is your party, and I need your address, Josh."

"Mom, do you still have the invitation in your purse?" Marissa opened the Fendi bag, then handed Lisa an envelope with her name, "Mrs. Lisa Lee" on the outside. "Mom was gonna mail you the invitation, but couldn't find out your address," Josh added innocently.

"Well, then it's especially lucky we bumped into each other today, isn't it?" Lisa took the invitation from Marissa's extended hand, and added, "I understand. Really, I do. I'd love to be at Josh's party tomorrow."

"Wanna come shopping with us now too, Lisa?" Josh asked, excited at the turn of events, oblivious to the undercurrents of pain the moment was precipitating for Lisa. She looked at the innocent face smiling up at her.

"I can't, sweetheart. I have a lot to do today, but I'll see you tomorrow. Okay?"

"Okay, Lisa."

"Have a good day. Both of you. Anything special you want for your birthday, Josh?"

"Nope. Mom said, I'm not supposed to ask for presents, and I should be polite to everybody even if I don't like what they bring me."

Lisa laughed. "Okay, then. I'll just try to come up with something on my own."

"You don't have to buy me a present, Lisa. Just come and watch me blow out all the candles on my spaceship cake."

"Okay, Josh. Bye you two. I've gotta run, but I'm glad we ran into each other. See you tomorrow."

Lisa spent the rest of the afternoon shopping. She was exhausted by the time she arrived home with an armful of packages. Her purchases included a complete aerospace set, with launching pad and rocket, fully automated by remote, for Josh. She wondered if Marissa was still as close to Yale as she'd been a year ago. She couldn't help feeling anticipatory, wondering whether Yale would be at Josh's party. She'd read articles stating he was back in L.A., after the closing of his failure on Broadway. However, auspiciously, nothing much else had been in the papers recently, and after Frank had died, it was weeks before she read a paper, magazine, or watched television.

Saturday, Lisa dressed in a bright coral jumpsuit by Donna Karan, coral snakeskin sandals, and stuffed her hair under a wide brimmed hat. She added a floral silk scarf of pinks and coral and arrived at Marissa's home at noon; just as the invitation read. Josh and Marissa welcomed her with such fanfare, Lisa was glad she came. It was the first time since Frank's death she'd accepted an invitation to anything social, and had to admit it felt good to converse with people in a house full of laughter and merriment. There were several familiar faces, including people she'd been introduced to during her marriage to Frank. Everyone was warm and friendly. She was being pulled by Josh, to see how big Buster had gotten, when she spotted Ruth sitting in a chair observing her. "Just a minute, Josh." She stopped in front of Ruth. "How are you, Ruth? It's been a long time."

"I've been better, Lisa. But, like you, I manage. I'm sorry about Frank. He seemed like a decent person."

"He was, Ruth. Very decent. Very special."

"Good," Ruth retorted, curtly. She appeared to have aged considerably in the last year.

"Come on, Lisa," Josh urged, tugging her hand.

"Excuse me, Ruth. Josh seems eager to show me Buster."

Lisa followed Josh out to the yard and soon was caught up in the child's excitement, as he showed her Buster and all the aeronautical decorations Marissa had filled the grounds with. She was biting into a hot dog when Howard Fixler approached her, extending a glass of punch.

"Hi, Lisa. It's nice to see you."

"Thank you. I didn't know you knew Marissa, too, Howard."

"Oh, I've known Marissa for almost five years. It's taken me four years to get her to notice me. We've been seeing each other for a while now. I'm crazy about the lady, and she's finally able to admit I have some endearing qualities."

"Well, she's a smart lady. I thought so the first time I met her, and my first instincts are usually accurate."

"What's accurate?" Marissa asked, approaching and putting her hand in Howard's.

"Nothing, honey," Howard chided. "I was just telling Lisa what a great guy I am. She agreed that's all." He winked at Lisa.

Lisa was smiling warmly, feeling good, and on her second hot dog when suddenly Yale staggered out of the house, yelling, "So where, the hell, is the birthday boy? Uncle Yale needs a hug."

"I'm here, Uncle Yale." Josh ran up to him. When Yale bent to hug Josh, he knocked Josh down on the ground, falling on top of him.

Marissa ran over and helped Josh up, while Howard extended a hand to help Yale up. "Sorry, Josh. How about a hot dog for Uncle Yale?"

"Okay, Uncle Yale. Come on. Lisa's here too, like she promised— remember?"

"Hi, Yale," Lisa said, as Josh brought Yale up to the table to give him a hot dog.

"Well…well…well…If it isn't Mrs. Lee. You look great, Lisa, in your fancy getup. Who says money can't make a person. Huh?" Yale was swaying, obviously drunk. When Josh handed him a hot dog, he dropped it on the ground. "Forget it, Josh. I think I've lost my appetite, anyway." He stood, swaying, staring at Lisa. He slurred, "Well, Mrs. Lee, I guess I should offer you my, deepest sympathy—but, I don't, actually, feel like it—so, I'll just go away, and let you all go on having a good old time, out here." He started toward the door wall, stumbled, falling, and passing out.

Ruth stood in the open door wall stoically. She watched, David Ross, Yale's longtime friend and assistant, and Howard Fixler, carry Yale into the house. They took him into one of Marissa's spare bedrooms.

Lisa tried to help Marissa restore joviality for Josh's sake, and to take her own mind off what had just occurred. After Josh had opened all of his gifts, and was involved in showing off his agility at operating the mini space craft Lisa had bought him, Lisa walked into the house to use the bathroom. As she passed the kitchen, she heard Ruth yelling. "No! No! I won't commit him. He'll be alright." Most of the guests had already left.

"Ruth, Yale needs help," Lisa heard David retort. "We can't keep pretending this will go away by itself. No one will put him on television again, since that last episode when he showed up drunk on Jay Leno's show. He can't get backing for a concert. He's gone through millions. And it's only getting worse. Please Ruth. We can't wait any longer. He hasn't been sober in months."

"No! I won't do it! I can't, David. I just can't!"

Lisa walked into the room, going directly up to Ruth, "I'm sorry for eavesdropping. Ruth, can I do anything to help?"

Can you reverse the earth's axis, Lisa, so I have my son back the way he was a year ago?"

"No, Ruth. But, maybe, I can assist, in some way, so the future looks a little brighter."

"Just tell me one thing, Lisa. Did you love Yale when you left here, a year ago, and married Frank?"

"Yes. I did, Ruth."

"Then why, Lisa? Why?"

"Don't ask me that Ruth. But trust me—please—trust me enough now, to help you and Yale, any way I can."

"Why should I, Lisa? Give me one—just one reason."

"Because I've never stopped loving Yale, or you, Ruth. And I've never lied to you, Ruth. That's two reasons."

Ruth crumpled in the chair. With her head bent, she whispered, "Alright, Lisa. You saved his life once before. Maybe, you can do it again. God knows, I can't. He's shut me out, and swears he'll never forgive me if I try to put him in a rehabilitation center or hospital."

"Ruth, you're his mother, and the only one who can legally have him committed. If you decide to do it, I'll be there every step of the way with you. We both know, we sometimes have to do painful things when loved ones are concerned. Don't look back, Ruth. Look at now—today. This is not the Yale I knew. This is not the Yale you want to see day after day. Let me check where the best place, with the least amount of publicity would be, and let's get Yale back on his feet."

"She's right, Ruth," Marissa offered. "You have to sign him into a medical care facility."

"Is there one where I can be nearby?"

"Ruth, I'll arrange it and go with you, if you'd like, but Yale would probably do better if he didn't feel the pressure of being watched. Can I call a good friend, in San Francisco—Dr. Harvey Stone, and we can ask his advice and help?"

"Okay, Lisa. I'll let you help. After all, you're the cause."

"No, Ruth. I'm not responsible. I take responsibility for my own actions—no one else's. Yale did this to himself. I'll be glad to help. But, not as a scapegoat. As a friend."

Lisa called Harvey Stone, asked him where the best rehab center was, which would provide the most privacy, and asked him to make immediate arrangements for Yale to be admitted under his care. She asked for his assistance, and arranged for Ruth and her to have accommodations nearby.

When she hung up, she said flatly, "Harvey Stone will handle the details, Ruth. He's a friend. An excellent physician. Now, you have to call this number, which Dr. Stone gave me, and a private ambulance will arrive for Yale. You'll have to sign the legal documents, Ruth. We'll pack and meet Dr. Stone at the Carmel Rehab Center, in Carmel, tomorrow morning.

"No! No! I'm not letting them take Yale alone. How dare you think I would—"

"Mom, what's going on?" Josh yelled, running into the room excitedly.

"Nothing, honey. Go back outside to your friends for a little while. I'll be right there." Marissa bent and kissed Josh's head.

"It's Uncle Yale, isn't it, mom? He's sick, isn't he? He fell two times today and smells yucky. Is he going to heaven?"

"No Josh, Uncle Yale is not going to heaven. But he is sick, and Lisa and Aunt Ruth are going to help him get better."

"Good," Josh said, then went up to Ruth adding, "Don't cry, Aunt Ruth. Lisa will help Uncle Yale. She helped me. Remember?"

"I remember," was all broken hearted Ruth could mutter.

"Lisa," Josh said, "thanks for the space ship. Mom said, I was too young to work it. She didn't want to buy it. But you knew I could do it, right?"

Before Lisa could respond, Marissa stated, more for Ruth's benefit than anyone elses, "I was wrong, Josh. Lisa was smart enough to know you could do something difficult, when I was afraid you couldn't. Maybe, if I need help for something, next time I'll call Lisa. Now go outside, honey. I'll be out in a minute."

"Okay, mom. I can tell when it's big people talk. Lisa, don't leave before I show you what I can make the spaceship do. Okay?"

"I promise, Josh," Lisa said tremulously.

Everyone was gone when Lisa, Ruth, Marissa and Howard watched Josh show off his expertise with the rocket. Only David was inside the house when the private ambulance, without its siren blaring, carried the violently screaming Yale, strapped to a stretcher, away from the grounds of Marissa's estate. A badly shaken David joined them in the backyard afterwards, trying desperately to maintain control for Ruth's sake. David put his arm across Ruth's shoulders gently, "Do you want me to take you home to pack now?"

"Yes, David. That's fine." She turned to Lisa, "Would it be possible for you to come with us, and perhaps arrange for us to leave for Carmel now?"

"If that's what you'd prefer to do, Ruth. I thought you might have some last minute details to take care of before morning, but I'll be glad to help you pack and leave tonight instead."

"Yes, I'd prefer it that way. Last time you said you were coming back, Yale was disappointed. I don't want to be disappointed now."

"I suppose you have reason not to trust me, Ruth. Perhaps, one day that will change. Come on. I'll go with you."

"Do you have anything you have to take care of, Lisa?"

"No Ruth."

"Tell me something, Lisa. Why did you marry Frank Lee if you didn't love him?"

"I never said I didn't love Frank, Ruth. I did. Don't make false assumptions, or put words in my mouth, Ruth. There are different loves at various times in our lives. I'm not sorry I chose to marry Frank. I'm sorry he's gone from my life. There's not a day I don't miss him."

"Maybe, some things are just a matter of timing, huh? What was good timing for Yale was always bad timing for you. Maybe, it's just destiny that things happen the way they do?"

"Maybe, Ruth. I don't ask myself such questions anymore."

"If I could have died today, it would have been easier than doing this, Lisa."

"I believe you, Ruth. Sincerely, I do."

CHAPTER 19

Once inside Ruth's apartment, Lisa asked if she could use the telephone, while Ruth packed, in order to expedite their travel arrangements. Lisa was uneasy being there with photographs of Yale looming at her from every wall. She wanted to escape the memories the apartment evoked, and felt she was not really welcomed there anymore. David was assisting Ruth in the bedroom when Lisa called Belle, asking her to pack a couple of suitcases, immediately, with comfortable attire. "I have to go out of town for a few weeks, Belle. Can you hold down the fort?"

"No problem, Miss Lisa. Do you need any evening clothes?"

"No, Belle. Just light, casual clothing. Anything important to relate?"

"Jean called from New York earlier. And Marc called about an hour ago. How was the party, Miss Lisa?"

"It was okay."

"Well, I'm glad you finally went out. You've done nothing but write and pick out furniture for long enough. You're too lovely to be alone, all of the time, except when you see your boys and your parents."

"Thanks, Belle. Listen, I'm in a hurry. I'll be there to pick up the suitcases in about an hour. I'll be in Carmel, but no one is to know. I'll call you with a phone number, in case of an emergency, in the morning."

"Okay, Miss Lisa. I'll go pack you up. Anything else?"

"No. Thanks Belle."

Next Lisa called to have the jet readied, then dialed Marc at the university.

"Marc, it's mom. Everything okay?"

"Yeh, fine. I was just worried about you today. You sounded sad yesterday."

"I'm fine, honey. You worry too much. I'm going out of town, on business, for a few weeks, so I'll call you between pit stops."

"What charity are you helping this week, Ma?"

"No charity. Just going to look at some real estate in Carmel."

"How was Josh's birthday party?"

"It was okay. How come you're home on Sunday?"

"Dad's coming up tonight, to take me and Steve to dinner, remember? I still can't believe you sent him that check to save his business."

"It's only money, Marc. I've got enough so I can share."

"A half million dollars, Ma? That goes beyond sharing."

"Big deal. So, where's your brother?"

"At Amy's; where else? He's definitely in love. Amy said his beard bothered her, so he shaved it off this morning. This must be true love."

"Well kiddo, I remember you once shaved your moustache for a special girl, after months of grooming it, and getting it just the way you wanted it to look."

He laughed. "Yeh Ma, I remember."

"Well, I gotta go, honey. I'll call in a day or two. Say 'hi' to Steve. Love ya. Bye."

"Love you too, mom. Have a good trip."

The last call Lisa placed was to Jean in New York. Ben Shinsky answered the phone. "Hi Ben, it's Lisa. What are you doing there?"

"The final edit of "Regrets" with Jean. We want your book out by September. Why don't you fly east and join us?"

"Sorry. I've got other plans. I'll be out of town for a bit. Jean called earlier, do you know what for?"

"Hold on, I'm putting you on the speaker. Jean, get in here. Lisa's on the phone."

"Lisa. Hi. How was the party?"

"Fine. What's up? I'm kind of in a rush. I have to go out of town on business for a couple of weeks."

"Nothing, honey. I just wanted to know how it felt to get out. It's the first time you've gone anywhere socially since—"

"It was fair, Jean. A lot of people looking me over actually. I wasn't very comfortable. I'd rather stay in and just write."

"Come on, honey. It'll get easier. You can't bury yourself, too."

"Jean, I really can't talk now. Can I call you—?

"Okay, Lisa. I won't push. Ben and I are almost done editing the manuscript. You want me to fax the few changes—"

"No. I trust you. Anything else?"

"You want a dedication in it?"

"Yes. Put—For Frank, who will live in my heart forever. There was silence on the line. "Are you there Jean? Ben?"

"We're here, honey. Frank would be more pleased, Lisa, if you did let him live in your heart, and stopped it right there. Are you going to join the human race again, Lisa? Are you coming to New York next week for the premiere of "Justices"?

"I can't, Jean. And it's not because I'm mourning. I have business in Carmel to take care of."

"Sure, Lisa. You always have business or some charity to aid. When are you going to do something that makes you happy?"

"I did. I went to a birthday party today, didn't I?"

"So why do I get the feeling you didn't have a good time. That it was a turn off instead of a turn on? Was Yale there?"

"Jean, I really have to go. I'll call in a day or two. I love you—you too, Ben—Bye."

She put down the phone before Jean could say more. She sat on the sofa, oblivious that Ruth and David had eavesdropped on her conversations. As she waited until Ruth was packed she couldn't help but feel sad and nostalgic.

When they reached her place Lisa didn't invite Ruth and David in. She merely said, "I'll be right out," and went in. While her chauffeur was putting the luggage in the limo, David got out of the car.

"Lisa, would you mind if I joined you and Ruth on the flight, and stayed the night. I'd like to see you both settled in?"

"Not at all. Perhaps, you should ask Ruth as well."

"I did. She's extremely anxious to be near Yale. I really don't have to pack for one night. If there's a man's shirt or sweater I could borrow, I'd appreciate it."

"I'm sorry, David. I have no men's clothing in the house." She climbed in the car. David followed, sitting next to her.

As the car headed for the airport, Lisa picked up the car phone and called Carmel Clinic. Harvey Stone was on the line in minutes. Lisa put the speaker on, turning the volume up.

"Harvey, I'm on the way to the airport with Ruth Frye and David Ross now. How is Yale?"

"The copter arrived as scheduled. I just arrived half an hour ago. I gave him a mild sedative and he's still out. He was vomiting in the ambulance. Apparently he's been taking pills, of some sort, as well as alcohol. Do you know what medication Yale was on?"

"I know he used to take some psychotropic medications—"

"Dr. Stone," David interrupted, "Yale has been taking Halcyon, in large doses, for several months. He said, it was the only way he could sleep."

"Anything else, David?"

"Not that I know of. That and a lot of vodka."

Ruth sat quietly, staring out of the window, while Harvey asked David how long this has been going on, and the quantities of alcohol and pills Yale had been ingesting daily.

"Lisa," Ruth finally uttered, "I have to see him tonight."

"Harvey, I need two more favors. First, we'll be coming straight to the clinic from the airfield. Ruth must see Yale, if only for a minute, before we go to a hotel."

"I understand, Lisa. I'll be waiting for you. I've got Dr. Hoburn covering for me, so I can stay for the initial meetings and consultations. Also, I was able to get you a vacated beach house which is less than a mile from the center's premises. It's a nice place; completely furnished, and has three bedrooms, all with terraces. It'll be stocked for you before you get there. It's Oceanside."

"Great. Thank you, Harvey. Thanks for everything."

"You requested confidentiality and privacy. What else?"

"David Ross is staying the night. He didn't have a chance to pack. I need a few men's shirts, medium, and some essentials."

"You got it. Anything else?"

"One thing. Not one word to Yale that I am in any way involved with this. Yale is only to know that his mother and David are helping him the best way they know of. Nothing else. If he suspects I, in any way, intervened he'll never forgive Ruth or David for allowing it. Ruth feels Yale's bitterness is partially a result of my betrayal in marrying Frank when he believed I was coming back to him."

"Does Yale—"

She cut him off. "Harvey, I never even told Yale I was getting married." He understood. She was subtly diverting the conversation away from any reference to her life with Frank. "Please, make sure Ruth can see her son, and I'll talk to you soon."

"Alright, Lisa. Page me when you arrive."

The plane was landing, in a private airfield in Carmel, when David gently shook Ruth awake. "We're here. Are you all right? How's your headache?"

"I'm fine. Where's Lisa? Still in that little room on the side?"

"Yes. She's been in there the entire time. Maybe, I should wake her?"

"No need, David," Lisa said, emerging in a matronly black polyester dress, silver wig, no make up, and spectacles. "I don't want any publicity. I've had enough lately. Even my dad didn't recognize me when I showed up in Florida, like this, last month. I look about fifty don't I?"

Ruth smiled for the first time that day. "Lisa, you look seventy—not fifty. You could pass for my grandmother."

"Good. Then no one will pinch my ass. Let's go."

They were nearing the clinic when Ruth finally asked, "Why didn't you at least call Yale before marrying Frank?"

"I couldn't, Ruth. I'm just not good at saying goodbye."

"Sometimes it's necessary, Lisa. It's cruel to leave someone you care about without giving them the chance to say goodbye back."

A vision of Frank drowning himself in the Pacific Ocean flashed across Lisa's mind. In a voice that was barely audible she replied, "I know".

CHAPTER 20

At Carmel Clinic, Lisa had Dr. Stone paged with an accented voice to disguise her own. "Please, tell Dr. Stone that Granny Kay is here. He's expecting me."

Harvey Stone guided Ruth, Lisa, and David to a private office, apparently familiar with Lisa's camouflaged appearance. He wasted no time, relating during Yale's lucid moments he was outraged at being committed and foul mouthed everyone in his presence.

"Let me be blunt, Mrs. Frye. Yale is lucky to be alive. He had enough medication, coupled with the alcohol in his system, to kill him, had he not regurgitated in the ambulance. Our initial assessment clearly shows a substance addiction and a clinically depressed individual. He is self destructive and unwilling to communicate with us presently. He may repulse you with his appearance, and disgust you with his vulgarity. This is not an abnormal response for those who do not enter the clinic voluntarily. I think Yale would loathe for you to see him now. I discourage you from talking to him until he exhibits some signs of acclimation, and a desire to conquer his illness."

"Dr. Stone, I cannot be more repulsed by Yale, now, than I have been watching him deteriorate these past months. I understand your apprehensions, but I am berated by Yale frequently, when he is quarrelsome or drunk. I have watched his smiles turn to sneers; witnessed his charm turn to scorn. I have allowed him to manipulate me with promises that were lies. And I am accustomed to his tongue-lashing. I respect your position. However, I will not leave until I see my son."

Harvey Stone studied Ruth's face. He contemplated such a reaction and understood the inner struggle of people forced to commit a loved one. He mellowed his approach with seasoned experience, inquiring, "Would you prefer to do the necessary paperwork, and Yale's medical history, before or after you see your son?"

"I'd like to see Yale first. Please."

They followed Dr. Stone to an elevator; then advanced down a long hallway to a private room in the multi-leveled complex. The walls were all warmly decorated with pleasing scenic paintings. There was an aura of informality, which lent itself to fortifying security. The regard taken to insure the clinic provided shelter without austerity was evident.

Dr. Stone opened the door, placing a hand on Ruth's elbow, as he entered Yale's room beside her. Lisa and David stood in the hallway outside the room. Ruth approached the bed cautiously. Male nurses were attempting to soothe Yale, and restrict his body from wrestling against the restraints on his arms and legs. Lisa and David's proximity allowed them to hear Yale's cursing and fury for being harnessed to the bed.

"Yale, I'm here," Ruth managed, as she got next to the bed. Yale spit at her, promising to kill her when he got out. He didn't allow her to speak, controlling the moment with unbridled recriminations until his maledictions were unbearable. His savage accusations and recitation that she was nothing but a fucking hag, who he never wanted to see again, finally drove her from the room. He was still screaming, "You feebleminded bitch! How dare you do this to me. I'll never forgive you—NEVER!" when Ruth walked out.

The weight of the day was taking its toll on Ruth causing her to become caustic by the time they were back in the private office downstairs. "How many damn forms are there?" she sputtered testily.

"Harvey," Lisa interjected, "Can some of this wait?"

"Shut up, Lisa. I don't need your interference," Ruth shouted. "You, who conveniently hides behind a costume, and frivolously plays with peoples hearts."

"That's enough for now, Mrs. Frye. It's late. And I won't allow you to avail your pain on Lisa. Please, meet me here in the morning to complete the paperwork." Harvey rose and resolutely said, "Mrs. Frye, I suggest you rest and prepare yourself for some difficult days. This is where your son belongs. The staff is competent. Defamation of Lisa will not generate Yale's recovery any. If you need time alone here tonight, I can arrange it."

"No. I don't need anything but my son to be all right. I'll endorse whatever you suggest to get Yale well." She rose and extended her hand. "Thank you for flying here to help Yale."

Harvey walked them to the door. "Lisa, how about a cup of coffee, then I'll drop you off?" He handed Ruth one set of keys to the house, and Lisa another. "I'd like to talk to you."

"Okay, Harvey. I'll see you in the morning, Ruth. Goodnight. Goodnight, David."

Lisa followed Harvey to the staff cafeteria. They sat in a corner of the room when Harvey asked, "Are you up to this?"

"I can handle it, Harvey. Ruth just needs to let off steam."

"You're right. She does. However, I'm not sure you should be her whipping post or companion. She doesn't seem to like you right now."

"She has reason not to."

"Well, if you continue to disguise yourself, she'll never trust you. She needs honesty, support, and a strong constitution to back her. You'll have to make a choice whether to go through this with her, as yourself, or you won't do her any good."

"I didn't want Yale to know I was involved. And I don't want any needless publicity."

"No, Lisa. You don't want Yale to hate you, and you're afraid to let your guard down in front of Ruth."

"What do you suggest, Harvey?"

"Be yourself. Yale will eventually learn the truth. So why not let him hate you now, instead of later. Now his anger and hate stem from his lack of control and his addiction, which is normal. Later, his hate would be a result of deceit. I think Ruth is aware of as much. That's probably one reason she lashed out at you in the office."

"But I don't want any more notoriety, Harvey. I'm sick of it. How do I, then, justify being here, without appearing in every tabloid across the country?"

"Become a volunteer patron. I could arrange for you to be listed as an aid."

"No. Then Ruth will think this is a charitable cause I'm supporting. Who owns this facility, Harvey?"

"There are five co-owners, I believe. Why?"

"I want to buy in. I'll invest, for controlling interest, and donate substantially, for a title and authorization to be actively involved. But it has to be done pronto—I want to be able to come and go as I please, and make inquiries without opposition or red tape."

"Why?"

"Then, I can be myself. I can be here without Yale requesting me not to be, and I can justify my reason for being here honestly. Can we get on it immediately?"

"Don't you want a financial report first, or to sleep on it, Lisa?"

"No. I want in—now."

"Let's go into the office then and make some calls."

It was dawn when Lisa woke Howard Fixler in L.A. asking him to finalize the immediate contractual agreement for her forty percent ownership of Carmel Clinic. She bought out two of the five shareholders for controlling interest in the facility. It had cost her twenty million dollars, plus a guaranteed million a year for ten years, to the rehabilitation center, to yield patient care improvement programs, including deferred rates to people who needed financial assistance. Howard would be flying to the clinic with the papers that evening to conclude the contractual agreement.

"I'm exhausted Harvey and grateful to you for everything. Can you just check if Yale is sleeping, comfortably, before taking me to the house?"

"You can check for yourself, Lisa. You're an owner of the center."

"Okay, wise guy. I'll be right down."

"When you care about someone; you care for life, don't you?"

"Yup," was all she said, as she walked to the elevator.

Lisa went down the corridor on the second floor and gently turned the knob to the room Yale was occupying. In her granny outfit, she quietly approached the sleeping figure in the bed, who was still in restraints. The male nurse in attendance, who was half asleep in a chair, didn't say a word as she put her index finger up to her mouth and whispered "Sh-Sh". Yale was pale. He stirred for the briefest of moments, opening his ladened eyes slightly, then drifted back into sleep. Lisa stared at Yale for a long moment, then turned and left the room feeling empathetic for the inner turmoil she assumed Yale must have been enduring. She stopped in the rest room to blow her nose, and dry her eyes, before going downstairs.

Harvey dropped her off. She kissed his cheek gently, "Thank you, Harvey." Ruth, who hadn't been able to sleep all night observed her from the living room window. Lisa removed the wig, tossing her hair, feeling free of the disguise she'd worn for the past twelve hours. She unbuttoned the top button of the atrocious black rag, allowing the fresh air from the ocean to wash over her as she exited the car.

"Get some rest, Lisa."

"Okay. Make sure you get some rest, too. I'll see you later, Harvey."

Lisa turned the key in the front door of the small white beach house. She entered quietly, trying not to disturb Ruth or David. She walked into the living room and was met by Ruth's cold glare and snarling sarcasm. "Did you have a pleasant night, Lisa?" She spat the words venomously then left the room, not even giving Lisa the opportunity to respond.

Lisa bumped into Ruth again when she came out of the one bathroom they'd be sharing. Lisa didn't want to argue. She didn't want to talk. She was exhausted and only wanted the comfort of a bed for a few hours.

"Dr. Stone must be close to you, Lisa," Ruth started, as Lisa exited the bathroom in a nightshirt and slippers. "He stocked the refrigerator and cupboards. He even had the shirts and sweaters here for David when we arrived, as you requested."

"He's a good friend, Ruth. I'm crazy about him. He's helped me through some difficult times."

"Perhaps, you should marry him next. He's got a fine reputation and he's quite handsome. By the looks of it, he's crazy about you, too."

"Harvey is already married, Ruth."

"Oh. I didn't know."

"Yes, Ruth. Harvey is married to medicine. And yes Ruth, there is a lot you don't know. Goodnight Ruth. I'm tired. I'll see you later."

She turned going to her bedroom. With the bay windows open, she climbed in bed, and let the sound of the waves from the ocean caress her to sleep. A warm breeze filtered through the room. The last sound she heard, before sleep cloaked around her, was a bird melodiously singing on the terrace.

CHAPTER 21

It was close to noon by the time Lisa approached the office filled with raised voices at Carmel Clinic. She wasn't prepared for the attack Ruth launched as she opened the door. "Well, here is "Sleeping Beauty" herself.

What's this I hear about you buying into the clinic, and that I can't see Yale for a week, or more? Who, the hell, do you think you are Lisa, and what—!

"Mrs. Frye, I should have let Lisa tell you herself about her arrangements regarding the clinic," Harvey Stone said, exasperated by this time. "I thought Lisa was going—"

Lisa interrupted. "It's okay, Harvey. Ruth wasn't much more civil to me last night than she is being here now. This must be Dr. Jay Dresler," Lisa said, turning to the other physician in the room, ignoring Ruth, David, and Harvey Stone for the moment.

"It's nice to meet you Mrs. Lee," Jay Dresler said, shaking her hand. "I'm chief of staff of Carmel. Apparently, Mrs. Frye feels the rules of our establishment are not ones she chooses to comply with."

"Well, Dr. Dresler, Mrs. Frye has no alternative." She turned facing Ruth and spoke succinctly, "You see, I heard Yale Frye threaten to kill himself and to cause bodily harm to others. He, obviously, is in need of medical evaluation, psychologically as well as physically, before we can release him to anyone's care. If I'm not mistaken, the only other option we would have at this point is to have Yale transferred to a state mental hospital, where he would have no privacy and, unfortunately, a substantially lesser quality of medical care than we can provide.

"All I wanted was to see Yale for a minute, after all these damn forms," Ruth shouted, waving sheets of paper in Lisa's face. "I'm his mother, for Gods sake. I just want to see him for a minute."

"Dr. Dresler," Lisa began, "I won't be finalizing my contract until this evening. I'd appreciate it if we could all go to Mr. Frye's room for a few minutes before we go any further with this discussion. I think I should advise Yale of the provisions and options before we go any further, and I'd prefer not to be repetitious."

"Lisa, that might not be wise," Harvey interjected, "Yale is going through withdrawal and is exhibiting—"

She didn't let him finish. "I know, Harvey. I stopped by his room before coming here. If Ruth wants to see Yale for a moment, I think we should make an exception to the rules this time."

They all walked to Yale's room on the second floor. Ruth did not wait for any of them as she pushed open the door to greet her son. Yale was still in restraints, convulsively thrashing against the bands, and soaked in perspiration. He was delirious, and drool was sliding down his chin. The nurse present was trying to soothe him. He was wiping Yale's face with a moist towel. Ruth had to grab onto the back of a chair for support as she looked at the ghastly sight before her.

"How is he doing, Jerry?" Dr. Dresler asked the male nurse, "Any problems with dehydration?"

"He's holding up, doc. We had to put the IV back in a few times, that's all. He's strong. He'll be better in a bit, Mrs.," He addressed Ruth. "The first few days are the worst."

Yale stopped thrashing for a second and began shivering until you could hear his teeth chatter. Ruth took David's arm and he led her from the room.

She made it back to the office and Harvey handed her a glass of water, from a desktop pitcher, as she crumpled into a chair.

"Ruth," Lisa said, more calmly than she was feeling, "The rules are that you go home now. Yale will be well cared for. You can't see him for the first week or until he's ready. I was told all patients have phones for outgoing calls, but no one can call in. There is someone with him, at all times, during the process of detoxification, and you can't ease the process by anything you might want to do. The choice is yours. Do you want Yale here? Or do you want Yale transferred to a state hospital? Yale, obviously, can't speak for himself right now."

"He's all that matters to me, Lisa. You know that."

"Then you know what you have to do, Ruth. Go back to the house and get some rest. I'll go with you."

"You know," she softly uttered, "You hear horror stories all the time. But you can't really comprehend some dilemmas until you go through the hell of one, like this, yourself. It's too bad understanding is often such a painful lesson."

Lisa left with Ruth and David. Harvey came to the beach house, later in the afternoon, to sedate Ruth when her state of hysteria wouldn't subside. Ruth was still sleeping when Howard Fixler came and left with the signed documents for Lisa's purchase agreement. And Ruth was still asleep when Lisa told David she'd grab a bite later, leaving him to keep an eye on Ruth, as she went out.

She didn't tell David she was going back to the clinic to check on Yale; just that she had to go out for a while. David had asked to stay a few days longer, and Lisa agreed, knowing Ruth was going to need a great deal of support from people she trusted; and she definitely didn't trust her at the moment.

Lisa paged Harvey at the clinic; spoke briefly with him and Dr. Dresler. She was given a white medical uniform and a plastic pin with her name and title as a staff supervisor written across it. She bid farewell to Harvey, who had to return to San Francisco that night, and whispered, "Thank you, Harvey, for everything. I hope I'll survive until you come back next week."

"You'll do fine, Lisa. But if you need me for anything, don't hesitate to call."

Dr. Jay Dresler was having announcements welcoming Lisa as a staff supervisor printed for disbursement in the morning. He was scheduling a meeting for all board members, and releasing a statement to the media of her involvement with the facility. After her conversation was concluded with Jay Dresler she excused herself, leaving the tall, handsome, dark eyed Armenian doctor, to go check on Yale. She declined Jay Dresler's dinner invitation for the following evening.

Lisa entered Yale's room without knocking. She introduced herself to Sherman Black, the nurse in attendance for the night shift. Yale was asleep and still in restraints when she entered. She was told he had been fitful most of the day, and his blood pressure elevated. She told Sherman Black to take a coffee break for twenty minutes, volunteering to stay with Yale until he returned. Since Sherman Black had already been apprised of Lisa's new position at Carmel Clinic, he didn't question her suggestion and left to get a cup of coffee.

In the dimly lit room, Lisa approached Yale's bed and stood looking down at him. She couldn't help remembering how it felt when she first got acquainted with him, and how life changed for her when they later shared a special time loving each other. He had amazed her right from the start. He was never the egomaniac so many superstars became. He was vulnerable, emotional, intelligent. He was giving, understanding, and so easily could ignite a fire in her which made the time they merged so passionate that she couldn't get enough of him.

Lisa was so lost in though for a moment, that she jumped when Yale stirred in the bed. She took a step backwards not wanting to disturb him, but it was too late. He opened his eyes and bitterly muttered, "Get, the fuck, out of here. I don't want to look at you now—or ever again."

She didn't move for a minute. "Can we talk for—"?

He cut her short. "Get out now!" "We have nothing to talk about. Get out! Get out!" He started pulling against the bands that held his hands imprisoned. "Get the fuck out of here!"

"No Yale. I'm not leaving yet. You can yell all you want. No one can force me out, Yale. You see, I'm part owner of this place."

He stopped thrashing and yelling. His face was wet with perspiration as he venomously sputtered, "You divorced one husband, buried another, and now show up to watch the suffering of someone who would have killed for you. I hope you rot in hell!"

The color drained from her face as she listened to his words. "It doesn't matter what you say, Yale. You can curse me—hate me—hurt me—but the fact is; you are here for a week. You can make it a time to clean up your act and go on; or you can fight it and go back to being a drunk when you leave. Either way Yale, I'm going to be around; like it or not."

Before Yale could say more, the nurse came back into the room, eliminating the need for Lisa to stay and take any more verbal abuse.

"He's all yours". She turned to leave the room.

"Wait," Yale yelled out. She turned facing him. He was beginning to shake again. "Just tell me one thing. What did Frank have that I didn't?"

"One thing for sure, Yale. Fewer days ahead of him to live life to it's fullest. He's dead and buried. You're not—yet. Good night." She left the room, leaning against a wall in the corridor to compose herself.

She left the hospital, and went directly to her bedroom when she reached the house. It was late. She hadn't eaten all day but knew the nausea she was experiencing wasn't from hunger. She put on a bathrobe and went out on the terrace adjacent to the bedroom. She sat down on the rocking chair and rocked, allowing the ocean air to calm her until she thought she could sleep.

Ruth was sitting over coffee when Lisa entered the kitchen in the morning. Ruth was a dismal sight to behold. Her eyes were swollen, her fatigue apparent. She didn't greet Lisa; just sat hunched over her coffee. Her amiable spirit was nonexistent. Self-pity had been substituted.

"Where's David?" Lisa asked, as she made a fresh pot of coffee and toasted some muffins.

"I think, he said, he was going to the store for something. I don't remember."

"I'm going to scramble some eggs, Ruth. How many do you want?"

"One's fine. Make a couple for David, too. I don't know if he's eaten anything."

"Okay. Why don't you take the car today Ruth? Pick up whatever you think we could use for a few dinners? I have to go to the clinic for a meeting soon."

"I'll see. Maybe I'll send David."

Lisa didn't respond. She bent, opening a couple of cupboards, in search of a frying pan, when the phone rang. Ruth made no attempt to get off the chair and answer it. By the fourth ring, Lisa picked up the telephone shouting, "Hello" with agitation.

"Lisa, is that you? It's Marissa. I didn't wake you, did I?"

"No, Marissa. Sorry if my greeting was unpleasant. I was just scrounging around for a pan. I don't know where anything is yet."

"I won't keep you, Lisa. I was worried about Yale and wanted to know how things were going."

"Not great, Marissa. Yale is going through withdrawal and all the symptomatic distress associated with being drug dependent. I saw him late last night. He didn't have any kind words for me then. I'll see him again later. Hopefully, today, he'll be a little better. I'll tell him you called. When he's ready, I'm sure, he'll call you. Patients aren't allowed incoming calls at the clinic."

"Howard said Ruth was sleeping when he was there with the legal documents and he didn't see her. Is she okay?"

"As good as any mother would be watching her child suffering."

Ruth sat listening, but didn't ask to talk to Marissa. She really didn't want to talk to anyone.

"Do you want me to come there, Lisa?" Maybe I could help, somehow."

"No, Marissa. Thank you. To tell the truth, there's little any of us can do, but let Yale know we care, and be available when he's able to reach out. Right now, he's angry, and feels powerless. Yale never liked situations where he felt he had to give up control. You know that. His reactions are normal and anticipated. How's Josh?"

"Great. He loved that you came to his birthday party. He's a little confused about his Uncle Yale, but Howard and I are reassuring him Yale will be better real soon."

"Good. Tell him I said hello, and that I had a nice time at his party, will you?"

"Sure. Listen Lisa, if you need anything—anything at all—please call."

"I will, Marissa. I promise. I'll give Yale your love and talk to you soon. Ask Howard to give me a call tonight, too, if you don't mind. I'd like to have him wire me additional funds from an account. I want to order some Gazebos for the grounds outside the clinic. I think, sometimes, people need to have a private place outdoors to collect their thoughts in, or just to go to when they need to be alone, or with a friend, or something."

"Okay. I'll have Howard call you later. Give Ruth my love too, okay?"

"I will. Thanks for calling, Marissa. It's the first friendly conversation I've had in a while. Talk to you soon."

Ruth sat mute, while Lisa placed muffins, eggs, and juice on the table. She was pouring herself coffee when David walked in, carrying a few bags of groceries. "Good morning, Lisa," he offered cheerfully. I got some juices, decaffeinated coffee, and a few things I thought we could use I didn't notice in the pantry."

"Thanks David. I really appreciate it. If I keep drinking this regular coffee, I'm going to get hyper. Sit down. I just whipped up some eggs. The only thing I can't find is napkins, so we'll have to use paper toweling."

Ruth got up from her chair for the first time. She opened a cupboard, taking out a package of napkins and bringing them to the table. "Here, I have a habit of keeping things like I would at home, even when I'm away, so I remember where I put them."

"Thanks," was all Lisa said, sitting down with her cup of coffee.

"Why didn't you tell me you saw Yale last night, Lisa? Why did I have to hear it in your phone conversation, just now, with Marissa?"

"You didn't ask Ruth, and didn't appear to want to talk to me at all when I came in here."

"You didn't say you were going to see him last night."

"You were asleep when I went out Ruth."

"And it wasn't appropriate to wake me, with news about my son, when you got back, I suppose?"

"I thought it could wait, Ruth. You needed some rest."

"Oh, I see. So now, you'll decide what I need too, huh? Pretty presumptuous aren't you?"

"What do you want from me, Ruth? Do you want a written report, everyday, of everything I do? This isn't a picnic for me either, you know."

"What is it for you, Lisa? Is this redemption for breaking Yale's heart, by marrying Frank, when Yale thought you were coming back to him? Is this your good deed for not even having the courtesy to call Yale, and tell him you weren't coming back, as any decent person might do? Is this to get Yale to forgive you for finding out you married someone else by reading it in a newspaper?" Her voice was escalating and her glowering eyes were livid.

Lisa got up from the table. "I'm not going to defend myself to you or anyone else, Ruth. I don't owe you, or Yale, anything. I'm trying to help—that's all. If you choose to dwell on the past—go ahead. I have better things to do. You're not the Ruth I knew. You're a self-pitying frail lady, who shrills accusations with a sharp tongue. Look in the mirror, Ruth, before you look at me. Your hesitation to commit Yale could have killed him. Your unwillingness and misgivings could have cost him his life. Your reluctance could have done more harm than anything I did. Now, if you don't mind, I'm leaving for the clinic. I seem to have lost my appetite!"

Lisa stormed out of the house minutes later and was still ruffled when she arrived at the clinic. She located Dr. Dresler, and asked for a complete report of the itinerary followed by the clinic, and what the daily routines consisted of. She wanted to know who was in charge of each department, and the techniques that were implemented that made the clinic so successful to date. She acquired a diagram of the facility, and asked that an office be made available for her immediately. She was on her way to the cafeteria when Sherman Black called out to her in front of the elevator. "Good morning, Mrs. Lee. Are you going to Mr. Frye's room? I'll tell you, I'm glad my shift is over. He's been bad-tempered all night. He had me place a call for him an hour ago, and it looks like he's got someone calling Dr. Dresler to have him released. He told someone on the phone that his mother was forced into putting him here, and that Dr. Stone was not his doctor, with no authority to admit him. I tried to tell him we wanted to help him and to reconsider. I won't even repeat what he told me to do."

"Who is with him now, Sherman?"

"A day nurse just relieved me. I think Dr. Dresler was going up, too."

"Thanks Sherman. I'll see you later."

Instead of the cafeteria, Lisa went to Yale's room. He was still in restraints, but calmer than he'd been the night before. A nurse and Dr. Dresler were in the room. Yale was mannerless when she walked in. "So, Mrs. Lee, it appears I'll be able to leave soon, and the next time I see you it will be in court, after you're formally served with a lawsuit for masterminding a plan to put me here, with the help of my unstable mother."

"Don't threaten me, Yale. I could care less whether or not you sue. You were brought here because you need help. No one did anything unlawful, and the criterion was legal. I had everything checked, Yale. The only one you can hurt is yourself, if you get yourself released."

"My choice, Bitch! Now, you can either let me leave voluntarily, or I'll be sure my unbalanced mother testifies you managed to, somehow, persuade her into doing this."

Before Lisa could respond, Dr. Dresler turned to her, stating, "He can't do anything, Mrs. Lee. I just spoke with his attorney and was about to explain, when you came in, that by ethics we have a moral obligation to ensure he doesn't harm himself. We have the power to evaluate his state of mind before releasing him. His attorney asked us to send him our determination as soon as possible."

When Yale heard Dr. Dresler's words, he became tempestuous and vigorously pulled against the straps on his arms and legs, wildly screaming, "You fuckers! You'll pay for this! You fuckers!"

"Stop it, Yale!" Lisa shouted. "Unstrap him, doctor. Release him. Give this bed to someone who wants to be helped."

Yale quieted and looked at Lisa. "Mrs. Lee, only his mother can sign the forms which would allow Mr. Frye to leave. You don't have the authority, and either do I—"

"Hold on, Dr. Dresler." She went to the phone and dialed the beach house. David answered the phone. "David, put Ruth on the phone, and stay on an extension" she began. "Ruth, I'm in Yale's room and he is insisting on leaving. Legally he can be forced to stay, but to tell you the truth, I'm sick of the bullshit. Why don't you and David come over to the clinic now? I'm unstraping, him and bringing him his clothes, but you have to sign the release forms before he can go. I've had it. I don't want to take any more crap from you, or from Yale. I've given up suffering, so come get him. We'll meet you on the main floor, in the office."

She put down the receiver and asked the nurse to get his clothes.

He was quiet, waiting. "Mrs. Lee," Dr. Dresler started, "This in not in Mr. Frye's best interests. His reactions are common—"

"Put a lid on it, doctor," Lisa interjected, "and stop speaking as if Yale wasn't in the room. If you want to tell him, it's not in his best interests—talk to him—not me. He's a big boy." She walked over to the bed and started undoing the restraints.

"Yale, I'm sorry you feel betrayed and victimized. Please, get dressed and come downstairs, to the office, with the doctor. After Ruth signs the papers, and you sign whatever is necessary, you can go. Please, don't cause a scene. When you leave here, please get Ruth's things at the beach house. I'll arrange for your flight home."

"Mrs. Lee, there are regulations, I can impose, to prevent you from doing this. I am chief of staff of the clinic and have been here a long time.

You don't have authority, simply because you just bought into the facility, to over-ride the doctrine of the center."

"Dr. Dresler, I suggest we put aside formalities or the conventional codes since Mr. Frye's mother is not in the best state of mind right now. She wouldn't be rational either."

"What's wrong with my mother, Lisa?"

"I think she's mourning the loss of her son, Yale." She undid the last restraint, extending her hand to help him sit up.

"I can manage," he said, declining her assistance.

"Fine. I'll see you downstairs then." She turned and left the room disheartened and concerned; doubting if what she was doing was right.

While waiting for Ruth and David to arrive, and weighing her options, Lisa was deliberating whether her decision was warranted. Pacing the floor, she spotted the alcoholic's prayer on the wall: **"God grant me the serenity to accept the things I cannot change, courage to change the things I can, and wisdom to always tell the difference."**

She sat down thinking how apropos the quote was, repeating the words again out loud, when Yale entered.

CHAPTER 22

Yale sat in a chair of the administrative office, worn, weak, and disheveled. He was unshaven, uncombed, haggard, and passive. Dr. Dresler was gathering the discharge forms with clauses, which dismissed the clinic from all responsibility for releasing him, before it was deemed appropriate by the trained staff of the clinic. He was announcing to Ruth and Yale, they would have to sign a disclaimer, relinquishing anyone affiliated with the center of any responsibility for his health, once he left against their opposition, and persuasive efforts that he continue with their program for rehabilitation.

Yale's hands were trembling; his brow beaded with perspiration. He sat gripped by abdominal cramping as Dr. Dresler explained he was being released against his advice and professional judgment. Lisa had left the office when Yale arrived, trying to avoid a confrontation with him or Ruth. She didn't speak to Yale when he had entered, just got up and walked out stating, "If you need me, Doctor Dresler, I'll be in the lounge. I have to make a couple of phone calls."

Ruth was in a state of confusion as Dr. Dresler continued to gather papers from various folders while pontificating on Yale's decaying condition, and self-destructive attitude. "Wait a minute," she yelled. "I don't understand what's going on here, and where is Lisa."

"Apparently, Mrs. Frye, Lisa is tired of fighting for some cooperation and is throwing in the towel. I don't blame her after the abusive treatment I've witnessed against her from Yale, and from the reports from Mr. Frye's attendants and nurses."

"Just get the fucking papers together, and shut up already!" Yale bellowed, as he sat hunched over, in obvious pain.

"Doctor, would you get Lisa for me. I'm not signing anything until I have a word with her."

"Ma, don't start. Just get me out of here, damn it!"

"Where is Lisa, doctor?"

"Down the hall in the lounge, Mrs. Frye."

Ruth got up and left the office. Dr. Dresler and David tried to keep Yale from following her, but when he wouldn't stop wrestling them, and continued verbally assaulting them, Dr. Dresler said, "Let him go. He's unwilling to be reasonable. I'll be surprised if he makes it to the lounge."

Yale rose unsteadily, yelled, "You're fired!" at David and walked to the lounge doubled over. He pushed the door open and stumbled to the nearest chair. Lisa was on the sofa, a nurse holding a cold compress against the back of her neck. Lisa's head was down between her legs. Ruth was next to the nurse.

"What happened?" Dr. Dresler asked approaching.

"Nothing, Jay," Lisa announced, straightening up, "I just got dizzy. I'm fine. Thank you," she said, pushing the nurses hand away from her neck. "I'm alright."

"Actually, Dr. Dresler," the nurse interjected, "Mrs. Lee fainted when she came in. Her pulse is still rapid. I just sent Carol, who was on break too, downstairs to get some fresh juice. Mrs. Lee said, she suddenly felt light headed; that she'd forgotten to take her iron supplements for a few days, and hasn't eaten anything since early yesterday."

"I'm alright. Really. Thank you, Amy," she said again, patting the nurse's hands. What can I do for you, Jay? Ruth?"

"I just wanted to find out what was going on," Ruth started, "I get a call to come get Yale. You were abrupt on the phone. I thought you'd at least explain when I got here…"

"Ruth, I offered to help you at Marissa's house. I never said I was going to be a sacrificial lamb. I've had it. You've been rude, insolent, and accusatory. You fight me on everything, and Yale has been just as bad. I love you, Ruth. And I love Yale, or I wouldn't have offered to try and help, but I can't take anymore. I've done all I can. I'm sorry."

"Look at him, Lisa," Ruth said tearfully, her voice cracking, pointing at Yale, who looked like he might pass out himself any second. "He's sick. He needs to be here. He's given up living. He drinks; takes pills, and spits at his mother. This is not my Yale—this is not my son—this is a stranger, who is killing himself, and killing me, day after day, having to watch him destroy himself. If you love us, how can you give up so easily?"

"It's not easy, Ruth. I'm just not going to let myself be violated or destroyed. It's called self preservation."

"I listened to everyone convince me that this was the best way I could help Yale. I was so afraid, I shut my eyes for months, hoping he would stop drinking on his own. I was wrong to wait so long. I see that now. But you don't know how hard it is to watch someone you love dying; feeling there's nothing you can do. Nothing."

Lisa reached for the necklace around her neck that Frank had left her, as Ruth's words unleashed pain and anger. She clutched the gold charm of the Ace, King, Queen, Jack, and Ten of Hearts, as she said, "It's harder when they're dead, Ruth. As long as the one you love is alive there is something you can do, Ruth—you can help them go on living, and take the reins when they're not able to."

"Then why are you releasing Yale when he can't take the reins right now?"

"I'm not, Ruth. You are. You have to sign the release forms. I'm just backing away from weak people who don't have the courage to fight. I'm a survivor, Ruth. I'm stronger than I knew. But I'm not a savior. You can't help people who won't let you in. Both you and Yale have been pushing me away. There's a lot you can do, and a lot Yale can do—you're both just unwilling, or afraid. I'm not sure which."

Ruth turned to Yale, stung by Lisa's words. "I'm not signing the forms, Yale. I'm not letting you leave here until you're cured of your addiction. If you don't want to see me again—fine. But I'm not going to be manipulated by you, and have to live with regrets, later, that I didn't do what I should have. I love you, Yale. Maybe, one day, you'll be able to love again. I hope so. Doctor, if you'll help him get back on his feet I'd be grateful."

Yale tried to stand up, to protest, but collapsed on the floor from weakness. "Ma, don't do this," he pleaded.

Ruth looked down at Yale; "I didn't do this to you, Yale. You did. Call me when you've come to your senses."

She turned looking at Lisa with new determination, "Will you stay and help me? Please? I need your help."

"Yes Ruth. I'll stay with you. Will you leave with me, now, and we can pick up something for dinner?"

"Sure. Why don't you go home and take your iron pills? I'll take care of dinner. You could use some rest anyway. I'll make you the toast and eggs, I didn't let you eat this morning, before I go to the grocery store."

Dr. Dresler handed Lisa orange juice the nurse brought up, felt her pulse and asked, "Are you sure you're alright?"

"Yes doctor, I'm fine. But if I need help I'm not so stupid I'd refuse it." She turned her eyes, gazing at Yale who was still on the floor.

She rose and took Ruth's arm. "Let's go. There's nothing else we can do here."

Yale yelled after them as they walked out. They didn't turn around. He made one last effort, "David, please help get me out of here. You've been with me a long time. David?"

"Sorry Yale. It's because I've been with you a long time, and because I care that I'm not going to help you get out of here. Anyway, I've been fired. Remember?"

CHAPTER 23

The following morning Lisa was on the phone with Harvey Stone when Ruth heard her talking to someone from the hallway. It was only six a.m. and Ruth couldn't imagine who Lisa would have called that early, unless she was checking on Yale. The phone hadn't rung so Ruth knew Lisa must have placed an outgoing call. Surreptitiously, she approached Lisa's room trying to decide whether she should just knock and inquire, or eavesdrop, and see if Lisa was going to be as open with her as she promised over dinner the previous night. She was next to the door when she heard Lisa saying, "But Harvey, even if you destroy all the records there are still people in the hospital who examined him, and know of his condition, who could disclose information. You could be doing it for nothing. And if it's ever discovered you removed files you could be charged with illegal tampering, and ruin your entire career. There are blabbermouths who would sell their mother for a buck. Don't do it."

Ruth stood very still; listening for a clue to what Lisa was talking about, surmising from what she'd just heard that Harvey Stone had access to something, which could be damaging to Yale if exposed. She heard Lisa's next response clearly. "No Harvey. You're wrong about this. You shouldn't have to be burdened with making a choice. Leave the records and forget it. If the tabloids are going to snoop around until they come up with something, it doesn't mean we betrayed him, or broke a confidence. Just let the pieces fall, as they will, and let's wait it out."

"Yes Harvey; I'm sure. This is best. I'm okay. At least, right now, anyway." There was a brief silence before Ruth heard, "No, I didn't go back to the clinic last night. I'm going to call in a while when Ruth gets up.

Well, at least she's being nicer, and last night we could speak civilly." There was another silence before Lisa answered, "No Harvey, she didn't know how much her words hurt me. I've had a lot of practice acting tougher than I feel. You know that. I'll be fine. I'll call you tonight then. You can let me know if anything else develops, okay?"

Ruth moved away, sensing the conversation was concluding, and returned to her room before Lisa hung up. She didn't hear Lisa's last words to Harvey—"Have a good day, Harvey. Frank wouldn't want you to suffer consequences, which could hurt your career. We're doing the right thing by placing the files in your desk, rather than destroying them. Talk to you later. Bye."

Ruth sat on her bed for the next hour. She decided not to say anything and do as Lisa said she'd be doing—wait it out, and see where the pieces fall. Ruth was reading the morning paper when Lisa greeted her in the kitchen. "Good morning. You been up long?"

"Not long. Did you get a good nights rest, Lisa?"

"Yes, but I woke up early. I've never been a late sleeper. I was on the phone with Harvey at six, and just hung up with Jean in New York."

"You called Harvey at six? Must have been important."

"Actually, Harvey is used to it. If you want to talk to him it's got to be before he leaves for the hospital at six-thirty, or after eleven at night, otherwise you have a hard time getting hold of him."

"How did you two become friends, Lisa?"

"Through Frank. I met him last year when I went to San Francisco for the fundraiser with Frank. Harvey and Frank were friends a long time. At the City of Hope function Frank introduced us. He came to the island often and I got close with him, too. He's like a brother to me. You know, he told me the only reason he knew Carmel Clinic was one of the nations best rehabilitation centers was because three years ago Frank introduced him to one of the co-founders, Dr. Bradly. Harvey then became actively involved, doing research for Dr. Bradly, on how long it took the average person to be dependent free of various substances physically. That's how he came to be an affiliate physician at Carmel. He said, Dr. Bradly fixed his "little red wagon" so he's listed as a clinical consultant, and has even less free time because of him. But knowing Harvey, he doesn't mind. He's a real humanitarian."

"He sounds like a special person."

"Special person? Did I hear someone mention me?" David asked, joining them.

"Yup, you qualify for a 'special person' title, in my book, David."

"Thanks Lisa. I feel the same about you."

They were finishing toasting bagels when Lisa stated, "Ruth, the only place I haven't called yet is the clinic. Do you want to get on an extension and I'll call Dr. Dresler to see how Yale's doing?"

"Thanks Lisa. I'll get on the line in my room. David, why don't you pick up a phone, too."

After twenty minutes on the phone with Dr. Dresler the pleasant atmosphere in the beach house vanished. Ruth came back to the kitchen, sullen and discouraged. Jay Dresler had related Yale was awake all night, staring at the ceiling, and uncommunicative. He felt Yale was apathetic and severely depressed. He related, Yale was asked if he would cooperate and they'd leave the restraints off, but Yale wouldn't respond. He added, Sherman Black, who was his night nurse again, removed Yale's restraints during the night and indicated Yale could shower and use the bathroom on his own, if he just left the door open. Sherman Black related Yale stayed motionless in the bed, with the restraints off, for several hours and eventually urinated in the bed, his eyes still fixed on the ceiling. He added, the breakfast tray was recently removed, untouched.

"Ruth, I'm going to the clinic. Will you be okay by yourself, since David has to fly back to LA this morning?"

"What are you going to do?"

"I'm not sure, Ruth. But remember how hard it was for Yale to perform and resume his concert tour a few years ago, after being mobbed and injured in England?"

"Yes. So?"

"Well, he did it, didn't he? I think he needs more coaxing. Maybe, I can get him to be responsive, somehow. I want to try."

"Will you call me, Lisa? I just can't sit here all day—" She was falling apart.

"I'll call every two hours, Ruth. I promise. But you have to promise to keep busy. Make a salad. Bake a cake. Prepare dinner. Okay?"

She nodded, taking Lisa's hand, and squeezing it.

After speaking briefly with Dr. Dresler, Lisa went to Yale's room. She asked the attendant to leave, and approached the bed. "Well, Mr. Frye, you look like shit. I hear you're not talking to anyone, so at least I don't have to take any verbal abuse from you. He kept his eyes focused on the ceiling. "I think they're planning to put you on IV again, since you're not eating. Too bad. The food here is not bad. I think you smell bad too, Mr. Frye, so I'll start by washing you. Since I'm here, I might as well make myself useful."

She filled a basin with warm water and carried it back to the bed, with soap, a washcloth, and two towels. She rolled the sheet and blanket off of him and started unbuttoning the pajama top; of the new pajamas, David purchased for him the other day. He didn't move or talk. His eyes remained fixed on the ceiling. She had the pajama top unbuttoned but couldn't get it off without some assistance. She went to the door and called for assistance. A nurse came in and together they removed Yale's top. "That's all; thank you," Lisa said, walking the nurse to the door. She came back and washed his face, neck, and chest. He remained motionless. She unsnapped his pajama bottoms and pulled them off. She washed his feet, calves, thighs, silently. She rinsed the washcloth, applied more soap, and said, "Well, at least your dick hasn't shriveled up, Mr. Frye, even if your brain has." She took the washcloth and started washing his genitals when he grabbed her wrist, sitting up, in one swift motion. He leered into her eyes and knocked the basin over with his other hand. She looked into his eyes, "You're hurting my arm." He didn't ease his grip, instead squeezed harder.

"You want me to cry out Yale; is that what you want? Go ahead, make me cry if that'll make you happy. I won't call for help." She was wincing. He eased his grip, still gaping at her. "Will you permit me to finish washing you, Yale, or should I get someone else?"

He let go of her arm and remained sitting while she refilled the basin and returned. She put a couple towels on the floor to absorb some of the spilled water. She took the fresh washcloth, soaped it, and extended it to him. He didn't take it; just stared into her eyes, then turned on his side. She walked around the bed and washed his back and waist. She took a towel and dried him off. She was rinsing the washcloth and wringing it out when he announced, "You missed some spots. If you're going to do something—do it right, or don't do it at all."

"Then lie down properly, Yale, and I'll do it right."

He rolled over on his stomach. She lathered the washcloth. She washed the backs of his legs, his thighs, and started moving the warm cloth over his ass in circular motions. She didn't speak. Either did he. She took a towel and started drying his behind when he asked, "Is my ass still cute and compact?"

"Yes Yale; but it's a bit flat from how much time you've been wasting on it."

He turned over swiftly and grabbed both her arms, "Then maybe you should find a different ass, again!"

She didn't miss the double entendré of his words, but kept her cool as she replied, "Maybe, I'm into flat asses I can help mold into great shape."

"Maybe, I like my ass the way it is," he retorted, flinging her hands away.

She walked around the bed, picked up the basin and towels, and flung the wet washcloth at him. "Then, next time, wash it yourself!"

She went to the door, opened it, and yelled to an orderly, "Get Mr. Frye's aid back in here, please. I'm hungry and want to go have lunch." She stood in the doorway until an attendant arrived, then said tartly, "You better get someone to help you get Mr. Frye back into his pajamas. There isn't much he does for himself these days." She glared at Yale, closed the door, and went down to the cafeteria.

Lisa was finishing a salad, after calling Ruth to relate what had transpired between her and Yale, when Sherman Black walked over and said, "Congratulations Mrs. Lee, you deserve a gold medal."

"What are you talking about, Sherman?" she asked, the beaming male nurse, whose smile showed every tooth in his mouth.

"You are the talk of the second floor. You got Mr. Frye to talk and join the human race, when the doctors feared he was going to end up catatonic.

Nice going. I just talked to one of the ladies who came down from the second floor. She said, she was called to help get Mr. Frye dressed, and he told them both to turn around, so he could dress himself, or he would—never mind—do something shameful."

"Come on, Sherman. I want Mr. Frye's exact words. What did he say?"

"He said, he'd piss on both of them if they didn't turn their backs until he got dressed."

Lisa laughed. "Sherman, I'm sorry I missed it. Thanks for telling me."

"It's a start. It's a good start—a great start—but now we gotta keep it rolling—know what I mean?"

"No. What do you mean?"

"We have to keep the fight alive. He has to start eating so they don't have to give him 'drip'. And he has to open up. The faster they start talking out their hearts; the sooner they heal."

"Maybe, before I leave here, I'll get a couple ice cream cups and take them to Mr. Frye's room. Do you think I'd be pushing too much for one day?"

"No ma'am. I think you're the best medicine for Mr. Frye right now. You already scored one gold medal. Why not go for another?"

"Good advice, Sherman. Thanks. See you later."

Lisa was in front of the elevator when Dr. Dresler exited. "Hi Lisa, I'm just coming from the second floor. Mr. Frye is fast asleep. I understand you were able to extricate some responsiveness from Yale earlier. I'm glad. It's an encouraging sign. It's also good he is able to sleep. He's made progress today. Indications appear favorable."

"Great. I'm really glad to hear that. Well, as long as he's sleeping, I'll put the ice cream and ginger ale in the lounge refrigerator, and use this time to familiarize myself with some of the staff; then get a good look around. I'll try to cajole Mr. Frye into eating later."

"I have some time, now, if you'd like me to accompany you."

"That would be helpful. Thanks Jay."

It was more than three hours later when Lisa concluded her tour with Jay. He had been paged several times and Lisa had accompanied him to a few of the calls, impressed with his diplomacy, and respectful of his knowledge. She was sitting in his office, having tea, when she asked if he would relate what he'd told her earlier about Yale to Ruth.

He said, he'd be glad to and Lisa got Ruth on the phone. When he concluded his conversation with Ruth, he handed Lisa the telephone.

"I thought you'd like to hear the good news from the doctor himself, Ruth. I'm going to be here a while yet, so if you're hungry don't wait for me."

"No. No. I'm not hungry, honey. I think I've eaten all the cookies in the cupboard already today."

"I'm going up to Yale's room again now, and try to get him to eat something. I'll call, if I can, to let you know when I'm leaving here."

"That's fine. Don't worry about me. I'm going to sit on the terrace with a book for a while. If you need to stay late, I understand. I feel so much better now. I can't tell you the relief—after yesterday."

"I know. Me too. I'll see you later then."

Yale was gazing at the ceiling again when Lisa approached carrying two containers of ice cream and a plastic bottle of ginger ale. She sent the aid on a break. "Mr. Frye, will you join me in dessert, or would you like a main course first?"

He didn't respond.

"Yale, will you talk to me?"

No response. She leaned over him so he would have to look at her instead of the ceiling and whispered, "Please Yale." He shut his eyes. She put down the ice cream and soda, pulling a chair next to the bed. She sat silently for a long time just looking at him. He continued to stare at the ceiling. She took her hand and started stroking his hair gently. She got no response.

"Once, we had so much to say to each other. Once, we shared our feelings and innermost thoughts. Once, we were able to bond. Once—"

He grabbed her arm and turned pained eyes to her, "Once, I believed you were honest. Once, I trusted you. Once, I believed you loved me. Get out of here, Lisa. Don't play on my vulnerability."

She stood up and leaned over him. "I never meant to hurt you, Yale. And I never stopped loving you—"

"Then you're a whore, and I'm no longer interested!"

She stood up trembling. She took out a piece of paper, with the phone number of the beach house on it, and placed it next to the phone.

"I'm leaving you the number of the beach house, Yale, in case you ever want to call—even if it's just to see how your mother is. I may be a whore in your eyes, but I never spit in my mother's face. You're a drunk and a low life."

He sat up and grabbed her hair so quickly she fell on the bed. "You should know what low is, Lisa; it's what my mother called you when she'd see a society picture of you and Frank in a magazine. "She's so low," she'd say, "that she sold her soul for stature.""

Lisa got up and was at the door before she spoke. "And you're so small, Yale, you not only believed it, but had to repeat it; just to hurt me."

She stood outside the door until the aid returned, then left the clinic to have dinner with Jay Dresler. She didn't call Ruth again, or return to the house until midnight. Ruth was dozing on a sofa, with a book beside her. Lisa grabbed a piece of paper, scribbled—I couldn't stoop low enough to wake you when you were sleeping so soundly—Yale is doing well! She placed the note in view, and went to bed.

Surrounded by darkness, it was still a long time before she could sleep.

CHAPTER 24

Lisa shuffled into the kitchen for some juice. Since it was so early, and David had returned to L.A., she came out wearing only her thin spaghetti strapped nightie. She was surprised to see Ruth already sitting at the table with the paper. The table was set for breakfast.

"Good morning, honey," Ruth greeted her. "Sit down. I've got a batch of blintzes I'll heat up. Your juice and medication are on the counter."

"Thank you, Ruth." She swallowed her pills and sat down drained of energy, her head pounding.

Ruth looked at her, noticing her arms and wrists were bruised, and Lisa's eyes appeared spiritless and droopy. She handed Lisa the morning paper, "You've made the front page, again, Lisa. You've made quite a reputation for yourself this past year or so."

Lisa looked at the caption: "Mrs. Lisa Lee acquires majority ownership of Carmel Clinic, in her continued humanitarian efforts, to fervently aid convalescing individuals, and lower medical care costs." Ruth watched Lisa cringe and put the paper down.

"How was Yale last night, Lisa?" Ruth inquired, as she took the tray of cheese filled pastries and placed them in the microwave.

"He's doing better, Ruth. He stopped staring at the ceiling and was willing to communicate when I left him last night." Her eyes were filling uncontrollably. "Listen Ruth, I'm not really hungry and I have a board meeting I have to attend, so I'm going to shower and dress."

"Those marks on your arms are from Yale, aren't they?" she asked perceptively.

"The marks visible will fade, Ruth. It's the marks which are not discernible that are more painful."

"Want to talk, Lisa?"

"I can't, Ruth. Let's call the clinic and see if Yale slept well," she answered, masking her burdens, while reaching for the phone. Ruth went to another room, picking up an extension.

"Good morning, Jay. I wanted to find out how Mr. Frye did last night."

"Good morning to you, too. The good news is, Mr. Frye ate the ice cream and soda you brought him last night, and the attendant reported he was cantankerous very early, demanding to shower and shave. He's combative, which suggests he's fighting back, and actively trying to conquer his addiction. The bad news is, I didn't seem to be able to amuse you at dinner last night. I'd like another chance. Can I take you to dinner tonight?"

"I'm sorry, Jay. I have other plans. I'm glad Mr. Frye is improving. I'm going to dress and I should be there by nine for the board meeting. Thank you for dinner last night, Jay. I'm sorry I wasn't better company. I just have several issues which require my attention, and am having difficulty channeling my energy. I'll see you soon."

Ruth was less jubilant that evening when Lisa returned from the clinic, indicating she hadn't seen Yale during the day, and she could call Dr. Dresler, herself, if she wanted an update on Yale's progress. She declined dinner and said she was going to bed, claiming to have a migraine.

It was the middle of the night when the phone woke Lisa and Ruth simultaneously. Ruth answered the phone seconds before Lisa. "Hello" she said quickly, alarmed something might have happened to Yale.

"Ma, it's Yale. Sorry I woke you."

"It's alright. What's wrong, Yale?"

"Nothing. I couldn't sleep and just wanted to hear your voice so I could tell you, I love you."

"I love you, too, Yale," she cried into the receiver.

"It's been a long time since I've said that to you, Ma."

"The important thing is that you're able to say it now. How do you feel, honey?"

"Like I've been away a long time, Ma. My hands are still shaking, but they say it's common. I still have trouble sleeping for long periods of time. How about you? Will you ever be able to forgive me for the hell I put you through?"

"I can forgive anything, Yale, if you start over. I love you unconditionally, but I couldn't go through a year, like this past one, again."

"You won't have to, Ma. I'm promising you that."

"Are you eating, Yale?"

He laughed into the receiver. "A little. My appetite still isn't great, but it's improving. How is Lisa—are you two getting along okay?"

"We're getting along. I didn't see much of her today. When she got back from the clinic she had a migraine, and went to bed without eating supper. She's been in her room since."

"Oh. I didn't know she was here today. She didn't come to the room."

"You want me to get her? I'm sure she—"

"No. No." He said quickly. "Let her sleep. I'll talk to her another time. I'll let you get back to sleep, too, Ma. I'll call you tomorrow, okay?"

"Yale, I'm glad you woke me. If you feel like talking again, you can call anytime—day or night, remember that."

"I'm sorry, Ma, for all the pain I've caused you." His voice was cracking. "Goodnight, Ma. I love you."

He hung up before Ruth could reply. Only Lisa, who was still on the extension, heard her say, "I love you too, Yale…Thank you, God," before she replaced the phone to its cradle.

Hours later, unable to sleep, Lisa dialed Michigan needing to hear the voices of her sons. She knew something was wrong as soon as Marc yelled, "Yeh" into the phone.

"Marc. It's mom."

"Oh, mom. Steve and I were just deciding whether to call you now or not. We didn't want to wake you in the middle of the night."

"What's wrong, Marc?"

"It's dad. Sue just called and said dad was in a car accident, late last night, on the way home from a business meeting. She's at Canton

Memorial Hospital with dad. He's in a coma." Marc started crying. "Sue said, dad lost a lot of blood, and he's AB negative, so they are tying to locate more blood. I guess they have a shortage, or something, of his type of blood. She was supposed to call us back after she talked to the doctor."

"Stay calm, Marc. I'll leave here now and fly to Canton. I'll meet you and Steve at the hospital. Get the next flight out."

She hung up and immediately called Harvey. "It's Lisa, Harvey. I need your help. Ronnie's been in an auto accident and is in Canton Memorial Hospital. I'm flying to Ohio now. He has AB negative blood. There's a shortage at the hospital. Can you do anything?"

"I'll get right on it. Who is his doctor, Lisa?"

"It used to be Stan Blau, when we were married, but—"

"Never mind. I'll make some calls. Call me in an hour."

"Thanks Harvey." She dressed quickly, left a note for Ruth, simply writing—Had to go out of town unexpectedly. Will call you later. She had contacted her pilot, and was on her way in less than an hour.

True to his word, Harvey Stone had made calls and AB negative blood was being flown to Canton the same time she was.

Lisa kept vigil with her boys, and Sue, for the next two days, until Ronnie regained consciousness. She was so involved soothing her sons, speaking to physicians, calming hysterical, useless, Sue, and summoning specialists to make sure Ronnie had not sustained any brain damage, she had completely forgotten to call Ruth. Fifty hours after rushing out, Lisa dialed the beach house. She was languid, unnerved, and spent. Ruth answered after the first ring.

"Hi, Ruth. It's me. I'm sorry I didn't call sooner, but I didn't have much of a chance to."

"Sure. Sure. No problem, Lisa. I'm getting used to your disappearing acts." Her voice was full of hostility. Lisa was too weary to argue or get into it with her.

"I'll be back tonight, Ruth. How's Yale doing?"

"Oh! Suddenly you're interested in how Yale's doing? Thanks for your concern," she added callously.

"Never mind, Ruth. I don't feel like defending myself to you. I'll see you later and explain then."

"Why bother? If it's newsworthy, I'll probably read about it in the paper. That's how I usually find out what's going on with you anyway." Her sarcasm irked Lisa and only added to her oppression. She lost her temper, yelling sharply, "Goodbye Ruth. Thanks for asking if I'm alright," and slammed the phone down.

Lisa slept for most of the flight back to Carmel, and munched on an apple, in the limo, on the way to the clinic. She had decided to check on Yale before going to the house. She didn't care that her outfit was soiled and wrinkled, or that she wore no makeup. The media had been advised she was at Canton Memorial Hospital anyway, and when she left the private room of the hospital, to get into a taxi, camera lights flashed, and she was forced into making a statement in the same unkempt fashion she was still exhibiting.

She went directly to Yale's room, without seeking out Dr. Dresler for an update, and walked right in since the door was partially open. She was surprised when she saw Ruth sitting in a chair opposite Yale, around a small table, sharing a meal. It had slipped her mind that this was the first day Yale was to be permitted visitors.

"Hi," she said self consciously. "Nice to see you're out of bed, Yale. You look good. Real good." She was very uncomfortable, not sure why. "Well, I just wanted to say hello. Sorry I intruded. I gotta go anyway." She started backing out the door.

"Wait, Lisa," Yale called to her. "Why don't you pull up a chair and join us?"

"No, that's okay. This is probably your first chance to visit together. I'll, uh, see you some other time." She didn't wait for either of them to have an opportunity to speak, rushing from the room to the elevator. She went to the little office she'd secured for herself, and sat in the heavy chair, feeling suddenly lonely and vacant. She dialed the main switchboard and asked where Dr. Dresler was. They informed her this was his day off, and Dr. Cooper was on call until tomorrow. She went to the staff lounge and poured herself some coffee. She said to an unfamiliar nurse, and the only other person in the lounge, "It's pretty quiet here today."

"It is every Saturday and Sunday when friends and family visit. Most of the people who are ambulatory go out for some private time with loved ones. There's a lot of activity in the social hall though. They'll be playing music, and serving refreshments in a little while."

"Maybe I'll go in there, too. This coffee is cold," Lisa said, tossing the paper cup in a receptacle and walking out.

She went back to her office, leaving the door open for better air circulation, and called Harvey. When his answering machine went on, she hung up. She tried him at the hospital. They said, he just left for the day. She didn't leave a message, figuring she'd be able to reach him later. She dialed Florida. Her father answered the phone. "Hi Pa. It's me. How are you?" She was unaware Ruth and Yale were in the corridor, having come in search of her.

"Okay, Lisa. What about you? You said, you were alright before you left the hospital, but in tonight's paper you look terrible."

"It was a long couple of days, Pa. I wasn't expecting cameras when I left the hospital."

"And Ronnie?"

"Ronnie's going to be fine. Marc and Steve are staying a couple of extra days. It was real hard for them, Pa; worrying they might lose their father—and so soon after Frank—" her voice wasn't concealing her emotions. Her composure was faltering. She bowed her head, and tried to mask her feelings, but wasn't credible. Her father knew her too well.

"You'll be alright, Lisa. I know this has been awful."

"Oh, Pa. Sometimes, I'm not as strong as everybody thinks."

"Lisa, you're a fighter. A survivor. If you don't know that by now, you never will. Why don't you come to Florida for a few days rest?"

"I can't, Pa. I can't leave here now. I bought into the clinic so I have to be here for some meetings."

"I don't know what you did that for, Lisa. You're involved in so many other charities."

"I bought in for selfish reasons, Pa, not to be charitable. I thought I could help Yale. Right now I'm wondering if it was such a smart move myself."

"Help yourself first, Lisa. Then you'll have the strength to help others. I know you, Lisa. I raised a special girl."

"Okay, Pa. I'll call tomorrow." She was crying. "I can't talk now, Pa.

Kiss Mom for me. Bye." She put her head down on the desk sobbing, when Ruth knocked. Yale was with her.

"Can we come in?" Ruth asked. "I owe you an apology, Lisa."

Lisa raised her tear streaked face. Her tears were falling unchecked, "What happened, Ruth? Did you read about my dilemma in a newspaper? Go away, both of you. I don't want your apologies. I don't need apologies. And what I wanted I can't seem to get from either of you. You both stopped trusting me a long time ago. What's the quote Ruth—"You can never go home again." Well, it's true. Once you leave, it's never the same when you go back."

"Maybe, it's time to build a new home," Yale offered. "One with a solid foundation; adding a brick at a time."

"I don't have any mortar left! Without cement the house crumbles, Yale."

"Then borrow some. I think I owe you a few bags myself."

"Stop being so noble, Mr. Frye. You're stepping out of character, aren't you?" She was afraid to let him get close after the way he reacted to her during the past week. "Your trite words can't erase what's transpired between us."

"It hasn't been a great week for me either, Lisa. I'm sorry I took it out on you. I wasn't myself."

She was so confused and tired, she said irritably, "Go to the social hall Yale, where you belong, and visit with your mother. I'm going home. I'm not myself now either."

"You always put barriers up, Lisa. I'm not sure who the real Lisa is? You tell people you love them, then run off without a word. You let people get close when they need you, but then back away when you need them. Why are you so afraid to admit you have needs?"

He hit a nerve and it caught her off guard. "Maybe, barriers are my protection, Yale. It beats the hell out of becoming dependent. I don't need you," she threw at him sarcastically.

"Come on, Ma," he said. "Let's go. I'm sorrier for you, Lisa, than I am for myself. I'm dealing with my situation and my problems. You don't even want to admit you might need someone."

"Well, Mr. Frye, I didn't see you seek help for yourself. You were forced into it. Who are you to preach? You're more believable when you're physically abusive."

"Well, Mrs. Lee, I hope someone helps you to deal with your pain. I think your hurt goes deeper than the bruises I left on your arms." They left the room and went to the social hall. Yale was distraught that she wouldn't forgive him. He was passive the rest of the day.

When Lisa arrived at the beach house, she was still thinking about what Yale had said. Maybe, he was right. Maybe, she was afraid to let anyone get close again. Maybe, more of her had died with Frank than she realized. Maybe, she still needed to suffer. It was what she seemed to do best. She went to her bedroom and tried Harvey's house again needing someone to confide in. "Hello, Harvey, it's Lisa. Am I calling at a bad time?"

"No. I just got in a little while ago. Are you back in Carmel?"

"Yes, and it's just as lousy being here as it was being in Canton. Just different people and different responsibilities."

"Lisa, I'm your friend, so I'm going to be honest with you. You're adopting all these responsibilities yourself. Did someone ask you to help Yale or Ruth? No. You volunteered. Did Sue call you for assistance? No. You didn't even wait for her to ask for your help. You took it upon yourself. Lisa, you have the capacity to give more than anyone I've ever known, but you're unable to believe you deserve anything yourself. Why?"

"That's not true, Harvey. I'm not lacking for anything, am I? Ronnie was my husband for many years. I had to do whatever I could. Yale was my love. God; the only man who I felt real passion with before I married Frank—"

"Listen to yourself, Lisa. You don't even hear what you're saying. You said it just now—I had to do whatever I could—those are your words, Lisa.—Had to—and—whatever I could. Don't you think it's time for you to take a turn? Stop feeling guilty, Lisa, for still loving Yale. Stop feeling guilty for leaving Ronnie. Stop feeling guilty that you couldn't keep Frank alive. Stop denying your needs. I think you're wasting a lot of valuable time, Lisa."

"I needed Frank, Harvey."

"No Lisa. Frank needed you. And you were there for him until the very end. But if you're honest with yourself, you'll admit that you might not have married Frank if he wasn't terminal—"

"How dare you! I loved Frank! You know I did—"

"Yes, I know you loved him, Lisa. And I know you did what you felt you had to by marrying him. I have the last letter Frank mailed that says it all—where he asks me to help you make the necessary transition; where he says he feels he cheated you; where he says he was aware you were in love with Yale when you married him; where he admits he took what he needed selfishly. Lisa, it's time to let Frank rest in peace and stop feeling guilty for doing it. Stop feeling guilty because you know, deep inside, that if Frank wouldn't have been dying, you might not have married him. It's nothing to be ashamed of. You're allowed to have those thoughts and feelings, Lisa. You're very honorable. You gave Frank so much. It's time to give to yourself, Lisa, stop punishing yourself for being human."

"You know, I tried Harvey. I tried really hard to make Frank happy. I came to love him; really love him. Then I lost him. I tried for a long time with Ronnie, too. But it ended. And Yale. Well, I'm not sure he'll ever trust me again, since he expected me to come back to him the week I married Frank instead. I feel empty-handed. Does that sound selfish? Part of me feels resentment, Harvey."

"No. It sounds like you're admitting something that's been eating away at you. I'm glad you can finally say it out loud. That's a start. Now, you have to decide where you want to go from here, Lisa. I can recommend a therapist, if you feel you'd like someone to help you put issues in perspective, Lisa."

"I think you just did, Harvey. Thanks. I think I'll sleep on it, then decide what to do next. Thanks for being here for me, Harvey. I love you."

"I'm nuts about you too, Lisa. I'll call you in a day or two."

Lisa was drained. She closed her eyes, lying on the bed, with the radio on, before readying herself for bed. The next thing she knew, Ruth was in her room putting a blanket over her.

"I'm sorry, Lisa. I didn't mean to wake you. I was worried about you. I knocked earlier. I heard the radio, but you didn't respond. I couldn't fall asleep and came to check on you again."

"What time is it?"

"Two a.m., honey. Why don't you put a nightie on and get under the covers? I probably shouldn't have come in."

"It's okay, Ruth. I was talking to Harvey and going to bathe. I guess, I was more tired than I realized. I didn't hear a thing. I've had more sleep these past six hours than I've had in days."

"Can I get you anything, Lisa? How about a cup of tea?"

"Sounds good. Want to join me, Ruth?"

"Sure. I'll boil some water while you change."

"Thank you."

"Lisa put a robe on and walked into the kitchen asking, "Are there any blintzes left? I'm hungry."

"In the freezer. How many should I put in the microwave?"

"Two for me. How many for you?"

"Two sounds good to me, too."

They were at the table eating, both quiet with their own thoughts, comfortable just being together for the first time in a long time, neither needing to expostulate on any given topic. Lisa ate the two blintzes on her plate and Ruth took one off her plate, placing it on Lisa's, "I'm not as hungry as I thought."

"Always the giver aren't you, Ruth" Lisa said knowingly, more as a statement than a question. "Thanks." She smiled at Ruth tenderly. "You know, I've decided to delegate the administrative responsibilities of the clinic to more qualified people than myself. I really think it would be best. Anyway, I'll probably go back to California in a week or so. Yale is on his way, and there's not much for me to do here."

"I'll understand, if you want to go home, Lisa. But Yale is far from on his way. He's depressed and frightened. He feels he's made a mess of his life and thinks he's destroyed his career. He's lost all confidence in himself. He was ashen today when he said, that as often as he's considered what it might be like to have a child of his own, he's grateful, now, he doesn't have any kids to witness what he's become. He asked me to go home, indicating he doesn't want to see the suffering he's put in my eyes. But, I said, I wouldn't leave, and I'd see him tomorrow. I'm going to have lunch with him at noon. Maybe, I'll bake the sour cream cake, he likes so much, before I go." She got up and placed the dishes in the sink. "Goodnight, Lisa. I'm going to try and get some sleep."

It was past lunch hour when Lisa knocked on Yale's door at the clinic, peeking in. "I smelled something wonderful from the other side of the door. Any of that cake left for me?"

"There's plenty of cake, just not much coffee."

"Well," she said walking in, "Yale, if you'll share some cake. I'll order some coffee."

"Sounds fair," he replied, looking at her amicably. "How's Ronnie doing?"

"Good. He's going to be fine. I talked to the boys. They said, he's been walking around already. How about you? How do you feel, Yale?"

"Angry."

"About anything in particular?"

"It doesn't matter," he replied, putting up fences; fixing his eyes on the cup in front of him.

She didn't push. "Well, I could order up coffee or we could have it outside instead. It's not too hot yet. You two interested in sitting outside with me? I haven't felt the sun in days."

"Go ahead. I don't have fresh clothing. I'll just stay in this shit all day." He was in the jeans he'd been wearing at Marissa's when he was brought in, with a pajama top over them. His tone was testy.

"I'll pick up a few things for you tomorrow, Yale," Ruth offered, trying to pacify him.

"Don't bother. I don't want anything. I'll get by."

"Honey, you lost so much weight, you'll probably need a few pairs of pants in a smaller size anyway."

"Thanks for pointing it out, Ma. Just what I need—another commentary on my appearance."

Ruth didn't reply and let it pass. Lisa couldn't. "Ruth, will you come outside with me for a little while. It's getting hot in here. Anyway, I want to show you the gazebos I had delivered here."

"Yeh, go on Ma. I'm tired anyway. I'm going to lie down for a while. Thanks for the cake."

"Don't you want me to be with you anymore? We still have hours of visiting time today. It's just a little after three."

"My how time flies when you're having fun, huh? Go home, Ma, okay? I'm tired."

"Come on, Ruth, Lisa urged, irritated. "Your son is feeling sorry for himself, and taking it out on you. My boys did that a lot, until they grew up. The best thing to do is leave him alone until he can be civil."

"Thank you, all knowing Lisa, for your words of wisdom. Go look at your gazebos. Make sure you got your monies worth." His hands started shaking. When he became aware of the tremors and realized his mother and Lisa also noticed, he threw his cup of coffee at the farthest wall, and stormed into the bathroom, shutting the door.

Lisa and Ruth left. On the way out Lisa said, "Forget the gazebos. I think we still have time to make it to a mall and pick up a few things for him. We can get some jeans in a couple of different sizes and bring them back, okay?"

"Thanks, Lisa. I don't know what got into him. He was fine when I got here, and happy to see me. Then, out of nowhere, he got in such a lousy mood."

"He told us what he was feeling, Ruth. When I asked how he was, he said angry. He must be frustrated as hell, Ruth, knowing he has no one to blame but himself for ending up in a rehab center. Maybe, he'll cool down by the time we get back."

They made it to a nearby mall and returned with several bags of clothing for Yale around the dinner hour. Lisa suggested Ruth go up to Yale's room alone, figuring maybe she wanted time alone with him, but Ruth asked her to accompany her. They opened the door gently in case he was sleeping and were met by Sherman Black, the nurse assigned to Yale. The room was in disarray. Things were trashed on the floor, and the walls wet with dripping liquid. Yale was asleep in the bed, his hands strapped down. "What happened, Sherman?" Lisa asked.

"He lost control. He got angry, throwing things and cussing up a storm. I called for assistance, but he wouldn't settle down, and began pounding his fists against the wall. We finally had to give him a mild tranquilizer. He just fell asleep."

"Did he say anything significant, Sherman?"

"He was shouting—"Stupid"—"Stupid"—"Stupid"—over and over again, as he was banging his fists against the wall."

Ruth had paled. "I think, I'll just sit in here for a while. In case he wakes up and wants to talk."

"Sorry, Mrs. Frye. He can't have visitors the rest of the day. Clinic rules. He'll probably sleep for hours anyway."

The only thing Ruth said, on the drive to the beach house was, "I think some of their rules are ridiculous."

Lisa had asked Sherman Black to call her on his break. After ten the phone rang. She and Ruth got on different extensions. Sherman related, Yale woke up a few minutes ago, but wasn't talking yet.

"Did you tell him we were there and give him the clothes?" Ruth asked hurriedly.

"Yes, Mrs. Frye, I did. He's just having a rough day. It happens. Maybe tomorrow will be better."

"Sherman, is Mr. Frye still in restraints?"

"Yes, Miss Lisa. He hasn't even asked for them to be removed."

"What time is your shift over, Sherman?" Lisa asked.

"In an hour. Then Clayton will be here for the night shift. I'll stay if you prefer."

"Sherman, connect me downstairs. I'm going to cancel Clayton's shift, and I'll relieve you in an hour. I'm going to take the night shift myself.

Please, remove Mr. Frye's straps. If there are no outbursts, just sit there until I arrive. Okay? Don't talk to him unless he talks to you first, please."

"This is kind of irregular, Mrs. Lee. I don't know about you being here, alone, for the night shift with Mr. Frye, after his outburst today. He might get violent again."

"I know what I'm doing, Sherman. Trust me. If I need help, I'll call for it."

"You're the boss here, Lisa. I guess, I have to follow your orders. But I don't like it. He's having a really bad day."

"I'll be there shortly, Sherman. Connect me downstairs."

As Lisa was walking out the door, she turned to Ruth, "I'll call you in a couple of hours. I know you won't sleep anyway. Why don't you make a fresh batch of blintzes. I'll probably be hungry when I get back."

She went up to Lisa and kissed her cheek, tears in her eyes. "Drive carefully, honey." She closed the door after her.

CHAPTER 25

Lisa had a nurse beckon Sherman Black into the corridor, then dismissed him from his shift. She walked into the dimly lit room and pulled a chair alongside Yale's bed. He hadn't stirred and she was unsure if he was aware of her presence. She sat speechlessly for many minutes before asking, "Life can really be a bitch, can't it?" She didn't wait for a response and continued, "I feel so empty sometimes. I divorced one husband, buried another, and lost the only man that ever ignited flames from every pore of my body. I've been asking myself a lot of useless questions lately, and formulating suppositions, but I don't seem to get anywhere. I'm sorry, Yale, that your going through such hell. I hope it's okay if I just sit here. You don't have to talk to me if you'd rather not, but once we could talk endlessly about anything and everything, so I'm here if you decide you'd like to talk."

He turned and looked at her for a long time, finally asking in a low voice, without malice or anger, "Can you just explain why? Why did you marry Frank Lee? I thought I knew you. You never gave two shits about status or big bucks. What was it then, Lisa?"

"I'll answer in four words, Yale, and beg you not to ask me anything else regarding Frank. To fill a void. I married—to fill a void."

"Obviously, a void you felt I couldn't fill. Did it work, Lisa? Was Frank able to fill the void?" She lowered her head, whispering, "Please don't ask anything else, Yale."

"I don't get it, Lisa. You say I'm the only one who extracted flames; that once we could talk about everything. Yet, I'm not allowed to ask questions."

"Please, Yale, can we try that new foundation you were talking

– 191 –

about the other day, and build from there. There's a lot I need to put aside or I'll never move forward."

"How can you expect me to just—. Never mind. Okay, Lisa, I won't ask you anything else, but can you even begin to imagine how I felt when I saw the newspaper announcing your marriage to Frank?"

"Yes, Yale, I've thought about it often. I'm hoping you can be forgiving."

He was suppressing his brittleness, looking at her and remembering what they once shared. "Is it compassion which motivated your actions and assistance in getting me help? I can handle battling to overcome my addiction, but I can't handle pity, Lisa."

"Frankly, Yale, I don't feel pity for you. I hate seeing you suffer, but I know you can conquer your problems with or without me. I'd like to believe that we were close enough to eradicate what was hurtful, and go on from here. I feel tenderness. I'm sensitive to what you're dealing with, but I'm barely managing to deal with the lunacy, which has surrounded my life. I hope, maybe, we can help each other."

He studied her face and absorbed her words. He couldn't deny he still loved her. "Times in the past I've wanted to kill myself for ever letting you return to Ronnie without fighting to try and change your mind."

"You know the kind of person I am, Yale. I had my sons, who were in their teens then, and too much guilt and responsibility I was afraid to shed. I knew Ronnie and I wouldn't be able to salvage our marriage the first week after I went back to Canton. But, I was terrified of change then. I only knew one way of life, Yale, and I think I was always intimidated by how worldly you were, and how little exposure I had in comparison. Sometimes, I've wanted to kick myself for always accepting the "Safe" life for so long."

"Well, you did a three-sixty, didn't you? Frank certainly provided exposure. He was a very powerful and influential man in many arenas."

She didn't say that had nothing to do with why she married Frank; afraid of additional questions, and let him surmise that which would terminate the subject, saying only, "Yes, he was very knowledgeable and sophisticated."

He saw pain in her eyes and refrained from asking more. She sensed he was aware of her discomfort, so to change topics asked, "Can I get you anything, Yale? Are you hungry or thirsty?"

"No. Thank you. I'm fine, Lisa."

"Well, I'll be back in a few minutes, okay? Why don't you try to get some rest?" She stood up. He reached, grabbing hold of her hand quickly.

"Don't go, Lisa. I need you to stay."

She sat back down, her hand still in his grip, "I was just going out to call Ruth. I promised I'd call her. Your mother was very concerned and distraught when we came back and found you restrained again."

"Will you call from here? I'd like to talk to her for a minute, too."

She dialed and told an anxious Ruth her son was better, and to get some sleep, then handed Yale the phone and listened as he choked out, "Sorry, Ma. I'm just having—uh—a bad time of it today. I—uh—I— thanks for the clothes. I—uh—I'll talk to you tomorrow, okay?" His voice trembled as he said, "I love you, Ma," handing the phone back to Lisa. After replacing the receiver, this time she reached for Yale's hand, and moved to sit on the bed as he pulled her to him. She cradled him. He buried his head in her lap relenting to sobs that racked his body. She held him tightly as he yielded to his misery. She maternally allowed him to alleviate some of his grief, consoling, and stroking his head and back. She didn't slacken her hold until his sobbing abated. "Oh God. Hold me, Lisa. Just hold me. Don't let go." She fastened her hold on him again, whispering, "It's okay, Yale. I've got you."

She remained composed, although he was extracting emotions with his nearness she couldn't deny. She soothed and comforted until he quieted. She waited, then asked softly, "Do you feel like talking?"

He moved, pulling her to him, bringing her down on the bed beside him, "Can we just lie here a while?" She was beside him on the bed, his body against hers, his face close to hers. "Close your eyes, Yale. I'm not going anywhere." He moved slowly, burying his face against her breasts. She placed an arm across him, protectively, and soon they both slept.

In the early morning hours he kissed her cheek and in a barely audible voice said, "I've missed you, Lisa. I've missed you." She kissed him back, and held him to her.

"Yale, I'm going to go now. What should I bring back for lunch?"

"Yourself."

"Okay. What else?"

"Surprise me."

She got off the bed, pulled the blanket around him snugly, and said, "Wear jeans. I'll see you at noon."

Carmel Clinic was less structured than many rehabilitation centers. There was individual counseling and several interaction therapeutic counseling programs provided, however, the principle guidelines were flexible. Since it was a smaller facility than most, with an outstanding reputation, and several noteworthy people who contributed large sums of money annually, it was able to offer the ultimate in care, without being as restrictive. There was no specific criteria for recovery, regarding length of stay, and each individual was encouraged to progress at a rate they were comfortable with. The staff worked diligently to induce candor and coax without badgering. Respect, equality, and humor were infused, while seclusion and isolation discouraged.

Lisa enthusiastically related Yale's ability to reach out to her while she was changing back at the house, and when Yale called Ruth later in the morning, Ruth was encouraged by his tone and attempt at joviality. He invited her to join him for lunch on Wednesday, stipulating he needed the next two days to try and stabilize his moods a little more. He asked her to make a few phone calls on his behalf, and requested her special cheesecake to gorge himself with. When Ruth watched Lisa purchase goods at the supermarket for an indoor picnic with Yale she was planning, her heart told her for the first time that everything was going to be alright. It was a smiling Ruth, Lisa kissed goodbye, as she hurried back to the clinic, already late, for the prearranged lunch date with Yale.

His desolate expression gave way to surprise when she entered his room. He was clothed, shaved, showered, and dubious. He greeted her bluntly with, "I thought something more important came up."

"Sorry I'm late. Your mother had to go back into the supermarket, twice, for items she'd forgotten to purchase. I think you're going to have enough cheesecake to feed half the population of Carmel." Her assessment was on target, as she added, "What did you think, Yale, that I wasn't coming back?"

"I wasn't sure."

"Well, I hope, eventually, you'll trust me a little more. Now, get your ass over here and bring your quilt. We're having a picnic."

He watched as she spread the quilt out on the floor, in the center of the spacious room, and removed plastic plates, silverware, napkins, fried chicken, potato salad, cole slaw, warm rolls and relishes, from a large bag. She opened the gauze drapes, letting more sunshine infiltrate the room, and placed the "Do Not Disturb" sign on the outside of the door. She set places for both of them, then handed him a bottle of apple juice and two plastic goblets asking, "Will you pour, please?"

He sat down next to her stating, "One thing is missing."

"What?" "What did I forget?" She asked, looking at the covered blanket.

"A hug," he answered seriously while his eyes smiled at her.

She leaned over and wrapped her arms around him tightly. "You look good, Yale, and smell great. What do you have on?"

"Baby powder" he laughed. "It's all I could find."

They ate ravenously, comfortable being together, enjoying the moment. He watched her intensely as she gathered the used plates and tossed them into the bag. She was aware of his scrutiny. "Want to go for a walk outside, Yale?"

"Nope. I like to recline after a picnic," he replied, summoning her to him. "Too bad there's not a tree to lie under in here." He pulled her down on the blanket beside him, and snuggled against her. He ran his hand down her body tentatively, waiting for a reaction; feeling his erection throbbing.

"Who says there's not a tree in here? I feel a hard trunk, or am I hallucinating?" She put her mouth on his, abandoning herself to his roaming hands. She ran her hands over his entire body hungrily, and eagerly returned kiss for kiss. She unbuckled his jeans and pulled down his zipper, reaching inside to hold him; hearing him moan. He had his hand inside her wetness and probed her mouth with his tongue, feeling their urgency mount. She stroked his shaft with sturdy fingers, feeling the fire spread through her body. His legs were entwined with hers, as his movements intensified. She started rubbing harder, and faster, feeling her own climax was close. He pushed hard against her stroking fingers while moving his hand expertly inside of her. He was panting between thrusts, consumed by need. She moved her hand closer to the head of his penis, vigorously massaging the rim, until the friction took him to the point of no return. She arched her back, and with a primal scream climaxed, as his semen spurted into her hand. She rubbed the secretion over his shaft delicately, listening to his carnal mellifluous sounds, as his mouth encased hers again, while he indulged in the sensations coveting his body. They remained cemented, serenity surrounding their embracement, neither expressing words of endearment nor love. With beads of perspiration still clinging to him, he placed his head in the nape of her neck quietly admitting, "I'm jealous of the year Frank had with you." She didn't respond, but for an instant ached to explain her final months with Frank. Instead, she touched Yale's face gently and sat up. He felt his words had shattered the moment and was immediately sorry he had expressed what he was feeling. She noticed his eyes cloud over. Intuitively, she suggested, "Is it okay if I come back for dinner with you around six? Or do you need some time alone, Yale?"

He helped her up and wrapped his arms around her. "Six is fine, Lisa. What are we having?" he teased, "another picnic?"

She looked at his crotch, giggling and countering with, "Depends what you'll be 'up' to."

When she returned, she relieved the night attendant responsible for overseeing Yale's needs for the late shift. She arrived promptly at six, carrying several bags. He smiled warmly at her, taking one of the bags, as she said, "I was almost late, again. Your mother closed the mall today." She opened one bag, extracting several shirts. "These are from your mother. Notice how colorful they are. She told me, cheery colors make for cheery moods."

He laughed, holding up the bright plaid and striped shirts he never would have picked out himself. "Could be worse. She could have bought matching slacks."

Lisa laughed, as she opened another bag and withdrew, bright, royal blue, glowing red, and white cotton slacks. "Do me a favor? Wear one of these when I bring her for lunch Wednesday, or I'm going to have to go back to the mall with her again."

"Maybe, the blue or white, with one of the striped shirts. But you have to toss the red slacks out." He chuckled, grabbing her ass in his hands and drawing her close. "You forgot my hug again, Lisa?"

"Don't you want to see what's in the other bags first, Yale?" She mocked, kissing his head, overjoyed at his good spirits.

He pulled her down on the bed, and kept a firm grip on her ass, answering, "No. I want you. Right here. Right now."

She wiggled her ass, cupped in his hands, and said hoarsely, "And what, pray tell, are you going to want next?"

"Whatever I can have," he replied, looking deep into her hazel eyes.

She couldn't resist giggling. "I brought Chinese."

"Later. I want desert first." He pulled her mouth down on his fiercely. He probed her mouth with his tongue until they were both breathless.

She had placed the 'Do Not Disturb' sign out already. She reached, and pushed his hands above his head, holding him down, as she kissed every inch of his face. She took her tongue and ran it across his lips, then nibbled on his ears, feeling the hardness of him beneath her body. She sat up, still straddling him, pulled her t-shirt off and removed her lace bra. She leaned over him, pinning his hands back, and offered her ripe breasts to his mouth.

He sucked gently, ran his tongue over her nipples, and tried to free his hands to cup her breasts. She whispered, "No" holding his arms down, and brought her mouth down on his. She heard his breathing quicken, felt his body thrust to meet hers, and press to feel pressure against his hardness. She sat up and unbuttoned his shirt, kissed his chest deliciously, and ran her tongue down to his belt buckle. She saw the desire on his face. She got on her knees and undid his pants. Teasingly, she ran gentle fingers around his genitals, until he pleaded, "I want you, Lisa. I want you now."

She pushed the bags on the floor, and stood up, undressing to his steadfast gaze. She licked her fingers, then placed them between her legs, letting him observe as she massaged herself in front of him. He pulled his pants off, grabbing her to him with ferocity. He tried spreading her for entry, but she kept wiggling away, all the while seductively running her hands over him. He was crazy with desire and used his strength to turn her on her back and mount her, pushing to get inside. She closed her legs, not allowing him to penetrate yet, asking, "What's the hurry, baby? Does your dick want to push and push and push?" She was rotating her hips, her hands rubbing his ass, breathing as hard as he was.

"Spread your legs, Lisa. I want you now. I want you."

She guided him in and held her thighs firmly shut, as he groaned; thrusting violently. She met each push and arched her body yelling, "Push. Push. Push hard, Yale."

He grabbed her hips and deepened his penetration, panting hard, grinding into her until he couldn't stop. She felt his sweat, the urge dominate, and his face contort as he screamed, "Now" exploding inside of her. She felt his member continue to pulsate inside of her afterwards as she kept him where he was, rubbing her hands over his back and behind. He wanted to tell her how much he loved her, but didn't. He was still afraid to say it. She wanted to tell him how much she loved him, but didn't; still fearful he wasn't ready to trust her again completely. Instead, she kidded, "You certainly have a lot to offer" rotating her pelvis beneath him, with a warm smile on her face.

"I always felt you had a lot to offer too, Lisa," he retorted with seriousness.

As the veil, again, shaded the radiance in her eyes, Yale was aware, he once more spoiled the magic. He rolled over and sat up, trying to act nonchalant. "So, are you going to feed me or just lie there? I thought I heard something about Chinese."

She couldn't mask her feelings and didn't want him to notice. She turned on her side, to hide her face, saying, "Just save me an egg roll," and pulled at the sheet to cover herself. He picked up the bag and removed the pouch of fortune cookies on top, taking one out, and cracking it open. "Hey, listen to my fortune. You will soon walk beneath stars, and sit in a gazebo."

She laughed, turned over asking, "What does mine say?"

He cracked another one open. Yours says: "You will spend the night in arms that love to hold you close." He pulled her up, kissed her, asking, "Do you think these fortune cookies have any validity?"

"Sure; but can you find one that says—you will eat first because you are hungry?"

They picnicked in bed, finger feeding each other the fried rice and almond boneless chicken, and laughing at the mess they were creating.

They showered afterwards, changed the sheets, then climbed back into bed nuzzling against each other. With the cover over them, they stroked each other's body, feeling serene and sated. Yale fell asleep first, with his head against hers. This time his arm was over her; protectively.

CHAPTER 26

Ruth was astonished with Yale's transformation at lunch the following day. He was witty, affectionate and loving. Several times, he reiterated how much he regretted what he had put her through, and spoke candidly regarding the therapy, explaining he was learning a great deal regarding stress management. He praised the care he was receiving and believed he had made substantial progress in the two weeks since he was admitted. He squeezed Ruth's hand frequently, in reassurance, when she spoke about her past fears and qualms regarding her ultimate decision to have him committed. She noticed the tenderness Yale and Lisa shared and was overjoyed they overcame the obstacles evident initially.

There was only a half hour left of their afternoon visit when they decided to walk around the grounds on this beautiful summer day. The air was dry, the sun bright. As they approached one of the many gazebos Lisa had contributed to the center, Dr. Jay Dresler approached asking if he could speak with her. She excused herself following Jay to his office. Since Lisa didn't return to the gazebo by the conclusion of the visiting period, Yale walked his mother back inside before leaving her for his two O'clock therapy session. Ruth and Yale were near the front of the structure when they heard part of a confrontation between Lisa and Dr. Dresler.

"I know what I'm doing Jay, and you're absolutely correct in your assessment. However, I am not capitulating to your expertise in this matter. I know what I'm doing. Stay out of it." Lisa's voice was raised; her tone tinged with bitterness. "I am the only outside link Yale is comfortable with."

"You can't make your own rules, Lisa. What works most effectively was established long before you came here. Dependency takes many forms and all of them are not substance related."

"Perhaps, Jay, more attention should be given to emotional needs, with less time devoted to analytical evaluations. Yale is building confidence right now, which should also be taken into consideration."

The phone rang in Jay Dresler's private office. He temporarily stopped their dispute to answer the telephone as Lisa said, "I'll be right back, Jay. I need a cigarette."

Yale took Ruth's arm, guiding her toward the elevator, before Lisa would realize they'd overheard the exchange. She went to the rest room to calm herself. When Jay indicated he was going to be on the phone a few more minutes, she stated she'd return after walking Ruth to the car, and saying goodbye to Yale. She found them in Yale's room.

"There you are," she said entering the room. "Listen, Ruth, I have to stay for a while. I'll walk you to the car and return to the house later."

"Something wrong, Lisa? Ruth asked innocently.

"No. Just administrative bullshit. I won't be long, and Yale is due to resume the itinerary now. Are we still on for dinner and a swim later, Yale?"

"Sure," he answered both perplexed and disappointed that she chose not to confide in them. She gave him a kiss and said, "I'll see you later then."

Ruth hugged him, whispering, "Call me later if you want to talk."

Lisa saw Ruth out then returned to Jay Dresler's office still miffed. He poured them each a cup of coffee before speaking. "Okay," he began, "you win. That was the head of psychiatry on the phone. He feels your idea merits consideration, and will try it for a few weeks to see if it has positive results. Maybe, the rules regarding children are too stringent, and it won't cause a child harm to have visitation privileges, no matter their age. You can call your friend, Marissa Myers, and tell her she can bring her son to see Yale. We're going to keep an open mind Lisa, but if results show even one child is traumatized by the experience, we'll have to formulate other possibilities."

"I just know Yale. I'm positive it would do him good to reassure Josh that he is fine. They have a special bond. I really think I know what's better in this instance, especially since I'm close to those involved."

"Alright, Lisa. I'm sorry I gave you a hard time, but I have to look at the whole picture, not just one case. Oh, before I forget, Harvey Stone called for you. He asked, if you'd call him at home after four. He'll be in a meeting until then."

"Thanks, Jay. And thank you for bending the rules. I'm in love with Yale, and I know, from my conversations with him, how horrible he feels about the condition Josh last saw him in. I wouldn't have pushed, if I wasn't convinced they both would gain from a visit, in the social hall, sharing time together."

"I still have some reservations, Lisa. Yale could feel he has to pretend in front of Josh, to reassure him. Yale's cure will be most effective if he does it at his own pace, not because someone needs him and induces subliminal pressure."

"My contention is still that this is not a dependency issue, but a form of support for both of them. Yale will feel better knowing Josh is aware he's better and vice versa."

They spoke for another half hour about impending personnel changes, and the woman being hired to handle a large portion of the administrative responsibilities Lisa felt she couldn't handle; then parted company.

Ruth left a note on the kitchen table of the beach house for Lisa, indicating she went to the supermarket. Lisa sat down at the table and called to find out how Ronnie was doing. She was pleased to be informed that he could go home in a day or two. She left love messages for her boys on their answering machine. She checked with Belle to see if everything was under control at home. She called her parents to tell them she loved and missed them, and then contacted Marissa advising her, she and Josh could come out and see Yale before Josh had to leave for overnight camp. She arranged to have her plane bring them to Carmel, Friday morning, and persuaded Marissa into staying at the ocean front property overnight with her son. She concluded the conversation with, "I'm looking forward to seeing both of you. I know the contact with Yale will be rewarding for all of you. I agree with you Marissa, Josh will be able to enjoy camp, much more, once he's sure his Uncle Yale is not going to heaven, and can personally give him a big hug."

It was about five when she finally reached Harvey. Ruth entered the house, in the middle of her conversation, carrying groceries. Harvey was updated on how well Yale was progressing, and her intervention to allow Josh and Marissa to visit. He agreed, in his opinion, it couldn't be anything but beneficial. She spoke about her budding relationship with Yale, and he teased, countering he was jealous it wasn't him.

"You know, I adore you already. And, besides, I need to be more social than you do." Ruth was listening while she put the groceries away.

"Oh Lisa, two things before I forget," Harvey interjected, "The yearly, City of Hope, fundraiser is Monday night. Are you planning on attending?"

"I'm not sure." Saturday, would mark the anniversary, to the date, that she first met Frank. When she opened the invitation days before, in the bundle of mail Belle forwarded to her, she felt an ache at the recollection of her first days with Frank, and the ensuing week they'd spent in San Francisco, bonding them physically and spiritually. "I don't know if I can."

"Too many memories, Lisa?" he asked perceptively.

"Something like that," she replied.

Ruth was curious what Lisa felt she couldn't do, what she wasn't sure about, and what—something like that—meant.

"I'd love to be your escort, if you change your mind," Harvey said at his end, adding, "besides I haven't been able to get away, and wasn't able to come there, as planned, last week. I'd like to see you. You know Lisa; there are good vibes here regarding Frank, too. The fun you had together. The way he showed you San Francisco for the first time. The way he looked when you were on his lap, telling him, you wouldn't settle for anything less than a royal straight. The devotion you showered him with."

Tears were falling as she listened to Harvey's words. She found it difficult to speak. "But there's still a lot of sorrow, too, you know. There are things that cling."

"I feel it too, Lisa. Most of it stems from the circumstances surrounding Frank's death. We both would have been able to deal with the loss with more of an adjustment if he hadn't taken his life. He tried to be sparing, but the consequences affected us oppressively."

She was crying openly now. "It's a hard thing to live with, and a lousy secret to keep."

"I know, Lisa. For me too. At least the media has stopped prying. You sure you won't come?"

"Let me think about it a little more, and get back to you. Okay? I love you dearly, you know. You're the only one who could possibly understand. I'll call you back."

"Okay, Lisa. If you want someone to be with on Saturday, so the day is less painful, I'm here. That's a year since you and Frank first met, right?"

"You are so insightful, Harvey. You give me the strength I need to adjust during the most turbulent times. Thank you. Thank you so much."

"Bye, Lisa. I'm here if you need me."

She wiped her face with the palms of her hands and looked up at Ruth from the chair. "Marissa's coming with Josh, Friday morning. Isn't that great?"

Ruth walked up to her, lifted her chin, pleading, "Let me help."

"I wish you could, Ruth." She rose and hugged Ruth saying, "It'll be okay. I better shower and change or I'll be late getting back to the clinic." She walked out, leaving Ruth disconcerted and concerned.

Yale was pensive when Lisa arrived. He did not badger her with incessant questions, but by the time they had finished their dinner, he was sullen and bad tempered. He had hoped she'd confide in him by now, and although he tried to entice her into conversations regarding the past year, she remained tight-lipped. He had been contemplating, all afternoon, whether or not to prod, and was piqued she was so reticent with him. He needed to know what had transpired between her and Dr. Dresler earlier, but wanted it to come from her voluntarily. She made no reference to the confrontation. She thought he was just having a difficult time of it, and attempted to lighten the atmosphere.

"You know what the cute dietician, who brought us our dinner, asked me when I ordered our meal. She asked, if I planned to keep you a captive in here forever. She's a big fan of yours."

"Why don't you get me her address and phone number, so when you decide to take off again, I'll have someone else to fuck?"

She checked her temper; determined not to let him get to her. "Are you trying to get rid of me, Yale? If you want to be alone, I'll go. I'm not in the mood for bullshit. You've been rude since I arrived."

"Sorry, sweetie. I'll try to behave myself," he sarcastically shot back.

"I'm leaving, Yale. I didn't do anything to warrant this kind of treatment, and I don't have to take it." She started for the door.

"Go ahead. Leave. Maybe, I'm spending too much time with you anyway. The counselors advise us against bonding too closely with people in the clinic during our rehabilitation. They say we need to be focused on recovering; first and foremost."

"Maybe they're right, Yale. Have a good night. Good bye."

She didn't hear from Yale that night and didn't visit the following day. Friday she brought Josh and Marissa to him and watched the love they exchanged. She remained distant and subdued. When she arranged a special barbecue for them Friday evening, Lisa didn't join them, explaining she had other plans she couldn't cancel. She didn't answer the phone when she arrived back at the house. Yale felt he was getting what he deserved when he put down the phone after there was no answer, and Lisa was justified not choosing to be in his company after his behavior two days ago.

After romping with Josh, Saturday morning, Lisa had the driver take Marissa, Ruth, and Josh for lunch with Yale. She sent along all the necessities for a picnic and had ordered a special cake, in the shape of a spaceship, inscribed with, "Have a great time at camp, Josh" to be delivered. She declined accompanying them, professing prior obligations, and went to a mall, by herself, instead. Ruth had asked Yale if he and Lisa had an argument, but after he said he didn't want to discuss her, Ruth changed the topic. She didn't press Lisa either, deciding it would be best for her to stay out of it. She had felt Yale's wrath, once before, when attempting to bring up Lisa's name, at a time when he was adverse to discussing his feelings. She didn't want to rock the boat, now, when he was making headway in his recovery.

Lisa, who always loved to go shopping, came back from the mall empty handed. She took a magazine on the terrace, next to her bedroom, kicked off her shoes, and leafed through the pages without interest.

Totally bored, she rummaged through the refrigerator and cupboards looking for something to munch on, but nothing looked appealing. She went back into the bedroom, turned on the radio, lying on the bed. The second song the station played was one of Yale's early hits. She thought back, about how excited she'd always become when she was going to one of Yale's concerts with Ronnie. She thought about their first meeting, after the assassination attempt on his life, during his comeback tour, by the radicals who met with their demise instead. She remembered how hard it was to ask him to let go, when she felt obliged to try and save her unsalvageable marriage. She heard the final words of the ballad now—"I'm never out of reach—never out of reach," and arrived at the clinic an hour later, asking, "Anybody save me some cake?"

"Oh, Lisa," Josh yelled, hugging her excitedly, "You're here." They were in one of the gazebos indulging in the cake. "Uncle Yale said you must have gotten me the space ship cake, 'cause he didn't. Did you?"

"Yup; I did. Is it good?"

"This one's even specialer than the one at my birthday party. Look, it has fudge and whipped cream and cherries all around the outside. The fudge is on the bottom, see Lisa, and the cherries are like lights and stuff, and the whipped cream is like foam for take off. The vanilla ice cream is inside it. Neat! Want some?"

"Sure do. That's why I showed up."

"Okay. Sit here, Lisa," he said, pointing to a spot next to him. "I'm gonna show you what we did. Can I do it, mom?"

Marissa laughed at his enthusiasm. "Go ahead, Josh," she replied, handing him a dish and spoon. He took out some vanilla ice cream from the center, put fudge over it, and topped it with whipped cream and a cherry. "Here, Lisa. Now it's a hot fudge sundae, except the fudge is not really hot, and we don't got no nuts."

She leaned over, kissed Josh's cheek, and said, "It's perfect. Thank you." Her eyes filled, as she looked at the sundae adding, "Just how I like it. With no nuts on top."

Yale and Ruth were studying her, while Marissa helped Josh wipe his sticky fingers. She kept her eyes lowered as she brought a spoon of the sundae to her mouth, but the tears that fell didn't go unnoticed. "Be right back, Josh," she said, rushing from the gazebo before he saw her crying. She returned minutes later wearing sunglasses to hide her discomfort. Josh was so spirited she didn't have to talk much, and managed to control her emotions effectively for the duration of time they spent in the gazebo.

"Uncle Yale, are we gonna watch the movie you got, now?" Josh asked, already restless, and ready to move on to the next event.

"Sure. Come on. Lisa, I hope you like Bugs Bunny as much as Josh and I do." Yale's eyes were begging her to stay.

"Actually, I'm a "Popeye and Olive Oil" girl, myself. But, I think, I can make an exception today."

"Who's Popeye?" Josh inquired as they all laughed, feeling the age gap that separated them.

During the movie, Lisa excused herself, and went to her office to call Harvey. Minutes later Yale took Josh off his lap and whispered, "I'll be right back," and went in search of her. He wanted to make amends, for his behavior of the other day, and had decided to tell her how much he loved her. The last couple of days had been torture; not being able to snuggle against her, or feel the caress of her hands on his face and body.

He found her in the hallway, hugging Harvey Stone, crying, "I can't believe you did this; you big lug. You're wonderful."

Yale tried to turn around, but it was too late. Harvey spotted him, calling out, "Hello, Mr. Frye. It's nice to see you again."

Yale approached, as Lisa wiped tears off her cheeks, "It's nice to see you too, doctor."

"Harvey; is fine. I'm not here as a physician. I've arranged to have someone cover for me in San Francisco, and decided to surprise Lisa, and see if I can seek refuge here for a few days."

"My place is your place, Harvey," she said, smiling up at him. "It's a great surprise. How's Bugs Bunny doing in there, Yale?"

"Josh is loving it, but I think I've seen it before. Excuse me, I just came out to use the john," he lied. "I have to get back to Josh and the movie before the ending. It's the best part." He walked away quickly, jealous, and tense.

Lisa led Harvey into her little office and sat next to him on a chair. "You're something else, Harvey. I think you're my only real friend.

The only person I don't have to pretend around." She filled him in on what had transpired between herself and Yale, confessed how much he meant to her, and how she had been fine all day, until Josh served her a hot fudge sundae. Harvey was familiar with the sentiment behind the sundae, from the times he'd visited Frank and Lisa on the island, and had also been told by Lisa's boys of their 'sundae fight' in Tahoe, when Marc and Steve first met Frank.

Yale was passing her office, on the way back to Josh, when he heard her saying, "I'm letting go, Harvey. It'll be bad for me if I don't. I have to. I know I do." Yale kept on going. He went back and finished watching the animated movie with Josh, feeling sick inside, believing what he just heard was Lisa telling Harvey that it was over between them. Meanwhile, Harvey was reassuring her, in Lisa's office, that Frank would be glad if he knew she was adjusting and going on with her life. She hugged Harvey, adding, "and if you'll still be my date, I'll go back with you on Monday, for the fundraiser in San Francisco."

"That's great, Lisa. I'm pleased you changed your mind. It'll give me a chance to introduce you to a special lady I've developed a relationship with, too."

"Harvey, have you been holding out on me?"

"Sort of. But it's a new relationship, and I'm still a little afraid of commitment, so I didn't want to say anything before."

"Is it Rebecca, the physical therapist, you've mentioned having dinner with a few times?"

"You know me too well, Lisa," he confessed, blushing. "She's very bright and gentle. She's a giving individual—a lot like you, Lisa, in fact. You'll like her."

"I'm looking forward to meeting her. I'm happy for you, Harvey. I hope it works out well. Now, come on, I'll say good bye to everyone, and you know what I need to do?"

"What?"

"Walk along the ocean with you. I look at the ocean from my bedroom terrace everyday, but so far, I haven't been able to get any closer. Let's find peace where Frank did. Okay?" He blinked away a tear and took her hand in his.

The goodbye's lasted over an hour. Josh remembered Harvey from the hospital when Tony had kidnapped him, and Marissa started commenting on how well the situation had been handled, and expressed her gratitude for his help at that time. Soon, Ruth was saying how young he was to be head of such a large hospital, and Josh was asking if he could get him a stethoscope, so he could listen to everyone's heart. The only one who said very little was Yale.

Lisa finally got up to leave. "Marissa, I'll see you and Josh at the house before you leave, okay? I'm going with Harvey for a while. Ruth, just call down when you are ready for dinner. They know what to do. She had arranged pizza for Josh, and ordered salads and various Italian dishes she knew Yale liked. "Yale, I'll see you tomorrow. David is flying in for the day. How about all of us having lunch together?"

"You sure you don't have anything better to do?" He replied sardonically.

"No, Yale. I'd like us to have lunch together. I'm going to San Francisco, Monday, for The City of Hope Ball, and I'd like to spend time with you, tomorrow, before I leave."

"What if I'd like you to stay here Monday and have dinner with me then?"

"Then I won't go to San Francisco," She answered truthfully.

"Why, Lisa? Is Yale, the charity case—more important than other charities—even The City of Hope?"

"Why are you doing this, Yale? You're not a charity case, for God's sake. What prompted this; all of a sudden?"

He looked at her, hurting. "Never mind. I'm sorry. I'm tired. Lunch tomorrow is fine. Come on, Josh. Let's go outside."

"Yale, do you want to talk?"

"No, Lisa. You're not willing to be open with me, and I'm not able to avoid what you don't want to discuss. See you tomorrow." He took Josh by the hand, turned, and left.

On the way out of the center Harvey asked, "What does Yale need to know that you won't talk about, Lisa?"

"Why I married Frank, when I vowed I was coming back to him."

"Maybe, you should tell him, Lisa. Frank wouldn't want you to suffer because of a secret you feel you have to keep."

"Maybe, if circumstances were different, Harvey. Right now, I'm afraid even if I did explain the last year, Yale would misinterpret my feelings as compassion instead of love."

"Are you sure it's love, Lisa?"

"I've been sure for a very long time, Harvey. I've never felt for any man, what I feel for Yale. I never will."

CHAPTER 27

Yale's intense securitization of Harvey made Lisa uncomfortable during lunch, but it wasn't until he intentionally provoked her, insinuating she could have her choice of bed partners that night which forced her to tell him to shut his mouth.

He continued trying to instigate an argument, by needling her regarding how influential she'd become since she married Frank, then becoming the rich widow. He attempted to lure Harvey into defending her. And when David suggested going out for a walk, Yale gave him the finger. Finally, Harvey stood up, angrily suggesting, "Mr. Frye, I recommend you call me when you'd like to share a pleasant lunch. I find you offensive and prefer to eat elsewhere today."

"Don't preach, doctor. I didn't invite you, and I certainly don't need you to lecture. So if you don't like it—"

"I'm not lecturing, Mr. Frye—"

"Shut it, you moralistic, self-righteous, pompous—"

"Go to hell, Yale!" Lisa shouted, standing up next to Harvey. "If it wasn't for Harvey's help, you wouldn't be rehabilitating in the best clinic in the country—"

"And if you had a conscience, Lisa, you couldn't be bedded so soon after your husband's death? Not a very long grieving period was it?"

"Yale. Stop—" Ruth yelled, trying to stop his outrageous, unwarranted, unscrupulous behavior.

"Get out of here! All of you! Get out and don't come back! I'm sick of the pampering, the niceness, the fakery—all of it—all of it—Get out!"

He was mounting a verbal attack, so hideous, without reason or regard for any of them. His voice was escalating so, that Ruth was petrified he was going to wind up restrained again. She couldn't stand the lack of stability he was displaying. When Dr. Dresler came in, with two attendants, to escort Yale back to his room, Ruth collapsed on the floor requiring oxygen. As she regained consciousness, she repeated, again and again, "I'm alright, really." She protested at the fuss afterwards, as Yale sat stupefied in a chair. He was aware his antics had caused his mother to pass out. When Jay Dressler helped Ruth into a chair, Yale sat passively, feeling deflated.

"I'm sorry. I better go to my room, where I belong. I'm sorry, Ma." He rose laboriously, his stress emphasized by the bulging veins protruding beneath the pallor on his face and neck.

"Yale," Dr. Dresler continued, "Would you like Lisa to remain in the vicinity? If she chooses—"

He cut Jay short, speaking brutally, "No. I've had enough of Lisa. I'd like her to go. I wish her a happy life. Get her out of here!"

"Yale," Dr. Dressler inquired, "Why is there such vehemence directed at Lisa? Has she let you down? Perhaps, we could to talk about it later?"

"There's nothing to talk about. I'm just sick of the calculated, compromising, things she does to extend herself on my behalf, so I'll have someone around to help me recover; when in truth she's completely artificial."

"Can you elaborate, Yale?" Lisa asked. "I'd like to understand, before I say goodbye. What have I done?"

"You really want it spelled out, Lisa? You must think I'm pretty stupid not to see how close you and Harvey are. A guy doesn't leave someone covering his position for him, spur of the moment, unless there's a special relationship going on. And you pretend I'm important one minute, then, minutes later, when I come in from lunch, the other day, I hear you and Dr. Dresler arguing. I heard your words Lisa—I know Yale; I know what's best for him—Let me handle this—I know what I'm doing. Those were your words, Lisa. I heard them. My mother heard them. More Lisa? You want me to say more? Sherman Black said, just this morning, unaware we had been previously involved, that he told you how you deserved a gold medal for your aptitude in drawing people out of their shell—I guess I owe you a medal, Lisa."

His voice was getting louder as he continued, "Then there was a conversation my mother mentioned to me, where you had a great deal to say to Harvey, one night, about keeping a lid on something. What Lisa? You want our relationship kept secret, so your reputation isn't soiled? Or, how about when I passed your little room here yesterday and you're telling Harvey—you have to let go, because it'll be bad for you if you don't. Is that enough, Lisa? You're a liar, Lisa. You're here under false pretenses, and as much as I had hoped we could pick up the pieces—Go home Lisa! Live your life! I'm going to make a new one for myself as well; only it won't be with delusions this time. I've been stupid long enough."

"Lisa," Harvey started, "I think it's time to clarify the misconceptions Yale—"

"No, Harvey!" She yelled. "No! I have nothing to say. Nothing! There's nothing I want to clear up. The problem here is deeper than Yale's interpretation of what he heard. It's mistrust. Until this minute, I wasn't cognizant of how little faith Yale had in me. I have nothing to divulge which would matter anymore. I have been complacent long enough. I have withstood all the abuse I am going to. I don't have to tolerate Yale's behavior. Nor do I have to deny of justify myself to him. Once, we understood one another—we had a special union. Now, there is doubt, distrust, and accusations of betrayal infiltrating the relationship in epidemic proportions. Good-bye, Yale. I am sorry for you, and sad at how long I've been a fool." She walked out.

As Ruth kissed Yale, advising him he could call her any time, day or night, he hugged her hard, saying, "I know."

Harvey listened, adding, "At least, Mr. Frye, that is something you do know. There is so much you don't know, Mr. Frye, and so much you've misinterpreted, I'm having difficulty understanding your interpretation of loyalty. Have you, for one moment, considered what motivated Lisa into purchasing the majority shares of Carmel Clinic, when it is a non-profit organization? She never even heard of this place until the day she contacted me, requesting the best location to help you. Have you, Mr. Frye, even once, asked yourself why she was here, exposing herself to burdensome individuals, when she has the means to be entertained like a queen for the rest of her life? Lisa's assessment is quite accurate, Mr. Frye. You are not even entitled to be corrected in your present frame of mind. This was not a pleasant day for you, Mr. Frye; however, I'm more concerned about the affect your words will have on Lisa. You see, Mr. Frye, Lisa is so in love with you that she wouldn't set the record straight to prevent you from having to deal with the guilt you'd feel consequently. Good luck, Mr. Frye. I hope, as the fog lifts, you see the sun. I really do."

"Would you like to be specific, Doctor, about my misconceptions?"

"I'm sorry, Mr. Frye. My loyalty is to Lisa. Since she asked me not to intervene, I respect the lady too much to speak against her wishes. Good bye, Mr. Frye."

They were eating tuna casserole in silence when the telephone rang. Lisa ignored the ringing, and Ruth sat motionless, with no interest in who was calling. Harvey finally answered the phone and handed the receiver to Lisa. "It's Jean. Something about your book. She says it's important."

"Hi, Jean. What's going on?"

"Nice greeting, Lisa. Thanks for asking how I am."

"Sorry, Jean. You caught me at a bad time. I've had an awful day."

"Want to talk about it, Lisa?"

"Not really. Everything I say, lately, gets twisted anyway; so why bother?"

"Lisa, I'm worried about you. What's Harvey doing there? Is something wrong with you?"

"No Jean, nothing's wrong with me, that a new brain wouldn't cure. How did you get the number here, Jean? I never gave it to anyone but Belle and—"

"Cool it, Lisa. If you're pissed because I called, say so, and I'll hang up. I was concerned and lied to some asshole at the clinic saying I was family, and it was an emergency. You know sweetie, if people dig, they can uncover a lot of shit."

"I'm not pissed, Jean. What's your point?"

"The point is the tabloids printed some shit about Frank having died while terminally ill. The next point is you've been offered big bucks for the rights to the manuscript, if you put the novel on hold, and allow

Universal to develop it into a screenplay first. Then there's the point that The New York Times ran an article, claiming you were in Carmel, to help Yale Frye, who admitted himself to conquer substance addictions, which presumably have destroyed his career, and nearly his life."

"Shit! I should have known nothing could be hushed up by now."

"How much of this is accurate, Lisa? And what can I do?"

"It's all accurate, Jean, and there's more. You can't do anything Jean—except, except—"

"Except what, Lisa?"

"Except, to put a contingency on the manuscript. Take the offer. I'll forgo publication if they agree to offer Yale a lead in the film. Everybody deserves a chance to start over. The rest of this I'll ignore for now, and see what else shows up in print. Jean, let me call you back in a little while. Are you going to be around?"

"I'll be here, honey, unless you want me to fly out to you?"

"I love you, Jean. Thank you. Stay put. I'll call you back later."

She placed the phone in its cradle. "Well, the day started off for shit, and is going to end the same way. The media disclosed Yale is in the rehab and that's why I'm here. The tabloids printed a story, just released, stating Frank was terminal when he drowned. I want to be out of here before morning, Harvey. Before the vultures attack."

"Lisa," Ruth asked, "When did you find out Frank was terminal?"

"The day after I left Yale to go to Tahoe with Frank. Harvey called and confirmed Frank's suspicion. The cancer was inoperable."

"That's why you married him." It was a statement, not a question.

"A primary reason, Ruth. Frank was aware of it. He even attempted to mail a letter to Yale, from Tahoe, but I intervened. Frank had given my son, two letters to mail. One was to Yale, an effort to explain why I was marrying him. The other, supposedly, a nuptial agreement to his attorney. I never wanted Frank's assets. At times, I've wondered if I destroyed the wrong letter. You're familiar with the story of the "Poor Little Rich Girl." Well, here I am. However, two major problems arose, Ruth. One: I fell in love with Frank. I went into the marriage knowing we had a year, at best, together. Frank was very special. He was able to admit he didn't want to die alone. And he adored me." She stopped, her eyes filling. "The second problem Ruth, was, he loved me so much, he wanted to spare me the final days when he could no longer mask his pain." Tears cascaded down her cheeks. "He chose to die in the Pacific Ocean, rather than in my arms."

She stood, looking into Ruth's eyes, "You know Ruth, you were absolutely right when you said it's important to say goodbye to people you care about. I don't know if I'll ever forgive Frank for cheating me out of my good bye." She left the table and went to her room.

"Oh my God," Ruth shouted. "I should go to her," she muttered, pushing her chair back.

"Why don't we give her a few minutes?" Harvey suggested. "This is the first time she's been able to say any of this out loud."

"Her parents; her sons; they don't know?"

"No Ruth. We vowed to keep Frank's secrets. Lisa and I are the only ones who have lived with the truth. That's what I was trying to keep a lid on, Ruth. The documentation and confidentiality Frank asked for. Yesterday was a year to the day, when Lisa first met Frank. That's why I came out. I didn't want Lisa to be alone. All her memories aren't easy ones to cope with."

Lisa returned more composed, and began clearing the table. When Ruth was about to assist her, Harvey touched her hand signaling her to remain seated. "You know Ruth," she began a minute later, with her back to them as she scraped the plates off, "I wanted to tell you everything. But Frank was so insistent about secrecy. I think he had this perception of himself he didn't want tarnished or something." She paused then added, "And you know, I've tried with Yale. I really did. I, uh, could handle the roughness the first weeks. I didn't care, uh, about the bruises or name calling, because of his condition, but, uh, I couldn't take it anymore when he, uh, made me feel like a whore." She paused again, trying to maintain control. "I have only been with three men in my life; Ronnie for more than fifteen years. Yale and Frank. Maybe, one day, uh, you could tell Yale, uh, that I am not, uh, easily bedded, and that, uh, he really hurt me when, uh,—she stopped unable to go on for a minute, then asked. "Am I a whore, Ruth, for sleeping with Yale when Frank has, uh, only been gone a short time? Am I wrong or is it some breach of etiquette, uh, to be able to love again so soon? Am I a tramp for wanting, uh, to feel alive? You know, uh, near the end, Frank couldn't, uh." She stopped again, overcome by emotion.

Ruth came up behind her, stroked her hair, answering, "Yale's actions today were brutal, honey, which I'm attributing to his illness. But Lisa, you didn't do anything wrong. You are anything but a whore. The fact that you can be demonstrative is a testimony to Frank. Instead of bitterness, Lisa, his influence has left you open for more love. That speaks volumes."

Lisa didn't like her vulnerability and abruptly moved away from Ruth. "Listen Harvey, I'm afraid I'm going to have to beg off going to San Francisco with you. The City of Hope will get a check. I'm just not up to being in public. I'm sorry. I hope you understand. I'll meet Michelle in a few weeks, okay? I'm going to pack and leave now. I'll call to arrange for the place to be left the way we found it, and send the plane back in the morning. I have to get away from here. I want to go home. Maybe I'll fly my boys out for a visit."

"Why don't I go with you?" Harvey offered. "I'd like to see what else you've done with the house."

"How about a rain check? I need some space."

"You're not able to keep your guard down yet are you? You make some headway, then go right back into hiding. Lisa, stop being so afraid."

"I can't Harvey. I've been knocked down once too often. I can't rebound at will. I'm already sorry for being as candid as I've been."

"Why? You're not betraying Frank by being truthful."

"I feel I am. He chose death to save me from suffering through his dying days with him. The least I can do is disappear until the media exhausts their articles regarding him, and moves on to someone else. I have to do this, Harvey."

"There are those words again, Lisa—have to."

"I can't help it."

She packed her bags and was gone in an hour. Her parting message to Ruth was, "Wish Yale luck. I really loved him, you know. But I never will again."

Tearfully, Ruth replied, "I wish you good luck too, Lisa."

With more than sadness Lisa responded, "My luck has run out. Once, I held a Royal Straight Flush. Now, I have a hand I have to throw in."

CHAPTER 28

The labyrinth surrounding Lisa did not prevail. She made a conscious effort not to dwell on what she knew would cripple her if she allowed herself to be languid. She engaged in organizing activities to occupy her days and traveled often. She met with Jean in New York, contributing ideas for the screenplay of "Regrets". She allowed herself to be persuaded into screen writing the mini series for television. Although there were days melancholy left her listless, she forged ahead. She spent time with Marc and Steve, when their schedules allowed. She saw Harvey and met his fiancé, and went to visit her parents, for a few days, every couple of weeks.

Yale had declined to audition for a role in "Regrets" according to Ruth, who Lisa spoke with regularly. Yale was fully recovered and was working with persistence on his music, enthusiastically structuring a new concert tour.

Lisa had not seen Yale since leaving Carmel, three months ago. She had Belle screen all her calls daily, always refusing to speak to Yale when he called. The numerous letters, cards, and wrapped packages Yale kept sending to the house, since he returned home, remained unopened in the bottom of a closet. Every floral arrangement was refused. And after bitter words with Ruth, Lisa was able to persuade Ruth to refrain from trying to smooth things out, threatening to refuse her calls as well.

"Lisa had built a fortress around herself which was impenetrable. There were only a few people she trusted. For the majority of the time she preferred writing, alone, in her study, to going anywhere she would have to interact with people. She slept little and had shed another ten pounds since she returned home. She made no new friends, but still generously sent donations to the charities she supported, and managed to remain involved with those most important to her. She was reclusive to all but a select few. Recently, she had purchased a puppy from a classified ad: **"Must sell, or put to sleep, eight week old Beagle, due to owner's poor health and lack of funds. Shelters already overcrowded."** The little, brown, black, and white Beagle, Lisa christened, "Matey." She was her only constant companion. She followed Lisa wherever she went, having been traumatized from birth with hunger and neglect. She would only sleep at the foot of Lisa's bed. If Lisa woke from a nightmare, Matey instinctively moved close to her, snuggling against her, until Lisa would sleep again. Matey could sense Lisa's moods from their onset, and knew when to be playful and when to remain subdued. Besides Matey, Belle was the only other face Lisa encountered daily. Belle, too, knew when to open her mouth and when to remain silent, but sometimes her concern for Lisa overpowered her so that she spoke up even when she was aware she shouldn't.

"Miss Lisa," Belle attempted, while her employer was hunched over a writing pad, in the study where she was never supposed to be disturbed, "I know I'm out of line again, but Marissa Myers is on the phone. It's the third time she's called in two days. Will you take the call Miss Lisa, and tell her yourself why you can't be at her engagement party—which I think you should go to—even if I shouldn't be sayin' it—'cause she's just gonna keep callin' back. She loves ya, Miss Lisa. You know she does."

"Belle, I'm going to replace you, if you don't stop this shit—I mean it. Tell her I'm out. Please!"

"Nope—I won't. Go on and replace me, Miss Lisa, 'cause I quit! I am tired of worrying over you, anyhow. Maybe, I can find me a job for someone, where I'll sleep better nights! I'll tell her I don't work here no more and she can try you again, if she wants, but that I thinks she should stop wastin' her time." Belle turned to leave, mumbling, "You gots money, but you ain't got a life. I sure wouldn't want to trade places with you, for nothin'."

"What did you say, Belle?"

"I said, I wouldn't trade places with you for nothin'. I still know how to find pleasure in life, even after losin' everything—including my kin. You don't."

"Okay, Belle, hand me the damn phone, and stay here. I'll tell Marissa why I'm not coming to her engagement party, and get you off my ass, so I can get some work done."

She picked up the receiver; while Belle stood there with her arms folded, watching her. "Marissa. Hi. Sorry I haven't been in touch, but I'm swamped with work."

"Sorry, is not good enough, Lisa. I thought we were friends. You saved Josh's life. You probably saved Yale's. You helped Ruth through the worst of times, and now you're shutting everyone out. I won't speak for anyone but Josh and myself. But we miss you, Lisa. We want you in our lives, and I'm not going to stop calling, no matter how many times Belle makes excuses for you."

Lisa's eyes filled. "Marissa, please understand. I can't come to the party. I wish you and Howard only the best, but I can't be there. I miss you, too, and I'd love to see Josh, but I'm still recovering. I can't be around reminders of dreams that died. I can't do it. I just can't."

"So, I'm being punished because of Yale? So, Josh is deprived of seeing you because of Yale. Do you think that's fair? What did we do to you?"

"You didn't do anything, Marissa..."

"Yes, we did do something Lisa. We loved you and still do. You, at least, spoke to me on the phone until Yale returned from Carmel. Now you won't even accept my calls. I'm hurt, Lisa. I'm a separate person—not an extension of Yale, for crying out loud! Just because he hurt you—is that any reason for you to hurt me?"

"I don't mean to hurt you, Marissa, but don't you see, Yale is a big part of your life, and I don't want to talk about him...I don't want to hear about him...I don't want to be around him..."

"Okay. Okay. I understand. I can accept that. If you can't be at the party, that's one thing—one night, but don't shut me out. Can we have lunch? Shopping? Can we visit? I promise, I won't even mention Yale. I'd just like to see you and keep the friendship we formed. We developed a bond, Lisa. I don't want to lose it. If you won't come to the party, will you come for dinner tomorrow night? It's Friday, so Josh can stay up later, since he doesn't have to get up for school, and Howard will be home at a reasonable hour. Please?"

"Okay, Marissa. Dinner tomorrow, and I'll bring dessert. What time?"

At six o'clock the following evening, Belle was standing in front of Lisa with her arms folded again, but this time the Afro-American, dignified, loyal, determined woman had a smile on her face. "You look great, Miss Lisa. My; My; I forgot how pretty you could look when you wants to."

"You are a pain in the ass, Belle, but I'm willing to overlook it, since you're probably one of the few people I still respect. Now, stop your gloating, and try my folk's number again, please. Maybe they're home now, so I can wish them a Good Sabbath before I leave."

Lisa entered the driveway to Marissa's home, in the gold, sports coupe Mercedes, Frank had bought her, feeling embarrassed so much time has passed since she last saw Marissa and Josh. She rang the bell, and seconds later felt the warm embrace of the woman who had become her close friend and a confidant. Minutes later, seated in the warm, comfortable, but elegantly furnished library, Josh was bombarding her with endless questions, and showing her what he had learned in his latest and most current passion—Karate. Howard finally had to ask Josh to help him serve the hor d'ores, to divert his attention to something less physical. Josh had apparently developed a close relationship with Howard in the past few months, and Howard's affection for Josh was evident. Lisa couldn't help feeling a little envious at the attentiveness exchanged between Howard and Marissa before, during, and after dinner. They were very much in love and it showed.

They were seated again in the Oriental accessorized library, over coffee, when Josh asked Lisa if she wanted to see his photos from summer camp. He pulled a chair next to hers, after gathering several albums from his room, and began explaining who and what each of the pictures represented. Halfway through an album, Josh pointed to a photograph of himself on Yale's shoulders.

"Here I am with Uncle Yale, Lisa. This is when we went to the San Diego zoo, last year. See the camels behind us?"

"Josh," Marissa interrupted, "Why don't you put your albums away. I think Lisa's seen enough for now."

"Just a few more, Mom, okay? I didn't show her the ones of us at Lisa's beach house, when Uncle Yale stayed there with us, after Lisa had to go on her business trip."

"Another time, Josh. I think—"

"It's okay, Marissa. I'd love to see a few more. They're wonderful photos, Josh."

Josh continued pointing at pictures, explaining the history of each one, until Lisa felt her throat tightening from the memories, some of them reincarnated. There were pictures from Josh's last birthday party, which was the day she assisted getting Yale admitted to Carmel Clinic. There were pictures at Yale's estate. And there were snapshots taken at the beach house, where Lisa finally said goodbye to her dreams. Josh was closing the album, having completed painting a mirage with his words, when a photo fell on the carpet. Lisa bent retrieving the snapshot of Josh and Yale sitting on the terrace at the Carmel beach house. They were smiling and holding hands. She handed Josh the photograph with trembling fingers, uttering, "This is one of my favorites, Josh. You and Uncle Yale look very happy in this photograph."

"It's one of my favorites too, Lisa. Aunt Ruth took it of us. Here, Lisa. You keep it. I want you to have it. I have copies 'cause Aunt Ruth made a bunch of them when she saw this one. She said this was how she wanted to remember the beach house in Carmel—you know—'cause me and Uncle Yale were laughing and fooling around, I guess."

Lisa swallowed hard before speaking. "Thank you, Josh. I'd like to have this one. It's a great photo and the way I'd like to remember the beach house too."

Josh reached for another album, ready to continue displaying other memorable times on celluloid for Lisa, when Marissa stopped him. "That's enough for now, Josh. Let's save the others for another time. It's getting late, Josh. Please put your albums away and get into your pajamas."

"Come on, Mom, just a few more."

"No Josh. Another time. Go on, and do as mom says," Howard added, supporting Marissa.

"Okay. Okay. But I'm not going to bed yet. Right? It's a late night, remember? No school tomorrow."

"I remember," Marissa said. "Just get in your pajamas, please."

"Alright. Lisa, next time I'll show you the rest, okay?"

"I'd like that, Josh. Thank you for this photo and for sharing your pictures with me. I'm going to keep this one in a special place."

"Do you got any pictures, Lisa? Mom keeps some in her wallet. Do you?"

"Yes, I have a few, including a couple of my new puppy, Matey, who I told you about during dinner. After you're in your pj's, I'll show them to you, if you'd like."

At the prospect of staying up later, and getting to see Lisa's snapshots, Josh scurried up the stairs to his bedroom to get into his pajamas; returning in a flash. Marissa was telling Lisa about the honeymoon she and Howard were planning in Monte Carlo, after their Thanksgiving Day wedding. When Josh bounced back into the room, he plopped himself down against Lisa on the sofa. He waited patiently, having been taught not to interrupt conversations, as his mom was explaining, "I've never been to Monte Carlo. I hear it's scenic and quite beautiful."

"It is, Marissa. I think you'll love it. It's a paradise."

"When were you last there, Lisa? Perhaps you can recommend some places to dine."

"Actually, I was only in Monte Carlo once. Frank loved it there. He took me there on our honeymoon. Unfortunately, it was one of the latter places we visited, and we had to cut our stay short since Frank's cancer was advancing, and he wanted to go home to the island."

"I'm sorry, Lisa."

"There's nothing to be sorry about, Marissa. To be honest with you, it's easier for me to talk about Frank now, since the media disclosed their findings regarding his health. I loathed all the crap printed and found it revolting that they tried to assassinate his character and mine. But I've learned to put it behind me and keep a lower profile."

"I'd like to say one thing, Lisa," Howard voiced, "I knew Frank for a long time; personally and professionally, and I don't need to hear or read anyone's version of his illness and death. I am just thankful God gave him you, to ease his departure from this world. I'm not at all diminishing your love for each other, Lisa. I might be presumptuous saying you made his suffering bearable, and the inevitable tolerable for him, but I hope Marissa and I will have as strong a support system in our marriage."

"I just wish I could go on the honeymoon too," Josh interjected seizing an opportunity to be heard.

"We explained Josh," Howard replied, "the first honeymoon is just for your mom and I, and you'll have a great time staying with Uncle Yale. You get to go on the second honeymoon, to Disney World, during your Christmas break from school. Remember?"

"Well, I don't know why I can't have two honeymoons, too, like you and mom. I never been to Monte Carlo either. And you heard Lisa. She says it's beautiful. Right, Lisa?"

"Yes, but there's not stuff kids like to do there. I'm sure you'll like Disney World much more. It's the best! I've been there six times, and can't wait to go again."

"Six times? Wow! It must be really neat. I invited Uncle Yale to come with us, after mom and Howard said I could. Maybe, you could come too. Mom, is it okay?"

"It's up to Lisa, honey. Of course we'd love her to join us, if she's free."

"Will you come, Lisa? Please. I could call Uncle Yale, right now, and tell him we'll all be going together and—"

"I don't think I'll be able to, Josh," Lisa quickly interjected. "I may be spending the Christmas vacation period with my boys."

"Well, why don't you just ask them if they want to come to Disney World, too?"

"Josh, it's getting late," Marissa attempted. "I think it's way past your bedtime."

"But I didn't get to see Lisa's pictures yet, mom. Just a few more minutes, okay?"

Lisa exchanged a look of warm understanding with Marissa adding, "Okay, Josh. If you'll get my purse, I'll show you the pictures, real fast, before you go to bed. I have to leave soon, too. I have an appointment very early tomorrow morning."

Marissa poured more coffee for them while Lisa opened her Chanel handbag, removing her wallet and two small gift-wrapped boxes. "Here Josh, this is for you. I almost forgot. And this is for both of you, Marissa, Howard. An engagement gift; with my love and best wishes."

Marissa opened the package, gasping in astonishment. Inside were "his" and "hers" matching Rolex watches. On the back of each, Lisa had the words—may love be timeless—engraved. Marissa and Howard kissed her warmly, then wrapped the watches around each others wrist. Lisa's moment of envy was broken by Josh's squeal of delight, as he finally managed to open his case, and extract a gold and onyx watch in the shape of a spaceship. Lisa helped Josh fasten the leather wristband, smiling at his delight. He asked, "Could you be my Aunt, Lisa, 'cause I love you?"

"Well, I could be a special friend, Josh. You're probably going to have many new Aunts and Uncles when Howard and your mom get married, aren't you?"

"No. I'm not. Howard doesn't got a family, just like my mom. Right Howard?"

"Right. I'm an only child, and everyone else is gone. But now I'm getting a new family—you and mom—and, hopefully, another addition in a year or two." He smiled tenderly at Marissa.

"I think, 'Aunt Lisa', sounds really nice, if you'd like the title, Lisa."

"Thank you, Marissa. I like the way it sounds too. Well, Josh, you just got yourself a new Auntie. Can we seal it with a hug and kiss?"

Josh climbed on her lap obliging, then ran up the stairs, forgetting about the pictures he had asked to see. Lisa put the wallet back in her purse and picked up her cup of coffee.

"I'm crazy about your kid, Marissa. He's enough to make me sorry I can't have more children."

"He's wild about you too, Lisa. He doesn't trust easily, especially since Tony kidnapped him. But he took to you from the start. I'm so glad you came tonight."

"Me too. Thanks for not giving up on me."

Josh came back into the room, minutes later, surprising them all.

"I thought you went to bed, young man. Come on, it's time to say goodnight. I'll tuck you in."

"In two more minutes, mom. I promise. I just want to see Aunt Lisa's pictures, and then I will. I gotta. Please?"

"Oh, Mom, it'll just take a minute to show Josh my pictures," Lisa teased, winking at Josh.

"Lisa, you are as bad as he is—maybe worse. Go ahead. Spoil him some more. I give up." Marissa threw her hands up dramatically, all the while grinning at the mischievousness of both of them.

Lisa showed Josh the most recent photos of Marc and Steve, answering several questions. She pointed to a photograph of herself and Frank, and asked Josh if he remembered Frank.

"Sure, I remember him. He had the neat airplane, and brought me back to Mommy. Why do you still have his picture in your wallet if he's in heaven?"

"I guess, because sometimes I want to look at his face, and remember all the fun we had together."

She flipped the plastic over to show Josh the snapshots of Matey, trying to skip a few photos, but he was quick to notice. "You missed some." He turned back the inserts she had attempted to pass, and said, "There's Uncle Yale and Aunt Ruth, Lisa. You almost forgot to show me those."

"Sorry. Now I want you to see Matey." She flipped to the next set of pictures. "Isn't she cute? She's already trained, and she loves to eat American cheese best of all. When I first got her, she slept a lot. Now, I can't get her to sleep unless I let her sleep on my bed with me."

"Does she do any tricks yet? Buster does lot's of stuff, remember?"

"She's just a puppy, but I taught her to sit when I say so. And only one other thing so far."

"What?"

"When I say—"Ahoy Matey"—she knows it's okay to jump on my lap."

Josh giggled, then asked, "When can I see her, Lisa? Can I come over?"

"Josh!" Marissa scoldingly cut in, "You wait until you're invited to someone's house. I've told you that before. You don't invite yourself over."

"I forgot, mom."

"Well, I'm inviting you now—all three of you. Will you come for a barbecue on Sunday? And Josh, you can bring Buster too, if you want. How about it?"

"Can we Mom? Huh? Please."

"Sure. That would be great. Now, kiss 'Auntie Lisa' goodnight, and head for the stairs. No more excuses, fella."

"But I'll miss the surprise, mom."

"What surprise? There are no more surprises tonight, Josh. Come on. Stop stalling."

"There is so a surprise, mom. I'm not stalling."

"Well, what is it, Josh?"

"I can't tell. It's a secret surprise and I promised Uncle Yale I wouldn't tell."

"What are you talking about, Josh? When did you talk to Uncle Yale?"

"When I was upstairs before. I called him up."

Before anything else could be said, the doorbell chimed. Josh said turning toward Lisa, "That's the secret surprise, I bet." He ran to the door followed by the housekeeper.

Lisa stood up, grabbing her purse, suddenly filled with anxiety and frenzy. "I have to go now. I'll see you Sunday. Marissa, Howard, thanks for dinner. Would you mind walking me to my car, Howard?"

"That won't be necessary Howard," she heard from behind her. "I'll walk Lisa to her car. I haven't seen the lady in a long time, and would like to have a few words with her."

She turned facing Yale for the first time in more than three months, replying boldly, "The lady asked Howard to walk her to the car, Yale.

And this lady doesn't care to have words with you, now, or in the future. Josh, one thing you should know about Aunt Lisa—she doesn't like surprises, honey."

She kissed Josh, then quickly walked past Yale. Without another word, she rushed to her car and drove off.

CHAPTER 29

Lisa's heart was racing as she sped away. She was so upset at having been caught off guard by Yale's arrival; she drove through two yellow lights, and accelerated while one traffic light was still red. Her breathing was labored, and she was afraid of bringing on a panic attack like those she suffered from years ago. Her palms were sweaty, her mouth dry. She needed to calm herself or she'd hyperventilate. She pulled the Mercedes into the next gas station, sensing she was losing control, and screeched to a halt, nearly running down an attendant.

"What, the fuck, is your problem, lady?" he shouted, "You could have killed me!"

"Oh, God. Sorry;" was all she managed to mutter when the young man realized she was in deep shit.

"You sick, lady? You don't look any better than I feel after the scare you just put into me. I'll call 911."

"No...No...Please." She leaned her head back on the headrest, breathing hard, "Water—could I have some water—"

"Sure, lady. Sit tight. I'll be back in a flash."

He returned with a paper cup of water in one hand, and a can of soda in the other. She gulped down the small amount of water saved from spilling in his rush to get back to her. He handed her the soda and watched her take a few swallows. "It's not diet soda, lady. You're not a diabetic, or nothing, are you?"

She was calming. "No. This is fine. Thanks."

"You sure I shouldn't call for help, lady?"

"Yes, I'm sure. I'm sorry, young man. Are you alright?"

"Yeh-yeh. Don't worry about me. You want me to call someone

for you? You shouldn't be driving any more tonight. Not the way you are."

"I'll be fine. Really. I'll just put some cold water on my face, and stand in the fresh air for a few minutes, if it's okay."

"Sure. No problem. Listen, lady, I'll be closing up in fifteen minutes, so if you'd like, I could tail you home? I'd feel better, if you understand where I'm coming from."

"Okay. Thanks. Do you own this place?"

"Name's Jack. And yup, this place is mine. Only eight grand left to pay on the franchise this year, then I can sock some bucks away for tuition. Going into computer programming."

She got out of the car and went to the rest room. Jack watched her and knew from experience she wasn't drunk or stoned. She walked around until he locked up. After reassuring him she was much better, she allowed him to follow her home. As she pulled her car in front of the electronic gate, once again she had to slam on the brakes. There, in front of her, was Yale, standing next to his black Jaguar, with one hand on the hood, his other hand on his hip.

Jack, who had stayed close behind her, all the way to the house, jumped out of his car and ran up to hers, "Shit, lady. I almost smashed up your car. You better put this baby in the garage."

"Sorry, Jack. I didn't expect to have someone in front of my gates when I pulled up."

Yale was walking toward her car, when it dawned on Jack who she was, and who he was. "I know you. Darn, you looked familiar, but I couldn't place it. I'm a real schmuck."

"Is there a problem, Lisa?" Yale asked, reaching them.

"Yes, there's a problem. You don't belong here. Please leave."

"Not until I say what I have to say."

"Well, miss," Jack said, feeling this was the time for him to split, "I'll be going now. I hope you feel better. Don't do any more driving tonight, okay?"

"Is she sick?" Yale asked, directing the question to Jack.

"She was, sir. She—"

"Never mind, Jack. You don't have to explain."

"Well, uh, okay. I'll be on my way then." He turned, not wanting to get in the middle of anything, when Lisa stopped him from leaving.

"Wait a minute Jack. Come back a minute. Please."

She opened her purse, removing her checkbook as he sAuntered back.

"What's your last name, Jack?"

"Daniel, miss. Like the drink."

She wrote out a check for eight thousand dollars and handed it to him. "Here, Jack. Thank you for helping me out. I'm sorry I scared the crap out of you. I'm very grateful for your assistance."

"Shit! I can't take this lady. I did what anyone else would have done. I'm just glad you didn't pass out before you hit your brakes at the station."

"Take it, Jack, along with my appreciation. Please. Otherwise, I'll have to back up and follow you home, driving again, in this condition, until you do."

"Okay. Okay. You win. I'll take the check if you swear you ain't gonna drive anymore tonight. Deal?"

"A deal." He thanked her profusely, left, and slid into his car, when the massive iron gates to her estate parted. She floored the Mercedes, pulling onto the road that lead to her front doors.

Yale managed to get inside the gates before they closed, and Jack pulled away before he would become further involved. "She's fucking crazy," Jack muttered to himself, driving off.

Yale ran toward Lisa's Mercedes hoping to reach her before she entered her house. He yelled out to her, panting, as she was placing her key in the lock, "I'm not leaving, Lisa, until you hear me out."

"Go away, Yale. I have nothing to say to you, and I'm not interested in anything you have to say."

"Lisa, please. Just listen to me. Let me apologize for all the lousy things I've said and done. I didn't know what you had gone through or that Frank was sick—"

She cut in angrily, her fists held high, her breathing quickening again, as she fought to ward off an anxiety attack, "Go to hell, you fool! I don't want your apologies. You don't know what the word 'trust' means. You don't know what real love is! You're so damn self-absorbed;

you only know what you go through! Get out of here, Yale…You make me sick…you've already put me back into therapy… Get out of here… Get out! Or I'll call the police!"

She was fumbling with the doorknob, feeling faint, aware Belle must have gone to her quarters already, when Yale moved closer, shouting back, "Who are you to talk about trust? I trusted you'd be coming back to me, and you went and married someone else, without a word—a phone call—a letter! And if you're in therapy, it's not because of me—it's because you have issues of your own to resolve. Don't try and blame me for your problems."

"Blame? I'm not blaming you—you asshole—I'm blaming myself for being so stupid as to let myself fall in love with a righteous, self-centered egomaniac! You were right about one thing, Yale. I was a whore. Because only a whore lets herself be used and abused! But you're even worse than a whore—because you'll fuck, just to satisfy your own lustful needs! You low life!" She turned, getting the key to unlock the door.

Her legs were giving out as she attempted to turn the knob. "Get out—" she managed to yell at him before collapsing in the doorway.

He rushed to her. Her face was soaked with perspiration. He was on his knees, brushing the hair off her forehead and trying to feel for a pulse, screaming, "Help! Is anybody here?" when she came to. "Lisa, what's wrong? Where's your phone? I'll call an ambulance."

She cupped her hands over her nose and mouth, and concentrated on regulating her breathing before trying to speak. Yale was getting up to find a phone and call for help, when a voice behind him scared the shit out of him.

"What's goin' on here? Miss Lisa, don't move!" Belle was standing in a robe, with red tattered slippers on the wrong feet, and a golf club in her hands, raised and aimed at Yale. "Put your hands up over your head, mister, and lean against the wall, or I'll clobber you right now, until you lay flat on this floor!"

The look on Belle's face and Yale obeying Belle's orders evoked a small chuckle from Lisa. "It's okay, Belle. I fell. I know him. Put the golf club down."

Yale put his hands down, feeling foolish, and stammered, "I'm Yale Frye. A friend of Lisa's."

"Then help your friend up from the floor, and Ill pour you both a cup of coffee. You been boozing tonight, Miss Lisa? You said, you don't touch the stuff."

"No, I haven't been drinking, Belle, and Mr. Frye doesn't want a cup of coffee. He's leaving."

"Actually, Belle, I'd love a quick cup of coffee or cold drink. You scared the hell out of me, appearing out of nowhere, and Lisa passing out in the hallway."

"Passing out? I thought you said you fell, Miss Lisa. Now that I think on it, you do look a bit peaked. Mr. Frye, I think you better help her to a sofa, and keep an eye on her, while I get those drinks. We best make sure she's okay, before you go."

Belle watched as Lisa ignored Yale's outstretched hand and stood up on her own, brushing hair off her forehead, and rubbing the back of her head with her hand. "Follow me, Mr. Frye," Belle directed, taking Lisa by the arm, and slowly guiding her to the sofa in the library. "I'll get some ice for your head, Miss Lisa. Just stay put for a minute. Mr. Frye, how do you like your coffee?"

"Black is fine. Thanks."

"Mr. Frye is leaving, Belle."

"He sure is, Miss Lisa. Right after he calms his nerves." Belle exchanged a glance with Yale, as she left the room, before Lisa could say another word.

"Yale, I would like you to go. You and I have passed the point of no return. We can't go back and change what's transpired, and I don't have it in me to forgive you. I know I made a lot of mistakes. My judgment wasn't always good, but I never hurt you intentionally. I never put you down the way you did me, and I never made you feel cheap and dirty, the way you did me. I can't love you anymore, Yale, and I need to distance myself from you to get over another dream that's been destroyed."

"What about what I've endured, Lisa? Can you, for one minute, consider why I acted as I did? I love you, Lisa. I have for so long, I couldn't stand the thought that you didn't love me as much as I did you. We belong together, Lisa. You're just fooling yourself if you think otherwise. Give me a chance to show you how I feel. The dream can still come true for both of us, Lisa. Don't shut the door. Please. I know you still have feelings for me or you wouldn't have reacted the way you did tonight. Let's build that new house Lisa, from scratch, one brick at a time."

"We can't, Yale. There are too many old bricks we can't toss out."

"Can't we build over them until they're buried and don't matter?"

"No, Yale. I can't. Those old bricks will still be there. Burying them doesn't make them disappear. I can't forgive you, Yale. It's over for us. We're different people than we once were, and truthfully Yale, I don't like who you've become."

Belle reentered the library carrying a tray, with a carafe of coffee, two mugs, and a platter of pastries. Lisa snapped angrily as she was placing the tray down. "Belle, Mr. Frye is leaving now! This is not a social call! Pick up the tray and take it back to the kitchen. Now! If you still want to be working here in the morning, I suggest you get me an ice pack and run me a bath instead of playing hostess!"

Belle never heard Lisa talk to her this way before, and decided not to respond to the outburst. She picked up the tray, without looking at either of them, retreating to the kitchen.

"That was pretty rude, Lisa. Maybe we both have changed. I'll go, Lisa. I'll call in a day or two. Maybe, during the next day or so, you'll think about what we once shared, and feel differently about wanting to see me again."

"Don't hold your breath, Yale."

"It's my breath, Lisa."

"You're wasting your time, Yale. I might as well be up front about this. It hasn't been announced yet, but Harvey Stone and I are getting married. Only a few people know, and for now, I'd like to keep it that way. So, please, don't call me, Yale. At least, this time, you heard plans directly from me, instead of reading it in a paper."

"I don't believe you, Lisa. My mother would have told me—" His shock was evident.

"She doesn't know. Only my immediate family has been told."

"I thought Harvey was involved with someone else—"

"That ended. We feel we'll be good for each other—"

"You don't love him—"

"Yes, I do. More than I knew. Look in here," she said, walking over to a closet, and opening the door. "These are gifts already arriving from some people who know—"

He stared at the gift wrapped boxes on the floor of the closet, then at her. "Good-bye, Lisa. I can find the way out if you'll just open the gates. Thanks for telling me yourself. I guess I deserved to lose you after the way I treated you. I hope you'll be happy, Lisa. I mean it. I'm sorry it's not me you'll be marrying, but I've changed enough to know we get what we deserve, and we have to deserve in order to receive."

He looked at her for a long moment, feeling the impact of loss. He walked out of the room without turning around again, and passed Belle who was carrying an ice bag on his way out.

Only Belle saw the anguish on his face before he left. He walked to his car and drove home.

Agony was etched on Lisa's face, as well, when Belle handed her, the ice bag. Belle didn't respond when Lisa looked at her from the sofa, still holding the remote control, that activated the iron gates surrounding the estate, and apologized for her attack. "Did you hear me, Belle? I said I'm sorry for jumping on you like that."

"I heard you, Miss Lisa," Belle said, still hurt for the verbal rebuking.

"Go back to sleep, Belle. Forget the bath."

"Alright, Miss Lisa. Your messages are on the counter. You know where I'll be if you needs me."

"Anything important?"

"Just one message from Dr. Stone. He left his number, in London, for you. He said, he and his bride, Michelle, had a wonderful honeymoon in Paris, and are looking forward to the reception you're having for them, next week, on the island."

"Thanks, Belle. I'll call him tomorrow. I don't feel like talking to anyone right now. I just buried another loved one. And myself with this one."

"Seems, Miss Lisa, the last one was terminal and his passing was a relief from suffering. It was probably a blessing for him. With this one,

I got the feeling no one is going to be resting in peace, and the suffering ain't terminated."

"They say time heals all wounds, Belle."

"Them, who says that, are fools, Miss Lisa. Time heals nothin'. It gives you hours and hours to ask yourself—what if—that's all."

Lisa got up from the sofa, uncomfortable with the truth of Belle's words. "I'm going to bed, Belle. Remind me to have these gifts in the closet, for Harvey and Michelle, sent out tomorrow, will you? And I was going to have a barbecue here on Sunday that I'll need to cancel. I'll be going to visit my folks instead."

"Okay, Miss Lisa. See you in the morning. Have a good night."

"Belle, I really feel badly about how nasty I was."

"I know, Miss Lisa. I feel badly about it, too. Maybe, time will heal it."

"Maybe, forgiveness would work, Belle?"

"It takes a big person to be forgiving, doesn't it, Miss Lisa?"

"Yes it does, Belle."

"I'm a big enough person, Miss Lisa. I wish you was. G'night."

"There are some things which are unforgivable, Belle."

"What fool said that, Miss Lisa? Probably, the same fool who believes time heals all wounds."

Chapter 30

Marissa wasn't surprised when Lisa canceled their plans for Sunday, but she was upset that Lisa had her housekeeper call, rather than calling herself. Belle diligently followed all of Lisa's orders, prior to Lisa's departure for the island, after viewing Lisa's face early in the morning. It was obvious Lisa had slept very little, and had been crying. Belle was concerned when she observed Lisa's hands trembling, and found the screenplay her employer had been working on, for weeks, shredded and lying in the trash.

Lisa arrived on the island in the early afternoon. It was the first time she had entered the home that she and Frank shared since his death. Previously, she had always arranged to meet her parents at the condo they still owned on the mainland. This time she decided to visit them on the island, and had prearranged a reception for Harvey and his bride, as the first celebration at the place that held special memories for both her and Harvey. The only variance was she was arriving days earlier than originally scheduled.

Her parents greeted her affectionately, as always, but her father knew instinctively his daughter was in a state of emotional upheaval. Her calm demeanor didn't fool him. "Want to walk around the grounds a little, Lisa? It's more than a year since you've been here."

"Maybe later, Pa. I'll just pour myself a cup of coffee now. Is it alright if I take the room that was mine and Frank's, or are you using it?"

"I'm not using it, Lisa. Ma and I use a room closer to the kitchen, so it's easier to grab a nosh when we feel like it. You sure you want that room, Lisa? It gets the sun early in the morning."

"I like the sun, Pa."

"Then why don't you have any color, Lisa? Her mother interjected. "I hear the weather has been beautiful in California recently."

"I've been busy. Maybe, I'll get some color while I'm here, Ma."

"It wouldn't hurt. You're pale. Did you lose more weight, too?"

"No Ma," she lied, "this outfit is slenderizing, that's all."

"It looks two sizes too big to me, Lisa. Go sit down at the table. I made a noodle kugel this morning. It's good. You'll have a piece with the coffee, okay?"

"Okay Ma. Thanks. I'll be right there. I want to wash up."

Her folks watched as she automatically headed for the hallway, which led to her former bedroom and bathroom silently, exchanging concerned glances with one another. When Lisa didn't return, her father went to fetch her. He found her standing on the balcony she and Frank had always had their morning breakfast on, with tears streaming down her cheeks. He put a hand on her shoulder gently. "You know, Lisa, you have to let go of yesterday to enjoy today. I think you should choose another room, honey."

"I don't have much that I care about today, Pa. Sometimes it's my yesterdays that make my today's bearable. I want to stay in this room, Pa."

"Fine. It won't be the same, Lisa. Frank has been dead for some time. The bed will be cold."

"I'm used to a cold bed, Pa."

"That's too bad, Lisa. But only you can change that. Perhaps, if you opened your warm heart a little more, the warm bed would follow."

"I tried before, Pa. Where did it get me?"

"Oh, so now we stop trying, huh? Lisa, you forgot how to forgive people for mistakes they make. Didn't you make some mistakes too?"

"What are you referring to, Pa? Frank?"

"No. No. Yale, I'm referring to. You said, you never loved a man more, yet you're here because you're running away from him, aren't you? I called Belle earlier. She mentioned you had an argumentative night with her and with Yale last night. True?"

"I had a bad night, that's all. I don't want to talk about it, Pa. Let's go have some of Ma's kugel, okay?"

"Are you going to shut everyone out, Lisa? Even me?"

"I'm not shutting you out. I wish you could help; that you had some answers. But you don't. No one does."

"You're wrong, Lisa. I have answers, and so do a lot of people who love you. The problem is, you don't want to listen. You'd rather run away. Too bad. You used to have so much spunk. It was a quality I admired in you. I thought you got it from me. I'll meet you in the dining room, Lisa. I like my kugel warm."

"Pa, I told you how Yale treated me when he was in the clinic. Do you honestly think he deserves to be forgiven?"

"You married Frank when Yale was waiting for you to come back to him, didn't you? Funny, he didn't ask himself if you deserved to be forgiven. He just loved you enough to forgive you..."

"Sure. Sure he did. After treating me like shit. After abusing me, than he, all of a sudden, sees the light of day."

"Well, Lisa, at least he finally saw the light. When will you?"

He left her standing on the terrace and walked to the door. "You know Lisa, if I thought, for one minute, that you didn't love Yale anymore, I'd keep my mouth shut. The trouble is, I know you're still in love with him. Go ahead; tell me I'm wrong."

She was silent. "I thought so," he said, leaving the room.

Lisa's attempts at being affable the remainder of the day didn't fool either of her parents. They were too perceptive, and knew her too well, not to be aware how tormented she was, and what a difficult time in her life this was. Her mother avoided prying, although she was curious if Lisa had been on any dates recently. Lisa volunteered very little, and feigned drowsiness before the eleven o'clock news was over, escaping to the solitude of her bedroom.

No mention was made the following morning about Lisa's screams during the night, although Lisa was certain her outcries must have been heard. By afternoon Lisa felt testy and was sorry she had come to the island sooner than originally scheduled. Every room brought back vivid memories. By nightfall she was so angry that Frank was dead, she moved her belongings to another bedroom in the mansion. Her parents noticed, but said nothing.

When Lisa had another nightmare, that night, Harry didn't stop

Rose from running to her as he did the previous night. Instead, he followed close behind and waited by the door as Rose went in to comfort their daughter.

"I'm okay, Ma. Go back to bed. I think it's harder for me to be in this house than I thought it would be."

"How about some tea, Lisa? Should I bring you a cup?"

"No Ma. I don't want any tea. Sorry I woke you. Go back to sleep. Please."

"I don't think it's the house that's giving you nightmares, Lisa. I think it's loneliness and fear."

"Well, maybe tomorrow I'll go stay at your condo and do some shopping in Boca. If I sleep better at the condo, then we'll both know for sure. Right?"

"You already know, and so do I. I'm not stupid. I used to have bad dreams, after the concentration camp, for years. They didn't stop until I had a new life, with new hopes."

"Were all your nightmares about the war, Ma?"

"No. A lot of them had nothing to do with the Holocaust. Some had to do with my childhood. Some dreams were about ruined dresses, or toys I never got. Silly, huh?"

"Ma, I just dreamt about the baby I lost so many years ago, when I was married to Ronnie. I dreamt I had a child calling out for help, and I couldn't find him."

"I understand. Bad dreams are a sign of not being fulfilled, I think. Turn on the radio, Lisa. It always helped you to relax when you listened to music. Since you were little. I'll go bring in some hot tea. It'll help. You'll see."

By the time Rose returned Lisa was asleep. The light was still on, and so was the radio. Rose put the teacup on the nightstand, kissed Lisa gently on the cheek, and tucked the coverlet around her. She turned the lamp off on her way out, but left the radio, with Yale Frye's voice singing—"Love is What Life is All About"—on.

With all the details for Harvey and Michelle's the reception completed, Lisa reiterated her desire to go to her parent's condominium the following morning. She couldn't tolerate the concerned expressions both her mother and dad exhibited. She wanted her father's brow to unfurl, and her mom to stop doting on her, but knew she wouldn't. By evening her composure was unraveling, and she felt totally useless and bored. Her parents didn't merit the nefarious comments she responded with, and her irrestrainable temper was getting to them. She packed a suitcase and said, with some agitation, "Look, I'm out of here. I need to be alone. Forget the condo. I'm going elsewhere. I'll be back in a few days, and we'll start over. I'm not good company right now."

"So, go to the condo and we won't go with you, like we wanted to, if that's what will make you happy. Your father and I just want to help, and keep an eye on you. To be close to you."

"I know, Ma. I'm sorry. I just need some time alone."

"What for, Lisa? Her father asked sarcastically. "You said, you threw out the screenplay you've been working on, for all these months, and Jean is having someone else do it. Before, you needed to be alone because you were writing. What do you need to be alone, now, for? You're not doing anything. Nothing."

"To clear my head, Pa. I need space to devise a course of action to follow."

"Go. Go then. Maybe, you'll think of something, that if you start it, you'll also finish it." Her father picked up the remote control and turned the TV on.

"Maybe, I'll just shop. I'll buy whatever I please! How does that suit you?"

"Big shot!" her mother yelled at her. Ornaments won't make you any happier, Lisa. What's missing from you life, Lisa, you can't buy—it's not purchasable."

"I know, Ma. Don't preach, okay? Just tell me to have fun and drop it."

Her mother didn't reply, instead left the room. Her father got off his recliner and followed her to the front door. "I don't understand you, Lisa. Maybe, you need seclusion to see how lonely it is. Go. I hope you come back in a better mood."

"I'll try," she said, kissing her father's cheek before getting in the limo.

She shopped for several hours on La Salles Boulevard, before checking into a suite, on the top floor of the new Palm Gardens Hotel.

She put out the—Do Not Disturb—sign, and removed the phone from its cradle, after calling her parents to apologize and advise them of her whereabouts. With her father's heart condition, she always made sure they knew where she was.

She ran the tub, consumed a glass of white wine from the stocked bar, and soaked until the water was no longer warm enough to be relaxing. She poured herself a second glass of wine, turned on the television, and decided to forgo eating as she climbed beneath the sheets of the bed. She had consumed four glasses of Zinfandel when she heard the entertainment broadcaster on the television announcing—"**Yale Frye opens his concert tour tonight at the Sunrise Theatre, in Fort Lauderdale. Mr. Frye will be at the Sunrise Theatre through Sunday. Yale Frye's premier concert is sold out for tonight, but some seats are still available for other performances. For more information, call Ticket Master or the Sunrise Theatre, during regular business hours.**"

Lisa turned off the television, poured herself yet another glass of wine, and impulsively called the concierge, ordering a limo for the evening. She put on the short, black satin, strapless dress she'd purchased earlier in the day, black fishnet stockings, and black sequined pumps. Forty minutes later she was swaying through the lobby, toward waiting limo, wearing much too much make up. Lisa looked more like a vamp than a lady, in the skin-tight dress and flaming red wig. She didn't even notice people staring as she told the chauffeur, "Sunrise Theatre, please."

The driver looked in his rearview mirror several times as he drove Lisa to the Sunrise Theatre, and noticed, his already sloshed passenger, drinking wine out of a bottle she had removed from the liquor compartment of the vehicle.

She didn't speak until they pulled in front of the theatre, when she slurred, "Wait here. I won't be long. I just have to take a leak." She laughed at her words, then steadied herself with the driver's assistance, as he helped her from the limo. "You know, kid, you're too cute to be a chauffeur. You should be in movies."

"Thanks, Miss," he answered courteously. "Are you alright?"

"Never better, kid. But I really have to pee. Escort me in, will ya?"

"Sure, miss. You can hold onto my arm, if you want."

"Great. Come on, before I have an accident, out here, on the sidewalk."

They approached the main doors and a young usher asked for her tickets. She laughed, replying, "I'm not here to see some asshole sing. I need a toilet." She pulled some bills out of her purse. "Here's two hundred bucks. Now point me in the right direction."

The usher, who only earned minimum wage, took the two hundred, adding, "You've got ten minutes lady, and you have to go in alone. Go down to the double doors, and the ladies room is on the right, just inside those doors. If you're not back here in ten minutes, I'll come and get you."

She laughed, walking past the usher, muttering, "And if you come get me, I'll report you took two hundred bucks, and my driver is my witness, creep."

She disappeared behind the double doors, and was still laughing mockingly, when she went into the ladies room.

The music, in the theatre, was piped into the ladies room. Lisa stayed in the stall listening, even after she was finished using the commode. Yale sounded great. He still had the magic. His voice was strong and sharp. And just as sharp was the pain in her heart while listening to him sing. She felt sick. She stumbled out of the stall and sat down on a velvet chair in the lounge. She put her head between her legs. The attendant asked if she was all right, just as the usher who had given her ten minutes to use the bathroom opened the door.

"Your time is up, lady—" he began, when he realized she really appeared ill. "Alice," he addressed the attendant, "get her a cold cloth, and let me know when she's ready to be escorted back to her car, will you?" He winked at Alice, shut the door and went back to his station. Alice turned to fetch a cold compress, for Lisa's neck, when Lisa rose from the multi colored floral upholstered chair and walked away. She was still nauseated, but managed to make her way into the darkened theatre. The only light was a spotlight on Yale, who was singing his closing number. He was dressed in a black tuxedo, standing center stage, and holding the mike in both hands. Lisa was familiar with the ballad Yale was performing. It had been one of his big hits, and a personal favorite of hers. She walked down the center aisle, very drunk, and started singing the song loudly and off key. People were looking at her, shushing her, but she ignored them, singing even louder, as she walked toward the stage. Two ushers approached her, in hopes of escorting her out, while Yale continued the number, trying to remain professional and unruffled.

As one of the ushers placed his hand on her arm, she shoved his arm away, yelling out, "Get your hand off me, putz. I want to sing!'

Yale recognized Lisa's voice and stopped singing; shouting, "It's alright. Escort the lady on the stage, please. If I have an ardent fan, this insistent on singing, I think, she deserves the opportunity."

The audience applauded his professionalism, laughed with him as he assisted the obviously inebriated woman over to his piano bench, and began the number again, sitting down next to her. Lisa sang the first chorus, oblivious to everybody, then got up and stumbled behind the curtains, passing out in David Ross' arms.

Yale completed the number to thunderous applause, receiving several standing ovations. He didn't return for the encore, as was scheduled, but walked alongside his personal assistant, as David Ross carried Lisa into the dressing room and locked the door.

Lisa was still out cold when David returned with the information he'd gathered, and the details regarding her stupored arrival at the theatre. And Lisa was still out cold when Yale carried her through a private entrance; into the suite she had reserved, at the Palm Gardens Hotel, and put her to bed.

Chapter 31

Listen, David, cancel this morning's rehearsal. Lisa is still out, and I don't want to wake or leave her. Were we able to keep this incident quiet?"

"It's been kept under wraps as far as Lisa's identity. I'm sure the cash helped keep the limo driver from talking. I don't think he even knew who his passenger was, but the money was good insurance to shut his mouth, from disclosing where he picked up his client, or dropped the two of you off. Lucky for us, he is an independent, who owns his own limo, and is accustomed to similar incidents. He has no 'higher ups' to report to. But the papers did include a line about "an unnamed fan disrupting Yale Frye's opening appearance," at the Sunrise Theatre."

"Shit. What else did they print, David?"

"Don't worry. It worked for us, not against us. They added how well Yale Frye handled the disruption, and what a pleasure it was to have a star of his caliber back on stage. That's all."

"Terrific. Just what I wanted. More help, even if unintentional, from Lisa. I'll call you later, David. I think I hear moaning coming from the bedroom."

"Did you get any sleep, Yale?"

"I dozed, on and off, in a chair. I'm fine. I'll get back to you, David. I think she's up. I want to find out what the hell this was all about. Lisa never drank before. I'm willing to bet this will be her first hangover. I want to make sure it's her last, too. I wonder where Harvey is. I think he should be informed about the condition his fiancé' was in last night, don't you?"

"Maybe, you should give it up, Yale. People change."

"I'll be in touch. The show was good, wasn't it?"

"Yes, Yale. The show was great. You've still got it."

"Thanks, David. I guess my insecurity is showing. Bye."

Yale walked to the bedroom door, peeking in, and found Lisa lying on her side, with a pillow tucked up against her, while she rocked, moaning in discomfort. "Good morning, Lisa. I hope you slept well. How about some breakfast? Why don't I order up some bacon, eggs, and pancakes? Yes. Pancakes sound good to me. How about you?"

Flashes of the previous night were penetrating. She looked up at Yale, but couldn't remember all the details. Why was he here? How did he get in? How did she get back to her room? The last thing she recollected was singing, or was she imagining it? "Go away. I'm dying," she finally uttered, still clutching the pillow; writhing on the bed.

"Go away? You ruin my opening night, make a spectacle of yourself, singing off key, yet, barely able to stand, not to mention that you didn't even have a ticket for the show, and you're telling me to go away? Where's your gratitude, Lisa, for getting you back here, and keeping an eye on you all night? I think you owe me an apology, and a "thank you" as well."

"Who asked you for help? Not me. Oh, I'm going to die. I think you better call for an ambulance. I'm sick. I'm really sick."

"Oh, now I should call for an ambulance? Am I hearing you correctly, Lisa? Are you asking for my help?"

"Oh, I'm dying. I think I have a brain tumor. My head hurts. It hurts bad. I'm not kidding. This is not a hangover. It's something awful. I'm sure of it. Call 911."

He walked to the drapes, opened them, allowing light to infiltrate the room, all the while controlling his urge to laugh at her innocence. "Come on, Lisa, it's a beautiful day. Get up. Let's have some eggs, or a cheeseburger. I'm hungry. You just had a little too much to drink. I'm sure it's not the first time. How about some strawberries and cream?"

"Go to hell" was all she managed to yell at him, as she leapt from the bed, and ran to hang her head over the toilet bowl.

His urge to sooth her was strong. His own experiences, however, had taught him that if someone had stopped him from violating himself with booze and pills, when he was out of control, he might never have had to be committed. He sat down on a chair in the bedroom and listened while Lisa puked and groaned in the bathroom. After her third call for help, he went to the bathroom door and asked casually, "Did you call me, Lisa? Do you want something?"

"Help. I'm sick, Yale. Call for help. I need a doctor."

"Who should I call, Lisa? Where's your fiancé?"

"Never mind," was her retort, as she remembered the lie she had fabricated about marrying Harvey. "Go away. I'll get my own help." She struggled back to the bed, holding her head with one hand, and her stomach with the other. "Leave already, will you? You're worthless anyway, you dumb putz!"

"Nice. Very nice, Lisa. I stay here, all night, to make sure you're okay, and this is how you thank me. Well, I'm going to order up some breakfast for myself, before I go. It's the least you can do to repay me, Lisa. Buy me breakfast, that is. I'll get extra in case you get hungry. Why don't you shower meanwhile, Lisa? You really do smell pretty raunchy."

"Go to hell, shithead!" was all Yale heard as he left the bedroom, shutting the door behind him. He called room service and was pleased when he heard the shower on minutes later.

When Lisa emerged from the bathroom in a terry robe, and her hair turban wrapped in a towel, he handed her a cup of coffee, and two aspirins, without a word. He sat down on the sofa, with half a bagel in his hand, and started leafing through the newspaper sent up with the breakfast tray.

"Anything important in the paper, Yale?"

"If you mean, did you get any publicity? The answer is no. David and I were able to keep your name out of the paper, so far."

"Thanks" she said, turning away.

"What's going on Lisa? What was last night about?"

She was quiet moments before responding. "Anger, Yale. Last night was all about anger. I'm sorry, Yale. I really feel badly. Excuse me, but I have to go back to bed, Yale."

"Wait a minute Lisa. Can we talk about this?"

She kept her back to him so he wouldn't see her tears surfacing.

"No. I don't think so. Please go, Yale. Thanks for your help, and thank David for me. I'm sorry. I'm really sorry." She rushed to the bedroom and locked the door once inside. She sat on the bed, ignoring Yale's repeated request for her to unlock the door, until he stopped calling to her. She heard a door open and close. When she thought Yale had left she slid beneath the sheets and rocked herself to sleep.

Yale, in fact, had not gone anywhere. He opened and shut the door hoping if Lisa thought he left she would come out of the bedroom. When she didn't emerge, he decided to wait it out on the sofa, until she was ready to communicate.

He had been dozing for almost an hour when the phone rang. After the third ring he picked up the receiver instinctively, "Hello," he said still groggy, "Who's this?"

"This is Dr. Stone. I think I've been connected with the wrong room..."

"Harvey? Sorry. It's Yale Frye. You have the right room. I was half asleep here on the sofa. I mean, there's nothing going on with me and Lisa, she just had a bad night and I hung around..."

"Yale, hold it. It's all right. You don't owe me any kind of explanation. If I called at an inconvenient time, I'll call back later. Or you can have Lisa call us. Michelle and I will be awake, packing, so Lisa doesn't have to worry about the hour."

"I'm a little confused, Harvey. Are you here, in Florida?"

"Not yet. I guess Lisa hasn't had the opportunity to fill you in. My wife and I were scheduled to meet Lisa on the island in a few days. Lisa insisted it was a perfect setting for our wedding reception. I called her home, and Belle, her housekeeper, stated she'd left for the island, abruptly, the other day. I proceeded by calling the island, and her father stated she was out of sorts, and gave me this hotel number."

"You're married, Harvey?"

"Yes. Michelle and I have been honeymooning. I'm surprised Lisa didn't mention it. Is she there, Yale? Is everything alright?"

"She's here, but she's asleep. She had a migraine. Can I have her call you later, Harvey? I'll tell her you called."

"Sure. Thank you."

"No problem, Harvey. Oh, congratulations on your marriage. I hope you'll be happy, and I get to meet Michelle sometime."

"Well, if you're here, we'd love to have you at the reception Lisa is having on the island. She said Michelle and I could invite as many people as we wished. My bride is a big fan of yours."

"Thank you, Harvey, but I can't commit myself. I'm tied to other engagements."

"I understand, Yale. It's been nice talking to you. I'm sorry I woke you."

"Don't be sorry, Harvey. I'm glad you did. It was time my eyes were opened anyway. Bye."

Yale put down the receiver. He sat staring at the bedroom door, deliberating over his conversation with Harvey, when Lisa opened the door. She was shocked to see him there and jumped. "I thought you left. Wasn't breakfast enough? You want lunch too?" Her voice reflected her dislike at being startled, but Yale also interpreted her reaction as annoyance that he was still there.

"I'm going, Lisa. This time for good. I'm glad I hung around though. I didn't know how much you wanted me out of your life, until just now. Funny. Inside, I kept hoping there was a chance, a flicker of hope I held onto, that you still cared." He looked at her with intensity before continuing. "Harvey called a little while ago. He'd like you to call him and Michelle back. He said not to be concerned about the time, that he, and his wife, would be up late packing." He waited, staring at her, but she said nothing. "You must really hate me, to fabricate such a story, in order to get me out of your life. God, I'm a fool. I am such a fool!"

"Yale, I…"

"Don't say a word, Lisa." He walked to the door and opened it. Without turning around, he flatly stated, "I hate you for lying to me. I hate you for destroying my illusions. But most of all, I hate myself for all the wasted time I've spent thinking about you, wanting you, loving you."

He walked through the archway, closed the door behind him, and left.

Lisa stood gazing at the door long after Yale left. She poured herself a mug of coffee. She held the cup, rolling it between her hands, then vehemently threw it at the door. "Mister Frye, I hate myself too. I hate myself for being afraid to admit how much I still love you."

She went back to bed and ignored the ringing of the phone. She didn't sleep. By dusk she understood what her father meant when he suggested seclusion might make her realize how lonely she was. She thought about Yale's words as well…he hated himself for all the wasted time…all the time he'd spent thinking, wanting, and loving her…

Lisa made three phone calls before checking out of the hotel at midnight. The first call was to her parents, asking their forgiveness for her rudeness, and advising them she had to fly to California for a couple of days. The second call was to Harvey and Michelle. She detailed the last two days for Harvey, concluding the conversation by asking him how she could start to enjoy her life again. Harvey's words were simple and honest. "Lisa, love yourself enough to feel you're entitled to pleasure. The enjoyment will follow."

The third call Lisa placed was to Marissa. She asked how Josh and Howard were, apologized for canceling their barbecue plans; then for the first time in a long time reached out. "Marissa, I need a friend. I feel alone and lonely. I'm hurting everyone who means anything to me. Can I see you tomorrow? I need to be with a friend."

Marissa's reply was simple and honest. "I need a friend, too, Lisa. I've got the prenuptial jitters. If you'll let me hold your hand, I'll let you hold mine. I'm glad you chose me to call, Lisa."

"So am I," Lisa responded before hanging up.

Lisa slept the entire flight back to California. She greeted Belle with a hug, "I can't run away from myself, Belle. Maybe, it's time for a new approach."

"Those are the smartest words I've heard you say, Miss Lisa. Welcome back, Miss Lisa."

"Take me to bed, Belle. And tuck me in, please. I need to be comforted. I'm scared. I don't know what of, for sure. I just feel afraid."

"It's okay, Miss Lisa. It's a good sign, I reckon, that you feel afraid. At least you're letting yourself feel. It's been a long time that you've been bottled up. Too long. I think everyone is frightened when they face new beginnings."

"You know what my dad said, when I said I was coming home and going to look at myself real hard before coming back? He said, "Lisa, let the war end. Even though, sometimes, it's easier to stay behind the barbed wires, since you know what you have to contend with there, cut the wires. Escape. Pa said, "there is safety without confinement," and he said, "There are pleasures to enjoy, if you accept survival as a gift of hope, not a chain of guilt."

"Your dad was speaking from experience, Miss Lisa, and you knows it. That's why the words stuck." Belle pulled the covers around her and turned the lights off. "Anything you need, before I go, Missy?"

"Strength. I need strength to cut the wires, Belle."

"You've got strength, Miss Lisa. I'm confident of it. And you've got the courage."

Belle watched from the doorway, as Lisa turned the radio on' and pulled a pillow up against her.

When Belle brought coffee to Lisa the following morning, she was grinning as she placed the tray down. Lisa was sitting, cross-legged, with Matey beside her, and giggling into the telephone receiver. She poured Lisa's coffee and overheard her saying, "Marissa, you are nuts. Wear a white dress for the wedding, if you want to. How many brides today are "Virgins in white" when they marry? Get real, Marissa. It's your wedding and your choice."

Belle didn't hear Marissa's words, but Lisa's next sentence was, "Get dressed and get your ass over here. I'll be dressed by then and we can do some serious talking. Maybe some shopping later, too, if we have time."

Lisa laughed again, hung the phone up, and smiled up at Belle before stating, "Marissa is as special as you, Belle. Thanks for the coffee."

"Your welcome, Missy. How about some eggs?"

"No thanks, Belle. Just coffee now, but will you prepare a salad for lunch? Marissa will be here in an hour. We're spending the day together. Also, I think Marissa and Josh will be barbecuing with me later tonight."

"Avocado salad for lunch okay?"

"Great, Belle."

"And what's going on the grill later—franks, burgers or steaks?"

"Steak, chicken and lots of fries, please."

Belle served lunch, and was whistling a cheery tune as she heard

Marissa and Lisa teasing each other, and poking fun at the outdated rules of etiquette, in a book Marissa had brought over with her. Lisa had eaten two full plates of salad, and four freshly baked pop-overs, which was more than Belle had seen her consume, at one meal, in months. The two spent the morning and afternoon together, and at three announced they were going to surprise Josh and pick him up from school together; then return.

When Josh entered Lisa's home for the first time, with Buster beside him, he yelled, "Wow! This place is beautiful. I like the fountain in front too. It's neat!"

"Thanks, Josh. Come on, I want you to meet Matey." Josh took Lisa's hand and walked with her to the library, where the little beagle was curled up in a corner of the sofa. It was Matey's usual waiting place for Lisa. Marissa kept the reins on Buster. It didn't take long and they were all laughing at Buster and Matey's playfulness, as they chased each other around the room.

Belle served the steaks, chicken, fries, corn on the cob, and salad, on the deck. She made a fast friend of Josh when she asked him to help her bring all the fixings for sundaes out, and praised him for the great job he was doing, when he prepared the sundaes himself.

"I've done this before, Belle. When my Uncle Yale was in a place getting better once, and I made sundaes, then, for everybody. Right Lisa?"

"You sure did, honey. I remember."

Both Belle and Marissa noticed Lisa flinch at the mention of Yale's name. And both were empathetic, when her eyes filled, as she brought the first spoon of the hot fudge sundae to her lips.

Lisa tried to brush a tear aside unobtrusively, and continue the evening with ambience, but Josh was too observant. He surprised them all when he went over to Lisa and kissed her on the cheek and said, "Aunt Lisa, I wish you wouldn't get sad when I talk about Uncle Yale. And I wish Uncle Yale wouldn't look sad when I talk about you. If you had a fight with each other, you should kiss and make up. Just like Mom and I sometimes do. Because, I know Uncle Yale loves you. I heard Aunt Ruth tell Mom so, last week, when they didn't know I was listening."

Lisa pulled Josh on her lap, and wrapped her arms around him, uttering quietly, "I was mean to your Uncle Yale a few times last week, Josh. I don't think he'll forgive me."

"Maybe he would, and maybe he wouldn't. But you should try and just say you're sorry. He might give you another chance."

"I'll think about it," Lisa responded, as she looked at Marissa, over the precious childs head.

"Out of the mouths of babes," Belle muttered, collecting some soiled plates, and sAuntered back into the house.

Lisa and Marissa bonded even more that evening, when Lisa went back to Marissa's house with her, and helped tuck a worn out Josh into bed. They sat confiding, revealing fears, desires, failures, and secret wishes, until dawn blinked on the hours of night.

They spent the entire next day together again, and since Howard was still out of town on business, they could talk about how different men's characters were from women, on several issues, without a male voice interjecting.

They took Josh to dinner with them, and after he went to sleep for the night, they sat talking again for hours. Lisa convinced Marissa to attend the reception for Michelle and Harvey, although Howard was tied up with business dealings, and couldn't accompany her. Marissa finally agreed, because Lisa promised to attend her wedding, and stop avoiding uncomfortable situations where she and Yale might appear at the same event. They agreed Josh would be Marissa's little date on the island, and Lisa's escort at her wedding.

Lisa admitted she was still in love with Yale during the course of their intimate disclosures, which didn't surprise Marissa at all. She added Yale was part of her past, adding she was going to have to accept it and move on.

Marissa eventually walked Lisa to the door, unable to stifle a yawn, at three in the morning. Lisa started to apologize for keeping her up so late when Marissa stopped her. "Lisa. I'm going to tell you another secret. This yawn is not due to the hour. You know that I'm a night owl."

"Bullshit, Marissa. I've talked your ear off. You're probably glad I'm leaving for the island tomorrow, so you'll have two days before you have to put up with me again."

"Wrong, Lisa. I'm going to call you a hundred times before Josh and I join you. I'm yawning because expectant mothers get tired easily."

"You shit! After all we've shared, now you're telling me you're pregnant. Now, when I'm walking out the door, and have so much more I want to say?"

"Sorry. I promised Howard it would be our secret. But I'm bursting with excitement, so you're the only one I'm telling. Now get out of here, and besides everything else I've asked your advice on, start thinking of girls names. I'll call you in the morning."

"How far along are you? It's a girl? Marissa, stop shoving me out the door. I need to know some stuff. Marissa. Come on..."

"Bye, Lisa. Talk to you in the morning. Get some sleep, Lisa. The godmother of my baby should be in good health too..."

"What? What? Godmother? Me? Marissa. Talk to me... Marissa..."

"Goodnight, Lisa..."

CHAPTER 32

Rose and Harry greeted a jubilant, glowing daughter at their door the following afternoon. Their skepticism eventually dissolved as they watched her gregariously welcome everyone to the island, for the reception for Harvey and Michelle. They were overjoyed with the apparent metamorphosis which restored Lisa to the frolicsome girl she used to be.

She handled her mothers grilling with good nature, and was more social than she'd been in a long time. She slept without the disturbance of nightmares, swam early each morning, and requested second helpings of food at meals. The night before the party was to take place Harvey and Michelle asked her if she was suppressing her unhappiness, of two weeks ago, for their benefit. She successfully assured them that was not the case.

"Harvey, you and I go back too far to fool each other. I have undergone a personal transformation. I've stopped agonizing and adopted a new attitude. I've suffered sufficiently for one person. I was asphyxiating myself with misery. I've decided it's time to embrace life again."

Her father, who wanted concrete evidence that his daughter was not just being obliging, picked up his cup of coffee and asked, "Does this mean you won't topple at the mention of Yale Frye's name, Lisa?"

"I won't topple, Pa. I'm still sensitive discussing Yale, Pa, but I have to confess I was as much to blame for the deterioration between us, as he was."

They were sitting in the spacious dining room of the home Lisa once shared with Frank. Her father put down his cup of coffee, inquiring, "Marissa and Josh should be arriving shortly, right?"

"Yes. Any time now." Her face lit up. "My boys too. That's all the people I've invited to stay here. Everyone else will be accommodated at the new hotel."

Frank had stipulated a hotel be erected, in his will, so others could observe the beauty of the small oasis, surrounded by water, once he was gone. It was completed and ready for this occasion.

"So, Lisa," her father continued, "how did you desensitize yourself, so well, to all which paralyzed you before? I'm amazed."

"Easy, Pa. I let the war end."

He smiled at her. Impulsively, she went and sat on his lap, putting her head on his shoulder. "The next step is going to be just as monumental, Pa. I have to create a new life; develop new goals."

"As a substitution, Lisa? Or as an act of liberation?"

"Both, Pa" she answered truthfully, rising from his lap as the doorbell chimed. She rushed to greet her other invited guests.

Lisa returned overflowing with delight. She merrily introduced Josh and Marissa to her parents, bestowed kiss after kiss on her boys, and created festivity and merriment, which enchanted and embodied them all.

Before retiring for the night, Harry approached Lisa, who was sitting on the floor playing 'jacks' with Josh, and kissed the top of her head. She looked up at her father lovingly, and noticed his eyes mist over as he stated, "It's been a long time since we've been in a house, together, where the atmosphere is "fralech," so full of joy. It does my heart good, Lisa."

"It does my heart good too, Pa."

The gala reception was beyond magnificent. Lisa looked radiant. She was a gracious hostess. Every detail had been handled with perfection. Exotic floral arrangements, and an enormous floral coated canopy of white gardenias created a warm embracing atmosphere. Dozens of white-gloved butlers, in tuxedos, served global delicacies to the hundreds of guests. The band played Reggae, since it was the music Michelle and Harvey favored. The magnificent ice sculptures were all designed to be symbolic of love, and each surrounded by mounds of exotic fresh fruits and fancy petit fours.

Josh followed Lisa everywhere to her delight. And several times during the party Marissa whispered little things in Lisa's ear, like: "I must have a "champagne pissing cupid," like this one, at my wedding," or: "Am I a pig, or what? I just downed ten chocolate covered strawberries, and want more."

Lisa giggled, since she was the only one aware of Marissa's pregnancy, and could empathize with the cravings, and frequent urinating implications Marissa was referring to jokingly.

Marissa had confided in Lisa, the morning Lisa left for the island, that she was only three months into the pregnancy, but a gut feeling, with perhaps a little bit of a personal desire, made her believe she was going to have a girl. She indicated she and Howard were ecstatic, and had decided to move the wedding date up, before she started showing. They agreed to still keep the pregnancy confidential.

Marissa and Josh stayed on after all the festivities were over. They were with Lisa when she sadly said good-bye to Marc and Steve, who had to return to the university. And they were around when Lisa fell apart, bidding farewell to the newlyweds. She hugged Harvey and Michelle, wishing them a blissful marriage, and bountiful life together.

"I'm going to miss living close enough to see you on short notice, Lisa. I hope you'll come to England for a visit soon."

"I'm going to miss you too, Harvey. But I'm glad you're going to be doing the research you've always been interested in. When Frank told me he was leaving you the castle in England, I knew someday this moment would come. You're like a brother to me, Harvey. If I know you're happy, I can accept anything, even your moving away. Just expect enormous telephone bills."

"I feel as close to you, Lisa. I hope, when you leave the island, tomorrow, you'll leave in search of the kind of life I wish for you. You've got so much love in you, Lisa. Don't waste valuable hours containing that love when it can benefit you, and those you shower it on. You had a royal straight flush once. You can have it again."

"I'm not one to gamble anymore, Harvey."

"You could be a winner again, Lisa. Or try a different game. The idea is, as long as you're in the casino of life already, you might as well try your luck. Otherwise, you'll always wonder, 'what if'.

"I'm a sore loser, Harvey."

"Then rake enough until you're hot, honey. Once you're more confident, and are willing to play the hot streak out, you'll go for it."

"Maybe, I won't hit a hot streak, Harvey."

"But maybe you will. I'd bet on you, Lisa. I wish you could believe in yourself as much."

"I love you, Harvey."

"I'm a safe bet, Lisa. That's why you can say it so easily to me. Now, take a chance on someone less safe, and tell him you love him."

They both knew he was referring to Yale. Harvey backed off then, sensing he had said enough, and gave Lisa a final kiss goodbye.

She was subdued the remainder of that day, and was glad to be going home in the morning.

On the flight home, she and Marissa concluded, Regina, was a beautiful name if Marissa had a girl. Now they had to see if Howard liked the name. Lisa had promised Marissa unconditional support, and as much time as she needed, for the next month, until the wedding took place. Marissa had directed the party planner to mail out the invitations a few days ago. She was frazzled because she still didn't know what to wear. Lisa vowed their first task would be finding the perfect wardrobe for Marissa, including the wedding dress, and new apparel for the honeymoon in Monte Carlo.

Josh fell asleep in the limo, twenty minutes from Marissa's estate. "It figures, doesn't it, Lisa. He's awake all night long, and feisty on the plane. Now he falls asleep, when we're almost home?"

Lisa laughed. "My boys were the same way when they were young. Steve was worse; He'd wait until we were, literally, one block from home before falling asleep. Then he'd get cranky as hell when he woke up, while Ronnie carried him into the house."

"Your sons are wonderful, Lisa. Their love for you is so apparent."

"They're good guys. I miss them a lot. It's been hard letting go. I miss all the commotion which surrounded us when they were growing up. Their friends coming over. The family trips and outings. You know, being a part of something solid and feeling needed."

They approached Marissa's house, entering through the gates, pulling to a halt in front of the main doors. "That's funny. Howard is home. His car is here. He's never home this early in the day."

Marissa was just about to wake Josh when Howard came out of the house, rushing to the car. Marissa opened the door. "Good. You can carry him in, honey. What are you doing home so early—did you miss me so much you couldn't wait—"

Howard cut in. "I have bad news, Marissa. I did miss you that much, but I'm home because David Ross called me at the office. Ruth had a heart attack, honey. She's in the cardiac intensive care unit of St. Joseph's Hospital. It doesn't look good. Yale is there now. David is with him."

"Oh God. Will you take Josh in? I've got to go to him."

"Want me to come with you?"

"No. Please, stay with Josh so he won't feel abandoned. Okay?"

"Marissa, I hate for you to be in a stressful atmosphere alone."

"She won't be alone," Lisa interjected, trying to remain composed. "I'm going with her. We'll call as soon as we know something. Okay?"

"Thanks, Lisa. I'll have dinner sent in when you get back. Marissa, remember, you're not supposed to overdo. Please!"

"I know, Howard. I'll be fine."

Marissa and Lisa held hands all the way to St. Joseph's Hospital, each filled with their own trepidation and anxiety. As a well-known humanitarian, and public figure, Lisa had no difficulty acquiring the assistance of officials at St. Joseph's to escort her and Marissa to the coronary intensive care unit, and to the private waiting room where Yale and David were seated.

Yale's face was ashen and unshaved. His eyes were red and swollen. He looked up at Marissa and Lisa. He didn't move from the black leather chair. He didn't speak. Marissa went to him, sitting down on a chair next to his, taking his hand. "How's she doing, Yale?"

"Not good," he said, lowering his head.

Lisa still hadn't spoken. She was rooted against the wall, just inside the door, of the small olive green cubical of a room. She didn't know what to say, or even what to do. But she felt a desperate longing to touch Yale.

Slowly she approached him, bent in front of him, and whispered, "I'm sorry you have to endure this pain, Yale. Ruth is strong. Don't give up hope."

He looked at her blankly and didn't respond. Lisa went and sat on a chair away from Yale. David went to her. "She's unconscious. The specialist is with her now."

"When did it happen, Yale?" Marissa asked.

"This morning. We were rehearsing the show in Atlanta. I wanted to change some of the material from the program we used in Florida. I got a call from Victor. He said a friend of Ma's went to pick her up, and found the newspaper outside the door, and no answer when she knocked. Apparently, the telephone had been busy for an hour before she arrived. Liz knew something had to be wrong. Ma's friend, Liz, was with her last night. It was their card night. Canasta. She said Ma was fine then. It must have been sudden. I didn't talk to her yesterday, with all the traveling and shit. Damn, I should have called her. Maybe she wasn't feeling well. Maybe she would have said something."

The door opened and a man in white garb entered, with a stethoscope around his neck, and a chart under his arm. Dr. Bruce Adams wasted no time as he approached Yale, who was already standing.

"Mr. Frye, your mother's only chance is immediate bypass surgery. The test results indicate four blocked arteries. She's stable. However, I won't lie to you. She's critical. The cardiograms and heart monitor suggest we have no time to waste."

Yale plopped back into the chair. "Go ahead, doctor. Do whatever you have to."

"There are no guarantees, Mr. Frye, this will…"

Yale stopped him. "I know. Just try. Please. Just try."

"Would you like a moment with your mother before we wheel her down to surgery?"

"No. I'll just wait here. Thanks."

"It'll be hours, Mr. Frye…"

Yale cut him off again. "Save it, doctor. I'll be right here until I hear from you."

Dr. Adams turned to leave the room. "Excuse me, Bruce," Lisa injected, knowing that he was an old friend of Franks, and had met him at many benefits previously, "I'd like to walk down with you and Ruth, if it's allowed. And if you could ask Dr. Weston to see that continual reports be brought in to Mr. Frye, I'd be grateful."

"Of course, Lisa. Follow me."

"Yale, is it okay if I walk down with Ruth?"

"On second thought, I'll go too." He got up, followed Lisa, who was right behind Dr. Adams, and walked into the ICU. They approached the bed Ruth occupied, between two hanging cloth partitions, and looked at the helpless, yet peaceful face, of the woman who always appeared invincible before. Yale stood at the foot of the bed, appalled by all the tubes and wires attached to his mother. He felt his mouth turn to parchment. Lisa approached Ruth and kissed her cheek, whispering, "Keep fighting, Ruth. I love you, Ruth."

Ruth was transferred to a gurney and then transported down to the operating rooms where Yale and Lisa had to part from her. Yale had not spoken since leaving the waiting room. Just before leaving, he touched his mother's face for a second, and choked out, "See you later, mom."

Lisa still wanted to touch him, to hold his hand, but he walked a few paces in front of her. He hurriedly entered the elevators, and then went directly back to the private waiting room. He said nothing.

True to his word, Dr. Adams sent Dr. Weston to Yale's waiting room, less than an hour later, to report Ruth was stable, and the entire necessary pre op was completed. He related surgery was about to commence. "Do you have any questions, Mr. Frye?"

"Yes. What are the odds, doctor?"

"Less then even, regretfully, Mr. Frye."

"Thanks for being honest, doctor."

"I'm always truthful, Mr. Frye. Lisa can vouch for me, How are you, Lisa?" he asked, turning his attention in her direction.

"I'm alright, Jason. I'm praying you won't have to be asked the same questions I had to ask you a year ago."

"I'll be back in a little while, Lisa. Have me paged if any of you need anything." He left the room, gently closing the door behind him. Yale looked at his watch. Marissa took his hand and kissed it. "I have to go home for a while, Yale. I'll be back later. Do you need anything?"

"No. Thanks. Go on, all of you. I need to be alone, actually. Please. David, you too. Take care of business, will you? Cancel everything."

Lisa walked out with Marissa and David, but after they were in the limo, she stated flatly, "I'm not leaving yet. Marissa, get some rest. I'll call you in an hour. David, I'll see you later."

She reentered the drab waiting room, followed by an aid carrying a few pillows and a couple of blankets. The aid put down the bedding and left. Lisa handed Yale a cup of coffee and sat down with the other cup of coffee she was holding. "The surgery usually takes several hours, Yale. Can I get you anything?"

He ignored her question, showing no surprise that she had returned, but casually inquired, "What kind of questions did you have to ask Dr. Weston a year ago?"

"How much time Frank would have had left if he hadn't died."

"What did he tell you?"

"That Frank probably wouldn't have lived another month, Yale."

"How did you handle it, Lisa?"

"I didn't. I called Frank every name in the book for killing himself, for cheating me out of the month, and most of all for not giving me the chance to say goodbye. I felt betrayed."

"You know, right now, I feel I cheated my mother out of seeing me become successful again. I needed her to see me at my best again."

"Maybe she still will, Yale."

"I'm terrified. I feel so empty already, and I don't even know what the outcome will be. It's strange."

"It's not strange, Yale. You're afraid to hope for the best, yet can't imagine handling the worst. I understand."

"Did you love Frank when you married him, Lisa?"

"Not like I love you, Yale. But I grew to love him. He protected me. I protected him. He made me feel needed, and I gave him a reason to live."

"Why would he marry you, knowing he didn't have long to live?"

"Because he didn't want to die alone. He needed to be part of a family, and feel loved, for himself, before he left this world."

"Would you have married him if he wasn't terminal, Lisa?"

"He wouldn't have married me, Yale. He was a proud man. I think he would have sent me back to you."

"Do you ever think he was selfish for marring you?"

"No. I think he was afraid, Yale. He loved me. He believed I was young and could go on to find happiness again, after he was gone. He gave me credit for being stronger than I am. He encased me like pollen between the petals of a flower. The petals stuck together. The flower never blossomed. We became what the other needed. Then he was gone."

"What will I do if my mother dies? She's the only permanent and unconditional love I've ever known."

"Don't cross bridges before you have to, Yale. It's hard enough to deal with the moment. Why don't you put your head down on a pillow for a little while?"

It wasn't what he wanted to hear. He wanted to hear she loved him unconditionally and permanently too. But she didn't. Suddenly, and furiously, he snapped at her. "Why don't you go home! If I need a pillow, I'm a big boy!"

"Okay, Yale. The pillows are here. I'm going to the cafeteria. Do you want something?"

He didn't answer.

As she rose to leave the room, the door opened. Dr. Adams entered. He walked directly up to Yale. "I'm sorry, Mr. Frye. Your mother didn't survive. She died, without regaining consciousness, a few minutes ago. We believe an aneurysm ruptured in the aorta. There was nothing more we could do. She died peacefully, Mr. Frye, and without pain. I'm very sorry."

CHAPTER 33

After the private burial services for Ruth in Boston, Yale flew back to his Bel Aire estate and remained secluded within the confines of his home. His mother had always said California was not home to her, and someday she would go home again. It was because of Yale she lived in California.

Yale put his mother to rest in the old cemetery where Ruth's parents were also buried. Only David accompanied him to Boston and back, and then was asked to leave. Victor was dismissed as well. The telephones turned off.

Yale didn't want to be comforted. He didn't want to talk about Ruth. He didn't want people around. And he didn't cry.

He hadn't shed a single tear, since Dr. Adams announced that his mother was dead. He withdrew, handling the necessary, immediate, arrangements methodically, and with total detachment. He had pushed Lisa's hands away when she ran to him, after the doctor's announcement. He walked out of the hospital hurriedly, driving to the ocean, and sitting in front of the vast expanse of water, transfixed for hours. When he returned home, hours later, and friends came over, attempting to console him, he felt suffocated, and that his privacy was being violated.

He couldn't stand the sympathetic looks on all their faces. He didn't want anyone to touch him. He didn't want anyone to kiss him. He didn't want to hear another—"I'm very sorry, Yale."

He told David and Marissa to get rid of everyone, and had gone to his room to make the final arrangements by phone. Now, alone in his home, he sat in the silence, wearing the same clothes he'd worn for the past two days.

He didn't allow himself to think. He didn't allow himself to feel. He didn't mourn. He sat. David came to the house periodically, letting himself in with the combination to the iron gates, and attempted communicating with Yale. By evening David was so concerned about Yale, he called Yale's psychiatrist for advice and help.

Doctor Ian, familiar with Yale's medical history, came to the house that night. After evaluating the situation, he suggested Yale admit himself into the hospital for a short stay. Yale refused, insisting the doctor leave. Yale reiterated, several times, he did not feel like harming himself, and merely wanted to be left alone. He told David to mind his own business.

Doctor Ian eventually left, but recommended David stay at the house, regardless of Yale's protestations, and he would return to see Yale the following morning.

Yale locked himself in his bedroom, while David sat in a chair on the other side of the door all night. In the morning, David forced open the door, then called Dr. Ian, who, again, strongly advised hospitalization after seeing Yale.

Yale was still in the clothes he'd buried Ruth in, and hadn't eaten in days. He spoke little and without animation. He threatened a lawsuit against Dr. Ian for unlawful entry and trespassing, and then calmly alleged he was an incompetent physician for suggesting Yale's behavior was self-destructive.

Dr. Ian was acquainted with the typical oppressive behavior Yale was characteristically using to get his way. He realized Yale's words stemmed from anguish, and were momentarily unauthentic. But he was uncomfortable that Yale was diffident and insouciant. He felt Yale's remoteness, if persistent, could become a distinct long-term problem. The barriers needed to be shattered.

"David, you have two choices," Dr. Ian concluded, "Either we have Yale hospitalized, or secure a mortician. He's killing himself. We must penetrate his concrete veneer. I detect evidence of dehydration. He has to get fluids into his body. He needs supervision and medical attention." David and the doctor were in the kitchen after Yale resolutely relinquished further communication, and pensively withdrew to a solemn marooned area of his mind. The doctor was emphatic as he spoke. "We have no time to waste, David."

"Okay, Doctor. Let me turn the phone on again and call Marissa, Yale's closest friend, and ask her to come over. Maybe, together we can get Yale to admit himself into the hospital voluntarily." David was at wit's end.

David dialed Marissa's number. Howard answered the phone. Howard related Marissa was under the weather and in bed. Howard didn't tell David the gynecologist sent Marissa to bed because she had started spotting, and was at risk of losing their baby. Howard put David on hold to answer the door, since the housekeeper was upstairs vacuuming.

"I'm back. Sorry, David. Lisa just got here. She's brought over some things for Marissa. Anything I can do for you, David? Or can I have Marissa call you later?"

Spontaneously, David asked to say hello to Lisa, wavering once she was on the line. "How are you, Lisa? I've been thinking about you? It's been a hell of a week, hasn't it? I hope Marissa's better soon."

"What's wrong, David?" Lisa asked perceptively. "The phones at Yale's place have been off, and I've been getting your recorder continuously for the last two days."

"It's Yale. The doctor thinks he belongs in a hospital, Lisa. He doesn't cry. He just lies there like a manikin. He doesn't eat. He doesn't talk. I don't know about a hospital though. What do you think?"

Lisa understood David's doubts and apprehension. She recalled Yale's reaction to being committed in Carmel. "I'm coming over, David. Don't tell Yale. Just let me in, okay?"

David's hesitation wasn't surprising. Intuitively, Lisa vowed if her presence created a problem, she'd leave immediately. "Alright. Thanks Lisa," he said, hoping he was making the right decision.

Lisa didn't tell Marissa where she was going. She simply said she had errands to run and would call later. She handed Marissa two novels, a stack of bridal magazines, and a book about Monte Carlo. "Stay put, Marissa. I've never been a godmother before, and I refuse to be denied this chance."

"Okay. Okay. You know, I could get used to being totally indulged."

"So take advantage of the opportunity. I'll call later."

Lisa arrived at Yale's an hour later. David apprised her of the situation, admitting he was afraid of how Yale would receive her.

"The doctor said Yale has to confront his feelings, Lisa. That the longer he remains in this state of denial and depression, the worse the ramifications could be. Dr. Ian wants to hear from me later."

"I'm going to him now, David. Keep the intercoms on, if you'll feel more comfortable. But give me some time with him alone, okay? I'm accustomed to Yale's tendency toward verbal attacks. If I can get a reaction out of him, even a negative one, perhaps he'll let go of this bottled up withdrawal. If I make matters worse, I'll leave."

She opened Yale's bedroom door and approached the bed slowly. She looked at the ravaged remains of the man she once dreamed would share her life and wanted to weep. He was unkempt and smelled of unseemliness and urine. His face had aged these past few days, and as she sat down on the carpeting, next to the bed, his foul breath repulsed her.

"Poor Ruth. She would turn over in her grave if she knew what you looked like now. This is the last thing your mother would have wanted, Yale."

He didn't respond or acknowledge her presence.

"I loved your mother, Yale. You know I did. I spent a long time living with her in Carmel. We had a special understanding parents develop. We knew sacrificing for our children often was really not a sacrifice at all, but a pleasurable way of perpetuating the happiness of those who meant the most to us. Ruth cared more about your happiness than her own. Don't destroy her dreams for you, by doing this to yourself, Yale. I beg you. Please, Yale."

"Get out of here, Lisa. You fucked up one of my mothers' dreams when you walked out on me. You're a stupid woman, Lisa. Get out. Leave me alone."

"I'm not going anywhere, Yale. Unless you force me out. And you're the stupid one, Yale. Ruth forgave me a long time ago. It's you who can't forgive yourself, for many things, just as I can't forgive myself for certain actions and some decisions I made."

"Like what? What can't you forgive yourself for?"

"The pain I caused some people unintentionally."

"Okay. I forgive you, Lisa. Now get the fuck out of here!"

"You really are dumb, Yale. I wasn't even referring to you. I can't forgive myself for the pain my children endured, at my expense, when I was in search of myself and broke up their family unit. I can't forgive myself for being naive enough to believe Frank, when he left the island, on the pretense of planning a surprise for me, and left me behind. Well, I got a surprise all right. He killed himself! Maybe you're right. I am ignorant, too. I should have been with him."

"You couldn't have known. You couldn't have stopped him. That's not something to blame yourself for."

"So, big shot, am I supposed to feel better now? You didn't know Ruth was going to have a heart attack while you were out of town. You could have stayed in the city instead of being on tour. Maybe, things would be different.

Huh? I shouldn't blame myself, Yale? Why are you allowed to do so, and I'm not?"

For the first time since his mother was pronounced dead, his eyes filled with unshed tears. His lips quivered as he fought to regain control. He clenched his fists, attempting mightily to hang on to his composure.

Lisa rose from the floor and sat on the bed, grabbing his clenched fists with her hands. "Open up, Yale. It's okay. Let go."

He stiffened. His body began to shake. The tears fell. And from the depths, he couldn't halt the primal screams, which erupted with volcanic force. "No...No...Ma...Ma" he screamed wretchedly. "Mom... Oh God...No...No...No. Ma...Ma...Oh God...No...No..."

Lisa moved, cradling Yale, and rocked him as the sobs which surfaced racked his body. Without inhibition, she allowed him to pull her down, and bury his face between her breasts. Simultaneously their tears poured, and in unison, their bodies shook with anguish and bereavement.

Lisa held him until the tears subsided and he finally slept.

David came into the bedroom, his own eyes swollen and red. He looked at Lisa tenderly, "Thank God you were able to get him to let some of his sorrow out. Can I do something? Please. What can I do?"

She answered softly, afraid of waking Yale. "Could you get some soup from the deli, and call Dr. Ian with an update? Ask him what we should do next to help Yale. I don't want to do the wrong thing or say the wrong thing. I'm scared to trust my instincts, David."

"Sure, Lisa. Anything I can get you?"

"A pitcher of water and two glasses, please. Maybe, Yale will drink some water in a while. We'll take it slow. He needs time to grieve. He and Ruth were so close." Her eyes began to fill again. "I'll stay here, for now, and stay close to him."

Yale slept fitfully, waking with a start a couple of hours later. Lisa placed her hand gently on his arm. "It's alright, Yale. I'm here." She rubbed his arm soothingly for several minutes. He didn't speak to her at all. Eventually when she started to sit up, he grabbed her arm with a firm grip.

"What, Yale?"

"Stay a little longer, will you?"

"I'm not going anywhere. I'm sitting up to pour you a glass of water; that's all."

She poured him a glass of water, and then another. She didn't leave his side. "What time is it?"

"About four, Yale. How about some soup and a slice of toast?"

"Later. I'm tired. I don't even have the energy to get up to pee."

"Come on. I'll help you to the bathroom."

"You're a regular Florence Nightingale, aren't you?" He said with more than a little irritability. He needed her. And he hated needing her. So he angered.

"David, are you there? If the intercom is on and you hear me, please help me out in here, and assist Yale to the bathroom, will you?"

David appeared as she sipped from a glass of water, which she then extended to Yale. He knocked it out of her hand intentionally and got soaked in the process. He tried to stand, but felt wobbly, which only irritated him more. Angrily, he sat back down on the edge of the bed, took out his penis and urinated on the carpet.

"Now I don't need either one of you to help me to the bathroom."

Neither Lisa nor David said anything; waiting to see what Yale was going to do next. The doctor had advised letting him release pent up feelings without restraint. Dr. Ian had said, "Suggest, but don't push."

"I'm going back to sleep. You can both leave. I wish you would."

"Do you really want time alone, Yale?" Lisa inquired calmly.

"I don't care one way or the other," he answered, lying down and pulling the quilt around him.

"Okay. I'll be in the kitchen, Yale. I could use a cup of coffee. Call out if you want something."

He didn't respond, and they left the room.

Lisa checked on Yale after drinking a cup of coffee. He appeared to be sleeping soundly. She decided to leave for a short period and stopped to check in on Marissa. She explained she'd been at Yale's, but refrained from going into detail about Yale's state of mind. Marissa claimed her spotting had stopped and the doctor felt a few more days of total bed rest should suffice. If there was no more bleeding, she could then resume moderate activity.

"I'm not as depressed as I was, Lisa. I think it's going to be okay—about the baby, I mean. I really am grateful to you for being with Josh so much this past week. He still gets frightened so easily. Ever since the time his father dragged him away, and the house was set on fire—He loved Ruth a lot, too."

"Shut up, Marissa. I love Josh. You know that. It's been a rough time for all of us who loved Ruth. Josh is young and has suffered several losses. He's been through a lot for a little guy. I know he adored Ruth. I just wanted to be around in case he felt like talking to someone else who loved her. I was glad to do it. There's nothing to thank me for. We're family."

"I love you, Lisa."

"Then follow the doctor's orders and I'll see you tomorrow. I'm going now. I have things to take care of."

"Like Yale, Lisa? He's not doing well, is he? Be honest."

"No. He's having a rough time of it. I feel so helpless. One minute he lets me get close, the next he's rude and insufferable. I feel like expressing my empathy, but I'm afraid he'll take it wrong. And if I say nothing, I feel a big gap is separating us. I didn't want to burden you right now, Marissa, but I figured you knew something was up."

"Follow your instincts, Lisa. Be yourself. Maybe, if your guard stays down Yale will follow suit."

"Maybe. Would you mind if I borrowed your little picture album? The one with all the duplicate photos Josh has. There are several nice pictures of Ruth I'd like to make copies of, if you don't mind?"

"Sure. It's on the bureau, over by the lamp. Got it?"

"Yes. I see it. Thanks."

"Will you let me know how Yale is doing later?"

"I'll try, Marissa. But if you don't hear from me, understand—okay?"

Lisa went back to Yale's place after stopping briefly at her house to change and pick up a nightgown. She'd decided after leaving Marissa's, even if Yale was rude, she would stay and tolerate his outbursts. After all, she had been able to get him to react earlier. Perhaps, he would open up again.

Yale was still asleep when Lisa reentered the house. David indicated he hadn't stirred since she left. Lisa felt a trifle troubled when two more hours passed and Yale was still sleeping. She called Dr. Ian, reporting Yale had been sleeping for the majority of the day. "Should we just let him sleep, doctor? I'm concerned Yale is using sleep as his escape. What should we do?"

"Try to get him up, Lisa. See if you can get him to eat. If he remains unresponsive, I still feel hospitalization should be a primary consideration. He really requires more intense therapy, to help him adjust, than house calls, office visits, or caring friends. I'm convinced he'd benefit from additional care from trained professionals, in a controlled environment."

"I don't agree, doctor. He doesn't need an isolated, sterile environment. He needs love and understanding. People who care about him and also loved his mother."

"Starvation is not normal behavior, Lisa. Denial is an escape, Lisa. Sleep is Yale's attempt at denial as well as deprivation."

"I want to keep trying for another day, okay? If he isn't any better tomorrow, then I'll let you decide what's in Yale's best interests. Maybe,

I'm deluding myself, but I feel he'll come around. He's tougher than he's been given credit for. He's a fighter. I know him well."

"Alright Lisa. I'll call in the morning. If you need to reach me before then, you've got my number."

Lisa prepared a tray of soup, toast and coffee. She left David in the kitchen and went to Yale's room alone. Yale was still asleep. She placed the tray on the nightstand closest to him then rubbed his arm gently until he stirred.

"You don't have to talk to me Yale. And I'll leave the room if you want, but Dr. Ian feels you belong in a hospital. I don't, Yale. I think you just need to mourn in your own way. Please eat something, Yale. I put a tray on the nightstand. If you get dehydrated, or physically ill, the doctor won't have a choice but to hospitalize you."

He didn't respond.

Lisa went and sat at the writing table. Yale went back to sleep. She left the room and returned with her purse and an ashtray twenty minutes later. Yale still slept and the tray remained untouched. She opened the Chanel handbag and withdrew her gold cigarette case, and the small photo book she'd borrowed from Marissa. She lit a cigarette and opened the leather bound album. With a sob, she muttered to herself, forgetting about Yale for a second, "Oh, Ruth. We never know, do we? So many opportunities go by when we can say how much someone means to us, and we take them for granted. Oh God. Ruth. I hope you know how much I loved you. How much I'll miss you."

Lisa sniffed unconsciously, took another drag of her cigarette, and was about to extinguish it when Yale startled her, "Give me a drag before you put it out, will you?"

She walked to the bed and handed him the cigarette and ashtray. He coughed spasmodically after inhaling. Lisa took the cigarette and put it out. She handed him a glass of water. He sat up and took the extended glass from her. She pulled some Kleenex out of the container on his night table. She walked back to the chair and sat down, closing the little album of photos. She blew her nose and lowered her head, as fresh tears seemed to surface out of nowhere.

Yale picked up a slice of toast, watching her. He took a bite, then asked, "What were you looking at?"

"A little picture album I borrowed from Marissa. It has some fairly recent photos I want to make copies of and have enlarged." She lifted her tear stained face. "Ruth was beautiful—really beautiful."

"Can I see it?"

"Maybe later would be—"

"Can I see it? Please!"

She walked over to the bed and handed Yale the little album. He took another bite of toast and responded with, "Thank you, Miss Nightingale." His tone was sardonic.

She looked at him, but said nothing. He finished the slice of toast and said, "Coffee, please," as if speaking to a subordinate. He hadn't opened the album yet, but kept a steady eye on her.

She poured him a cup of coffee from the carafe and handed it to him. He took it from her without a word, and as if excusing her turned his attention to the picture book on his lap. She returned to the chair she had been occupying.

He looked at a few pictures carefully before commenting. "Yes, my mother was beautiful. Inside and out. She was the most giving person… never judged…never hated…never quit trying to please. Unselfish. She was like a fictional heroine in a novel. There aren't many like my mother."

Lisa took a cigarette out of her case.

"Don't smoke in my room."

She put the cigarette back in its case and closed it.

"Mom loved Tommy Dorsey music. She never really related to mine. She loved the Big Band Era. Funny that I should think of that now."

"I think she liked Johnny Mathis a lot, too. A couple of times I caught her singing along to one of his classic hits, when we were in Carmel."

"Yeh…and 'West Side Story'… she loved to sing all the songs from 'West Side Story', too."

He smiled with tears in his eyes. He looked at a few more photographs silently, then closed the album abruptly. "Celluloid. I'm left with memories and celluloid. What do I do now, when I need more than that?"

"Try to go on, I guess. Treasure the special memories."

"You always have all the answers, don't you? Well, Miss Nightingale, not everyone has your constitution. Some of us cave in during and after tragedy strikes!"

When she replied with, "I know" Yale took it as an attack on his character, rather than the admission of having been there herself which Lisa meant. He looked at her with bitterness and retorted, "You know what else I loved about my mother? She wasn't self righteous or pompous like you."

"Okay. If that's how you see me—I can live with it. Now, why don't you shower? You smell. I'll change the bed while you shower."

"How much do you charge, Miss Nightingale?"

"I'll send you a bill."

"What's the matter—no freebies—for an old friend? You didn't go through all of Frank's money already, did you?"

He was hurting her, but she was determined not to let it show. "No. I've got plenty of money. My book did quite well, thank you. I haven't even needed to touch Frank's gift to me."

"You took his house and turned it into something that's been in every "House Beautiful" magazine on the market, didn't you? Why didn't you just leave it the way it was? You must of spent a fortune."

"Because it was empty, Yale. Literally empty! There was nothing in the place but a fucking mattress! Now, if you're done being so inquisitive, why don't you go wash yourself? You stink!"

"Why did you stay in the place if it was empty? My mother said you didn't leave the place for a long time. I thought it was because you wanted to surround yourself with Frank's things."

"I stayed because I had no place I belonged. Frank sold, or gave away, every other residence of his in his will. I didn't want to burden my boys—my folks—and I had no friends, other than Harvey, who pushed me into starting over. I was alone. A part of me needed to suffer, until I couldn't suffer anymore. I hated Frank for deserting me after I devoted myself to him. I hated him for not letting me have the chance to say good-bye. And I felt bitter and perplexed. God, Yale, I'm only now able to say any of this aloud. Cave in after a tragedy? I know all about caving in. I wasn't just saying it. They wrote about me—the benefactor. Me; the heir to a fortune. And I had nothing I gave a shit about! Nothing!"

Suddenly he realized how he had misinterpreted her earlier words and felt badly about his callousness. "I'm sorry, Lisa."

"Don't feel sorry for me, Yale. I'm moving forward. I learned the hard way that forward is all there is. I hope it won't take you forever to do the same."

"My wounds are fresh, Lisa?"

"They don't ever heal by themselves, Yale. They stay open sores until you do whatever it takes to aid in their healing."

She walked to the door. "I'll be back in a few minutes." She left the room.

She'd taken her purse, so Yale surmised she was going outside for a smoke. He got out of bed and wearily walked to the window. He parted the blinds and looked outside. He was taken aback when he saw her sitting on the ground, hugging her knees, crying. He watched as she finally removed a tissue from her purse and wiped her face.

He cracked the window when he saw David approach her, and listened as David asked if she was all right.

"Maybe I'm the wrong person to try and help him, David" Yale overheard her say. "Once we understood each other. But that time has passed.

Maybe, Yale's right. I did become a "Florence Nightingale" of sorts, when I married Frank. Perhaps it stuck. But that's not enough for me anymore. I'm a woman. I need to feel like a woman—not a nursemaid. I'm only staying tonight. After that, I'm out of here. I'm not as strong as I thought. I can't stay and have to defend every word I say. Yale and I are antagonistic toward each other. I can't handle it. I want to help him, David. I just don't know how. He won't let me in. He doesn't trust me anymore."

"Why don't you express yourself as candidly, as you did just now, to Yale?"

"Because I don't think he knows how to listen. He only hears what he wants to, David."

"What now, Lisa? Do you just give up? Are you walking out on him, again, when he needs you?"

"He doesn't need me, David. Unfortunately, the person he needs now is the person he just laid to rest. You can't give someone 'fight'. It comes from within, David. He'll be fine in time. Ruth will guide his days, until he can walk on his own again. Trust me, David. Her strength will transfer itself to Yale. The kind of love they shared doesn't get buried. It's carried on. Yale and I do have one thing in common, David. Ultimately, we're both survivors."

CHAPTER 34

When Lisa heard the shower running and found Yale's bed vacated, she changed the sheets and pillowcases, and took the tray back into the kitchen.

"Well, at least he ate something, David. That's encouraging. He's still in the shower, so I didn't tell him you were leaving for a while. Go on. I know you're reluctant to leave, but I'm not running off. Take care of the things you have to do. I'll page you if I need you."

Yale feigned sleep when Lisa returned to check on him, carrying a fresh tray of food and drink. She placed the tray down and left quietly.

He was lying on his side, with the lights off, and the room dim. He heard Lisa dialing out on the phone, having accidentally hit the speaker button to on before getting in the shower. The smell of her perfume lingered in the room. He felt remorse for his behavior as the fresh linens surrounded his body. He knew she was right when she told David they were both survivors. But he wasn't sure he wanted to endure. His life felt so empty. He had no purpose. At least his fame and fortune had made life easier for his mother before. She could have luxuries because of him. But who needed him now? Whose life would he enhance now? He was so very tired. He just wanted to sleep. He reached to turn the speakerphone off, when he heard the familiar voice.

"Pa. Hi, it's Lisa. I was about to hang up. It rang so many times, I thought you were out."

"No. I'm here. I just don't move so fast anymore. Ma's in the bathtub. I was going to ignore the phone. Now I'm glad I didn't. How are you, sweetheart?"

"I'm okay, Pa. I'm at Yale's place. He's going through hell."

"Such a shame, Lisa. His mother was still a young woman. Much too early...she died much too early. And the night before Rosh Hashanah. A nice New Year, huh?"

"I loved her, Pa. Ruth was unique. She had her heart in the right place, Pa."

"Tell Yale how sorry we are, Lisa. We missed having you here for the holiday. We'll be there for Marissa's wedding, though. Just like we promised. We'll be together then. How's Marissa and Josh? You said they were very close to Ruth too."

"Marissa's still a little under the weather, but getting better. Josh is doing better too. He finally stopped asking why so many people go to heaven all the time. He said, he doesn't ever want to go to heaven. He has a hard time accepting the finality of never seeing someone he loves—ever again."

"Don't we all feel the same way, Lisa?"

"I suppose, Pa. You know, the day Yale was burying Ruth in Boston, I received a Jewish New Year card from her in the mail. Ruth must have mailed the card out a day before she died." Her voice cracked, as she continued, "You know what Ruth wrote, Pa? "To the daughter I never had. May the coming year be happy and bright—and your burdens light. May all you pray for be yours, and all you dream for come true. Don't be afraid of asking for too much, Lisa. Because if anyone is entitled to receive—it's you!"

"Don't cry, honey. You've cried enough, Lisa. I'm sorry I didn't get to know Ruth personally, but somehow I feel I knew her. I hope you'll invite Yale over when we're in California."

"I don't know, Pa. Yale and I always seem to be fighting the same war, but we're on different continents."

"So ask for a transfer, Lisa. Better to fight beside a comrade, than amongst strangers."

"Maybe we've been apart too long already, Pa. Maybe it's time to make friends with strangers."

"Only you know that, Lisa. Some decisions have to be made without interference or influence. You, then, are the only one accountable for the results of your choices."

"I know, Pa."

"Oh, Lisa, I talked to the boys. Marc and Steve called for New Years and sent us a plant. Such good boys. You should be proud."

"I am, Pa. You're right."

"Also, we got a huge basket of fruit from Harvey and Michelle, with a beautiful note. And then Jean called here, just two days ago. What's this she tells me about you wanting the rights to the screenplay of "Regrets" nullified? You didn't say anything last time we talked."

"I changed my position, Pa. I want it back and released as a novel first. Then, if I decide to have it developed for the screen, I'll do it myself. I put too much into writing it, to let it be handled any other way. Anyway, I still think Yale would be perfect for the lead male role, and I want control of what happens with the adaptation."

"Now you're using your head, Lisa. Why take a chance on someone else's interpretation, when you're qualified to develop and represent the script as you see fit. I always believed if you give birth and life, you have an obligation to nurture. By nurturing, we love. And by loving, we are able to nurture. Do you agree?"

"Okay, Pa, you're a wonderful philosopher. I get the message. Now go make sure Ma didn't drown in the tub, and give her a hug and kiss for me. I'll talk to you in a day or two."

"And where's my hug and kiss, Lisa?"

"It's there, Pa. It's always there. I love you."

"A zees yur, Lisa."

"A sweet year for you too, Pa."

Lisa walked back into Yale's bedroom after concluding her conversation with her father. She approached the bed and found Yale awake, tears streaming down his face. She craved to sit down and hold him, but refrained from doing so. Instead, she remarked, "Florence Nightingale is back again. Is there anything I can get you, Yale?"

He looked at her with such suffering etched upon his face she had to look away or surely, she would succumb to the torment she too felt. He reached for her hand and whispered, "I don't know if I can handle this. I don't know if I can go on, or if I even want to."

"Why don't I call Dr. Ian, Yale? Talk to him, okay?"

"Can't I talk to you, Lisa? Can't you even be a friend anymore?"

"If I wasn't a friend, Yale, I wouldn't be here. If I didn't care, I wouldn't take your shit and turn the other cheek. I don't know what to do for you, Yale, and I'm afraid of doing the wrong thing. I feel you'll attack me no matter what I say or do. I didn't come over to add to your plight, but you treat me as your enemy. Yale, tell me what you need. Tell me what I can do."

"I need to hold someone, until I'm ready to let go. I need someone to hold me back, and not let go. Can you be that someone, Lisa?"

She sat on the bed, still holding his hand, and let him pull her down beside him. He yanked at the quilt until he could cover them both beneath the soft fabric, then wrapped an arm across her protectively and whispered, "hold me". She embraced him and kissed his wet cheek, feeling desire involuntarily mount. She felt his breathing quicken, and knew he, too, felt the hunger and yearning. "This feels so right, Lisa. I need to feel alive."

She stoked his hair and kissed his face repeatedly, wanting to make his pain vanish. He moved a hand between her thighs and forced his mouth on hers.

She opened her mouth to his tongue, and tightened her thighs around the hand that had moved up between her legs. He rubbed his hand against her crotch and let his tongue mingle with hers. She took her hand and placed it inside his briefs, finding the hardness that was waiting to be engulfed. She stroked his shaft, feeling the moisture of her own body beckon to the sliding hand between her legs.

"Help me feel alive. Replace the pain, Lisa."

She rubbed his shaft in steady, firm strokes, until he moaned. She was wet and breathing hard. "More. More, Lisa. Make me come." She forgot about her own needs and heeded his plea. She encased the rim of his penis and stroked in rapid succession, listening to his mounting, urgent uproarious squeals. She compressed her fingers, applying more pressure to his thickness and felt him thrust faster, his body crying for release. He was breathless as he pumped rapidly. She continues to stroke, feeling his body tensing. He was ready to surrender to the passion and yield, when unbelievingly he pulled away, and in amazement denied himself from the ejaculation.

In astonishment, Lisa watched him suppress his need until he lost his erection and was in control, without capitulating to the climax. "Just hold me, Lisa. I can't let myself go. I need to suffer and not surrender. I can't explain it."

"Yale, talk to me about this. I don't understand. Denial is not a rational way to work out your feelings. Why are you doing this?"

"Don't become my shrink, Lisa. Just be a friend, okay?"

"I am your friend. But I don't get it. First, you beg to feel something other than pain, then you inflict pain on yourself intentionally? Why?"

"I'm punishing myself. It doesn't take a genius to figure it out."

"And you're using me and sex to help you?"

"Whatever works. Right?"

"Yale, you need help." She got up from the bed. "I don't like being used. I'm calling Dr. Ian and explaining what just happened, and then I'm calling David to come over. I don't know how to help you. I don't want to be part of an approach that padlocks emotions. If you ask me, you'd probably find it beneficial to unfasten the floodgates."

"How dare you determine what's good for me!" He leaped from the bed and grabbed her by the shoulders. "Who are you to tell me what's in my best interests?"

"Let go of me, Yale!"

"Not until you promise me that what went on here will go no further." He kept a firm grip on her shoulders, his eyes blazing.

"Sorry. I'm your friend. Remember? I think you need to talk to Dr. Ian about this. I know, I do."

"No!" he shouted, pushing her down on the bed and pinning her hands down. "This is our business and that's how it's going to stay."

She struggled against him. "Let me up, Yale. You don't want to talk to the doctor—fine! But I do! Now, get off me, Yale! You're hurting me!"

"No. I'm not getting off until you swear you'll keep this between us."

She struggled against him with ferocity. "Get off me! You are an idiot! Your mother should have seen this bit—her son denies himself release to insure further suffering—"

"Shut up, Lisa!"

"Get up Yale! Get off me! You're crazy if you thought I'd sit by and watch this kind of sick behavior! Get off me, before you get another erection and have to fight to control yourself."

"Tell me this is between us, Lisa! Say it!"

"No! I won't pacify you!" She struggled and fought to get him off her, realizing he did indeed have an erection. "You used to be a good fuck, Yale. Now you're just a fucker!"

"Shut your mouth, Lisa! You sound like a whore!"

"Well, maybe, a whore is what you need, Yale! Someone you can manipulate for money! Maybe, you'd come with a whore and feel it was fine then!"

"Just shut your mouth, Lisa."

"Make me! She struggled again, then pushed her body upwards and against him. "Hard, aren't you? Too bad you prefer wasting such a good erection, Yale. You used to like deep penetration. Now you can't even enjoy a hand job!"

She saw rage in his eyes. She had pushed him to the limits. She felt him press the weight of his body on hers, and knew what was happening. She egged him on. "Go ahead, Yale. Get yourself real close. I feel you. Go ahead and rub yourself against me. But make sure you don't come—you fool!"

He tore at her clothes and she fought to get him off. He grabbed her breasts, now bare, and bent to suck the nipples. She writhed beneath him, shouting, "Get off me, you jerk! Go suck on yourself, Yale. God knows you're not doing a thing for me!"

"Shut up, Lisa!" he yelled, covering her mouth with his, fiercely probing her mouth with his tongue. He pulled her slacks down, destroying the zipper, and pushed her legs apart. She pulled on his hair, hard enough for him to remove his mouth from hers. "Stop fighting me. You asked for this, Lisa."

He pushed himself into her and began thrusting violently. She had her hands held down by his. "Go on, putz, push. But be sure to pull out before you get too close!"

He kept pumping, feeling the point of no return was near, and wanted to stop, but couldn't. He pushed again, breathing hard, and forced his mouth down on hers. She didn't resist this time, but opened her mouth to greet his tongue, and thrusted to deepen his penetration. He pulled his mouth away and screamed… "No" as he climaxed, his body controlling and ruling him.

Yale was mortified afterwards. He looked at Lisa's transfixed face, and felt hideous and unscrupulous. He moved off her and stood up. She remained immobile. He looked into her eyes but saw only stormless, unruffled eyes looking back at him. "I have no excuse, Lisa. I've never been a brutal or callous man. I must be mad. Forgive me."

With composure and without agitation she replied, "I asked for it, Yale. Don't denigrate me with an apology."

Just as placidly, she added, "This can stay between us, Yale. I'm fine. You didn't hurt me, Yale. I made some cruel remarks. Let's not become erratic over one incident."

He was confused. Apparently Lisa wasn't. She sat up, pulled the top sheet off the bed and wrapped it around her. It was only when she went into the bathroom that Yale saw the blood on the bed and panicked. He burst open the bathroom door screaming, "You're bleeding! My God, what have I done? I've lost my mind!"

She attempted to sooth him, but he refused to listen. "Yale, I provoked you. Do you understand? I'm alright. It's just a little blood. Yale—"

He was paralyzed with fright. He wouldn't let her talk. He ran to the telephone and called Dr. Ian's unlisted number. Dr. Ian answered the phone at his home on the second ring.

"It's Yale. You have to help me!" He shouted into the receiver. "I raped Lisa! I raped Lisa! She's bleeding!"

Yale was still ranting when Dr. Ian arrived. He refused to be absolved of guilt from Lisa, and hysterically insisted she go to the hospital for an examination. He nullified Dr. Ian's attempts to minimize his shocking behavior, and tongue lashed himself derisively.

It was his fervent spontaneous plea, which finally convinced Lisa to relent to a medical examination. "I'm not one to beg, Lisa. But for my sanity, I beg you to let me come with you, and have you checked out. If you refuse, I will be tormented until I am resting beside my mother."

Lisa thought Yale would be sensible after the physician assured him she was not internally injured in any way. She thought he would understand that bleeding sometimes occurs with deep penetration, and repeated thrusting against dry walls, or sometimes when an individual has not had intercourse for a prolonged period of time, or when the male member is larger than the female can accommodate comfortably, or even by robust activity involving an unusual or variant position. But he didn't. He repeatedly admonished his behavior and berated himself. He refused to believe any of the reasons presented to him.

After hours of self-castigation, he resolved to make himself a worthy person and asked Lisa for one more favor. "I want you to leave, Lisa, and not come back. I can't be around anyone right now, especially you. I need time to get my shit together. And to be honest, you're not helping me. You see, I need you, and I resent needing you. I feel mothered by you and I try to resist it. I had a mother. Lisa, I'm not whole, and you seeing me less than I want to be hurts. Selfishly, I am asking you to show me one more merciful act. Leave. Tonight I did something I thought I was incapable of. Friends don't hurt each other the way we have. Please leave, Lisa. And try to forgive me."

Dr. Ian felt Yale might have relinquished enough of his impenetrable veneer to make progress with therapy at this point, so he interjected. "Lisa, I feel there is no advantage to your staying with Yale currently. I concur with his suggestion, that you go, and allow him to pursue the necessary treatment, which will enable him to feel in control of his decisions, with an affirmative attitude and fewer apprehensions. I trust you understand Yale's current request is a positive effort he's initiating, in order to regain stability in his life, which has been severed by his mother's sudden death."

"I understand, doctor." She picked up her purse and stood in front of Yale. "You know, Yale, I really did ask for what happened in the bedroom. I wanted you to share yourself with me, completely. I thought if I could get you out from under that veil, I'd be helping you. I provoked you, intentionally, every step of the way. But this, Yale, hurts me to the core. I feel rejected. I feel discarded. And I feel hurt. I'm sorry you feel I hindered rather than helped. Forgive me, Yale. Forgive my stupidity. "There's nothing you need to be forgiven for."

She looked at Dr. Ian a moment. "You know, doctor, being a psychiatrist does not give a physician the license to heal one person while injuring another. I, too, am fragile. As you are well aware, interaction is a vital part of therapy. Perhaps, you should review your texts, doctor. I think that I deserved some consideration here. I, too, have feelings."

She walked herself to the front door, pushed the combination to open the thick black gates, and drove home.

She was up most of the night. She took out her prayer book and said the mourners prayer for Ruth. She sat, clutching the pendant with the royal straight flush on it and cried. "Why God, do I constantly overstep the boundaries? Why do I think I can fix everything? I was so desperate to help Yale. Oh God, the few drops of blood on the sheet are nothing compared to the way my heart is bleeding. Help me. Please help me."

CHAPTER 35

Lisa made a concious effort not to dwell on what transpired with Yale. She was at Marissa's early the following morning. Howard was elated to see her, explaining he had two business meetings scheduled, and was afraid he was going to have to cancel them. He explained, Josh woke up with a fever, and the housekeeper took the day off to attend her child's first parent/teacher conference. She shoved him out the door, "Go on. I'll be fine. Just don't come back tonight empty handed. I expect pizza and spaghetti for retribution."

"I adore you, Lisa. Call if you need me and, please, please, keep Marissa in bed. She's feeling helpless and guilty for having to lay low. She was up half the night."

"Well, if I have to deal with Marissa too, you better add garlic bread and salad to my dinner order. Now, go already. I think I'm capable of holding down the fort." He hugged her, then left.

Lisa went to the refrigerator, opened the freezer compartment, removing a large carton of fudge-nut-carmel ice cream, then marched upstairs holding the ice cream and three tablespoons. She heard Marissa soothing Josh in Marissa's bedroom, and entered cheerfully.

"Hi, I'm back. And it's party time! I hear you two are not up to par. I figured, when I feel lousy, ice cream always makes me feel better; so grab a spoon, and let's have breakfast."

"Lisa, you're nuts." Marissa laughed, her face lighting up at the sight of her dearest friend, who was standing before her in faded jeans, an oversized sweatshirt, and her hair pulled up in a ponytail. "Ice cream at eight o'clock in the morning?"

"Oh. Sorry. You want to wait until eight-thirty?"

"I don't," Josh proclaimed, standing up on the bed; moving toward her and the ice cream.

"Me either, Lisa stated. Now give me a kiss hello, and I'll give you a spoon. If your mom doesn't want any now, that's fine. There will be that much more for us."

"Oh, no you don't! That's my favorite flavor. You're not getting all of it. Give me one of those spoons, Lisa."

"Not until you kiss me good morning too, little mother. I need some affection."

The hours sped by as Lisa took charge and, with a revolutionary style, all her own, kept Marissa and Josh entertained and comfortable all day.

By nightfall, Josh's fever was down and Marissa had made a final selection for her bridal gown from one of the many exclusive catalogs she and Lisa examined earlier. Before Lisa left for home, she arranged for two leading designers to meet her at Marissa's the following day, with apparel, to complete an entire trousseau for Marissa.

Marissa had stopped worrying and was in good spirits when Lisa kissed her goodnight. Although Marissa kept insisting Lisa was her guardian angel, and the reason she felt so much better, Lisa knew the doctors visit during the day, confirming the pregnancy was on the right course again, and that she was progressing satisfactorily, had a great deal more to do with her elation.

Lisa had managed to be evasive on the subject of Yale all day, but now on the drive home her thoughts were revolving around how Yale was, and whether she should attempt to contact him once more.

When Lisa entered her house, and Belle informed her David Ross just called, the decision was made for her. She dialed the number David had given Belle, recognizing it as Yale's house number. David answered before the first ring was completed.

"Hi David. It's Lisa. I just got your message. What's up?" She tried to sound more casual than she felt.

Yale's in the hospital, Lisa. Dr. Ian had an ambulance summoned to the house when he came to see Yale earlier and found him unconscious in the bathroom. I was gone for half an hour, picking up Yale's mail at the P.O. box, at his request, and arrived back at Yale's the same time as

Dr. Ian. Yale seemed a little better today. I swear he did! The next thing I know, we walk into Yale's room together, and Yale's on the bathroom floor unconscious. The doctor then proceeds to call an ambulance. When Yale came to, he said, he'd just gotten dizzy, but Dr. Ian insisted he be placed in the psychiatric unit of St. Joseph's. Yale finally said, "Do whatever you want, doctor. I don't give a shit." I think Dr. Ian acted a little prematurely, but who was I to interfere?"

"Calm down, David. You're speaking so rapidly you're making my heart race. It's done. All we can do is wait a day or two, and call Dr. Ian to see if Yale is doing any better. If Yale was so weak he passed out, perhaps the hospital was the best decision, and where he belongs."

"Lisa, Dr. Ian said Yale couldn't have any visitors for a few days; until he deemed it the appropriate time."

"He's Yale's doctor, David. We'll just have to wait then. If Yale trusts Dr. Ian, I think, we should stay out of it."

"You know, Lisa, Yale really did seem better. He ate today and talked about Ruth often. He even asked me to pick up his mail. In the ambulance he looked at me stating he went in the bathroom to shave, and the next thing he remembered was coming to, on the floor. I told him I was sorry I left him alone. He said, eventually his ugly reflection would have knocked him out anyway. He said, for me to stop blaming myself."

"Sounds like his self esteem is really low, doesn't it? Well, he's right that you shouldn't blame yourself. Why don't we wait a day or so, and see how things are then? Okay?"

"Alright. I'll call you if I hear anything—I mean, if you want me to."

"Thanks. If you can't get me here, try Marissa's. I'm there a lot."

The next day Lisa related her conversation with David, to Marissa, and then Marissa brought it up again the following day, inquiring if there was any new information.

"No. Nothing, Marissa. David said, Dr. Ian never called him back, and the hospital blocked his attempted entry into the psychiatric unit yesterday."

"So, what are you going to do, Lisa?"

"I suppose, I'll pick up Josh from school now, then pick up the

Chinese food for dinner. Since Howard's working late, and we've completed selecting your wardrobe, why don't you take a nap? I'll see you in a bit."

"That's not what I meant, Lisa, and you know it."

"I'm not doing anything about Yale. It's out of my hands. Why? Do you have any suggestions?"

"You have pull at the hospital, Lisa. Why don't you see if they'll allow you and Josh to see him, as long as you're out already. Anyway, Yale should be advised that you're watching Josh while Howard and I are on our honeymoon, since he's unable to, don't you think?"

"I don't know—"

"Josh would feel better knowing his Uncle Yale was okay. You know how glad he was to see Yale at Carmel Clinic, and he understood it was a place where you get well. I'm sure you could arrange a quick meeting, in a private room, so Josh isn't exposed to more than he can comprehend."

"I don't know what condition Yale is in, Marissa. Maybe, he's unkempt and withdrawn—"

"One phone call to St. Joseph's and you know you can find out everything you need to know."

"Okay already. I'll call."

"Lisa, Yale needs you. He loves you. You're the only woman who has ever meant anything to him. You belong together."

"Funny. He once said those very words to me—we belong together. It seems so long ago."

Lisa, place the call. After several connections with various department heads, she finally was connected with Dr. Elijah Beck, head of the psychiatric division of St. Joseph's, and informed Yale Frye signed himself out of the hospital, against his doctor's advice, and had left the facility a couple of hours ago. She then dialed Yale's house, expecting David to answer, but Yale answered the phone himself.

"Yale, is that you? It's Lisa."

"Yes. It's me. I'm on the other line. Can I call you back?"

"If you don't want to talk to me, it's okay. I was just about to pick Josh up from school, for Marissa, and called the hospital to see if you were up to seeing Josh, but—"

"I'm up to it, Lisa. I really am on the other line. It's not a brush off. Can I change and come over there?"

"Sure, Yale. Marissa will be delighted. So will Josh. I'm picking up Chinese—"

"Good. Then get some almond boneless chicken for me, and I'll see you in an hour."

"Great. Anything else you'd like, Yale?"

"Yes, Lisa. Your forgiveness. But I have to earn that, and I will. See you soon."

Lisa put down the phone, turning to Marissa, "What do you make of this?" The speaker on the phone had been on so Marissa had heard the exchanged dialogue.

"I'm not sure, Lisa, but I better tell the housekeeper to set another place at the table. Well, get going, Lisa. Josh will be looking for you. And why don't you go home and change. You've had the same jeans on for the last three days."

"They're my favorites. What should I change into, pray tell? Perhaps a slinky black dress, asshole?"

"I wouldn't go that far. But one of your Donna Karan sweaters and a pair of nice slacks wouldn't be bad."

"Thanks "Mom". Just what I need—more advice! Go take your nap, Marissa, and I promise I'll be the picture of elegance when I return."

Lisa was out the front door when Marissa yelled out, "I'm going for my nap now. Do something with your hair, too, before you come back, will you?"

"Anything else, creep?"

"Yeh. I love you, Lisa. You're one of a kind."

"Then, maybe, you should dump Howard and marry me!"

She got in the Mercedes and drove off while Marissa stood in the doorway laughing.

By the time she pulled up at the school Josh was standing with his hands on his hips, his head cocked to one side, and a frown on his face. She opened the door and he slid in, fastening his seatbelt.

"Sorry I'm late Josh, but I was on the telephone. Your Uncle Yale is coming over to join us for dinner. We have to stop at my place, then pick up Chinese."

His face lit up. "At least you have a good excuse. I'll forgive you this time. Why do you have to stop at your house?"

"To change my clothes."

"Good. You've been in those jeans for the last three days."

"Another country heard from."

"What did you say, Lisa?"

"I said, I love you, Josh. You're one of a kind."

It was dusk by the time Lisa and Josh returned to Marissa's. Yale's car wasn't there, so Lisa was shocked when she walked in and found Yale sitting next to Marissa, in the study, near the entrance of the house.

"Uncle Yale. Uncle Yale. I'm so glad you came over," Josh heartily expressed, running to Yale, and climbing on his lap.

"I missed you too, big fella. Give me another a hug."

Lisa and Marissa exchanged glances as they watched the currents of love venerating between Josh and Yale. Marissa rose and took one of the bags from Lisa. "Oh, I smell something good in here, Lisa."

Yale got up, holding Josh by the hand, and took the bag out of Marissa's arms with his other hand. "Sit down, Marissa. Josh and I can take the stuff into the kitchen. Josh, want to take the other bag from Lisa, please?"

"Thanks Josh," Lisa acknowledged, handing Josh the other bag she held. "I'll go out to the car and get the rest."

"Why don't you sit down, Lisa? Josh and I can handle it. Right, big guy?"

"Right, Uncle Yale."

It was the first exchange of words, which included Lisa. As she looked at Yale she could only say, "Thanks". She walked to the sofa, and sat herself down.

When Josh and Yale were out of sight, Marissa said, "He looks pretty good; considering. Don't you think so?"

"I suppose."

"He's been here for almost an hour. I swear, he kept looking at his watch, and listening for you to pull up."

"Yeh; Josh was rushing me as I was changing too. He was excited about seeing his Uncle Yale."

"I don't think Josh is why Yale was clock watching, Lisa."

Lisa attempted to change the course of their conversation. "Did you nap at all, Marissa?"

Marissa nodded affirmatively, then casually retorted with, "You can look damn good when you want to, Lisa," a smile turning up the corners of her mouth.

"Shut up, Marissa. I only changed to make you happy."

"Sure you did, Lisa. And Yale is the picture of GQ just for me too. Right?"

"Probably."

"Probably, what?" Yale asked offhandedly, returning to the room with Josh beside him.

"I was asking Lisa if she thought—"

Lisa cut in quickly, "If it's going to rain tonight or not."

"Really? Probably, you say, Lisa? The weatherman said the drought was expected to continue earlier."

"I might have heard wrong. Don't pay any attention to what I say. I'm usually way off base."

"I don't know about that, Lisa," Yale responded, looking directly at her with intensity, "You're the one who said you didn't agree with Dr. Ian a few days ago. You felt I needed continued personal interaction rather than hospital isolation. You were right on target then, and my therapist, with all his years of training and expertise, was wrong. And you weren't off base on several other occasions I recall vividly. You shouldn't be so tough on yourself, Lisa. Trust your instincts a little more."

She was speechless, and stared at Yale gaping, wondering if this was the same person of a few days ago.

"Something wrong, Lisa?" he asked with a gleam in his eyes.

"No. No. I was just wondering if you underwent a lobotomy, Yale; that's all."

He laughed aloud. "That's one of the things I love about you, Lisa. You are always obscenely up front. What you feel—you say."

"Well, I'm starved. How's that for up front? Are we going to eat soon?" She was dubious about this sudden about-face of Yale's, and needed time to absorb some of what she was finding hard to comprehend.

They were around the table, feasting on the various selections of Chinese food, when Howard called Marissa to say he would be very late, and not to wait up for him. Marissa was perturbed. "He's working too hard, trying to tie up as many loose ends as possible before the wedding. I think our honeymoon is the first vacation Howard will be taking in years."

"I'm working very hard in school. I think I need a honeymoon too, mom."

"Josh, we've been all through this. You're staying with Lisa while Howard and I are gone, and you're going to Disney World for Christmas vacation."

"I still don't know why I can't have a honeymoon too."

"Because a honeymoon is for a husband and wife. We talked about this already, Josh. Remember?"

"Sure. Sure. And first, I'm staying with Uncle Yale. Then that's changed and I'm staying with Aunt Lisa. Maybe, no one really wants me to stay with them!" He pushed his chair back, knocking it over, and started to leave.

"Hang on Josh," Yale shouted. "I'm confused too. Why aren't you staying with me?"

"Ask my mom, Uncle Yale. She's the one who changes everything around, all the time. Even the movies we were supposed to go to last week. She promised. Then, all of a sudden it's—another time, Josh—another time for everything—another time! Another time! If Howard wanted to go to a movie I bet she wouldn't say—another time—to him!" He ran from the table crying and yelled, "I hope your honeymoon is awful."

"What now? You said I could expect Josh to be jealous of Howard, since he's had so much turmoil in his life, and had me all to himself for so long. What do I tell him, Lisa? How do I let him know he's not being replaced? I forgot about the movie. I was so worried about losing the baby. What now? Even if I try to explain, and tell him I'm pregnant now, he'd probably feel more threatened that some other person will be coming along, to take his place in my life. I don't know what to do at this point. Lisa?"

"Are you up for a game, Marissa? All three of us have to convince Josh we want him. Yale, I offered to have Josh stay with me, since the wedding is less than two weeks away, and we didn't know how you'd be feeling. You weren't communicating a few days ago."

"I understand. I'd still like Josh to stay with me. I feel better, Lisa. And quite frankly, I'd love his company now, more than ever."

"So what are we going to do, Lisa? Barter for my son?"

"Exactly. We're going to start a pretend argument of sorts, expressing we love him, and both want him with us, because he's so special."

"Then what, Lisa? Make Josh choose? That's not a good idea."

"He doesn't have to choose anything if Yale and I agree, in front of him, and together, that because we both love him, we'll both be with him, and then do just that. Yale can take him to school—I'll pick him up. We'll both be there for him, and spoil him so badly you'll regret not taking him to Monte Carlo. What do you think, Yale? Marissa?"

"I think it's a great idea," Yale injected," and there's a new sci-fi movie I'm sure Josh would enjoy."

"Good. Then you can take us both to the movies. I like science fiction too."

"Are you sure about this? Yale, you've just gone through—"

"Ready, Lisa?" Yale interrupted. "You want to start or should I?"

They moved closer to the staircase. "What do you mean you love Josh more than I do, Yale?" Lisa yelled loudly. "I love him just as much as you do!"

"Well, just because I didn't feel good, for a little while, doesn't mean I'm not better! I still want Josh to stay with me! We have lots of fun together!"

Josh appeared at the top of the stairs.

"Well, Josh and I have fun too. I even thought we could play miniature golf and go on an overnight camping trip."

"Lisa, I like to do those things too. And I wanted to take Josh to that new Sci-Fi movie opening next week."

"Well, I love Josh a real lot too. I'm glad you're better Yale, but it's not fair if you get to have Josh all to yourself. I want to be with him too. Couldn't we be with him together? Couldn't we love him together? Couldn't the three of us do all kinds of neat stuff together, until Marissa and Howard get back from that Monte Carlo place?"

Josh ran down the stairs to them. "Stop fighting over me already!

I think it's a great idea. We could all do stuff together. I could make a list, like Mom and I do, and we can take turns picking out what we'll do that day."

"Okay with me, Lisa. But since I've known Josh longer than you, even if you love him just as much as I do, I get to pick the first nights activities. Okay?"

"I guess so. What do you think, Josh?"

"Sounds fair to me, Aunt Lisa. Go ahead, Uncle Yale, you plan the first night, and we'll sleep at your house the first night. Lisa, you can have the second night, and we'll sleep at your house…and then I'll plan the third night. And we'll just keep doing it like that."

"Okay, big guy. Come here and let Uncle Yale hold you. I love you trillions and zillions. I'm glad that's settled!"

Yale lifted Josh up and carried him, over his shoulder, back to the dinner table. As he put Josh on the chair, he kissed the top of his head. Lisa and Marissa were already in their perspective seats when Josh said softly, "Uncle Yale, I bet Aunt Ruth is happy, in heaven, that you're all better, 'cause she loves you as much as I do."

Yale swallowed hard before he could speak. "I bet you're right, Josh. In fact, I'm positive you're right."

Yale took his seat and looked down at his plate, hoping to get a grip on himself. Josh saw a tear fall on Yale's dish, and left his chair to go climb on Yale's lap. The young boy put his arms around his Uncle Yale's neck and wept. "I miss Aunt Ruth too. Do you think she knows how much we miss her?"

Yale let the tears fall openly now, hugging Josh to him, "She knows, honey. She knows."

"I wish she didn't have to go to heaven yet, Uncle Yale."

"Me too, Josh. Oh, me too."

Josh put his head against Yale's chest. Even after the tears subsided, he stayed, while Yale held him tightly, receiving as much comfort as he was giving.

There was quiet in the room for a long time. There was no need for further words. The silence spoke to each of them, individually and jointly. And somehow, new barriers were broken, more wires were cut, and they each felt the solemn encasement of a shared speck of time.

Chapter 36

After Yale assisted Marissa tucking Josh in bed, they returned to the quaint study, where Lisa had remained, and found she was still on the long distance, call with Jean.

"Look Jean, you're a great friend, wonderful with PR; not to be reckoned with in the publishing arena, but I'm not selling. "Regrets" is my baby, and I personally don't give a shit if I'm forgotten as a writer, because I'm delaying the publication, by not "putting out" fast enough by your, or anyone else's standards. I want to change the ending. I'm not satisfied with it."

Lisa was quiet; obviously listening to Jeans rebuttal, but clearly unwavering, when she replied, "I'm sorry you feel I'm letting you down Jean, but I'll be letting myself down if I put out "Regrets" the way it is. It has a vague, hatchet ending, Jean. Frank was dying. He loved to read my galleys, so I rushed to write enough for him to see something viable, as proof that I was doing more than coddling him. Frank's dead now. I've read and reread the manuscript. I want to improve it. I'm not cashing in on a previous success. And that's final!"

There was another tense moment of hesitation before Lisa spoke again.

"Jean, when I'm happy with the results is the best I can offer. I can't give you a date. I can give you a novel we'll both be proud of. Allow me to take pride in my craft. Don't cash in on my name. Not you, Jean. Please."

Following another pause, Lisa concluded the conversation angered. "Goodbye Jean. We have nothing else to say to each other. Not ever!

You, of all people, know how much I sacrificed to get my first novel published. And now, you—the last person in the world I would have believed capable—are accusing me of being lax because of my money. Shame on you, Jean! Shame on you!"

Lisa slammed the receiver down. "I'm a real idiot. I trust and get mowed down. And worst of all, I never learn. I go and trust again. There must be a cure for this! Maybe, it's just not trusting anyone...Ever!"

She picked up her goblet of wine taking a large swallow. Yale came over and took it out of her hand. "You're a lousy drunk, Lisa, if you'll recall. That's no solution anyway. Trust me. I know."

She laughed. "Well, you got three out of four right, Yale. One: I am a lousy drunk. Two: It's no solution. Three: You know. But the fourth—Trust you? Sorry. I think I'll pass!"

"I understand," was all he said in response.

She looked in his eyes and knew she hurt him. She didn't mean to. The evening went so well. They had been able to talk. They were comfortable. They, even, got past some of the old bullshit—and now she had to go and spoil it. "I'm sorry, Yale. I really am. I think it's time for me to say goodnight. I seem to have lost my ability to relate anymore tonight. My tolerance for disappointments seems to be at an all time low."

She picked up her purse and let Marissa hug her.

"Would you mind dropping me off, Lisa? David brought me over. I wasn't comfortable getting behind the wheel, since I just came home from the hospital today."

"Sure. No problem Yale, if you can still stand to be around me. Jean! Damn! I can't believe she's more interested in the a publication date, than with the results of my work. I don't understand. I don't get it."

Marissa walked them to the door. "Lisa, you sure you don't want to stay over? I hate to see you go home like this."

"I'm fine, Marissa. Thanks. Go to bed. I'll see you around nine-thirty, and we'll select a hotel for the out of towners and make the arrangements. You want fresh bagels?"

"Yes, and some of that cherry strudel you brought over the other day. That was great!"

"I know, pig. You didn't leave me one little piece!"

"So bring more than you did last time, fool!"

They kissed each other, as Yale chuckled, then left.

"You and Marissa have become really close," Yale commented once they were in the car.

"I adore her. She's my only real friend."

"I'm glad. It's nice you can trust her implicitly, and she you."

His words didn't miss. "It took me a long time before I could admit I needed more than I had. I finally reached out to her and she embraced me."

"Marissa told me about the pregnancy, before you and Josh arrived back at the house. She said, you're the only other person she's confided in."

"Yes."

"Marissa feels you've been her guardian angel. She told me you were there when she started bleeding, taking over in areas she couldn't, and helping in countless ways, not to mention being with Josh limitlessly."

She glanced over at Yale as she halted for a red light. "Yes, I'm a regular "Florence Nightingale," I guess."

He turned away from her gaze, as if slapped, understanding the hurt he had inflicted on her days before. He stared out of the window, at the traffic, without any effort at defending his former actions. There was nothing he could say to rectify what was. Sadly, he realized it.

Lisa was sorry she'd thrown the remark in his face seconds after she did. "I'm sorry, Yale. I'm touchy tonight."

"You're not the one who should be sorry, Lisa."

"There are worse names I could be called, and have been, than Florence Nightingale. One that hurt me badly, years ago, was when Ronnie continually referred to me as "a child" when I told him I needed to seek out my potential, and strive to obtain goals. He put me down, time and again, for not accepting my life as it was. "Ungrateful Child. That's what you are, Lisa" he'd say so often. "You don't know how good you've got it—you child. Grow up, Lisa," he'd repeat until I, almost, believed he was right."

"But inside you knew Ronnie was wrong, didn't you? You proved to yourself, and to Ronnie, that you were capable of more. And you succeeded."

"He wasn't completely wrong, Yale. I was, in part, a child. Just as part of me is probably a little like "Florence Nightingale". But, perhaps, it's not all bad, Yale. If I hadn't dreamed of more, as innocently as a child, I may never have had the guts to try. And if I didn't have a little of the "Florence Nightingale" in me, Frank might have died without feeling cared for. The problem is, I'm more than child or nurse, and need to be seen in entirety. I don't want to be capsulated."

"I've hurt you a lot, Lisa."

"And I you, Yale. But it wouldn't have hurt as much if we didn't care about each other."

They were approaching the gates to Yale's estate. She stopped the Mercedes so he could enter the code to open the gates. "I wish we could start over" he said, as she drove up to the double doors.

"We can't start over, Yale. But we can move ahead from here, and see where it goes."

"Could you ever trust me enough to let me in, Lisa?"

"If you try to be honest with me. If you trust me in return. If we can be open without fear of some kind of reprimand. If we can listen to each other without misinterpretation."

He looked at his house, then at her. "I don't want to go in, Lisa. I dread having to stay in my own house alone."

"Do you want me to come in for a while? Maybe, Victor will fix us some coffee."

"I haven't asked Victor to return yet."

"So you can make me a cup of coffee then."

"You don't understand, Lisa. I don't want to be in there. My mother is in every room. I see her rearranging food in the refrigerator; sitting on the sofa; fluffing up a pillow. I feel her hands on my face; her lips against my forehead."

He stopped, feeling the sorrow mounting, and sighed heavily. "I know I have to get past this. But it's so hard. I think I understand, for the first time, how you must have felt going into an empty house after Frank died. I've never felt so deserted. So empty. So lonely. I can't find solace. Not from anyone or anything. I knew the hospital wasn't going to help. I wasn't ready to talk or be talked to. But this house—it's desolate and threatening too. Do you understand?"

"Would you like to stay at my place, Yale? Belle is a great cook, and

I have a stack of all the latest novels in the library. You always loved to read."

He put his hand on the door handle. "Maybe, I should just go in and try to get used to it. I can't keep running away."

"Maybe you should stop pushing yourself so hard."

"And when will I get over this loss? When will I want to go in the house?"

"You'll never get over the loss, Yale. We both know it. You'll adjust, then go on. As for your home, it's here. When you're ready, you'll open the doors. No one said it has to be tonight, tomorrow, or even next week."

"You really wouldn't mind, Lisa?"

"If you become a pain in the ass, I'll call you a cab. Fair enough?"

"I don't even want to go in for some clothes. Sounds crazy, doesn't it?"

"No. It sounds truthful. You can call David in the morning and ask him to bring you what you need. So, what do you say?"

"I say, thank you. Thanks a lot."

He watched the traffic on the streets, silently, until they reached her place. With understanding, Lisa, didn't invade the quiet.

Belle handed her the stack of messages when she entered the kitchen with Yale. "I just hung up the phone, Missy. Jean called again. She's called four times in the past hour, Miss Lisa. She didn't believe me, I'm a thinking, that you weren't here. She begged me to ask you to call her, no matter how late you got in. Did I do wrong to give her Marissa's number? She was on your little list of people I could give the number to."

"You didn't do anything wrong, Belle. Just cross her name off my list of forwarding callers. She's on my "shit list" now.

Belle glanced at Yale, remembering the last time he was in the house, and wondered if he was going to be kicked out again, and new trouble was brewing.

She knew better than to ask questions, when Lisa started biting her lower lip unconsciously, so only answered with, "I'll take care of it, Missy."

"You remember Yale, don't you, Belle? He's the one you almost clobbered with a golf club, when you thought I was being harmed a while back." Lisa chuckled at the memory, putting Belle a little more at ease.

"Yes, Miss Lisa, I remember. Hello, Mr. Frye."

"It's okay, Belle. Relax. Yale's off my "shit list" this week. Jean is on it! So you can leave your golf club in your quarters, unless, of course, Jean shows up—which won't happen."

"Thank the Lord! I'm opposed to violence. I feels much better just knowing I can leave my golf club where it is."

Both Yale and Lisa laughed as Belle raised her eyes to the heavens in relief. Yale extended his hand, "Please call me Yale, instead of Mr. Frye, Belle. I'm pleased to meet you, officially, this time."

Belle shook Yale's hand and noticed his palm was moist. She felt his hand tremble slightly as he withdrew it from hers. "I'm pleased to make your acquaintance as well, Yale. And I'm glad you ain't on Miss Lisa's "shit list" this week. Makes things a little simpler for me, God knows."

"Yale will be staying here for a while, Belle. Could you prepare the guest room next to mine, please?"

"Right away, Miss Lisa. Can I see you alone a minute, Miss Lisa, before I go upstairs. I need to ask your advice on something private."

"Sure, Belle. Sit down, Yale. I'll pour us some coffee in a second, then show you around."

Lisa followed Belle from the room and out of earshot.

"What is it, Belle?"

"First, I wanted to say I was sorry about his mom, but didn't know if it would be proper. But more important, Missy, when Mr. Frye shook my hand, his palm was wet, like when you're weak or ailing, and his fingers felt like they were trembling a bit. If I should mind my business, say so Missy, but I just wasn't feeling easy not tellin' you."

"Thanks, Belle. I'm glad you told me. I think Yale's acting stronger than he feels. He's been through hell. Why don't you get the room ready, and put a pair of Steve's pajamas on the bed. They're about the same size. I'll pour us a cup of decaf. Then when you're through upstairs, would you fix a tray of cheeses, fruits, and sparkling water, and place them in Yale's room? I think he's going to need a little help getting his strength back."

"Right away, Missy."

Lisa returned and poured two cups of coffee. She put a cup in front of Yale asking, "So what should we pig out on? Cheesecake, or some of that cherry strudel I didn't take to Marissa's?" She giggled wickedly.

"I'll try the strudel. If it's so good the two of you are hoarding it, I better have some while I have the opportunity."

He was about to get up to help her. "Stay put, Yale. This is an informal "pig out". She brought over the strudel, wrapped in waxed paper, and two forks. She knew he would resist being waited on, so she unwrapped the strudel, handed him a fork and ordered, "Dig in".

He smiled at her. After they knocked off the strip of strudel he commented, "This is great strudel! Flaky crust with lots of filling. Just the way I like it. I may just show up at Marissa's tomorrow, so I can have some more."

"I knew you'd be hooked, once you tasted it. Tell Belle. She made it. It's my mother's recipe, but Belle's got it down pat. But I'd never admit that to my mother. She'd be heartbroken."

Belle appeared moments later, inquiring, "Any special soaps or shampoo's you prefer, Mr. Frye—Yale?"

"No, Belle. Whatever is in there will be fine. I would, however, love to have some more of this cherry strudel next time you make some. It's terrific!"

"Oh, good; another customer! There's about two dozen in the freezer. Some are apple and cinnamon. Lisa's mom's recipe, you know."

"Can I put in my order for some of both for tomorrow, Belle?"

"Sure can. Any other requests?"

"Not yet. But give me time, Belle."

"All right, Yale. Don't be shy with me. People, who get to know me in this house, know I learned from Miss Lisa to speak my mind. And I appreciates the same in return. Even Josh has learned he won't be getting any sundaes from Belle unless he, at least, tries the vegetables I serve him before deciding whether he likes them or not."

Lisa and Yale were getting up from the table when the phone rang. "I'm not in, Belle. Not to anyone but my folks and the boys."

"I'll bet it's Jean again. Sometimes, I wish I could just tell people when they're on the "shit list" and stop all this calling!"

Yale couldn't help laughing as Belle answered the phone. Belle pushed down the loudspeaker button, answering, "Lee residence."

"Hello, Belle. It's Jean. Have you heard from Lisa? It's really important I talk to her."

Lisa ran over and scribbled on a piece of paper.

"Yes, Jean. I spoke to Miss Lisa and gave her your messages. She said, if you call again to tell you that you're on her "shit list" right now, and to give her time to cool off."

"Okay, Belle. Tell her I'm sorry that I was such an ass. Ask her to forgive me. Please, Belle. Will you?"

"Yes. I'll give her the message, Jean."

Belle put a hand on her hip after concluding the conversation. "Go on, Miss Lisa, let me have it if you wants to."

"Belle, why did you add the last bit about me wanting time to cool off? Why didn't you just say it the way I wanted? That she's on the shit list—period."

"Because I couldn't. You can say what you like, but I know by next week you'll be mellowing—no matter what happened tonight. If I'm wrong, I'll just tell her you ain't cooling off."

"Come on Yale, before I get on Belle's case. I'm tired. And I'm sure you must be too. Want to pick out a book to take upstairs with you?"

Yale winked at Belle, before following Lisa to the library. He chose two novels he'd been meaning to read, and they went upstairs. She led him into his room and watched as he appraised his quarters.

The massive room was warm and inviting. The king size bed was centered around built in wall units, with every imaginable necessity provided. Reading lights were built into the headboard over the bed, and an electronic device illuminated the lights to the desired voltage. The plush black and white carpeting was at least six inches thick, ran through the dressing area, and covered the bathroom floor as well. The television and stereo system were built into the wall, across the room from the bed, and there was a black leather recliner, with forty adjustable positions near the door wall.

Bay windows spanned an entire wall. There was a writing table and two chairs. The two bay windows closest to the center of the room opened to a carpeted terrace, and overlooked a fountain, and manicured portion of land. At night a control covered the wall of windows with a panel of blinds, and another button filtered the sound of ocean waves through the room, to soothe and comfort, or when sleep felt elusive to visiting guests.

Yale was noticing the beautiful etchings and paintings when Belle knocked, and asked if she could come in. Belle walked over to the table and placed a sterling silver tray down, beautifully arranged with finger foods, and fruits. She took a few ice cubes from the crystal container and poured him a glass of Evian, handing it to him with a smile. "Goodnight, you two. If there's nothing else, I'll be going to my quarters now. I still have two chapters to read before I go to my anatomy class tomorrow night."

"Goodnight Belle. Thank you. I think we're all set. Remember Belle, one chapter until midnight. The other one tomorrow. You're already a whole chapter ahead of the assignment."

"I know. I just get nervous about falling behind still."

"You're not going to fall behind. I told you, when you need more time, we'll make sure you have the time you need. Now, give me my hug and go on."

"Can I have one too—hug that is—Belle? Or better yet, can I give you a hug instead, and say thank you for your kindness?"

She allowed Yale to hug her, and hugged him in return. "Get some sleep, Yale. You too, Missy. I got better things to do than worry about the weariness in other people's eyes."

When Belle left, Yale sat on the bed totally exhausted. He lowered his head. His shoulders sagged. He felt near tears and didn't want it noticed. He was drained. He was vulnerable. And he was so sad. Lisa sensed his need for privacy. "I'm going too, Yale. If you need anything, let me know. I'm wiped out." She touched his shoulders gently. "Goodnight, Yale."

She heard him crying before the door was closed behind her, but decided to give him some space, and time alone to grieve, rather than go back to him.

She undressed in her room and slipped on a nightshirt. Her puppy was still at the vets, after being stung by some insect, which had caused Matey to convulse. She washed the makeup off her face, and was about to climb beneath the quilt, when she remembered she hadn't taken her nighttime medication. Belle had stopped leaving the pills on her nightstand since she spent so much time at Marissa's of late. She was about to go downstairs for her pills when she wondered if Yale had taken his prescribed meds. She knocked on his door before going downstairs. When he didn't answer, she opened the door and entered.

Yale didn't even know she was there. He was sitting, as she had left him, with tears falling from his eyes. He was rocking slowly, and his eyes were shut.

Lisa ran downstairs, dialed David, to confirm what medication Yale was ingesting, took her own, and returned to his room. "Stand up, Yale. David said, you always keep some of your medication in your wallet."

She got him up and undid his pants before letting him sit back down. She removed the pills from the plastic pouch in his wallet and handed them to him, with a glass of water. He swallowed methodically. She started to put him down on the bed and he whispered, "Please don't. Please."

"Then get undressed, Yale. And get under the covers."

"I will."

She decided to let him have his way and left. But she left the door to his room open.

She was in her bed when he walked in without knocking. He was in pajamas, holding a book in his hands. "You know, I think this was the last book my mother read. She said it was good. Did you read it?"

"No. Not yet."

"Well, I'll let you know if it's as good as she said."

"Okay. Thanks."

He bent and kissed her cheek, then pulled the quilt around her. "Goodnight Lisa."

He turned and left the room. He didn't close her door, and when she peeked out, minutes later, his door was also ajar.

When Lisa got up to use the bathroom during the night, she groggily went to check on Yale. She became alarmed when she noticed his bed was empty. She rushed to his adjoining bathroom, fearing he may have passed out again, but the room was vacant. Wide awake now, she rushed down the stairs, her heart pounding, and was relieved when she found him on the sofa in the library.

She checked her temptation to yell at him, for scaring the hell out of her, and inventively asked, "You couldn't sleep either?"

"I think I slept for about an hour, but something startled me awake. Probably a dream. When I couldn't fall asleep again, I came down here. I found your manuscript of 'Regrets' on the table. I've started reading it. Do you mind?"

"No. Actually, I'd appreciate an honest appraisal of the manuscript when you're done with it. Then tell me, if what I have in mind sounds like it might make a significant difference, will you?"

"Sure. I'd be glad to. Why are you up at four in the morning? Am I adding stress with my presence?"

"No. No. You're not the problem," she lied. "Matey, my little Beagle is still at the vets. She's been sick for a week already. I guess, I've just gotten used to having her at the foot of my bed."

"So you weren't upset when you found I wasn't in the bed, Lisa?"

"A little. I thought you might be distressed or—how did you know I went to look in on you?"

"I heard light footsteps suddenly become running feet down the staircase. You forget, a musician has an ear for sounds others don't."

"Well, I do miss my puppy too. Matey is so cute and cuddly."

"I can be cute and cuddly, Lisa. Can I sleep at the foot of your bed?"

"Sure. And if you snore I'll push you on the floor, with my feet, like I do Matey."

"I think I'll stay where I am then. This sofa's not bad. Probably not great for the back, but I'll make do."

"What's wrong with the bed? The mattress too firm?"

"No. The bed's cold. I couldn't get warm. That's why I've got this afghan of yours over me."

"Your mother made that afghan for me, Yale."

"I know. It's similar to one I have. I feel warmer beneath this than the quilt upstairs." His eyes misted.

"Can I get under it too? I can use a little of Ruth's warmth myself."

He lifted a corner and she snuggled beside him, under the beautifully stitched work of art, Ruth had hand crafted. She placed her head on his chest, and draped an arm across him as she found a comfortable position on her side. She placed her feet between his legs. He pulled the afghan around them, and pushed the remote to turn the lights off. They stayed side by side, listening to each others breathing, until sleep finally accompanied them back into the night.

CHAPTER 37

Neither Lisa nor Yale heard Belle enter in the morning. So deep in sleep were they that Belle's proclamation of "Lordy; Lordy; a dozen bedrooms in this place, and the two of them are glued together in the littlest room, on half a sofa, lookin' like a couple of peas in a pod."

Belle was grinning to herself as she retreated into the kitchen and prepared breakfast, taking special pleasure dividing several slices of strudel and placing them decoratively on a crystal platter.

After calling the veterinarian, she turned the ringer on the telephone system back to off and left it flashing. Then she asked the gardener to refrain from cutting the grass for a couple of hours. She requested he just bring her some fresh flowers, and the morning papers, for now.

When Belle heard their voices on the intercom, she turned off the system, and nonchalantly, carried a readied tray of brewed coffee, freshly squeezed orange juice, and the morning papers into the library, announcing, "Breakfast is ready any time you two are" and left.

Lisa stifled a laugh, since Belle was fully aware she never ate breakfast, and rarely had time to read the newspapers until evening.

"Is that clock accurate, Lisa? Is it really after ten?"

"How should I know? My eyes aren't opened yet?"

"Didn't you tell Marissa you'd be over around nine-thirty?"

"Yes. But I never said what day."

"Lisa, are you going to sit up soon.? I have to pee."

"So climb over me, Yale. I think I'm paralyzed."

He did just that, commenting, "Something smells good," as he got up.

"Well, it isn't your armpits, that's for sure!"

"Are you trying to tell me something, Lisa?"

She giggled. "That's what I love; a bright man, who catches on quickly." She pulled the afghan over her head. "Wake me tomorrow. I'm going back to sleep. I think I'll skip today."

He laughed as he made his way to the doorway, "Where's a bathroom down here?"

"Turn right and you can't miss it" she mumbled from under the coverlet, then giggled as she remembered it was supposed to be—turn left; not right, from this room.

She finally got up and poured coffee for them. Yale came back in smirking. "Remind me never to ask you for directions in the morning. A closet is to the right. The bathroom to the left. I almost pee'd in a pair of patent leather pumps."

They were having coffee when Belle walked in with two terry robes, placing them over a chair. "Marissa's on the phone, Miss Lisa. Do you want to call her back?"

"No. I'll get it in here. Thanks. And good morning, Belle."

"Good morning, back at you, Missy. Don't forget your pills, next to the juice."

"Okay. Thanks. Belle, there's a plastic pouch on Yale's dresser upstairs with a few pills in it. Would you mind bringing it down? We'll be in for breakfast shortly."

Lisa pushed the telephone speaker to on. "Hi Mariss', how's the little mother this morning?"

"Bored! Bored! Bored! Where are you?"

"I'm home, jerk. Remember, you called me?"

"What happened to nine-thirty, Lisa?"

"I skipped nine-thirty today. Sorry. How do you feel?"

"Fine. Are you alright, Lisa? What do you mean you skipped nine-thirty?"

"I overslept. I guess, I got jealous of how an indulged person must feel just lying around, reading magazines, being waited on, and thought I'd try it. Did Howard take Josh to school this morning?"

"Yes, and it's the housekeepers day off, so I'm all alone with the list of out-of-towners, and no itinerary prepared yet. We were supposed to call the hotels about accommodations remember?"

"Are you dressed, Marissa?"

"No. I'm still in a robe. Why?"

"That's cool. Get your list and go to the front door. I'm sending my driver over for you. You need to get out of your house—but don't bother getting dressed because Yale and I are in robes too. You'll have breakfast here, and then we'll handle the arrangements. You need a change of scenery, I just decided."

"Oh" was all Marissa said at the other end.

Lisa laughed. "Just call Howard and tell him you'll be here. I'm sending a car for you now."

"I could do it alone, if—"

"Don't give me a hard time, Mariss'. We have things to do, and I think Belle just opened a restaurant in my kitchen from the aromas floating around here. So, be a good girl and call Howard. I'll see you in half an hour. Byeee."

Belle was humming to herself as she merrily cleared the breakfast plates from the table where Marissa, Yale, and Lisa were still sitting, disheveled and in bathrobes.

Belle just kept on humming when the gate tone sounded and Lisa commented, "Wow! David got here quickly."

Belle activated the gates to open, and was still humming as she set a fresh place at the table before answering the front door. She returned to the kitchen with a smile, and a bundle, announcing, "I reckon this one won't be wanting any coffee," handing Matey to Lisa with a big grin.

"Oh, Matey. You're better. Look how happy she is to be home, Belle? Why didn't you tell me?"

"Hard to talk to sleeping people, Miss Lisa. Oops, there's the gate again. I suppose it's Mr. David this time."

After David had devoured the last piece of strudel on his plate and told Belle, "he couldn't possibly eat another piece, but she could wrap a couple of slices for him to take home for later" they all went into the library. Yale went crazy over Matey, and the little pup seemed very content to stay next to Yale.

Even after Lisa and Marissa concluded the last of the wedding plans, and Marissa went to say goodbye to Yale, the little beagle didn't move from Yale's side. Yale had been in the library with Matey and the manuscript of "Regrets" for nearly three hours.

Marissa bent and kissed Yale. "I'm going now. Lisa lent me this jogging outfit. Her driver is taking me to pick Josh up from school and take him home. I want to spend some time with him alone, for the next couple of days, and try to give him back a little of the sense of security he seems to have lost lately. Talk to you later, Yale."

Yale kissed her back, smiling. He was still in the robe, but at least his eyes weren't puffy, and his spirits seemed better.

After dinner Lisa snatched the manuscript out of Yale's hands proclaiming, "You've read enough of this today! Let's walk outside."

"It's getting dark," he countered, reaching to take the manuscript back.

"I'll get you a flashlight if you need more light. Come on."

The air felt good. The evening was cool and dry. They didn't say much, just walked, hand in hand, with Matey beside them. When they returned and Matey jumped up on Yale's lap, Lisa said, "Looks like you've got a new friend, huh?"

He looked at her, stroking Matey's coat, "I have more friends than I realized."

Belle came in to tell Lisa she was leaving for her class, and she'd see her in the morning. She was carrying a cardigan sweater, two books, and a notebook, with a pen attached to it.

"Good luck on the exam, Belle. You'll do fine. Just take your time, and remember to read each question carefully."

When Yale lost himself in the manuscript again, Lisa ignored it and went upstairs. She took a bath, dried her hair, and climbed into bed. She was almost asleep with the radio on, when Yale came in, wearing fresh pajamas. He had showered and shaved, and was holding Matey in his arms. "Can we both sleep in here tonight?" He tilted his head to one side, and panted, with his tongue out, copying Matey.

She smiled, lifting the quilt, and they both took their prospective positions; Matey at the foot of the bed; Yale against her. Yale put an arm across her tenderly; "Thank you for a good day, Lisa."

She checked her emotions before responding. "You're welcome."

Yale was already in the library, his nose between the pages of her manuscript, having coffee, when Lisa came down. She hadn't even heard him get up. Matey jumped off the sofa greeting her with licks and a wagging tail. Yale merely looked up from the manuscript, for a second, acknowledging her presence with, "Good. You're finally up. Now I won't have to eat my pancakes alone."

"Good morning to you too" she said sardonically, picking up her pills and juice from the tray, then leaving the room.

He appeared at the kitchen table, minutes later, sitting down across from her. "I asked Belle for blueberry pancakes. You don't mind, do you?"

She was going through several days of mail. She looked up with detachment and said, "Enjoy," then left Yale at the table.

Lisa continued going through the postmarked envelopes in the library when she heard Belle and Yale laughing uproariously. She pushed the intercom on to eavesdrop. She heard Yale. "Don't get up yet, Belle. Sit another minute. I have another great story. I think I was only ten or eleven, and my mother was late for work. I really wanted the blueberry pancakes she'd promised to make me. Me and my favorite childhood breakfast. Anyway, Mom says, "Yale, today I don't have time to make you pancakes. I'll be late for work.""

"So what did you do this time?" Lisa heard Belle ask, with a chuckle in her voice.

"I faked a soar throat, so convincingly, not only did I get my blueberry pancakes, but Mom didn't go to work, and I got to skip school."

"You were naughty as a child, weren't you, Yale?" Lisa heard Belle ask him.

"Not naughty really, Belle. But, I knew, there was nothing my mother wouldn't do for me, even then, and I was only a kid. Maybe, that's why I had a craving for these blueberry pancakes this morning. The association of something, with someone, who knew no boundaries in loving me."

Lisa felt stupid after listening in. She had reacted too quickly, and now it was too late to salvage the situation. She felt tears sting her eyes, but was too slow in brushing them away when Yale walked in. "What's wrong, Lisa? Something happen?"

She shook her head. "Nothing. Don't mind me."

She kept her eyes lowered, opening another piece of mail on her lap.

"Am I wearing out my welcome already, Lisa? Are you upset because of me?"

When she shook her head, still keeping her eyes from meeting his, he didn't believe her. "Why don't you try being honest, Lisa? It's like pulling teeth to get you to tell me what you seem to be able to say to everyone else. Why are you upset? What aren't you telling me? Have I done something?"

She looked at him. "I'm upset, because I'm jealous. Belle got to hear your stories instead of me, okay?" Her voice grew louder. "I'm jealous that Matey spends more time on your lap, than I do, okay? And I'm fucking sorry I ever gave you that damn manuscript—because I'm even jealous of all the time you're spending reading it, instead of talking to me!"

He bent in front of her and kissed her lips gently. "That's the most beautiful yelling at I've ever had, Lisa. You do still love me, don't you? You're not just empathic?"

"You're a fool, Yale Frye" she retorted, rising and leaving the room in a flurry.

He found her on the deck, with a pad of paper on her lap. She was lost in thought, looking like a schoolgirl, in a blue jersey sweater over jeans, with her hair pulled back by a scarf. She didn't acknowledge his presence.

He pulled a chaise alongside hers, and with her manuscript of "Regrets" in his hands, and sat down next to her.

The radio was on, but she seemed oblivious to the music. "It's nice back here, Lisa. Tranquil."

"Sometimes" she replied, without looking at him. "Other times it's lonely."

She wrote a few lines on blank paper, tore the sheet off, crumpled it, and placed it next to her.

"You want to be alone, Lisa?" He felt intrusive.

"I am alone, Yale. I hate to deal with it most of the time. But when you cut to the core, I've been alone a long time."

"I know the feeling, Lisa."

She kept her eyes from meeting his, and chose to doodle squares and circles on the pad. Glancing at her Rolex, she assessed, "Lunch should be ready in a few minutes."

Diverting from the nonsense, he extended her manuscript to her, "Here. I've finished reading your book. It's good. Really good."

After a quiet moment, she calculatingly responded, while continuing to scribble, "There's plenty of reading material. If you don't like any of the novels you chose, feel free to select something else."

"I don't think you should change one line of "Regrets," Lisa. It's perfect, as is. Who did you picture playing the female lead, opposite me, when you wrote it?"

She stopped doodling, turned her head to look at him, "Does it matter?"

He ignored her response. "I picture Debra Winger in the role. She's got the right combination of fire and ice for the part."

She chuckled. "Frank once said, it was too bad I couldn't act, because I'd be perfect for the part. He was right, you know. I can't act. People see right through me. I've never been able to balance how much of myself I want exposed and how much I do expose. I guess, I lack control or discipline."

"Why do you see your openness as a fault? It's what enables others to be so candid with you. I think it's a strength, Lisa."

She looked skyward. The clouds seemed low in the sky. The song coming from the radio was one of Yale's first platinum hits. "This is a good song, but I always thought it would sound better as a ballad. The words are so pretty."

"I agree. I originally wanted to record it in a rhythm and blue's mode, but the "big wigs" said it wouldn't be commercially profitable. They nixed my composition. Someday, I'll show you how I really wanted to record it."

"What if I don't like your composition?"

"I'd ask why. Your opinions are important to me."

"What did you like about "Regrets," Yale?"

"The life you gave each character. Everything was real. The love for Melonie, Shawn was able to display. The family. The principles and values the characters held to—all of it. It's a wonderful story. Wonderful!"

She continued to watch the clouds.

"Are you going to keep me at a distance Lisa?"

"Are you able to let me in, Yale?"

"I think so. I'm not afraid anymore. But I need a little help from you. I need to give as well as take. I don't want a lopsided relationship. I want to feel needed, not just in need of."

"I need you."

"Then why won't you look at me and say it? Why are you staring at the sky when I'm right here?"

"Because I'm frightened, Yale. Terrified, one day you'll decide to leave me. I don't think I could survive it. You have the ability to hurt me. That scares me, Yale. It scares me a lot."

"Does that mean you're going to remain guarded the majority of the time?"

"Whatever works."

"What works is connecting. Bonding. What works is expressing your needs, and allowing people to get close enough to help fulfill those needs."

"Now you're a "maven". Suddenly, you have all the answers?"

"No, Lisa. I don't have all the answers. I just want us to try a little harder, sharing our feelings without restraint. We've both been afraid too long. I want, so much, to spend a day—an entire day—in bed beside you, talking, touching, holding, understanding—"

"Then why don't you? Why are you telling me this now when you've been in bed with me and said absolutely nothing? You were next to me all last night, Yale. Did you expect me to beg you for more? I'm tired of longing for what I need! I'm sick of feeling disappointed! I don't need to deal with rejection, too."

"And I'm still man enough, Lisa, not to take unless I can give in return. Do you understand? I will only allow you to be caretaker of my soul, if I can be caretaker of yours. I'm not Frank. I don't need convalescent care until I die. I don't need love based on dependency. I need to feel whole on my own, and give as much as I am capable of to another whole person."

"Let's have lunch, Yale. I don't want to talk about this anymore. You're sabotaging all that Frank was with your preconceived notions. Dependency? Frank was man enough to admit when he needed me! He was strong enough to give me all of himself!"

"Sure, Lisa. He gave you control to manipulate the relationship, and meet all of his needs, because he knew your time together would be short. You guided, and you provided, until the end was inevitable for him. What did you get out of the relationship?"

"A royal-straight flush! A man who tried to mail you a letter, at the very beginning of our relationship, to explain he was dying and needed me! A man who wasn't afraid to admit he needed! A man who gave up control when he knew my strength would get him through! A man who responded to my manipulation because he trusted me! A man who gave me purpose and forced me to grow up! A man who was strong enough to be selfish, when he had to be! A man who allowed me to play the part of harlot when his manhood was threatened! No, Yale. Frank's love was not dependency—it was filled with substance—not bullshit! He died a happy man because of me! He died feeling whole and loved because of me! Sure, there was game playing—but we both were aware of it, and used the games to our advantage. It was a give and take kind of love, where neither of us kept score, Yale. We didn't need scorecards. We were united."

"Sounds like a hard act to follow, Lisa."

"That's where you've got it all wrong, again, Yale. You are a star. You don't follow another act. You have your own show. There's no one you have to compete with, or against. You told me to trust my instincts a little more, just the other night, at Marissa's. Why don't you try taking your own advice, Yale?"

"Because, like you, I'm often leery of the reaction I'll elicit. Funny, you tell me I don't have to follow anyone's act, when that's what I seem to be doing since we met. First, there was Ronnie; then Frank. Then, the fakery you invented about marrying Harvey. Is it any wonder I'm cautious about following my instincts?"

He had a point. She had no answer. The doors in her head were swinging back and forth from the tallying. How could they move ahead when the chains around them were so heavy? "Can we stop this,

Yale? There's no point." She picked up the crumbled paper, her pad of paper, and the manuscript. "Let's have lunch. I don't want to rehash old material. I'm not perfect. I'm human. I make poor judgments at times, and say the wrong things. But, so do you. I've come too far to start being defensive, all over again, about what was. Can we put it to rest?"

"Fine. But I'd like to say one more thing."

"Save it, Yale," she said, moving to the door wall and opening it. "Another time. Please!"

As she passed through the door, leaving him behind on the deck, he called after her, "I just wanted to say I love you, Lisa. No matter what, I always will."

She didn't turn around, or react. She had shut the door wall after herself. He didn't know whether she had heard him or not.

CHAPTER 38

Yale showed signs of restlessness the remainder of the day. He didn't open another book, and played with the remote several times, each time finding nothing of interest, ultimately turning the television off. He hadn't joined Lisa for lunch, and barely ate at dinner. Lisa was on the phone with Marissa when Yale announced he was calling it a night. It was only nine-thirty.

Lisa placed a couple of calls, then reread a few portions of her manuscript of "Regrets" before climbing the stairs. She noticed light at the base of Yale's closed bedroom door, but decided not to knock. They had said enough for one day.

She was relaxing in the tub when Yale appeared in the doorway. "I don't want to sleep alone. Can I stay?"

"Yes, you can stay, but there's a stipulation. Will you wash my back?" She looked up at him coyly, wondering if he would take kindly to being seduced.

He got on his knees and lathered a cloth. She sat up, exposing ripe breasts, then hugged her knees waiting to be soaped. "Lay back, Lisa. I'm not ready to do your back yet."

She obeyed.

He lifted her right leg, and caressingly sponged it with slow smooth strokes. He repeated the process on her left leg. She closed her eyes and purred. He put down the cloth, soaped his hands, gliding his palms over her neck and shoulders. Her nipples rose above the water level as she arched her back. He took advantage of the motion, leaning forward, and with gentle fingers rubbed the soapy solution under, around, and across her breasts.

She felt the longing for him in every pore. He tenderly kissed her face and mouth. The throbbing in his loins was undeniable. He rinsed her body with delicate hands and grabbed the soft pastel bath towel from the heated rod for her. He patted her dry, while kissing her, until they both felt their knees weaken. He guided her toward the bed. "Let me love you, Lisa. Love me back. I need your love."

"Don't talk, Yale. Show me. And I'll do the same."

He undressed and moved close beside her on the bed. "I want you, Lisa. I'm just jealous of everyone else you've loved."

She pulled him closer, feeling the heat, and ran her hands up and down the back of his torso. "We've both been forlorn long enough. Give me yourself, Yale. I want all of you."

He moved over her, his body craving hers, and took her like a virgin experiencing lovemaking for the first time. He touched every part of her, then penetrated gradually, feeling her muscles tighten around him. With slow rhythmical movements, they built a fire neither could extinguish.

In the morning he took her again, claiming, "I can't get enough of you, Lisa."

She nuzzled against him, feeling secure. Side by side, the morning hours slid into afternoon as they shared all that was relevant to understanding what the other experienced, during the times they were apart. She couldn't look him in the eyes when she admitted, honestly, "Part of me is so scared to love you completely, Yale. I want to. I'm just frightened."

He rubbed her arm, understanding completely what she meant.

"I don't want to lose you, Yale, but with all that's happened, all we've been through, can we believe our lives can have a fairytale—"They lived happily, forever after"—ending?"

"We could start with the—living happily—Lisa, and see how that goes."

She raised her chin and looked at him. "Okay, Yale. I'm ready to let happiness back into my life. Are you?"

"I don't want to be miserable anymore."

"Answer my question, Yale. Are you ready to let yourself be happy?"

"I just lost my mother, Lisa."

"I know."

"I may need help, Lisa."

"I'm here."

"I don't know how to ask."

"You don't have to ask, Yale. You just have to be able to accept it when it's offered."

"I love you, Lisa."

"Enough to let me love you back, Yale?"

"Yes."

"Good."

She smiled and kissed him tenderly before resuming her former position, cradling as close to him as she could get. He felt her warmth seep into the pores of his skin. And the last words she heard before falling asleep were the identical words her own heart spoke. "Thank you, God. Thank you."

Lisa wasn't sure if Yale's manhood, pressing against her back woke her, or her dream about his making love to her did. But she knew regardless of what initially brought her out of slumber, at that moment, she craved loving him. Slowly, yet methodically, she slid down, allowing her body to rub his member as she moved. She was beneath the quilt, kissing his inner thighs, when she first heard him sigh. She moved her mouth, engulfing him, and felt his hands stroke her hair. She let her tongue and lips covet him until his urgency could no longer be contained. Afterwards, he slipped beneath the covers and sought out her flesh with his mouth and tongue.

With the blanket keeping daylight out, and passion in, she begged him to never stop loving her.

"I need you, Yale. I need what you make me feel. I want the— forever after—too."

"I'll give it to you, Lisa. I swear I will. I know you're afraid to believe it. But I'm not going away. Not now—not tomorrow—not ever. We belong together."

"I wish I could give you a baby, Yale. You're so good with Josh. A part of me envies Marissa and Howard."

"I don't want a baby, Lisa. I'm too selfish. I don't want to share you. I want you to myself."

"Would you say that if you knew I still could bare a child?"

"Yes. All I want is you."

She didn't believe him, but didn't press the issue, instead asking, "Should I ask Belle to bring us a tray or are you tired of eating in bed?"

"No, I'm not tired of eating in bed," He chuckled at the innuendo. "Why? Are you?"

"Very funny, putz. You tell Belle this time. I'm going to shower."

She kicked at the quilt until it was on the floor, exposing their naked bodies to fresh air, then harmoniously they quickly retrieved the blanket and snuggled against each other, laughing until they felt warm again. Yale pushed the intercom on, and asked Belle to send up dinner. Both he and Lisa laughed again, when Belle was heard outside their door, obviously delivering a fresh tray, while removing a prior one, all the while muttering, "Lordy, Lordy, Lordy. One minute they be fighting, the next they be locked in a room all the day long. I'll never figure them two out."

Lisa rolled on top of Yale, mockingly pinning his hands down. "Lordy," she mimicked Belle, "I do believe I'm hungry, Mr. Frye. I just don't know what for—you or the food on the tray."

"You can have both, little lady," he teased, wrapping his legs around her in locked formation. "But do your want dessert before, or after?"

She covered his mouth with hers in reply.

Later on, they were nibbling on strudel and laughing as Yale tried to teach Lisa to sing in tune with songs on the radio. "Come on, Lisa. Listen closely."

"I am," she laughed. "I'm singing just like Whitney."

"Don't ever tell Whitney that. I think you've invented your own key."

She bellowed louder. "One—moment—in—time, to—be—all—that—I—can—be—"

"Stop! Stop! You're destroying a beautiful song."

"Oh yeh;—"Just—one—moment—in—time—"

"Please—Please—no more—"

"—Then—I—will—know eternity—" she bellowed, while Yale roared at her dramatic attempts to put feeling into her presentation.

So caught up were they in the musical demonstration and hilarious mischief they created, that neither heard the raucous on the stairs. Lisa was groping for a strong finale', along with Whitney Houston, when the bedroom door flew open and Harry and Rose stood there.

Lisa and Yale grabbed to cover their nakedness, while Rose bellowed, "Surprise, honey. We're here."

Lisa couldn't help laughing hysterically, as she took Yale's hand, yelling back, "Surprise to you too. This is Yale."

Yale sat mute, not sure what to do, unable to move.

Harry, who had followed Rose in, looked as uncomfortable as Yale. To break the tension he stated flatly, "Sounded like a fire broke out in here. We heard screeching."

"That was not screeching, Pa. I was singing. Now, be nice and say hello to Yale. Yale, these are my folks." She fell backwards on the bed giggling.

"It was screeching, Lisa. And it's nice to meet you, Yale," Rose continued, as if this was a normal occurrence. "I see the two of you are having strudel."

"Yes. Yale loves your strudel, Ma," she giggled, "Don't you?"

"Yup. Sure do. Great strudel—just great! The best!"

Belle was standing in the hallway, with her hands on her hips, shaking her head and muttering to herself again. "Lordy. Lordy. This be one for the books."

Harry looked at Yale and winked. "So, Yale, I hope you can teach Lisa to sing—not screech. You think there's hope for her?"

"No sir. Not as a singer. I think Lisa has many special 'talents' but singing isn't one of them."

Lisa slapped him on the back.

Harry laughed.

"See, honey," Rose injected, quite innocently, "We always said, a singer you're not. Now a professional agrees. Stick to writing."

"Okay, Ma. I guess I'll take a "professionals" advice. Yale thinks I should try to improve, though, so I have to practice trying to sing in key…"One—moment—in—time. Give—me—one—moment—"

"Rose, come on. Let's unpack. I think I'm getting a big headache."

"Good idea. We'll be downstairs, Lisa, if you decide to get out of bed. If not, we can find whatever we need ourselves. Nice to meet you, Yale. If you want more strudel don't be ashamed to say so."

"Nice to meet you—" he mumbled as they both exited, closing the door behind them. "Oh shit," he declared, lying down next to the still giggling Lisa, and burying his face in a pillow.

"Well, I guess my singing lesson will have to wait until later. Come on, Yale. Get your face out of the pillow, and your ass off the bed. We better get downstairs before my mother starts rearranging the furniture."

"Don't they knock, Lisa?"

"Once in a while, but not usually. You better start locking the bathroom doors for the next week, too."

"You're joking, right?"

"Nope."

She got out of bed, slipped into a red silk robe. With nothing else on, she went to the door challenging, "Do you have the balls to come downstairs or not? They're going to have a lot of questions, Yale. After all, I'm still their "little girl". As she was closing the door smirking, she heard Yale doing his Belle imitation on the other side of the door.

"Lordy; Lordy; Lordy; I feel like a teenager, caught with my pants down, in my girlfriend's bedroom."

Lisa opened the door seconds later and tossed Yale a shirt and pair of jeans from his room. "Two things honey. You're not a teenager. And secondly, you weren't caught with your pants down—you were caught with them OFF!"

Lisa was sitting at the kitchen table, with her parents, when Yale sheepishly entered. He sat down at the table. Belle swiftly brought him a cup of coffee. He looked up at the gentle face with gratitude, and took a sip of the brew. Lisa was telling her folks what had transpired with Jean regarding the manuscript.

"Maybe, you're overreacting about this, honey," Harry concluded. "After all, I read "Regrets" too. And I think it is fine—better than fine—just the way it is. What could make it better?"

"I agree," Yale daringly contributed, looking at Harry with respect for speaking his mind.

"See, Lisa. Yale and I are of the same mind." He looked at Yale briefly, then asked his daughter, "So, tell me already, what do you want to change?"

"The ending. It's a trite ending. Too simplistic. I could build on it."

"No Lisa. You know it's the right ending, and perfect as is. Maybe, you don't want to let go of the manuscript for other reasons? Huh?"

Yale watched tears fill her eyes, and Harry reach for her hand, squeezing it.

"Lisa, I know you."

"I know you do, Pa." The tears fell down her face and onto the table, leaving wet droplets on the marble top.

"Lisa, start a new book. This book is completed. There are no more chapters. Frank is dead. You can't give him life with more chapters. And you can't keep punishing yourself, because you weren't there when he died."

"I know, Pa. But if the book is published, and it's not a success, I'll feel I let Frank down, in another way, for the rest of my life. "Regrets"— is all I have to give to the memory of Frank."

The tears on the tabletop were multiplying rapidly.

"Lisa, you gave Frank more—much more than one thing. What— you think because Frank knew you were in love with Yale, when you married him that it diminishes what you brought to his life? Honey, you're wrong. So wrong. What about time, Lisa?"

She looked at her father questioningly, as the tears continued to cascade from her eyes.

"Yes, Lisa. Time. You gave Frank time that you can never get back. Every day you gave to, and shared with Frank, was a gift that was his alone. Honey, he took your gift of time, until he couldn't anymore. Let go already. Frank knew when he had to."

"Maybe, there are no more books in me, Pa."

"How will you ever find out if you don't try again, Lisa? You're wasting valuable time, aren't you? Move on to a new story, honey." He took out a handkerchief, from the pocket of his slacks, and extended it to her.

She blew her nose and raised her eyes to look at Yale while she directed her words to her father. "Yale thinks Debra Winger would be good for the female lead, if the book is developed for the screen, Pa. What do you think?"

"I don't know about the female lead. However, Yale would be my first choice for the male lead, since the character stems from your feelings for him."

"I'm an entertainer, Harry. A singer. I've never been a lead in a movie."

"So, you don't like the idea, Yale?"

"No. I mean, I like the notion. I don't know if I could do the part justice, that's all."

"So, Yale, it seems there's only one way to find out. Right?"

Yale looked back at Lisa before responding. She smiled at him with misty eyes. "Well Harry, I'm not getting any younger. I've always wondered about making movies. Maybe, I shouldn't have rejected the part the first time it was offered to me. If it comes my way again, I'll consider your implication very seriously, and find out if I can handle the part. Thanks for your vote of confidence, Harry."

"Don't mention it. I have good instincts, Yale. I know people. Stick around—you'll see."

Rose, who had been unusually subdued, suddenly broke her silence. "I know people too, Yale. But I let my heart guide me, like Lisa. That's why we get hurt so easily. We give away too much of ourselves. Maybe, it's not a good trait."

"I love your daughter, Rose. I'm not going to hurt her."

"Good. She's suffered enough."

"So have I, Rose."

Harry pushed his chair back from the table and stood up. "I'm going to catch the National News now. Rose, come on. Let's see what's going on in the rest of the world."

"Harry, do you want a coffee in the den?"

"Yes, Rose, I could use another cup. Thanks."

"Yale, would you like a fresh cup, as long as I'm pouring?"

"No. Thank you, Rose. I'm coffee'd out. I think I'll just go upstairs and read for a while."

"I'll be up in a minute, Yale."

"It's okay, Lisa. Visit with your parents. I'm tired anyway."

"I guess I wore you out today," she teased, sensing his tenseness, and attempting to lighten the atmosphere.

"No. You didn't wear me out. I just feel sick inside, Lisa. I just felt this wonderful connection between you and your parents. I witnessed parental love and caring, and suddenly it hit me that I'll never know those feelings again. God, I took so much for granted."

He left the room while Lisa, Rose, and Harry, stood together, as the family unit they were. He felt alone again, and knew the emptiness he was experiencing was not going to diminish for a long time. He didn't read in his room. He turned the lights off, locked the door, and cried.

CHAPTER 39

"Unlock the door, Yale. I know you're awake. Come on, Yale. Let me in. It's after ten, and you never sleep this late. Yale, open the door please, or I'll get the master key. I left you alone last night, Yale, but I'm not going to now. Yale, talk to me. Yale…"

"What's going on up there, Harry? Why is Lisa yelling?"

"I'm not sure yet, Rose. I heard her shouting and walked over here by the staircase. I think they slept in separate rooms, and he locked the door, without letting her in."

"Why?"

"What am I—a mind reader, Rose?"

"Yale, open the door! Yale—"

"Okay. It's open. Are you happy now?"

"I was worried about you, Yale. Why didn't you let me in last night? Are you alright?"

"Fine. I'm fine, Lisa. I just need some space. I called David. He's picking me up. I have to go home for a while."

"Why, Yale? Because my parents are here? What's this about?"

"It's time, that's all. I need to be in my own home, not someone else's. I need—."

"Someone else's? Yale, you make it sound like you're in a strangers house. Yale, it's me. Why are you going?"

"I have to, Lisa. I just have to. I don't belong here now. Your boys will be here soon too. Your parents. I'm an outsider, Lisa. Don't you see?

To them, I'm a stranger. You are one big happy family, Lisa, and I'm a guest. A visitor."

"You're and asshole—that's what you are! How are you ever going to get to know my parents, or my boys, if you run away? You just said, a few days ago, that you couldn't stand the thought of being in your own home now. That Ruth was everywhere…that you saw her rearranging food in the refrigerator …kissing your forehead…"

"I know what I said, Lisa. But this is just as bad. I see a family, when I have none. I see a mother—when mine is gone. I see love, respect and concern. I can't stay, Lisa. I see everything I'll never have, and it hurts. It's too painful. Please, try to understand…I need a few days… Please!"

"No! No! I won't try to understand, Yale! I need you! You said, you needed me. You said, we belong together! This is being together? You locked yourself in here and shut me out last night, Yale. I'm not going to let you shut me out again! I don't want you to leave, Yale. I want you here with me—here in this house—here—in one bedroom—our bedroom. Don't run off Yale…don't leave!"

He went and picked up the suitcase David had brought over a day ago, and kissed her cheek softly. "I'm sorry, Lisa. I can't stay. There are ghosts in this house too. Only here, I don't know any of them. At least in my own home the ghosts are familiar, and I know their history."

"Yale. Don't go. Please…or take me with you, if you don't want to stay here. I don't want you to be alone. Yale, you're going through a difficult time…Yale…"

He stopped at the top of the stairs, looking back at her in front of the room he'd cried in all night long. "Lisa, I'm not Frank. I don't want to be taken care of until I die. I don't want to be taken in because I'm alone. I'm not up for adoption, Lisa. Don't feel sorry for me…"

"I do feel sorry for you, Yale, because you're stupid and pathetic! You're not being taken in because you're alone or sick. You're here because I want you here…because I love you…because I need you, as much, if not more, than you need me."

"I wish I could believe that, Lisa. I'll call you."

He walked past Harry and Rose at the bottom of the stairs, without a word, appreciating they made no excuse about being where they could hear what was going on. He poked his head into the kitchen. "Thanks for everything, Belle. Especially, the blueberry pancakes and your good company."

He bent down and stroked Matey at the front door. "Go on Matey. Lisa has a treat for you. Go on."

As the pooch turned to look for Lisa, Yale pushed the button for the gates, opened the front door, and walked toward David approaching in the BMW, down the driveway.

Inside the house, Lisa stormed into the kitchen yelling, "Belle, there's been a change. Put Yale back on the "shit list". I'm busy when he calls. And, I swear, if you interfere you'll be looking for a new position elsewhere. Now, get a car over here for me, please. I have shopping to do. I need a few things for my trip to England, after Marissa's wedding. I'm going to go see Harvey and Michelle before their baby is born. Why wait?"

"Okay, Missy," was all Belle said, exchanging glances with Harry and Rose.

Lisa immersed herself in so much activity until Marissa's wedding day that she was able to function without evidence of frailty. Her hours were consumed. Her heart impenetrable. She had reached an impasse, and until she could sort it all out, she immunized herself to feeling. She told her parents to refrain from even trying to talk to her about Yale, and closed the subject.

She briefly tolerated Marissa's inquiries, ending all speculation that time apart might make them see how much they needed each other, by retorting—Yale was not man enough for her. She declined to discuss Yale with Marc and Steve, after their arrival. Only the commitment that she and Yale take daily turns watching Josh, while Marissa and Howard were honeymooning, remained unaltered. She decided to put off calling Harvey and Michelle, about a visit, until after Marissa's honeymoon, and had begun writing a new novel to fill the late night hours, when sleep was a fugitive.

The day of the wedding Lisa was as nervous as Marissa, only her anxiousness was attributed to having to be with Yale, for the first time, since he left her home. She was Marissa's maid of honor, and Yale was giving the bride away. They would be linked all day, and seated together at the head table for the reception. She prayed to God, on the way to the ceremony, to give her the strength she needed to maintain her composure, and not spoil anyone's time. She and Marissa had agreed not to see each other until it was time to walk down the aisle that day, for fear of becoming too emotional. But they had managed to call each other more than a dozen times since early morning.

Limousines lined Marissa's driveway as everyone arrived to witness the couple exchange vows. Lisa entered Marissa's estate with her parents in front of her, and Marc and Steve beside her. The first person she spotted, as she looked toward the floral covered banister, was Yale. He looked magnificent in his black tuxedo and peach ruffled shirt. His blue eyes sparkled as they met hers. He approached her immediately, and quite unexpectedly.

"You look absolutely gorgeous, Lisa. As pretty as the bride upstairs, who is having a hard time with Josh. He refuses to put on the tuxedo."

She giggled. "It figures. I'll go see what I can do, Yale. Will you escort my folks and boys in?"

"Sure. Hi Marc; Steve. It's been a long time." He extended his hand. "You grew up nice. You're both handsome. Hello Harry, Rose. Nice to see you again. Follow me and look around at the flowers your daughter had flown in, from the island, for Marissa. They've created an exotic splendor."

"It is pretty, isn't it Harry? It's easy to understand why Frank loved the island so much."

"Big deal. Flowers."

Yale laughed. So did Marc and Steve. "Come on Harry, they're beautiful. Frank was a lucky man. Waking up beside Lisa every morning. Seeing her beauty next to him, and the beauty of majestic nature outside his window as well. What more could anyone ask for?"

"I don't know. Why don't you tell me, Yale?"

He looked into Harry's eyes with sadness. "To feel you belong in the beauty of your surroundings, Harry."

Yale seated them in the front row, only feet away from the floral canopy, which had been designed especially for the occasion. The seats were filling quickly in the floricultured area behind Marissa's estate. Yale excused himself as he heard Howard call him, and walked past the rows of armless chairs, seizing a moment to take a deep breath.

"Yale, we've got a problem. Lisa got Josh to put on the tuxedo, but he'll only walk down the aisle if you and Lisa walk down with him. He doesn't want to go it alone in front of all the people."

"I don't blame him, Howard. Where is he?"

"Upstairs with Lisa. In his room. She didn't want Marissa hysterical before the ceremony, so she took Josh to his room. He's being a 'Royal' pain."

"I'll go up, Howard."

"We've only got a few minutes."

"Don't worry, Howard."

Yale went up to Josh's room and found Lisa playing "go fish" with Josh on his bed. "Okay, Lisa, do you have any tens?"

"Yup. I've got two tens. Here."

"Lisa, do you have any three's?"

"Nope. Go fish, Josh."

"Excuse me, you two, but the wedding is about to begin."

"We know, Uncle Yale. We're ready. I'm walking with you and Aunt Lisa. She said so. I just can't let Buster come to the wedding 'cause he might bark too loud. Right, Lisa?"

"Yup. That's right. Now, Josh, do you have any fives?"

"Nope, go fish, Lisa."

"Oh, I think I hear the music starting. We'll have to finish our game later, Josh. Leave the cards here, and go give your Mom a kiss for luck. Tell her we're ready."

"No! I'm still mad at her for locking Buster up."

"Go kiss your Mom now, Josh, and tell her we're ready, or I'm leaving this room and never playing with you again!"

"Okay. Okay. I'm going. You don't have to get excited."

He walked to Marissa's room, as Lisa stood with her hands on her hips, in her apricot lace Givenchy dress, watching him. He knocked on the door. Marissa came into the hallway.

The white chiffon gown seemed to float around her as she kneeled to kiss Josh. The layered dress concealed the waistline Marissa swore was expanding daily. She looked happy and angelic. Soft auburn curls rested on her shoulders, and a woven ring of tiny white rosebuds cloaked the top of her head.

Josh took her hand and kissed it. "We're ready now, Mom. Come on. I want everyone to see how you look."

Marissa was so affected by Josh's spontaneous words of approval; she couldn't suppress the tears that sprang forth. "You look pretty terrific too, Josh. Thank you for putting on the tuxedo."

"It's not so bad, Mom. Anyway, Lisa decorated it inside. She put a Ninja Button on the shirt. See. No one can see it, but I get to smile when I walk down the aisle with her and Uncle Yale 'cause I know it's there, and nobody else will."

She took Josh's hand and approached Lisa and Yale. The music began. Her couturier rushed to her with the bridal bouquet. She kissed Yale, then Lisa.

"Before I walk down these stairs, Lisa, I want you to know how much—"

"Not now, Marissa. I'll lose it, completely, if you start. Come here, Josh. It's time."

They were at the floral archway. The violins began. Lisa squeezed Josh's hand softly. "Where's your smile, Josh?"

He looked up at her with a big grin.

She looked at Yale. He smiled. They walked down the aisle and took their places. Josh next to Howard; Yale facing her on the opposite side of the chuppah.

Lisa didn't hear the exchange of vows. She was lost in reverie for all but a few words. It was only when Howard kissed his new bride and whispered, "I love you. Sincerely, I do" that she jolted back to reality.

Yale had not taken his eyes off Lisa for one second during the rites. He was captivated by her elegance, stirred by her delicate, yet firm, handling of Josh, and moved by her warmth. She embraced so easily; so completely.

Josh walked between Marissa and Howard up the velvet center aisle after the matrimonial ceremony. Lisa was on Yale's arm. He was taken aback when halfway up the aisle she murmured, "This feels so right" that he blurted, "What?" wanting to make sure he'd heard her correctly.

"Nothing, Yale. I was just thinking out loud."

She let go of his arm almost immediately thereafter, and excused herself as she rushed away.

Marissa thought Lisa's tears were tears of joy for her. She hugged her dearest friend tightly, and promised to be as supportive when Lisa remarried, which only caused fresh tears to sting Lisa's eyes.

"I love you, Marissa. Just be happy, every single moment, of each and every day."

"If you don't stop, Lisa, I'm going to fall apart. See. Now my mascara's going to run. Do you have a tissue?"

"Allow me" Harry offered, taking a handkerchief out of a pocket. "Mazel Tov, Marissa. Mazel Tov, Howard. A long and happy life together."

"And that goes double for me" Rose added, placing a hand on Lisa's shoulder affectionately. "Maybe, I'll live long enough to see my Lisa married again. I can only pray."

Lisa felt knifed and overreacted. "You'll need ten lifetimes before you ever see me say "I do" again, Ma! My days as a wife are over. My motto is: Use them. Then lose them!"

She hurried off, brushing her father's hand away; nearly knocking Yale down in her haste.

"I don't know why she's talking this way. I don't believe my ears."

"It's alright, Rose. She's a little tired today. I saw her yawning before. I'll go find her."

"Harry, I know my way around here. Would it be alright if I get her instead?"

"Go ahead, Yale. But I'd appreciate it if you ignored what Lisa said."

"She said it wrong anyway, didn't she, Harry? It's more like—they need her; then desert her—wouldn't you agree?"

"Yes, Yale. I agree. I'm glad to see you're not only a fine entertainer, but a man of wisdom as well."

"Not always, Harry. But I'm learning. I never should have left her house, Harry. Running in circles never gets you anywhere."

"Also spoken wisely, Yale."

He found her smoking a cigarette in Marissa's bedroom. She was standing in front of the triple dresser, her back to him, looking at the numerous framed photographs covering the bureaus top.

"Marissa's going to need a bigger dresser, for all her photos, pretty soon. She's always been a pack rat. I remember, when the fire ruined the house, I tried teasing her, by telling her; at least she got rid of some of her junk. She got furious. I guess I didn't time my comment appropriately. She was back in the house less than a week, and I remember vividly, she'd already scattered numerous collectibles throughout. I was amazed."

"It's nice. It makes a house—"homey". What do you collect, Yale?"

"I used to like collecting old records and original sheet music. Lately, all I collect is self pity. I think the latter is more difficult to dispel. It clings to you like garlic."

She turned to face him and took another drag of the cigarette.

"I once collected stamps. Foreign and American. It got boring. Now, I collect clowns. They're fun and more—me."

"I have a clown for you, Lisa. It's big and sort of goofy. It's an original, but I don't know it's worth. It's kind of lonely all by itself. Maybe, you'd be able to make it feel special; make it feel—homey. I think it could use your special handling."

"Really? I'd like to see it."

"You're looking at it, Lisa. So—what do you think?"

"Originals are hard to come by, Yale. But they make me nervous. What if I lose it? What if I get attached to it, and I go to look at it, and it's gone? It's happened to me before."

"I don't think you have to worry, Lisa. This clown doesn't want to stay hidden anymore. It wants to be appreciated. To feel a part of things. It's been miserable alone, wrapped in cellophane, and kept in storage. It needs love."

"Does this 'clown' dance?"

"I think so. But it's been in storage for so long, I really don't recall how well."

"Why don't we find out, Yale?"

CHAPTER 40

Harry and Rose couldn't take their eyes off the dance floor. Even Marc and Steve were transfixed watching Lisa and Yale mambo, waltz, jitterbug, cha-cha, conga, samba, and two-step, as if they had choreographed a eurhythmic event for the occasion. They moved around the floor like swans on water. And when the beat gained momentum, their steps were so synchronized that Arthur Murray would have been jealous that he couldn't take credit for being instrumental for their graceful floatacious symmetry. Some of the gyrations raised Rose's eyebrow, and turned more than a few pairs of eyes green. The two whirled oblivious to everyone except each other.

When the band stopped for a break, Lisa took Yale's hand and breathlessly tugged him toward their table. "I haven't danced this much in years, Yale. My feet are killing me."

She sat down next to her father, kicking off her shoes. "I'm pooped, Pa. I must be getting old."

Yale was standing beside her smiling. "I'm exhausted from just watching the two of you. But you dance nice together. Very nice."

"Thanks, Harry. Rose, your daughter wants to sit the next one out. Will you dance with me?"

"Sure, Yale. But no fancy stuff, please. I'm a lot older than she is."

When the music resumed, Yale waltzed around the floor with Rose, while Harry and Lisa watched. Marc and Steve found some pretty young women, and they were also on the dance floor.

"Ma looks good, Pa. She always loved to dance."

"Both of you dance well, Lisa. But neither of you can sing worth bupkas."

"Very funny, Pa. And you have such a great voice?"

"No. But better than yours. Want to dance with me, Lisa?"

She put her shoes back on, and followed her father onto the dance floor.

"You know, Pa, it's been years since I've danced with you. You're not bad. Not bad at all."

He guided her toward Yale and Rose, and purposely bumped into them. "Excuse me, Yale, but could we exchange partners. I think you're holding my Rose too close. I'm getting jealous."

Harry winked at Yale, as he handed Lisa over to him, and took Rose in his arms. "Come closer, Rose. With me it's allowed."

Lisa laughed as she went back into Yale's arms. "They are so cute together. Aren't they great?"

"Yes. They're special people. I think they'll be wonderful in-laws."

Her eyes darted up to meet his. "What did you say?"

"I said marry me, Lisa, the only way I could."

She stepped on his toes and stumbled. He helped her get her balance back. He pulled her closer to him.

"I shouldn't have left your house the other day. I was wrong. I can't run away from what hurts, and we've both wasted enough time apart. I want you for my wife. I want us together. Forever. Marry me tonight, Lisa. The Rabbi's still here. Your family is here. I don't want to wait another day. I love you."

"Okay."

This time, he stepped on her toes. "What?"

"I said, yes, Yale. I'll marry you tonight. I don't want to spend another night, for the rest of my life, without you beside me."

He stopped dancing and stood looking into her eyes in the middle of the dance floor. "Really? Tonight?"

"Yes, Yale. I love you. I'm not letting you get away again. Not ever."

"Will you feel cheated out of a big wedding, Lisa?"

"No, Yale, I won't. Will you be happy to spend your honeymoon at the house—with my folks—and my boys—and Josh?"

"Sounds like a great honeymoon to me, Lisa."

"Well, I guess we should tell the family and get the Rabbi then."

"Rings. We need Rings, Lisa."

"Oh, right. Does this mean we have to wait then?"

"Nope. Come on, Lisa."

He took her hand and led her back to their table. She sat down. He placed his hands on her shoulders, as he stood behind her. He turned to her parents, "Harry, Rose, I've got a problem. I just asked Lisa to marry me. Tonight. I hope you approve."

"You have no problem, Yale. Rose and I give you our blessings."

"Thank you, Harry. But there's another problem. We don't have rings, and Judaism dictates wedding vows should be exchanged in plain bands. Everything we're wearing has gemstones. Any suggestions?"

"Yes, Yale. I suggest you ask me to lend you my plain gold wedding band; the one I wore when I married Rose, forty-eight years ago. I further suggest you wear it for the next forty years, and be as blessed, in you marriage to Lisa, as I have been in mine, married to her mother."

"Bless you, Harry. And thanks."

"I am blessed, Yale. And you're welcome. Rose, it looks like your prayers have been answered. I bet, even you, are surprised at how quickly."

"I'm not surprised by anything, anymore, Harry. Lisa, I have my gold wedding band at the house. If you'd like, I would be happy to see you wear it."

"I'd be proud to, Ma. Yale, could we ask the Rabbi to come to the house and be married there, privately, after Marissa's reception? I'd prefer to keep this to ourselves tonight. Marissa will never leave Josh with us if she knows we're getting married. I don't want her to feel anything, but completely happy, and carefree, tonight. I know her. She'd end up changing all her plans around."

"See why I love her so much, Harry. She's concerned about everyone. The lady is selfless."

By midnight, all the guests departed. Lisa was helping Josh pack a few more 'must take with' items in a duffle bag. He was excited about taking Buster, and staying at the house with her and Yale.

Yale was downstairs getting Buster. Her parents and boys had already left for home, and were going to ready a makeshift chuppah for her nuptials. Marc and Steve had been delighted by the news. They liked Yale and knew their mother really loved him.

Lisa and Josh were almost done packing when Lisa heard yelling coming from Marissa's bedroom, where the bride and groom had gone to change for their flight.

"I said, no, Howard! Never! Never! This is my business—not yours!"

"It's my business, now, too. I'm your husband, Marissa. I'm not going to keep quiet just because you say so!"

"Stay out of it, Howard! I'm warning you—"

"Warning me? What is that—a threat, Marissa?"

"Please, Howard. We'll talk about it later. Don't start—"

Lisa looked at Josh who had become sullen and quiet. "Ready, Josh?"

"I guess so, Lisa. Do I have to say goodbye to them?"

"I think it's a good idea, Josh. I think Mom is going to miss you a lot while she's on her honeymoon. Maybe, she needs a big hug, huh?"

"She doesn't need a hug, Lisa. She doesn't even need me no more. She's going to have a new baby, and Howard told her to stop spoiling me." His eyes filled.

"Josh, maybe Mom and Howard need time to talk about their differences. I know they love you very much. Sometimes, grownups say things because they're upset too. They need you, Josh. A new baby can't take your place. Not ever."

"Sometimes I hate them, Lisa. They've been screaming at me to leave them alone a lot. They send me out of the room—but—but—I hear the shouting. I don't care if they ever come back from their dumb honeymoon!"

She moved closer and wrapped her arms around Josh who was crying openly now. "It'll be okay, Josh. We'll have a great time while Mom and Howard are away. I promise."

Yale jAunted in with Buster beside him. He immediately went up to Josh, realizing some difficulty had developed, and plopped down on the bed. "Hey, big guy, I'm too tired to make a bunch of trips up and down the stairs. Think you can give your Uncle Yale a hand, carrying some of the stuff to the car? I sure could use your help."

"Yeh. Sure. It's better than staying up here and listening to Mom and Howard fighting. Will you come with me, Uncle Yale, to Mom's room? I gotta say good-bye. Lisa said, I should."

"Sure, sport. Get on my shoulders and we'll all go say good-bye together. Okay?"

They knocked on Marissa's door and eventually said their farewells. Marissa promised to call everyday. Howard said, maybe every other day. Marissa promised to send postcards. Howard said, not to expect too many postcards, since he was going to keep Marissa "too busy" to do too much writing. Marissa promised to bring Josh back a present from Monte Carlo. Howard stated, he couldn't imagine what kind of kids stuff they could find in Monte Carlo, but surely Marissa would find something to buy. Marissa hugged Josh, saying she was really going to miss him. Howard said, Josh should behave himself and not be any trouble. Marissa ran down the stairs, and out to the car, to give Josh one more kiss. Howard stayed in the bedroom, putting last minute paperwork in his briefcase to take along.

Josh stroked Buster's coat in the back seat of the car. "Sorry you had to be locked up, Buster. It wasn't my idea, you know."

Lisa and Yale exchanged glances, in the front seat of the vehicle, both empathic to the tribulations Josh was experiencing.

"How about some pizza, Josh? Why don't we stop and pick one up on the way to Lisa's place? I'm a little hungry. How about you?"

"Could we get it with pepperoni, Uncle Yale?"

"Sure. Do you like pepperoni on your pizza too, Lisa?"

"Sure do. And lots of cheese."

By the time they got to the house, each one of them had already devoured three slices of pizza, and an Italian ice. Josh was in a better mood, and as he helped Yale carry his things into the foyer, he seemed very wide-awake considering the hour.

Josh's cherubic face was glowing as Yale and Lisa exchanged wedding vows. He was as enthusiastic as Marissa would have been had she been there.

His appearance, from his auburn hair, to his delicate features, and full mouth, were so like his mothers that to Lisa it felt, in a certain way, that Marissa was indeed watching her wed the man she adored. Even Josh's expletives were duplicates of words Marissa would have used.

"Yes! Oh yes!" Josh wholeheartedly rejoiced when his Uncle Yale sealed the marriage with a long hard kiss on Lisa's waiting lips.

Lisa could hardly believe she really married Yale after the timetable that had kept them apart for so long. But, somehow, she felt this was the suitable time, and appropriate surrounding. What more could she hope for? Her parents and sons were there. Belle was on hand. And Josh provided the same vivaciousness his mother would have. Even his smug smile was so like Marissa's. Lisa never really appreciated their strong facial similarities before.

Sagaciously, Harry said, after the Rabbi left, "This calls for a toast to my daughter and new son-in law. Then, my fine young man, Rose and I will tuck you into bed, Josh, and let the bride and groom have a little time alone together. Tomorrow is another day."

It was after three, when Yale finally carried his bride into the bedroom. Lisa was reluctant to close her eyes as she snuggled against Yale. He felt much the same as he sought to feel the gold ring on her left hand.

"I told you, we belonged together, Lisa. I'm never going to let anything come between us. I worship you, Mrs. Frye. I finally feel whole."

She stroked his bare chest softly. "It took long enough for this moment to arrive, Yale. Now, I know you're mine. I've got you for good, Mr. Frye, and I don't intend to share you with anyone, ever. I've waited too long to take what I needed to make me happy. I intend to stay as elated as I feel right now."

"I want you, Lisa. Passionately. I want you like I've never wanted anyone. Come here. I want to consummate this marriage."

CHAPTER 41

Marissa and Howard were arguing between sips of cappuccino at the airport. They were sitting in the VIP lounge, waiting for clearance notification of their flight. Dense fog had delayed their departure. Marissa was pleading with Howard to put off leaving for Monte Carlo, for one day, and take her home.

"No. I want us to leave as scheduled, even if we have to wait another hour, or two, for the fog to lift. If you go home, you'll call Josh, and we'll have to deal with all the good-bye crap, all over again. This is best. Just drink your coffee. It can't be much longer."

"I'm tired, Howard. I'd like to get some sleep. We could be here for hours. Can't we, at least, get a room nearby until the fog lifts? There's a hotel less than a mile from here."

"Let's wait another half hour. If the fog is as dense then, and it looks like the delay will be longer than anticipated, I'll get us a room. But I won't have you calling Josh. Do you understand, Marissa? As far as he's concerned, we're on our honeymoon. I don't need to deal with all the whimpering you go through every time you deal with him. You know you're too close to that kid of yours, don't you? It's not normal."

"Don't tell me what's normal, Howard. How would you know? You've never been a parent!"

"Shut up, Marissa! At least I know the consequences screwing around can create. Want to sling mud, Marissa?"

She flung her empty cup at him and stood up. "I'm getting a room, Howard. I'll take a taxi to the Shelby Hotel. Call me when you get word that we can take off. I'm not sitting here all night. Nice wedding night!"

"Alright! I'll get us a room and have someone notify us when there's flight clearance. But I won't have you calling Josh. I'm only agreeing to this because you're pregnant and could use some rest."

"How big of you, Howard!"

She followed him to the exit. Because of the numerous departure delays, availability of a limo or taxi was backlogged. Marissa again followed Howard until he halted in front of a car rental counter; rudely demanding the clerk, expeditiously, have a car brought to them. He was being loud and crude. She was humiliated by his arrogance, and totally outraged by the time she took the passenger seat in the only subcompact vehicle that had still been available.

"What's the big deal, Howard? I don't need a Mercedes to go back and forth from the airport in. I just want to sleep for an hour. Stop acting like such a schmuck!"

"Don't tell me how to act, Marissa. If you weren't carrying my baby I'd have waited in the lounge, rather than go through all this shit. I can't even see where I'm going."

"Turn the headlights off, Howard. They make it harder to see in a fog."

"Do you want to drive, Marissa? If not, just shut your mouth and let me handle this!"

"Yes, Howard. You handle everything so well! I couldn't even leave my wedding reception feeling good because you couldn't understand how frightened Josh was, at being left behind. Maybe, I would have been better off losing this baby when I started bleeding! Your insensitivity shocks me!"

"Shut up, Marissa! I don't feel like listening to your stupidity right now. Is that the exit?"

"Don't tell me to shut up, Howard! I've already been in one abusive marriage. And I'll tell you, right now, that I won't stay in another relationship where I don't get treated with respect. Baby or not! Do you understand—?"

"Watch out, Howard! Oh God—Howard—Howard—"

CHAPTER 42

Dawn was unveiling, but Yale and Lisa didn't notice. They hadn't slept. Instead, they spent the hours of darkness exploring each other's bodies and minds. The goose-down, pastel comforter covered their nakedness, while their heads shared one pillow. The satin sheet beneath them couldn't have felt any warmer had it been flannel instead. The smell of lovemaking dominated the expensive perfumes they took to bed with them hours before. And the stubble on Yale's face felt good against Lisa's cheek as she sighed, content, against him.

"Can I change my mind about something, Yale? I've decided I really do want a honeymoon. I'm jealous of Marissa and Howard. They get to be alone—all alone—together—just the two of them—for hours and hours. Can we go away, just the two of us, when they get back?"

"For how long?"

"Forever."

"You've got a deal. Where do you want to go, Lisa?"

"Anywhere I can have you all to myself. The location isn't important."

"Can we go to Boston first?"

"Sure, Yale. But I think Ruth knows without us having to be there."

"Maybe. But I didn't say goodbye the way I need to. I was too upset. I felt the only woman I could count on had left me. This issue with trusting is a tough one for me, Lisa. I'm so afraid of betrayal, I can't get close to people the way I want to anymore."

"You promised me earlier, Yale, that you wouldn't run away again. Did you mean it?"

"I won't run, Lisa, but I can't swear that the urge won't be there."

"If we try to be this straightforward with each other, all of the time, perhaps the trust will follow."

"It's funny. I trust men more than women—and that's not much—even though my father was my first experience with desertion."

"Yes. But your mother was always there. She made up for him."

"Probably."

"On a scale, of one to ten, how much do you trust me, Yale?"

He was silent.

"Come on, Yale. Open and honest. Remember?"

"We've been through a lot, Lisa. There's been so much turbulence—"

"Don't be afraid, Yale. Tell me, truthfully, on a scale of one to ten—"Three."

"Then I'll have to work hard to get to ten, won't I?"

"Are you upset?"

"No, Yale. I understand. What about your mother? On a scale of one to ten—"

"She went from ten to zero by dying."

"Okay. What about Marissa? On a scale of—"

"Let's not do this, Lisa. It's making me uneasy. Okay?"

"No. Not okay. What about Marissa? Surely, you must trust her more than a three—come on; be honest."

"I've had a deep, loyal, relationship with Marissa. We go back a long time. We have a history that wars didn't alter. It's different."

"I understand, Yale. That's good then, isn't it? Marissa is a woman you trust. She's always been there—right? She's never lied to you—right? Seems like a good place to build on the trust issue to me. Focus on someone who will stimulate the positive side of trusting. Focus on how lucky you are to have Marissa in your life, and you in hers. She's got to be close to a ten on the scale, wouldn't you say?"

"How much do you trust me, Lisa?"

"About a seven—maybe even an eight. My father and Harvey are ten on the scale. But they're the only ones."

"What about Marissa?"

"A nine."

"What about Howard?"

"A four, Yale. He's hard to know."

"What was Frank?"

"A ten after we were married. But he went to zero when he killed himself."

"And Ronnie?"

"Only a five or six when we first married, but I had hoped he'd grow to a ten. Instead, I trusted him less and less, and he finally became a zero on my list."

"I guess, Marissa is close to being a ten, on the trust scale, right now. But I think you're more than a three. I think—"

"Yale, you don't have to change it. It's okay. I know. I understand—"

"No, you don't. You see, just by allowing me to be this candid, and to open up, completely, you've already moved up a notch. I love you, Lisa. I love you ten—plus! I just need time and help in the trust department."

"I love you ten—plus, too, Yale. The rest will follow. Now, come here and kiss me. You're ten—plus—in the lovemaking department, too. And I want more. Much more."

It felt as if they had just dozed off when Josh knocked on their door close to eleven. Lisa hurriedly slipped a cotton nightshirt on, while Yale pulled the comforter snugly around him. "Who's there?"

"Me, Uncle Yale. It's me. Can I come in?"

"Sure, Josh. Come on in, but leave Buster and Matey out there."

Josh opened the door wide enough to squeeze himself through, all the while yelling, "Stay. Stay," to the hounds that weren't complying with his commands. Once inside, he quickly shut the door and ran over to the bed, still in his bright green Ninja Turtle pajamas. "That was a close call! Buster almost knocked me down!"

"Well, climb up here and catch your breath, Josh. Then we can decide what we're going to do today, big guy."

"Okay, Uncle Yale. Can I be in the middle?"

"Sure. Lisa, will you give Josh a little more room. I think he's crowded."

"Nope. Not until I get a good morning kiss. Sorry."

Yale leaned over to kiss her.

"Not you, silly. I want a good morning smooch from the "big guy." Well, Josh, do you have a peck for me?"

Laughingly, Josh hugged and kissed her. "Aunt Lisa, you are the bestest. I never got to stay up as late as you let me last night. Wait till I tell Mom!"

"Sure. Sure. You just want me to get in trouble. But I think your Mom will forgive me when she finds out Uncle Yale and I got married. Don't you?"

"Yup. She loves you, so she'll forgive you. That's what Mom tells me all the time—"I love you enough to always forgive you, no matter what.""

"Smart Mom you've got, big guy. I always new Marissa was the cream of the crop."

"No. You are, Uncle Yale. So, how about we get dressed and go to the mall. And if there's enough time, maybe, we can stop at the arcade too."

"Sounds like a great idea Josh. Lisa, what do you think?"

"I think we're wasting time, and the last one down for breakfast has to pay for all the games we play in Arcadia!"

Belle had the dining room table elaborately set in honor of the bride and groom. The Lennox china and Stueben crystal were lustrously placed on a French lace tablecloth. The sheen of the sterling denoted that Belle had been up very early to give them fresh luster, and the floral centerpiece was resplendent and colorful. There was merriment around the table this festive morning, although Lisa was going to have to say goodbye to Marc and Steve in an hour. They did promise, however, to return for more frequent weekend get-togethers if Belle would promise to prepare the same banquet of marvelous, delectable dishes she now brought out.

Even Rose was impressed as they all voraciously devoured the crabmeat salad, salmon mousse, cheese and vegetable quiches and soufflés; not to mention the assorted bagels, cream cheeses and herring Harry and Rose favored for brunch.

Harry opened a bottle of Don Perignon for the occasion and toasted

Lisa and Yale simply. "May your days be bright; your love strong; and your troubles small. L'Chayim."

They all laughed as Josh rubbed his nose, and made a face, when the expensive bubbly annoyingly tickled his nostrils.

Over coffee, Rose placed her hand on Yale's. "Welcome to the family, Yale. I know, no one can ever replace your mother, but I hope, in time, we can fill a part of your heart so your loss is less painful."

He had difficulty getting the "Thank you" out. Empathically, Rose patted his hand saying, "I know. I know."

Yale was moved again when Marc and Steve embraced him before getting into the car to head for the airport. They had been able to have brunch leisurely since their confirmation call to the airlines indicated their flight was delayed, and wouldn't depart as originally designated, due to the dense fog earlier.

"Take good care of my mother," Marc shouted as the car pulled away.

"See you both in a couple of weeks," Steve added. "You too, Josh."

"Call us," Rose yelled after them. "Let me hear from you two more often."

"What did you give them this time, Pa? I saw that sneaky hug and handshake."

"Nothing, Lisa. A little spending money for a movie or something."

"How much, Pa?"

"I don't know whose picture was on the bill, Lisa. Honestly. I didn't even look."

"I saw, Aunt Lisa. It had a five and two o's on it."

Harry laughed, then tousled Josh's already curly head of hair. "Wise. This one is very wise. And the spitting image of his mother. Twin faces. Even the freckles are in the same spots."

Harry took a fifty out and extended it to Josh. "Here. I'm giving you a five with one 0 after it. When you're older, you'll get the other 0. Now, Rose and I are going to rest; then take a walk. It looks like it's going to be a nice day after all. Go to the mall, the three of you, and there's no need to rush back. We ate so much for brunch, I'm not going to be in a big hurry for dinner today."

"So, tell me, Josh, what are you going to buy with the fifty dollars my husband gave you?"

"A camera. I'm going to buy a new camera and take bunches and bunches of pictures to show Mom when she gets back from Monte Carlo, so she can see what a fun time I had, even if Howard didn't want me to go on their honeymoon with them. I bet I'm having more fun then they are. It's 'funner' to be with Aunt Lisa and Uncle Yale than with Howard anyhow!"

"Well, in that case, Josh, here's another twenty-dollar bill for film. I hope Rose and I can be in one of your pictures, too."

"Sure you can. You can even come play the games at Arcadia if you want to."

"I'm not so good at those games, Josh. I think Rose and I will wait here until you get back, okay?"

"Okay. But don't forget if my Mom calls to tell her I'll call her back later. She promised to call me with her phone number in Monte Carlo."

"We won't forget, honey," Rose promised, "and we'll tell them you miss them."

"No! Don't say that, 'cause I don't. I hate them! They don't care about me no more. I hear them fighting. I just want the phone number. That's all. I don't care if they stay in Monte Carlo forever! And I hope it rains, there, all the time too!"

"Josh, why don't you go grab a parka in case it gets cold later. Yale, would you get the car? I'm going to grab a sweater and purse."

"Okay, Lisa. We'll have to stop at my place, sometime today, so I can pack a bag or two, and bring some essentials over until we decide which house we're going to sell."

"I told you last night, Mr. Frye, I don't care where I live, as long as you're beside me."

"Well, hurry up and get back down here, Lisa. And don't take long, alright?"

"What's the rush, Yale?"

"No rush, Mrs. Frye. I just want you where I can see you. I love looking at you. Especially with that gold band around your finger."

"Oy; mush, mush, mush. Rose, did we ever act like that?"

"Who remembers, Harry. Almost fifty years together and you expect me to recall?"

"I recall, Rose. You said the sun wouldn't rise without me."

"It wouldn't, Harry. And there wouldn't be a moon either."

"That part sounds familiar, Rose."

"It should, Harry. I just said it to you last night!"

"See what you kids have to look forward to." He kissed Rose tenderly.

"I see, Harry. And I hope Lisa is looking forward to it as much as I am."

"I'll bet you a five, with three o's after it, that she is, Yale. I know my daughter. I know her well. Sincerely, I do."

CHAPTER 43

Lisa was acutely aware that something significant was wrong when the three of them returned from their afternoon of fun and frolic. Her mother was rubbing her left arm with the, all to familiar, consistent strokes, Lisa grew up observing as a definitive signal that she was troubled and didn't know how to express her discomfort. Her father had only to look at her with his penetrating, unblinking gape to let her know she should brace herself for unwelcomed news. His face always advised her that he acknowledged what he had to say was going to shake her, but she should prepare herself, because it was unavoidable.

Fear gripped her heart as she uttered, "The boys? Pa? Did you hear from my Marc and my Steve?"

Yale observed as Harry's eyes bore into Lisa's with unflinching steadiness, while he stoically declared, "The boys are fine. Josh, why don't you go wash your hands, and put your jacket away? Then you can show me and Rose what's in the bags. Okay?"

"Okay. Then I'll take some pictures of you. Alright?"

"Sure, honey. Go on. Rose, why don't you give Josh a hand. There's a lot of bags there. Put them in his room for now."

As soon as Josh and her mother were out of earshot, Harry said, "Sit down, Lisa. It's bad. There's been an accident."

Harry lowered her onto the sofa with solid hands. "Howard and Marissa were driving to a hotel near the airport, this morning, when their flight was delayed because of fog. Howard made a wrong turn. The car hit a six wheeler, head on. Sweetheart, Howard died before the ambulances arrived, and Marissa is in critical condition. Honey, she lost the baby she was carrying and her chances are slim. She's lost a great deal of blood, hemorrhaging."

A croak escaped from Yale's throat, as his knees buckled, and he slithered down beside Lisa in one swift motion.

She reached for his hand automatically and locked fingers with him. "Oh, dear God. What do we do? Pa, what hospital is Marissa in?"

"Providence Hospital. Intensive Care Unit."

"Josh. What do we tell Josh? Yale—Oh God!"

"The boy has to be told, Lisa."

"Not yet, Harry. Lisa and I will go to the hospital first. We'll call you from there. Can you keep Josh entertained until we let you know if Marissa is conscious and Josh can see her?"

"Of course, Yale. What are you going to tell him now?"

"That Lisa and I have to pick up David from the airport. He'll believe that. I'll tell him that Lisa and I want to show David our wedding rings and surprise him."

"Where's Belle, Pa?"

"Church. She asked if she could go pray for Marissa after the call, an hour ago. She'll be back soon. I tried your cell phone, Lisa, then noticed it on the kitchen counter."

"Yale, I'll call for the driver and car. Will you tell Josh—"?

"Tell me what, Aunt Lisa?" Josh asked, dashing into the room, with his new Polaroid camera and the handful of snapshots he'd already taken, earlier, at the mall.

"Aunt Lisa and I have to go out for a little while, big guy. David was expecting me to see him when he arrived back in town tonight. Well, since Aunt Lisa and I got married while he was gone, we are going to pick him up at the airport together, and surprise him real good by flashing our rings in his face. Harry and Rose will keep you company until we get back, sport. And if you play your cards right, maybe Belle will let you make a sundae after dinner."

"Can I stay up until you get back, Uncle Yale?"

"I'll tell you what. Tomorrow is a school day, so if Aunt Lisa and I see we're going to be out too late we'll call. But you can stay up until we call or get back. Fair enough?"

"Fair enough, Uncle Yale. I'm gonna take more pictures while you're gone. I'm gonna take some of Buster and Matey, and Belle. Of everybody! Wait till Mom sees all the pictures I took when she gets back. She'll be surprised, I bet."

Yale bent and kissed Josh. "Save some of your film, okay? See you later, Josh."

Hand in hand, Yale and Lisa entered the sterile facility, with walls of brick that had been whitewashed. Providence Hospital was one of the oldest hospitals in the state. While embellished with less contemporary furnishings than the newer hospitals, the health facility maintained a proud reputation with able-bodied, highly qualified doctors and nurses. It had a convalescent home adjacent to the forty year old, nine floor, hospital. Lisa was acutely aware of the antiseptic odor and abundance of nurses on the floor as she and Yale followed Dr. Bush to the third floor, critical care unit.

Yale was only aware of how loud Lisa's heels sounded on the tiled floor as they walked hurriedly to the end of the long corridor where the double doors had a sign posted: "Admittance Without Personnel Prohibited." His palms were sweating, and he could feel perspiration oozing from his temples.

Lisa had called ahead from the car phone and advised Dr. Bush, the surgeon handling Marissa's case, that they were on their way.

Dr. Bush, a stout, dark skinned man in his late fifty's, had been expecting their call. His blunt manner did nothing to calm either of them as they had absorbed his words, over the speaker, during the drive. His reiteration now was just as alarming. "I wish I could offer you more hope," he flatly stated, "but Marissa's condition is grave. She has not regained consciousness since admittance. We don't know, conclusively, whether or not she has sustained any permanent brain damage. The fetus died on impact. I'd estimate she was beginning her second trimester. The hemorrhaging, during the hours in surgery, was extensive. We had to resuscitate her twice in the operating room."

"Doctor, was the fetus male or female?"

"It was a girl, Mrs. Lee."

"It's Mrs. Frye now, doctor. Lisa Frye. Thank you for telling me."

"She's in bed four, Mrs. Frye. The next cubicle. Don't be alarmed by all the equipment. It's necessary. Mr. Frye, are you alright? Your pallor concerns me."

"Yes," was all Yale managed to blurt.

Lisa heard Yale gasp as they reached the foot of the bed Marissa occupied. Dr. Bush grabbed Yale's elbow as a nurse quickly provided a chair for him. Lisa stood frozen against the base of the bed, her eyes glued to the sunken figure before her. She felt nauseated. Hospitals are always hot. Why did she feel so cold? Her mouth got suddenly dry.

It was minutes before she managed to move closer. She approached the side of the bed, and leaned over, kissing Marissa's cheek. "It's me, Marissa. It's Lisa. I'm here. Yale and I are both here. We love you, Marissa. You're going to be fine. Keep fighting, Marissa. Josh needs you. I need you. Yale needs you. Do you hear me, Marissa? We're here. We love you. We'll be right here until you wake up."

She touched Marissa's hand. It was warm. That surely must be a positive factor. She touched her cheek, then brushed a few auburn curls off her forehead. "Marissa, I have a surprise for you. Yale and I got married. Can you hear me, Marissa? I love you. I love you."

The tiny body on the bed was so still. Marissa's face was bruised in several places; her lips chapped. There were tubes in her nose. There was another tube in the corner of her mouth. And there were several— several—tubes going to various parts of her body. Some from machines. Others for the blood and IV drip.

"It's good we didn't bring Josh here tonight, Yale. It'll be better for him to see Marissa when some of these machines are removed. It would have frightened him, don't you think?"

He looked at her pained eyes, which were brimming with tears, but couldn't reply.

"I know what you're thinking, Yale. But you'll see. She's going to be fine. We just have to wait. She's very weak after what's happened. It'll just take some time. Right, Marissa? I'm going to sit right next to you until you wake up. I have so much to tell you. This is the longest period of time we haven't spoken to each other in months. Do you realize that, Marissa? I'm right here. I love you."

"Mrs. Frye, why don't you and your husband get a cup of coffee? We'll get you if there's any change."

"No, doctor. Thank you. I'd just like a chair, please. I want to be here when she opens her eyes. It'll make her feel better to see a familiar face. I know it will. I know her."

Yale rose from his chair. "I'm going down to the chapel, Lisa. Maybe, this time, God will hear me."

"Okay, Yale. I'll get you when Marissa wakes up. I'll sit with her. She'll be fine. You'll see, Yale."

Yale brought Lisa a cup of coffee, watched for a retched moment as his wife stroked Marissa's hand with gentle fingers. He called Josh, lying that David's flight was going to be late and that he should go to bed soon, then went down to the main floor of the hospital and sat listlessly in the first row of the chapel. The nondenominational sanctuary provided relief from the horrifying sight of Marissa. But the room offered no solace to his ungalvanized heart.

There were only three other people in the sanctum. Yale observed that they were all praying. His mouth was parched, and there was an uncomfortable tightness in his throat. He looked around hoping to feel spirituality engulf him. But it did not. "Please God," was all he uttered as his mind replayed the loss of his mother, just weeks ago.

He watched an elderly woman walk toward the display of candles. The woman crossed herself and lit a candle, as she religiously intonated some biblical words of prayer. She clutched a crucifix in her hand tightly, and swayed slightly, as if off balance. Yale watched the wrinkled hands open an old worn handbag and remove a bill, depositing the money in a little dish. He felt hypocritical being there. It felt foreign. He was embarrassed.

Yale didn't know why, but some time later, when he was alone in the chapel, he went and lit all the remaining candles. Afterwards, he emptied the entire contents of his wallet in the dish. Subsequently, he resumed his seat on the long fixed bench, closed his eyes, and lowered his head. "Please. Please, dear God. Not again," he begged.

As Lisa's vigil continued on the third floor, she continually spoke to Marissa, believing Marissa heard every word she said. She explained how Yale had proposed to her, on the dance floor, at the wedding reception, and how he almost tripped when she said, yes. "I really love him, Marissa. I know you're happy for me. Open your eyes, Marissa,

and tell me you knew we would end up together. Please…Marissa…
Please…"

Lisa poured herself a cup of water from the plastic, drab green,
pitcher the nurse had provided for her. With a trembling hand, she
raised the cup to her mouth. She thought she heard Marissa make a
sound and quickly called a nurse over.

"She made a sound. I heard her. Can you see if any of her vital signs
have changed? It was like a sigh. A high-pitched sigh."

The nurse empathized with Lisa, but was accustomed to hearing this
type of remark from loved ones who were in denial at the prospect of
losing someone close to them. "There's no change. I'm sorry, Mrs. Frye.
Her pulse is still very weak and her breathing labored. What you heard
might have come from one of these devices. Can I get you anything,
Mrs. Frye? Coffee? Tea?"

"No. No. Thank you. I'm sure I heard her make a sound. I'll just
wait right here. Maybe, she'll come to in a little while. She's a fighter,
you know. Marissa's a tough lady. She'll come around soon. I know
she will. You know how it is with a best friend, I'm sure. You know
each other so well that it's difficult for others to sometimes understand
the connection—you know—the link you share. Thanks. I'll call
you if I hear her make that sound again, okay? I'm sure it wasn't the
machines."

The nurse nodded with understanding, and returned to her station,
feeling sorry for Lisa and what she was going through.

Less than ten minutes later Lisa was sure Marissa's eyes fluttered.
She bent forward and kissed Marissa's cheek softly. "I'm here, Marissa.
I love you. You're going to be okay, honey. I know you can hear me,
Marissa. You know, I felt funny not waiting for you to get back from
Monte Carlo before marrying Yale, but I was afraid he wouldn't ask a
second time. I love you, do you hear—"

"Lisa…Listen—"

"Oh, God! Thank you, God! I'm here—"

"Listen…please…"

Marissa's eyes opened slightly. She was trying to tell her something,
but the tube in her mouth made it difficult. Lisa took her hand, and

leaned very close to her. "I'll get the nurse. I have to tell them you're awake—"

"No…Please…Lisa…Listen. This is…very important…Listen… Now…"

"Okay, Marissa, I'm listening. But don't push. You've been through a lot, honey. You need your…"

"Listen… Lisa…I have to tell you…"

"Okay. I'm here. What is it, honey? What, honey?"

"Listen carefully…"

"I'm listening…"

"I didn't want to tell…before…now…I must…"

"Alright, Marissa. Take your time…"

"My purse…My purse, Lisa. Take my keys. In my safe…at home… is a tape." Her breathing was uneven. Her pain evident. "Listen to it… first."

"Okay, Marissa. Don't worry. Just rest. I'll take care of everything. Tape…I'll get the tape for you."

"No, Lisa, you have to listen to it…very important.—Please."

"You need rest—I'll listen to the tape. I promise. Please rest…"

"No! Listen to me, Lisa. I've lived a lie. A—big lie. A… horrible… lie. Tony left me a note when he kidnapped Josh…he took Josh just to make me suffer. He wrote—he was sterile—and had been since a teenager…From mumps…Do you understand? Josh wasn't his child. But I didn't know who—the biological father was until recently—you see—Tony and I once were heavy drug users…Wild…Sick…sick…sick people—"

"It's okay, Marissa. That's behind you. You made a fresh start. You're a wonderful mother. Josh is so splendid because of you—"

"Listen…Please…Lisa…Listen…When I realized I was pregnant… and Howard and I were going to be married—Lisa, I had all of us go through complete physical exams…and blood testing. Howard and I wrote wills…We were doing…paperwork. When Howard looked through our medical documents…you see, I slept with other people to hurt Tony—back—when—"

"I understand, Marissa. I love you, Marissa. I don't care about the sordid details of long ago. It's not important. Rest. Please, rest."

"Listen—Listen—it's very important, Lisa, because Howard and I—" She took a breath—"were able to confirm, without question...Yale is Josh's real father. It was only one wild night, Lisa...But I've known for a couple of months—Both RH negative—Both—"

She was struggling to speak. Her eyes begged Lisa to hear her out.

"What? How can you be sure? What are you saying, Marissa?"

"I had genetic blood tests done—on Josh's blood—and compared to Yale's blood...You know, when Yale went into the hospital—after Ruth died. Lisa, Howard had it checked and rechecked several—times. Yale is Josh's father. All the information is on—tape."

"Why didn't you tell Yale? Why—Why are you telling me now?"

"I didn't know how...I love you, Lisa. I couldn't—Lisa—oh, Lisa—I'm—sorry—I love—"

Marissa's eyes closed. She took a short breath and was gone. The heart monitor went to that awful straight line. The sound was dreadful. She couldn't move. Her best friend was dead. Gone. And again, she was left with secrets no one else knew. She was numb. She couldn't even cry. She was riveted to the floor. She scouted the faces rushing in—"Bring her back," she yelled. "Bring my best friend back!" she shrieked.

She viewed a lot of people, and pushed a nurse aside to kiss Marissa, her best friend, good-bye. Someone, she didn't know who, eventually escorted her from the room. She pushed hands away and leaned against the cold hard concrete wall in the corridor. Finally, she made her way to the chapel on the main floor where Yale had been all this time. She approached him and gently placed a hand on his shoulder. "Let's go home, Yale. God was too busy today. Marissa's gone."

They were almost home before a word was spoken. Yale put his hand on her arm to get her attention. She had been staring out of the window vacantly since they'd left the hospital. In her arms, she was clutching a plastic bag. The contents held Marissa's purse and the jewelry removed from her body at the hospital. Howard's body had been taken to the morgue earlier. His personal effects had been temporarily released to his business partner, and close friend, after it was verified that neither he nor Marissa had living relatives—other than Josh.

Howard's partner had presented notarized documents to all officials, which gave Lisa and/or Yale custodial rights of Josh, and all holdings belonging to both of them. As an attorney, Howard had prearranged documents written out, in the event that neither of them was able to care for Josh, due to a death or a permanent debilitating illness.

"Lisa, I knew she would never regain consciousness after I saw her. I couldn't sit there and watch her die. I'm sorry."

She didn't turn around and look at him. She just kept staring out of the window. "I understand," she said quietly.

"How are we going to tell Josh? He's going to be mortified. He's going to feel abandoned."

She still didn't turn to him. "I don't know, Yale."

"We have to talk about this, Lisa. There are arrangements—"

"I know. I know, Yale."

"Should we wake him up as soon as we get home? Talk to me, Lisa. Now's not the time for us to mourn. We have to think of Josh. We have to handle the next few days first."

"I know." She still didn't turn to face him.

He broke down. "I can't go through this. Dear God. First, my mother. Now, Marissa—and Howard. I can't handle this."

She finally turned and cradled him against her. "I'll handle it, Yale. It'll be alright. Josh has to be told when we get home. He has a right to know, right away. We'll help him get through this."

She still hadn't shed tears. She still didn't believe it.

Her parents tried to console them when they entered the house. Yale was receptive to Rose's beckoning arms and cried openly. Lisa pushed her father's hands away, "Not now, Pa. Please."

Belle's puffy eyes met Harry's as they watched Lisa climb the stairs with the plastic bag clutched against her. Neither of them could suppress their anguish as they saw Lisa struggling to the upper level as if weighted down by barbells. Was it just a day ago when Lisa was glowing as a new bride? Was it just twenty-four hours ago when merriment surrounded them all?

Lisa placed the plastic bag with Marissa's items in the closet and returned downstairs. Yale was fighting to get himself under control. She approached him and extended her hands. "Come on, honey. We have to tell Josh."

They entered the bedroom together and approached the sleeping child. Rose, Harry and Belle stood just outside the open door, ready to offer support. Lisa gently stroked Josh's hair until he sleepily opened his eyes. Yale sat down beside him. Yale's eyes filled again. His body sagged. Lisa turned the bed lamp on dimly. Josh looked at Yale with fear.

"What's wrong, Uncle Yale? How come you're crying?"

Yale couldn't speak.

Lisa got on her knees and leaned close to Josh. "We have to tell you something very sad, Josh. It's real sad news, honey. Your Mom and Howard were in a car accident, Josh. They had to go to heaven."

She waited for a reaction, all the while stroking his head, just as she had stroked Marissa's head an hour ago. "Do you understand, Josh? Mommy and Howard can't be here anymore. But Uncle Yale and I will take care of you and love you. Mom and Howard didn't want to leave you, Josh. They didn't have a choice. It was an accident."

Yale was sobbing so hard his shoulders heaved. Lisa placed her other hand on one of Yale's. She remained composed. "I'm real sorry, Josh, to have to tell you such awful news."

Josh sat up and leaned against his Uncle Yale. "I don't care. Mom didn't need me no more. She had Howard and that new baby, pretty soon. I don't care...I don't care..."

His eyes shed tears as he spoke. He looked at Yale imploringly. "Where am I gonna live, Uncle Yale?"

Yale wrapped Josh in his arms. "Here, Josh." His voice reassured. "Lisa and I will take care of you forever and ever."

"Can Buster stay too, Lisa?"

"Of course, Josh."

"Mom shouldn't have gone to Monte Carlo. She shouldn't have married Howard. If she wouldn't have left me, God wouldn't have taken her to heaven. I hate her! I hate Howard, too! I don't care that they went to heaven...I don't care..."

"Yes, you do, Josh. You care, and it's okay. Uncle Yale cares too. That's why he's crying so hard. It's okay to be angry, Josh. I'm angry that your Mom and Howard are gone, too. I'm going to miss them a real lot..." Her voice cracked for the first time. She lowered her head.

"Uncle Yale, I'm scared. I don't want you to go away. I don't want to go to school. Can Buster and Matey and you sleep in here? Don't cry,

Uncle Yale. I'm scared…I hate Howard…It's all his fault…He wanted to go to Monte Carlo…I hate him…He yelled at Mom…He made Mom go…Uncle Yale…Why did Mom go with him?…Why didn't she stay with me…Uncle Yale…Aunt Lisa…Is Mom with Aunt Ruth now?… Is she?…Is she…?"

"Yes, sweetheart. Mom is together with Aunt Ruth. They'll be watching over us from heaven. They're together. They loved you very much, Josh. Aunt Ruth didn't want to leave Yale, just like your Mom didn't want to leave you, Josh. They couldn't help it, honey. They couldn't help it."

Yale and Josh clung to one another, rocking and sobbing. Lisa removed Yale's shoes and told them both to lie down. She pulled the blanket over them and turned off the light. She walked out of the room, leaving the door partially open, and heard Yale say, "It'll be okay, Josh. I'll never leave you…I promise…You'll always have your Uncle Yale."

CHAPTER 44

Harry went to check on Lisa during the night and found her going through the plastic bag with Marissa's belongings on the bed. She had a cigarette in her mouth, and from the looks of the ashtray, had been chain smoking for hours.

He hadn't knocked, but that was typical. "I figured you might be awake. Nice honeymoon. Your husband has to sleep in another room. Your best friend died. And you are in here alone, going through hell."

"Stop it, Pa. I know your tactics. Don't try to break me. I don't need to fall apart. I don't need to get all bent out of shape. I have to take care of a lot of stuff—"

"Stuff? Lisa, we know each other. I know when you're going into hiding. I know when the pain is so unbearable you try to deny it exists. What's wrong with shedding tears over a tremendous loss in your life, Lisa? What's wrong—"

"Please, Pa. I can't feel anything more than I do right now. Please go back to bed, Pa. I need to be alone. I want to be alone."

"What about the child, Lisa? Are you prepared for what lies ahead? You are going to have to make some serous decisions."

"The decisions are already made, Pa. It's the disclosure of specific findings which is scaring the hell out of me."

"What do you mean, Lisa?"

"Nothing Pa. I'm sorry. I'm just trying to sort things out in my head. Forget it, Pa. Please. We'll talk another time, okay?"

She put out her cigarette with a trembling hand, immediately lighting another one.

"I'm worried about you, Lisa. Don't shut me out. Is there something you'd like to share—"

"No. No. Not now. Please, go back to bed, Pa. We better get a little sleep. The days ahead are going to be hard ones."

He kissed her head, watching, as she fought to maintain her composure. "I'm here if you need me, Lisa. Remember that. I'm here for you."

She hugged her knees and started rocking. She couldn't look her father in the eyes. She knew she was close to crumbling. "Good night, Pa," she managed, and waited for him to leave the room.

He stood outside the door a few minutes, waiting to hear if Lisa finally gave way to her anguish.

She didn't. He finally went back to bed. "Is she alright, Harry?"

"As well as can be expected, Rose. Get some sleep. She'll be alright."

He turned over, hoping his lies would turn to truths, and his daughter would really be alright. Eventually he slept.

Upstairs, Lisa continued to smoke, cigarette after cigarette, as she stared at the set of keys from Marissa's purse. The keys Marissa asked her to take, in her final words. She put out the cigarette, left the bed, and dropped Marissa's keys in her own handbag. She knew what she had to do.

With dark circles under her eyes, Lisa entered the kitchen very early in the morning and poured herself a cup of black coffee. Belle was already there. With a cigarette in her mouth, she sat down at the table feeling the exhaustion no sleep perpetuated. "Are we the only ones up, Belle?"

"I think so, Missy. It's not even seven yet. I thought I heard your dad a few minutes ago. But he might have gone back to bed."

"Where's the morning paper, Belle? It's usually on the counter when I come down."

"Somewhere, Missy. Can't rightly recall where I put it. How about a slice of toast, or a muffin, Miss Lisa?"

"No. Thanks. Just the paper, Belle. Give me the paper."

"Want your juice now, Missy. It wouldn't hurt you none to take your pills a little earlier today."

"The paper, Belle. Just the damn paper!"

Belle opened the cupboard underneath the sink and pulled out the newspaper she'd hidden behind some bags. She handed it to Lisa with pained eyes.

Lisa unfolded the paper and stared at the headline—"HOLLYWOOD STAR DIES ON WEDDING DAY." Below the caption was a picture of Marissa and Howard smiling. Next to the picture was a photograph of the collision site and the demolished vehicle Marissa and Howard had been in when the accident occurred.

Footsteps alerted Lisa and stopped her from reading further. She quickly folded the paper in half, and leaned across it, as Yale approached. He kissed her. "Did you get any sleep, Lisa?"

"Yes," she lied. "Is Josh still sleeping?"

"Yes. He wet the bed. I put a towel down for now. Buster and Matey are next to him."

"Okay. I'm going to get dressed, Yale, and go over to Marissa's house. I have to pick out some clothes for Josh to wear to the funeral. It's probably best if you stay here with Josh. I'll call the funeral home, from upstairs, to make the arrangements."

"Alright. I'll get David to help us out, too. Are you sure, you can handle going into Marissa's place by yourself, Lisa? Maybe, I should go with you."

"I can handle it, Yale. Josh is going to need you to be with him. I'm okay. Really."

Lisa left them all sitting around the breakfast table and drove over to Marissa's estate. She declined her father's request to accompany her, and grabbed a slice of toast off the plate to pacify her mother's fervent plea to eat something before she gets sick. She tossed the slice of toast in the shrubs as soon as she walked out the door. Belle was troubled as she watched Lisa discard the bread before driving off, while she stood at the kitchen window. "Poor Missy," she whispered to herself.

Josh had said very little since coming down from his room. Lisa had explained she was going to pick up a suit for him at the house for the funeral, and asked if he wanted to come with her. He shook his head negatively, asking only if she could bring his picture albums back with her. She promised she would.

As she entered Marissa's bedroom her breathing felt hampered, and her skin was cold. She sat down on Marissa's bed and took a few deep breaths. She surveyed the room feeling Marissa's presence engulf her. Even the aroma in the room still had the scent of Marissa's favorite perfume lingering in it. Only two nights ago Marissa was donning her bridal gown in this very room. Only a week ago they were giggling on the bed together, like two schoolgirls. Only days ago Marissa was jubilantly looking forward to a new baby.

Marissa had been right. It would have been Regina, the name they had picked out for the baby together.

With trepidation, Lisa took Marissa's keys and inserted the special key to unlock the safe in the back of Marissa's closet. She entered the code letters, J-O-S-H, and heard the click. She opened the second steel door, and removed two metal boxes from the unit. The first container held jewelry, some cash, and several personal treasured mementos, including a childhood drawing Marissa once made for her mother, and a high school graduation pin, of blue and red.

Lisa replaced the items and placed the box back in the safe. With clammy hands, she fumbled to open the other case. On top of a stack of documents was a single cassette in a plastic holder. Lisa removed it and read the words Marissa had written and then taped to the top: **To be opened only in the event of my demise by Lisa Lee. Confidential.**

After placing everything else back in the safe, and locking it, Lisa took the cassette downstairs and put it in a recorder. She sat back on the sofa, in the warm familiar room, and pushed play. Marissa's voice shot a current through her, so intensely, her reflexes jolted and her body stiffened. She listened to the entire tape, as Marissa detailed the complete story. The story she only had time to summarize before she died in the hospital bed.

Lisa's head was pounding as she heard the evidence and mellifluent voice enlighten her:

And so you see, my dearest friend, that I have been torn these past few weeks, between being honest enough to tell Yale what Howard and I have determined to be conclusive, with undeniable evidence. Yale is positively Josh's father."

The tape went on:

"I searched my heart, Lisa, and am convinced you and Yale will someday have a life together. And because I love you and Yale so very much, I have decided to keep this secret until I die. I would never want anything I've done, in my past, to effect your lives in the future. I hope, if ever you hear this tape, you will understand and forgive me.

I will let your heart guide you, in your decision as to whether it should be shared with Yale or Josh. You have always been wiser than me."

Lisa pushed rewind and listened to some of the beginning of the cassette again:

"So, here I am, about to be married, and Howard is already trying to dictate what I should do. I emphatically told Howard the decision is mine to make, but he feels differently. I think he's even lost respect for me, because I really didn't know Yale was Josh's biological father until recently. But how should I have known? Tony never told me he was sterile, until just before he died. And he was so crazed at that point, I never knew when he was lying and when he wasn't. And Josh, thank heaven, has never been hospitalized. Who pays attention to blood types, or any of that stuff, when you don't have to? I had no reason to be up on medical data when I had good doctors, and a staff who, literally, took care of most of my needs, since I became a celebrity.

Perhaps, it was stupidity on my part, Lisa. I'm not sure. I only know, when I married Tony, I loved him deeply and trusted him. I had no reason for doubt."

Lisa pushed fast forward, and again listened to the dialogue, which fortified the probability of Yale's lineage to Josh:

"There were no formalities back then. Anything went, Lisa. I know it must be incomprehensible to someone who led a "normal" life. But, we drank, got stoned, and during the course of that one night copulated with more than one person. I remember fraternizing with Yale, as well as Tony. I distinctly remember our cohabitation ending with Yale's ejaculation. It was the first, of only two times, Yale and I had sex together in all the years we've known each other. We were so high on grass, and high on being famous back then, that morality sometimes went to hell. Please try to understand. I know how it sounds. There is no way to rationalize, or excuse, what sounds like obscene behavior. But be mindful that sex sometimes anesthetized us against other fears, and was a release for pent up emotions. I'm not trying to condone my life back then, Lisa. This is not a copout. This is an explanation of a party night, when young people were unmindful of what could happen, and sought the pleasures of the flesh. Yale never loved me romantically, or I him. But we have loved each other, like family, for as long as I can remember. How could I, now, tell him that he is Josh's father. He might hate me. It might change all our lives…"

She pushed fast-forward once more:

"I, Marissa Myers, would like to end this disclosure, with the hope that if it ever becomes necessary to play this tape, that my best friend will find it in her heart to forgive me, love me, and remember me, as the person she knew. My dearest Lisa, forgive me for this secret. I did what I thought I had to do, although, Howard doesn't agree. I always told Josh—if you love someone enough—you can forgive them anything. Please, Lisa, forgive me.

And do what you must."

She rewound the cassette, replaced it in its plastic holder, and dropped it in her purse.

After gathering Josh's photo albums, a suit, and some of his favorite books together, she returned home. She had been gone almost three hours. She couldn't neutralize the queasiness in her gut.

The burial service was the most difficult to get through. Josh didn't comprehend everything, and tried to make himself obscure, by hiding behind Yale, when he was most uncomfortable. Yale, too, attempted to conceal the magnitude of his pain from the professional lenses he'd spotted in the cemetery. It was only when the procession of more than 100 vehicles separated, after the service, and Yale and Josh were back at the house that the two unleashed their grief.

Lisa still hadn't cried.

When Yale was sure Josh was asleep that night, he joined Lisa, Harry, and Rose in the library. "Another day from hell," he commented, as he sat down next to his bride. "Josh asked me how come his Mom had to be buried next to Howard. He said, he didn't like it. I told him, it was because they were married. You know what Josh said." Yale didn't wait for a response. "He said, his Mom shouldn't have married Howard, or be buried next to him. That if she never would have married him, she wouldn't have died. He said, they had been yelling a lot about a secret, but he didn't know what the secret was.

Only, that Howard kept saying that she should tell, and his Mom kept yelling—- "over my dead body—." He asked if I knew what the secret was."

Lisa's face drained of blood. She was chalk white. "What did you tell him, Yale?"

"The truth, Lisa. That secrets don't cause people to die. That it was an accident, because of the fog, which was responsible for what happened."

Lisa removed a cigarette from the pack on the cocktail table, and lit it. Yale was rubbing his forehead and didn't notice her hands shake, or her lips tremble. But Harry and Rose did.

"Yale, why don't you shower and go to bed, honey. You look exhausted. I know how hard it is for you—and so soon after Ruth. I'll be up in a little while."

"I think I will, Lisa. I can't see straight, anymore, today. Why don't you come up with me, Lisa? You've been carrying so much of the weight. I see the toll it's taking on you. Come on, honey. You look like hell."

After Yale fell asleep, Lisa came back down to the library. She picked up one of the photo albums she'd brought back with her from Marissa's, and leafed through some of the pages. She hadn't been able to fall asleep, and knew, in part, it was due to the disclosure she was going to have to share. She stared at some pictures of Yale and Josh laughing, knowing there was no way she could avoid revealing the truth to Yale. Even if it meant more havoc would result consequently. A final thought drifted through her mind, as sleep finally pounced on her exhausted body. Would Yale ever trust anyone, completely, after he discovered the one person—the single closest person to being a 'ten' on his trust scale—had planned never to reveal what he rightfully was entitled to know; That Josh was his son?"

Lisa woke with a start. She quietly crept into the bedroom, and dressed without waking Yale. She rushed out of the house and promptly got into the Mercedes. She was sorry she hadn't taken a sweater along, since the sun had not yet ingressed on the day, and the air was cold. She drove to Marissa's house and unlocked the safe again. She removed the container, which had held the cassette, and read through some of the documents that had been beneath the cassette. There, in black and white, were the medical reports, which validated everything Marissa stated on the tape. She unfolded another paper, and read a hostile letter Tony had left Marissa, when he kidnapped Josh, denying he ever loved her or Josh. It stated, he merely used them. His vile words ripped Lisa's heart apart. How awful it must have been for Marissa to read such treachery from someone she once loved. How horrible it must have been for Marissa to accept that she had been a fool, and so easily manipulated by someone she loved enough to marry. How dreadful it must have been for Marissa to feel so ashamed, of old mistakes, that she couldn't confide in anyone. Lisa placed the incriminating evidence of Yale's lineage to Josh in her purse next to the cassette.

After gathering a few more articles of clothing for Josh, she left.

Instead of returning home, Lisa drove to the burial ground where they had put Marissa to rest. She approached the spot where the casket had been lowered, and sat on the sod next to the still moist soil, which covered the coffin. There was no hearse today, or the hundreds of mourners that filled the area yesterday. There were no pallbearers. There were no rites being read now. And there was no one there to invade Lisa's private requiem. She smoothed the soil with her hands, and swayed back and forth in slow motion. Then, when the pain was more than she could bear, she slumped over on the dirt where her best friend was buried, and shrieked, "No. No. Marissa, I need you."

Her body convulsed as she screamed, "Oh, my Marissa, how could you leave me? Marissa. My dearest friend. Why—why did this have to happen? Why?—Oh God—Marissa—I finally let someone into my heart, after so long, and you're gone…Gone. Oh Marissa, I need you—I need you—Why—Why—Why? Oh God, I can't seem to keep the people I love in my life. Oh, Marissa, what am I going to do without you? Oh, dear God, how could this happen? Why?—Oh God—I can't believe I've lost you—Marissa—Marissa…"

She sobbed for all the hours of grief she couldn't release before. She shrilled at the injustice of it all. She yelled at the God who took her best friend from her. She tongue-lashed the God who could do this to her. She ranted at how unfair it was. "Oh, Marissa, how do I accept this—How—?" She hugged the ground, racked with grief. "Was this because of me, Marissa? Would you be alive if you and Howard weren't arguing about the secret—Oh God, Marissa—I love you so…You were like a sister…Why?—-Dear God. Why—?"

She admonished herself for getting so close to someone. She let her bruised heart bleed. She unfurled the rage she could no longer conceal. The high-pitched outcries poured from her endlessly, until she felt two hands support and lift her from the earth.

"Come, Lisa. I'll take you home. Someone will come for the other car. Come on, honey. Let daddy take you home."

Covered with dirt, she let her father guide her to the car, and hold her, as the driver took them home. He put his sweater around her shaking body, and embraced her, while she put her head against his chest. It wasn't until he helped her from the car that she whimpered, "Pa, take me to my room, then send Yale in alone. I have to tell him that Josh is his son. That he is the boys' real father. He has to know."

"Oh, my daughter, some day life will be filled with less obstacles for you to overcome. And, I, my child, will witness it. Come on, Lisa, I will put you to bed, and try to keep other demons away. Your severed heart will heal."

Blinded by his own tears, Harry walked Lisa up to her room. When she requested, again, he fetched Yale, who now was in a fresh state of apprehension and confusion.

"Here, Yale. Lisa asked me to give you this cassette recorder. She wants you to bring it up to the bedroom. She needs to talk to you alone."

CHAPTER 45

Yale's face resembled, what one might conjure up in their imagination, a face might resemble if an apparition were to unexpectedly and suddenly appear before them.

When Josh approached him, tugging at his arm, reproaching, "You've been in the bedroom with Aunt Lisa for hours, Uncle Yale. When are you going to call my teacher? You already missed lunch." Yale beheld the diminutive figure as if casting eyes on him for the first time.

"I'm sorry, Josh. Aunt Lisa needed me. She's not feeling so good today."

"What's wrong with her, Uncle Yale? Can I go see her now?"

Yale gazed at the face, still in shock from the revelations on the cassette, and the documents he examined upstairs, and didn't realize he hadn't answered the child who was looking at him imploringly.

"Uncle Yale, what's wrong with you? Didn't you hear me? Can I go see, Aunt Lisa? Does she need medicine?"

"No, Josh. I mean, no; she doesn't need medicine. And, yes, you can go in for a few minutes. But don't stay too long. I want Aunt Lisa to get some sleep today. She's very tired and needs to rest. Okay?"

"How come you were in there so long then, Uncle Yale? Maybe, you shouldn't have talked so much if she's tired."

"Maybe, Josh. Go on up. I'm going to call the school. I'll be up in a minute. I want to get a pot of tea for Aunt Lisa. She said, she's cold."

"Okay. I'll keep her warm, and tucked in, 'till you come up, Uncle Yale. Mom always said, when I was sick, she'd keep me "snug as a bug in a rug". And it made me get well faster. We can do it for Aunt Lisa now. I bet it'll work."

"I bet you're right, Josh. I'll be right up."

His eyes followed Josh, as he considered the magnitude of the revelation heard on the cassette. He was a father. A dad. He had a son. Josh was his child. His boy. His link to immortality. A person who was a blood relative—family.

Lisa slept the afternoon away submissively. Fate had once again conquered a loved one, and presented new hurdles for her to overcome. She felt short changed and defeated. Rather than dodge more bayonets, it was easier to amputate herself. Sleep provided the trench for all her dissected parts, and shelter from piercing eyes that were interested in resurrecting the dismembered pieces. Sleep provided a sanctuary.

Over the next forty-eight hours, Lisa only left the bed to use the bathroom. She spoke briefly to Marc and Steve, convincing them to stay at the university, and allow time to help Josh heal. She reconciled her differences with Jean, and told her agent she'd advise her about releasing "Regrets" for publication soon. And she confided in Harvey, when Yale was engaged with Josh in an outdoor activity.

Harvey offered to fly over immediately, but she asked him to refrain for her sake. "Not yet, Harvey. I'm not ready. I need time to adjust. If you're here, I'll become dependent on you. I know myself, Harvey. This isn't my first loss. I don't let go easily."

"Then I'll stay in England, Lisa, if you promise to ask for my help if you need it. I do so care about you. I'm at a loss for words to express how sad I feel for all you're faced with."

"I know, Harvey. Stay where you are; beside Michelle. If I see I'm unable to cope, I'll call you. Other than my father, you're the only one I've confided in. I don't know when Yale plans on telling Josh he's his real father. Yale has slept with Josh the past two nights, since Josh's nightmares began. And to be honest, I'm in avoidance. I feel, for every step forward, I'm punished, and have to take two steps back. I need more time, I guess."

"You, of all people, know how precious time is, Lisa. Don't waste time on the backward steps, honey. Keep forging ahead. You wound up marrying Yale, didn't you? The forward movements have been rewarding, ultimately. Concentrate on the rewards, Lisa. My life was significantly better for the years I had Frank as a friend and mentor. So, although, the loss remains monumental, I will always be grateful for the time we did share and love for one another."

"I hear you, Harvey. I just lack resilience at the moment. How many times can a person be knocked down before they stop wanting, to even try, to get up again?"

"It seems you have reasons to bounce back, Lisa. Now, more than ever. Your husband needs you, and loves you. And Josh is depending on you. You've never been one to be self-indulgent. Your fortitude will not stay dormant when loved ones are in need. After all, Lisa, would you really be fulfilled if you weren't needed? We both know the answer, don't we? You've never been, merely, an observer, Lisa."

"Good-bye, Harvey. I get the jest. Kiss Michelle, and I'll be in touch. Hopefully, I'll see you when the baby arrives. I love you, Harvey."

"I love you back, Lisa. See you soon."

Six days after Marissa's burial, Lisa emerged from the bedroom. And a week later, she desperately wanted to go back into hiding. She had lost Yale. He was immersed with Josh, and Josh's doings, around the clock. She might as have not existed. Yale wouldn't have noticed.

Yale ate and slept with Josh. He professed it was because Josh had frequent nightmares. Yale followed Josh around everywhere. He had become obsessive. And Josh was becoming manipulative.

Lisa tried to convince herself this was a temporary situation. Soon, Yale would realize he was neglecting her, and alter the patterns she observed as unhealthy.

Her parents and Belle attempted to make up for Yale's inattentiveness by catering to her. They agreed to take Josh shopping, more than once, hoping to give Yale and Lisa some time alone. But Yale always intervened, stating if Josh wanted to go shopping, he'd take him.

Yale had taken Josh out of school and hired a private teacher. And, although, the instructor was highly qualified, Lisa felt Josh belonged in a classroom with his peers.

A month after Marissa's death, Yale announced at breakfast that he had placed his estate, and Marissa's, on the market, for sale. He still hadn't told Josh that he was his father. But Lisa was sure it wouldn't be long now. When he asked her, nonchalantly, if she would go to Marissa's place and gather all of Josh's things together, she lost her temper for the first time since the funeral.

"No. I will not go to Marissa's place and get the rest of Josh's things, Yale! When Josh is finished with his lessons, you take him. And while you're there take a good look around. Maybe, there's more than Josh's things you should bring back with you."

"What are you yelling about, Lisa? All I suggested was for you to get Josh's belongings together. I don't want him to ever go into that house again."

"Why, Yale? To protect him? Or to protect yourself? That was his home for nine years. That's where he was raised! That's where he was mothered! That's where he was nurtured—not suffocated!"

He knocked his cup of coffee off the table in fury. "Don't tell me what you think, Lisa! I didn't ask for your opinion!"

Harry and Rose stood, to leave the table, when Lisa pleaded, "Don't go. This is important, and I want you here. I have no one else." They sat back down.

She turned her attention back to Yale. "You're right, Yale. You didn't ask for my opinions. You haven't asked me for anything lately. Not a kiss. Not a hug. You get whatever you need from Josh, apparently. But you're not doing him a favor. He needs friends. He needs to interact. And most of all he needs to grieve for his mother! You are stifling all the things that will allow him to move on. Don't you see what's happen—"

"Don't give me that crap, Lisa! I know what I'm doing. I know what Josh needs! He's my s—!"

"And I'm your wife! I've stood by as long as I'm going to. I'm tired of an empty bed, Yale. I'm tired of being excluded from decisions. I love you, but I won't be put on the back burner. Go to Marissa's place, Yale, like I had to. Take a good look around. Look at the pictures. There's a history in that house, Yale. Josh's history. Marissa's history. Important memories that shouldn't be cast aside—"

"I know what's in the house! I don't need to see it to remember! I spent plenty of time in that house—"

"Yes! As Uncle Yale. And as Marissa's friend! It's a little different now, isn't it? Why do you think Marissa left the tape for me, instead of you, Yale? She knew you'd get frenzied! She knew all our lives would be affected! And she knew you would have trouble coming to terms with the truth!"

He stood up seething. His face was red with rage. "She deceived me. She kept, from me, what I was entitled to know. She married Howard, knowing—"

"What should she have done, Yale? Marry you! Marissa died! I'm sorry you feel betrayed, Yale. I'm sorry you can't see how much she loved us instead! She loved us enough to keep this secret, so we could have each other, Yale! She was afraid to share her discovery. And rightfully so! Look what's happened in just a month. You've lost all perspective, Yale. And I've lost you!"

He stormed away.

She sat, calming herself. Her parents sat with her. None of them spoke. There was no need.

A new hand had been dealt. Lisa had put her cards on the table.

She had to wait. She had to wait to find out if she had a winning hand.

Yale already had a pair of aces—Josh and himself.

Would a "full house" win? Or "three of a kind"?

She wasn't going to "fold". She, once, had a royal straight flush. She was going to play the hand out. But were the odds in her favor?

Only The Dealer knew.

CHAPTER 46

Since Josh was under thirteen years of age, he was not obligated to observe the Jewish laws of Torah regarding the mourning period. Lisa felt, however, that Josh might have benefited from the fourth stage of mourning known as sheloshim, the thirty days following burial, when mourners are allowed, even encouraged, to resume their place in society. Instead of the gradual process of returning to some normality, Josh's grief was still in a vacuum because of Yale's protectiveness. She was afraid for Josh.

After storming away from her earlier, Yale kept himself distanced from Lisa. He was gazing at a portion of the grounds from an upper level study, while Josh was completing his tutoring for the day, when he spotted Lisa gathering flowers in a basket. It was the first time she'd been outdoors in days. He observed, as she clipped a rose from a branch and brought the delicate flower closer to relish it's fragrance. She had lost weight, and the jeans she wore were sliding from her waist. He felt passion in his loins as he watched her wiggle, tugging the pants up to wear they belonged.

His desire for her was mounting as he observed the delicacy with which she handled each flower. She seemed to caress every blossom individually. When the basket was overflowing with foliage, she sat on the grass and concentrated on the clear sky. Yale felt a throbbing behind his zipper gazing at Lisa's refined beauty. She was sculpturesque. Her well-shaped breasts were pushing against a cotton jersey. She was so pleasing to the eye. He rubbed his hand over his crotch as his urge intensified. The pressure felt good but only added to his already stimulated state. He turned from the window, nervously, at the sound of the approaching voice.

"There you are, Uncle Yale. I'm done. Miss Nelson says she wants to talk to you for a minute. I don't like her. She keeps telling me I'm not paying attention. I want a new teacher."

"Go downstairs, Josh. Belle will have your snack ready. I'll be down shortly."

Yale called Margaret Nelson into the study and closed the door. The lanky, middle-aged tutor declined to sit down. "I'll be brief, Mr. Frye. I'm already behind schedule. Josh is very bright. His school records indicate as much. But he is lost in an abyss. He isn't able to concentrate or retain the material we cover from one day to the next. When I asked him to pay attention to a problem in division we were going over today, he snapped, and asked me not to tell him what to do. I attempted to reassure him, and explain the problem again, but he became belligerent and claimed math was dumb. When I said it wasn't dumb, he snapped at me again, saying I was dumb, too. I told him, I wouldn't allow him to speak to me in such a manner. He yelled, that I wasn't his mother, and he didn't have to listen to me. I think we have a problem we're going to have to iron out. Any recommendations, Mr. Frye?"

"Yes, Miss Nelson. Give him time. That's my recommendation. Josh is going through a difficult transition. He needs time to adjust. Don't magnify his insolence. It will pass."

"I'm not magnifying anything, Mr. Frye. And I don't think—it will pass—as you put it, without confrontation."

"I'll take care of it, Miss Nelson. Anything else?"

"Yes, Mr. Frye. One more thing. If the disrespect, and lack of attention persists, I will recommend you seek another teacher for Josh. I have too many students who want an education, and give me due respect, as well as the support of their parents when I indicate we need to address a specific situation, to waste time in homes where my authority is not supported."

"Good afternoon, Miss Nelson. I'll have a talk with Josh. Perhaps, he's having a bad day, and he's not up to par."

"I don't think that's it, Mr. Frye, but I'll let you be the judge. Please advise Josh that I expect a note of apology in the morning. Good afternoon, Mr. Frye."

He watched the skinny legs, beneath the blue plaid skirt, walk out of the room. He was pissed that a tutor thought she knew so much. Josh was suffering. He just needed love, patience, and time. "Dumb bitch," he muttered to himself as he went to join Josh.

Lisa was arranging the flowers she had gathered, while Josh was having a tantrum, when Yale entered the kitchen.

"I said, I don't want peanut butter cookies, Aunt Lisa! I want the chocolate swirl ones!" He threw the cookies on the floor. "I hate these cookies!"

"Lisa, calmly declared, "Get the broom, Josh, and clean up the mess you've created. I told you, these are the cookies you're getting today. We're out of the chocolate swirls, and you've been eating too much chocolate lately, anyway."

"No. I won't! Tell Belle to clean it up. It's her job!"

"Oh, no it's not, Josh! Belle has enough to do without cleaning up after you! You threw the cookies on the floor, and you'll clean up the mess you've made! Now!"

Josh's eyes filled and he stomped his feet. Yale intervened. "It's okay, Josh. I'll clean it up myself. Go into the library, and I'll fix you a fresh snack—"

"No, you won't, Yale! I asked Josh to clean up after himself. I expect you to support—"

"Stop it, Lisa. He's just a kid. Come on—"

"Sorry, Yale. This is between me and Josh. Belle will not clean up this mess. And neither will you! I expect Josh to do it, as I've asked. And there will be no other snacks today. I don't reward fits of anger. Now, Josh, get the broom, or I'll find another punishment for you!"

Yale stared at her as defiantly as Josh had. Finally, he concurred. "Go on, Josh. Get the broom. When you've cleaned up your mess, I'll take you for a ride. We both could use some air."

Lisa watched Josh sweep up his mess, and replace the broom in the closet. "Are you happy, now, Aunt Lisa? Come on, Uncle Yale. Let's go for that ride," he added triumphantly afterwards.

"Get a jacket, Josh. It's cooling off."

"I don't know what you think you're doing, Yale, but if you're not going to back me up, when I discipline Josh, we're going to have major problems."

"Give it a rest, Lisa. Okay?"

"No..." was all she managed to reply before Josh returned with a jacket.

"I'm ready, Uncle Yale. Where are we going?"

Lisa opened her purse and removed a set of keys to Marissa's place. "Here" she said, tossing the keys at Yale, "These are the keys to Josh's other house. As long as you're both going out, why don't you two get some of Josh's sweaters and things. I'm not going in that direction. I'm taking these flowers to Marissa's grave. See you later."

She walked past them.

Belle turned her attention to finishing the salad she was previously preparing, as Yale and Josh walked to the front doors. When they drove past the kitchen window, Belle mumbled, "Lordy. Lordy. Miss Lisa's got her hands full again. I'm stayin' out of this one."

Yale wasn't prepared for the impact walking into Marissa's house would have on him. Either was Josh. They clasped hands, and went directly to Josh's bedroom. Josh looked around awkwardly. He felt like crying, but didn't.

"Where do you keep your sweaters, Josh?"

"Over here, Uncle Yale," he indicated, opening a drawer of the mahogany double dresser, which had Ninja Turtle and Batman paraphernalia scattered on top of it.

"Okay. Well, why don't you pick out which sweaters you want to take with you, Josh."?

He looked up at Yale with sadness. "Can't I take them all, Uncle Yale?"

"Sure. Sure. You're right, Josh. A person never has enough sweaters. What else would you like to take along, Josh?"

The child scanned the top of the dresser, then looked at Yale for help.

"Well, maybe we should get some boxes, Josh. There's lots of neat stuff in here. We can take it all. Okay?"

He nodded agreeably.

"Do you know if there are any empty cartons anywhere, Josh?"

"I think Mom had some in her bedroom closet, Uncle Yale. The ones she always saved for the stuff she gave away to charity."

"Okay. You put everything you want to take on the bed, while I go look. Alright?"

Yale walked down the corridor he'd walked through so many times in the past, but for the first time was aware of all the portraits lining the hallway walls. There were shots of Josh since birth. His first steps. His first birthday. His first dog. His second birthday. His first day of school. The first drawing he signed by himself.

He felt a dull ache, having to accept all that he'd missed out on as a father, and never could recapture. He didn't realize how long he had been looking at the photographs, until Josh approached him.

"What are you doing, Uncle Yale? You didn't even get the cartons yet."

"Sorry, Josh. I was looking at the pictures."

"Why? You got the same ones, don't you? And you took a bunch of these yourself. Remember? Like this one, Uncle Yale, when I started school. I remember, Uncle Yale. I didn't want to go. You came over 'cause Mom was crying that it was my first day of school. She got all mushy, and stuff, and you kept her company 'til I got home. You took that picture, too, Uncle Yale, didn't you? Dad was out of town, or something."

"Yes. You have a good memory, Josh. I took this one of you when you first got Shotsy too, didn't I—and this one at your third birthday party, when you were afraid of the clown your Mom hired to do magic tricks for everyone."

"Yup. And this one, too, Uncle Yale, when I got Buster."

"Want to take the pictures with, Josh? We could hang them in your new bedroom if you want to."

"Can we take the ones on Mom's dresser too? Those are even specialer. They have you, and Aunt Ruth, and Aunt Lisa, and Mom on them. Come on, Uncle Yale. I'll show you."

Yale's dull ache became a sharp pain when he and Josh walked into Marissa's bedroom. Across the bed was the bridal gown Marissa was married in, and the crown of rosebuds, which had adorned her hair.

Only now, the rosebuds were brown from aging. Next to the bed were several pairs of shoes, which Marissa always had the tendency to leave lying around. Yale was so shaken by the sight of Marissa's belongings that he didn't notice the suffering on Josh's face immediately. It was only when Josh picked up the dry rosebud laureate and watched some brittle petals fall, and lie withered on the carpeting, that he saw the glassy, vacant look, in the boys eyes.

"Do you want to go, Josh? We can do this another time."

He extended the stale crown to Yale. "Mom had this on her head, Uncle Yale." His face had paled. "Look, Uncle Yale. It got dead, too. Mom liked it. She liked it a lot. It made her head look extra nice. She said so, when I asked how come she was wearing it." Yale took the dried crown and placed it back on the bed.

"Come on, Josh. Let's go home—"

"I don't want to, Uncle Yale! I want this home! I like this home! It has all my stuff—and Moms!"

"We can take everything you want to your new home, Josh."

"Except Mom, right?" He didn't wait for an answer, but ran from the room, down the stairs, and out into the backyard. Yale ran after him, but didn't stop Josh. He watched the child go to the floral garden and gather a handful of flowers. He returned to Yale with pleading eyes. "Can we take Mom these flowers, Uncle Yale? Those ones she had on her hair are dead. I want to bring Mom good ones, like Aunt Lisa."

"Sure, Josh. Your Mom would like that."

"I know. Will you help me get some more, Uncle Yale? I want to bring her lots of them."

Lisa was sitting next to the burial site, talking to Marissa, when Josh and Yale approached. Josh was carrying an armful of flowers. He started placing them across the plot. Lisa felt the hurt Josh was experiencing and couldn't handle.

"You know, Josh, the flowers you brought your Mom are much better than mine. Most of your flowers have their roots. If we plant them, like Mom did in back of your house, they'll probably grow and multiply. It could make Mom's spot look really pretty. I think she would like that. Do you think we could plant them together? Then we can come back in a few days to see how it looks, and see if we need to plant any more."

"I don't know how to do it, Aunt Lisa."

"Can I show you? Then you can do the rest by yourself, if you want to."

"Okay."

When all the flowers were embedded in the soil, Josh sat down beside Lisa and Yale.

"Well, Marissa, we've decorated your special spot. Josh did most of it by himself. He did a great job, Marissa. It took a long time. We'll be going home soon, Marissa. It's almost dinnertime. I miss you, Marissa. I miss you, so much, that sometimes I'm still angry that you're not here to talk back to me. You know what's the hardest part for me, Marissa. I didn't get to say goodbye to you, and I didn't get to show you my wedding ring. You always knew I would marry Yale, Marissa. Well, I did. And, now, Yale and I are going to take care of Josh for you. You'll always be his Mom, Marissa, but I'll try to give him a lot of love for you and, of course, my own love too. I'm going to miss you, forever, Marissa. No one will ever take your place in my heart." Tears cascaded down Lisa's cheeks.

"Lisa, why are you talking to Mom? She can't hear you all the way from heaven."

She took Josh's hand. "Maybe, I just want to believe she can, Josh. Anyway, I feel better telling your Mom what I feel inside, Josh. It helps me, and makes me feel close to her. Is there anything you feel like saying to Mom, Josh?"

She moved closer to Josh, still holding his hand, understanding how difficult this was for him. His lips were quivering and his eyes were filling.

"Before we go, Marissa, I think Josh has something he'd like to say. I hope it's real quiet and peaceful in heaven, Marissa, and you're listening. What do you want to tell Mom, Josh? It's okay, honey. Let it out."

"I—I wanna tell Mom, I didn't mean it—when I—said—I hated her."

She urged him on, keeping a firm grip on his little hand. "Tell her, Josh. Tell Mom."

"Mom, I'm sorry," he unburdened. "Mom, I never hated you. I just was mad, 'cause you went away. Mom, I want to be in my old house. I want all my stuff. But, I don't like it there without you. I—I know it was an accident, Mom, and you didn't want to go to heaven yet, but I miss you all the time. Maybe, if you didn't go with Howard, you still would be here with me. I wish I could see you, for one more minute, Mom. I forgot to hug you, before you went to Monte Carlo. I hope you're not mad at me, or nothin, 'cause I love you, Mom."

Lisa wrapped her arms around the young child, and held Josh as he purged the grief from his heart. She encouraged him to unburden his sorrow, while bundled in her arms.

Yale displayed his own bruised heart, but appeared lost in thought.

When Josh, eventually, calmed and his modulation ended, Lisa, sensitively, inquired if he was ready to say goodbye to Mom and leave.

When he didn't respond, and remained in her hold, she made no attempt to move, accommodating his need to remain a bit longer. "You know what your Mom told me the day before she went to heaven. She told me, that she loved you more than she loved anybody in the whole world. Mom said, Josh has a mind of his own, and sometimes I have to remind him to do something more than once, but he is the best son a mother could wish for. He has a wonderful, warm personality, and a great sense of humor. Josh loves to trick me, your Mom said. He's always playing jokes on me. And he is a good person to go places with. Josh is fun to be with. She said, you had just decided you wanted to be a soccer player."

He looked up at her surprised. "That's right, Aunt Lisa. I did tell Mom I was going to be a soccer player. She said, I could sign up for soccer lessons, if I wanted to."

"Where at, Josh?"

"My school. I was gonna bring home the paper so I could sign up."

She looked at Yale for a minute.

"You'd need a uniform wouldn't you?"

"The school sells all the stuff. You even get to have your own locker for your stuff to go into. The only thing is, it costs fifty dollars to join a team."

"I've got an extra fifty dollars, Josh," Yale volunteered. "What if we told Miss Nelson not to come to the house anymore, and you went back to your school instead. We could sign you up for the soccer class. Would you like that?"

He sat forward, displaying some enthusiasm for the first time. "Yeh. I could become a real good soccer player and everything. And if you want to, Uncle Yale, you and Aunt Lisa could come and watch the games. I bet I could get good at it. I already run real fast, and you have to be fast for soccer."

"When does the session start, Josh?"

"I don't remember, Uncle Yale. It's on a paper in my old bedroom."

"Do you feel like stopping to pick it up? I'll go with you."

"Will you come too, Aunt Lisa? I got a lot of stuff in my room I wanna ask you if I should bring with me."

"Sure, Josh. Are you ready to go now?"

He stood up and took another look at the grave solemnly.

"Good-bye, Marissa. We have to leave now. We'll come back another time. I still have lots of stuff to tell you. I love you, Marissa."

Josh took Lisa's lead. "Bye, Mom. I'll come back to see if the flowers are growing. If some of them die, don't worry, 'cause I'll plant new ones. I love you, Mom. I wish you didn't have to be in heaven."

As fresh endless tears poured from Josh's soul, Yale's heart constricted. He swept Josh into his arms and kissed his wet face. "Let's go, big guy. We'll come back again whenever you want to. Lisa, do you want to leave your car here, and we'll have it picked up later? I'd like us to stay united."

His words didn't miss. She smiled at him for the first time in weeks.

CHAPTER 47

Lisa grinned when close to midnight Yale entered their bedroom and climbed in bed beside her. "Well, Josh is sound asleep. I'm not sure if it's because he's exhausted from rearranging his room, or because he uncorked his sorrow, but the little guy, actually, admitted he was tired. That was a great idea, Lisa. Having all his bedroom furniture brought over, and creating a familiar room, with all of his own things. It seems to have made a big difference. This is the first night he didn't mind me leaving the room. Maybe, the nightmares will stop too."

"And I'm glad the soccer sessions didn't start yet. That the class still had some openings. It was nice of his teacher to call back and tell Josh, personally, how everyone missed him, and how glad she was he'd be returning to school on Monday."

"Should I go into the school with him on Monday, Lisa? Maybe, he'd feel more comfortable if I did." He didn't wait for a reply. "I think I will."

"Try not to smother him, Yale. He needs room to blossom."

"It's easy for you to say. You've had the privilege of watching your children go through all their various stages. I haven't. My son was denied the opportunity to bond with me. We missed out on a lot."

"Did you? She casually asked, turning on her side, her back to him.

"What's wrong, Lisa? Tired?" He tried to sluff off her last remark, which was more comment than question.

"Yes, I'm very tired, Yale. Tired and troubled. But, this too, shall pass."

"What's that supposed to mean? Talk to me, Lisa, if there's something you have to say. Don't turn your back on me, for God's sake! I'm not a mind reader. What's bugging you—that I have a son? That I want to connect with a child that's mine? That's pretty selfish, isn't it? How would you feel?"

"Does it matter how I feel, Yale?" She stayed, with her back to him. "It hasn't mattered, to you, for weeks. Sorry…I forgot. You're the only one allowed to agonize. Got to sleep, Yale. I don't feel like talking anymore. I'm sick of everything."

"That's nice. Thanks, Lisa, for being so understanding! I come to bed hoping to share my feelings with you—hoping we could hold each other—and you turn away! And you're acting like the injured party—I don't get it! I really don't!"

"I'm not surprised, Yale. Good night."

He sat up and turned on the lights. "No. Not good night! Let's have it, Lisa. I want to know what, the hell, your problem is? Why can't you understand how I feel? I'm a person, Lisa. Haven't I been through enough? I feel cheated! I feel denied!"

She still didn't turn over. "That's the problem, Yale. I feel all the same things, just for different reasons. Think about it. Just for one second, Yale, put my feeling out there too. "I"—"I"—"I"—that's all I've heard. Where's the—"you"? Where's the "We"? Please, Yale. Turn off the lights. I'm tired."

The need to seek refuge from hurting took Lisa into slumber almost immediately after Yale turned off the lights. She was drained. Her escape from pain was to hide in darkness, where she could avoid dealing with issues not easily resolved.

Yale, on the other hand, could not sleep, or even find a comfortable position in bed. After an hour of tossing, he checked on Josh, and opened a book on the main floor library sofa. He read the first chapter, without the vaguest idea what the twenty pages consisted of. His mind was too absorbed with other thoughts. He was considering ways to tell Josh that he was his real father when Harry walked in, wearing a robe; carrying a folded newspaper.

"So, I'm not the only one up, in the middle of the night, eh? What's your excuse, Yale? Mine is; I'm an old man. And I probably took too long of a nap in the recliner during the day."

"Mine is a head full of thoughts I can't dispel, which I just keep going over, Harry."

"So, talk, Yale. If you speak of the thoughts dancing around in your head, perhaps clarity will follow, so you can stop moving in circles."

"I'm thinking about Josh. My relationship to him. What to tell him, Harry. How to tell him. What this means to me. How it will affect him. How it will effect Lisa. A whole lot of garbage, Harry."

"You were doing okay until the last few words, Yale. We both know it's not garbage. It's important issues, which can change your life, the child's life, and Lisa's life—forever. Have you spoken with your wife, Yale?"

The set jaw, and sudden pulsation on Yale's temple, gave Harry his answer. "I see," he stated, going on. "What is it which plagues you most, Yale? Having to make the disclosure to Josh, or fear of the unknown consequences which may develop as a result?"

"I think Josh would be happy, Harry. We've been like family since he was born. I've been there for all the special occasions. For holidays, birthdays, trips. He's been as close to me as he would have, had he known from birth what my claim is. I've been more of a father to Josh than Tony ever was, Harry."

"So, if I understand correctly, Yale, you will not benefit from the explanation, as far as the closeness you and Josh share, correct?"

"That's not the point, Harry. He's family—my family. A person to carry on, after I'm gone. A link to the future. A part of me. I've already missed out on enough."

"I'm a little confused, Yale. Would you ask Josh to change his name?"

"No. That might cause too much confusion for him to deal with at such a young age."

"Okay, Yale. What about this link to the future—or the past. Regardless. Pick one. Either, Yale. Will Josh's knowledge alter what will be; or what was?"

"Maybe, Harry. Not the past, so much. But it may have an impact on the future."

"I'm still confused, Yale. As a child, you already won Josh's love, respect, and trust. Correct? You were a big part of his past. Correct?"

"Yes."

"Then, I ask myself what have you missed out on, and who will benefit from this disclosure? The answer is simple, isn't it, Yale? I cannot help you, I'm afraid. You see, as one man to another, my pride from the knowledge that I created a life would probably make me want to shout it from rooftops. I might be so full of joy—that I had a son—that I wouldn't care what it did to others, or how anyone else felt."

"Then, you understand, Harry, don't you?"

Harry paused. "Yes, son, I understand. I'm also starting to get tired. I hope, Yale, you didn't object to my calling you son, just now. We are not bound by blood. You are not my child. Yet, you are like a son. Funny, isn't it, the weight and significance we sometimes place on words."

He kissed the top of Yale's head. "Goodnight, Yale. I prefer actions, to words, myself. A word can be scratched out. Covered. Erased. An action is not so easily transfigured. It takes discipline to conclude what actions to take in situations which effect more than ourselves."

Thoughts nagged at Yale the remainder of the night. When everyone else was coming to the table for breakfast, Yale was going to bed. To sleep.

Resolutely, Lisa pretended everything was fine all morning. She explained, "Uncle Yale is just tired," to Josh, and ignored her mothers' implication, that perhaps a weekend alone would do wonders for the newlyweds.

Marc and Steve called before noon, West Coast time, and put sunshine into Lisa's morning. "Terrific. I'm glad you both can get away. I'll see you later, then. Yes, Josh is here. Hold on."

"Josh, hi. It's Steve. Marc and I are coming out for the weekend. Are you going to have some free time to spend with us?"

"Sure. Why? What do you want to do?"

"We love the ocean. I thought we could go "beach it" tomorrow. Maybe, do some surfing. We heard the weather's supposed to be good. How about it?"

"Yeh. I love the beach too! Could you show me how to sail, maybe? Mom was gonna take me sailing with her and Howard when they got back from Monte Carlo. Howard said, he had a sailboat called "Nifty".

Mom used to go sailing a long time ago. But now they're in heaven, so I don't got no one to show me what to do. I don't think Uncle Yale goes sailing. He said, once, his music keeps him too busy for doing other stuff."

"Sure, Josh. We sail whenever we can. Marc and I used to hoist sails off the island Mom and Frank lived on, when Frank was alive. Frank taught us a lot. Mom was never interested. She liked sunbathing, or just floating on a raft. She always said sailing was too much work."

Josh laughed. "I bet, Aunt Lisa would like it if we did all the work. Right?"

He laughed again, to whatever it was Steve said on the other end.

"Well, we'll see you tonight, Josh. We're very sorry about what happened to your Mom and Howard. If you ever feel like talking about how you're feeling, Marc and I are here for you. Okay?"

"Okay. But I don't gotta talk about it. I planted flowers on Mom's spot, and already talked to Mom about missing her. Uncle Yale took me to the cemetery yesterday. Aunt Lisa was already there. I think she goes to talk to Mom a lot. Mom was her best friend, you know. Aunt Lisa misses Mom, just like me, and she said I can go to Mom's spot whenever I want to. Aunt Lisa cries about Mom going to heaven more than me. More than anybody, even. Maybe, she would need to talk to you about Mom. She's lonely for Mom. I can tell."

There was a short hesitation and Josh said, goodbye. He replaced the receiver and approached Lisa, hugging and kissing her. "That's from Marc and Steve. They said to do it, and tell you they love you."

"Thanks, Josh. Do you have one of your own hugs and kisses for me too?"

He obliged, asking afterwards, "Did I bring my bathing suit here?"

"Go check. If not, we'll have to go get you one."

Josh returned wearing a bathing suit, he'd outgrown. "It's tight, Aunt Lisa. And the other one is lost. I looked in all the drawers."

"Well, get your jeans on and we'll go shopping. You could use some new things for school, too. You said, you needed sweats for the soccer practices, didn't you?"

"Right. Should I tell Uncle Yale to wake up?"

"No. Let him sleep. We'll show him our purchases when we return. And do your laces up, please, before you come back down, not afterwards. I don't need you tripping on the stairs."

Yale found himself alone in the house when he woke. He was close to hysteria when Belle came in, carrying bags from the supermarket. "Where, the hell is everyone? Nice of somebody to leave me a note!"

"I'm sorry, Yale. I thought I'd be back before you got up. The lines in the store were—"

"Never mind that, Belle! Where's everybody?"

"Miss Lisa took Josh shopping for some clothes. Rose and Harry went to the Jewish Community Center. They're seeing a play about Stalin's rise to power. I had to pick up some extra—"

"When did Lisa and Josh leave? Why didn't they wake me?"

"They left about one, sir. And I don't know why they didn't wake you, sir. Anything else?"

"No. Not a fucking thing!" He stormed away, returning to the bedroom and slamming the door shut.

He was seething by the time he saw the car slowly approach the front doors from an upstairs window. It was after five, and he hadn't even had a cup of coffee yet. Like a raging bull, he antagonistically bombarded into the den. "What, the hell, is wrong with you, Lisa?" He launched. "Where is your head? I went nuts when I came down and the place was empty! Where's some consideration for me? I can't believe you!" He didn't stop shelling her with his rabidity. "Couldn't you wake me? Couldn't you ask me if I wanted to go? Couldn't you even leave a damn note, so at least I'd know where the hell everyone was?" His ranting was endless.

Rose and Harry entered in the middle of Yale's tirade and only caught part of the uproar. They stood in the doorway stupefied, refraining from making any overtures to quiet Yale, until Josh ran to them overwrought and flinching nervously.

"Enough!" Harry shouted over Yale's guttural howling. "Yale! Enough!"

Yale turned from Lisa, toward the gruff voice, and was about to break loose with force on Harry, when he saw the look on Josh's face, as the boy gazed at him open mouthed, while clinging to Harry. He shut up.

"Come, Josh. Let's get a snack while Uncle Yale calms down. Rose, how about some coffee?"

Josh slackened his hold on Harry, now that his Uncle Yale had stopped yelling. He took Harry's hand and gawked at Yale with scowling eyes. "Why are you being so mean to Aunt Lisa, Uncle Yale? She didn't do nothing. She even bought you a new bathing suit, too, when we were shopping. She didn't wake you 'cause you needed the rest, Uncle Yale."

"I'm sorry. I'm sorry, Josh," he sputtered. "I didn't mean to upset you." There was a heaviness in his chest. His lungs felt as though they might explode.

"You should tell Aunt Lisa you're sorry, too, Uncle Yale. You talked bad to her. You made her smile go away."

He looked at his wife. "Forgive me, Lisa. I shouldn't have—"

"Forget it, Yale," she interrupted. "Go on, Josh. Have your snack. We'll be having dinner later than usual, since Marc and Steve are coming out."

"When did this come about? No one told me—"

"Sorry. You were sleeping when the boys called, Yale. Belle must have forgotten to mention it."

He looked from Lisa to Belle, before meekly admitting, "I think Belle tried to tell me. I guess, I wasn't very receptive to her conversation earlier. Sorry, Belle. Excuse me, please. I—uh—think, I should go outside, for a few minutes and cool off. I seem to have gotten up on the wrong side of the bed, or something."

He sat on the deck petulantly while everyone else was inside. Eventually, his annoyance turned inward, and he peevishly acknowledged to himself that he was a swine. His actions were that of a pig. His temper tantrum had no justification. And Josh was right. He'd seen the smile on Lisa's face from the upstairs window, and with his tirade, he'd taken that smile away.

Lisa opened the door wall and stepped outside. "Here, Yale. Belle fixed you a sandwich and coffee. She said you haven't had anything to eat all day."

He accepted the plate from her with calm reserve. "I seem to have an identity crisis on my hands, Lisa. I don't know who the fuck I am. I don't know where to go from here."

She looked at him angrily. "You have another problem, Yale. One that I can't be complacent about. All I'm still hearing is, "I—I—I—and it's making me sick. Try on someone else's shoes for a while, Yale. Maybe, your identity crisis won't be so all consuming! Now, it's your turn to excuse me, Yale. I don't feel like being in the company of an asshole!"

She avoided being in the same room as Yale until Marc and Steve arrived, and it was unavoidable. She had been dodging his attempt for a reconciliation, by sidestepping around the house for hours.

He felt awkward during dinner, and inferior for his lack of temperance earlier. She was so full of courage; totally audacious. She didn't shirk responsibility for her errors as he did. She didn't circumvent excuses for herself. She was authentic. Genuine. And he felt unworthy.

Yale went to bed early. He wasn't really tired. Just hollow. He did not attempt to manufacture an excuse. "Well, I'll let you guys catch up on all the news. Josh is finally asleep. I'm going to hit the sack, too. See you in the morning."

"We're about ready to call it a night, too, Yale. Anyway, newlyweds don't like to go to bed without each other, do they?"

Steve hit a nerve, but Yale casually parried, "I can make an exception to the circumstances for you two. After all, it's not every day you get to see your mother."

"True. True. And I, sometimes, envy friends who live near their parents and can see them, whenever. Know what I mean?"

Yale swallowed hard. "Yes, I understand the feeling. Well, goodnight guys. Goodnight Harry, Rose."

She undressed in the dark. She knew Yale wasn't asleep yet, but didn't want to talk. She took her time in the bathroom, then climbed beneath the quilt silently. He was the one who couldn't remain mute.

"I guess, it's hard for your boys to be separated from you for such long periods of time, Lisa."

"It's, probably, harder on me, Yale. They have lives. Full lives. Good night."

He didn't turn over. He didn't try to touch her, although he desperately wanted to. And it was hours before he could sleep.

CHAPTER 48

Marc and Steve noticed undercurrents of tension between their mother and Yale the following morning. Breakfast had gone smoothly, but now, when they were debating which beach would accommodate all their needs best, Yale seemed distant and Lisa condescending.

"That's fine, Marc. I'm sure you chose as good a place as any. As long as I have a towel and radio, I can find a spot to suit me."

"Well, Yale, what do you think?"

"Sorry. About what, Marc?"

"The beach—you know—"

"Oh. Actually, I'm not sure about the whole thing. I don't know anything about sailing. Are the two of you knowledgeable enough to take Josh out on the water yourselves?"

"Yale, I wouldn't entrust Josh to Marc and Steve's supervision if I wasn't sure they were capable—"

"I didn't mean to suggest, Lisa, that you would. I'm just—"

"Can we just go, already? Uncle Yale, I'll have the life jacket on; remember? And I'm a great swimmer. Mom always said, "I was like a fish in water.""

"Okay, Josh. But you have to promise me you'll listen to Marc and Steve, at all times. And I don't want you guys going out too far. Just be sure to stay within eyesight. I'll feel better that way."

"Aunt Lisa, will you tell Uncle Yale to stop treating me like such a baby? I'm nine, already. I think he got up in a bad mood again, or something."

"That's enough, Josh. Yale is merely being cautious. It is your first time out. It has nothing to do with being nine, ten, or twenty. Now, all of you, get your gear together, and kiss grandma and grandpa goodbye. They're probably glad we'll be out of the house for a few hours so they can have some quiet."

Harry and Rose didn't comment, but exchanged private looks only the two of them, and their forty-eight years together, would understand.

Belle had packed a picnic basket for them. Even she sighed in relief when they finally left.

Lisa was relaxed near the ocean. She even dozed off for half an hour under the sun's cloak and the soothing sounds of the water teasing the sand. Yale spent the afternoon dashing from spot to spot, acting like a watchtower in motion. By days end, Yale was taut with tension and fatigued.

Since lunch was consumed before they rented the sailboat, everybody was ravenous by the time they got home. Everybody but Yale. As Lisa, Marc, Steve, and Josh emptied bottles of soda, and downed bags of potato chips dipped in peanut butter, Yale sat idly by with a cup of coffee and a stomach ache. He popped an antacid tablet in his mouth under Harry's scrutinization.

"So, Yale, I understand Josh is a natural. Marc and Steve said he did great. A fast learner."

"I did. I loved it, Harry. Uncle Yale was watching the whole time. I had so much fun! I can't wait to do it again!"

Yale popped a second antacid in his mouth.

Harry chuckled, patting Yale on the shoulder.

"Okay; all of you, out of my kitchen," Belle shouted, good-natured. "You've dropped chips on this floor, made a mess on the table, and dragged enough sand in here to fill a litter box. Go on, and shower, while I get the grills going. You won't be able to eat your steaks if you don't put them chips away. Miss Lisa, you are one bad influence here. Get your hand out of the peanut butter jar already."

Like a child, Lisa sat there licking her fingers, one at a time, while Belle stood in front of her with her hands on her hips and feet apart, until Josh burst out laughing.

Josh's laughter was contagious. He was giggling so hard the

infectious sound spread until they all were uproariously caught up in a amiable moment.

"Aunt Lisa, you are so funny. You got peanut butter on your nose. And you got a potato chip stuck to your hair!"

"Yeh. Well, that's nothing, Josh. I got sand in my tush, too!"

"Mom!" Marc yelled, as the laughter mounted, "You are sick!"

"No, but I am getting this yucky feeling!" She wiggled on the chair, until even Belle couldn't help but chortle.

Josh's mirth was bordering on hysterics. Lisa was deriving eminent pleasure watching him beam with happiness. "Okay, Yale. Take the snickering kid and dump him in the shower, will you? He's making fun of me. I'm going to soak in the tub. I think my back got too much sun. It's starting to sting."

She pulled her t-shirt off and tried to look over her shoulder.

"Oy, Lisa, you're all red. Didn't you put on sun screen?"

"I forgot, Ma. I think I fell asleep on my stomach."

Yale looked at her back guiltily. He was so busy guarding the sailboat from the shore; he'd neglected her all afternoon. Now her back was blazing.

"Put cool compresses on it tonight, Lisa. Yale, spray her with the stuff in the medicine cabinet."

"Don't worry, Ma. It'll be fine. Come on; let's get cleaned up fella's. I'm starved. Josh, wash your hair this time. You forgot yesterday."

"I don't like the shampoo, Aunt Lisa. It burns my eyes. I don't got mine. You keep getting the wrong one."

"Belle got you the kind you like yesterday. Belle, is it in Josh's bathroom?"

"Yes, Missy. The monster soap, too."

"Thanks, Belle. No excuses now, buster. Get!"

Yale was subdued during dinner. He watched as Lisa tousled Josh's hair. He observed their exchange of warm smiles. He wouldn't have thought of getting Josh the shampoo he was accustomed to using. Or the monster soap. He wouldn't have thought of giving Josh his vitamins, as Lisa did. He wouldn't have thought of making Josh go change his shoes when he appeared in the ones he'd taken to the beach. He didn't even notice. There was so much he had to learn. And so many things he had to make amends for. Lisa was hurting from the sunburn. He could tell. She was refraining from sitting back against the cushion on the chair. But she was enjoying having Marc and Steve around. She was listening to everybody with real pleasure. She wouldn't do anything to spoil their time together. She knew how to love. Really love.

She looked at Yale and caught him off guard. "Are you alright, Yale? You didn't eat much."

He tried to smile, but his eyes gave him away. "Saving room for desert, Lisa."

She didn't push. "Josh, some vegetables, please, before Belle clears the plates."

"I don't gotta. I don't like 'em."

"You heard, Aunt Lisa, Josh. Some vegetables or forget desert."

"Okay, Uncle Yale. But not all of them. There's too much."

Lisa smiled at him. He understood. It was the first time they were suggesting something for Josh in unity. He wasn't displaying his previous elitist attitude. They were showing support co-jointly. He smiled back at her, as Josh finished the mound of mixed vegetables on his plate.

They were all watching the movie Marc and Steve had bought Josh for a gift, prior to their arrival, when Josh conked out on Yale's lap. Yale picked the little boy up, whispering, "I'm going to tuck him in."

Marc pushed pause on the VCR. While waiting for Yale to return, Marc probed, "Does Yale mind us being here, Mom? I'm getting strange vibes."

They didn't know Yale had turned the intercom on in Josh's room.

"No, Marc. Yale's just going through a bad time."

"He seems to be off somewhere else, all the time, Mom. Like he'd rather be alone. Know what I mean?"

"It's been rough on him, Marc. First, his mother passed away. Then Marissa. Both suddenly and unanticipated. And they were the two people closest to Yale. The ones he loved and trusted most."

"What about you, Mom? It hasn't been a piece of cake for you either. And Yale doesn't seem to be touching you, or hugging you, the way he did the night you got married. Is he off, somewhere else, all the time with you, too?"

"Pretty much, Marc. He's lost a lot of his enthusiasm lately. He stopped reading. He never goes to his office, and cuts phone calls short. He's made no mention of wanting to resume performing. I'm hoping time will rectify things."

"Are you two going to adopt Josh?" Steve interjected. "He has no other family. Right?"

"I don't know, Steve. We're taking it a day at a time."

"He's a neat kid, Mom. I know you love him. You know, gramps, Josh asked us, on the sailboat, if we thought you'd care if he called you and grandma, his grandpa and grandma too. He said, he never had grandparents, and that Mom lets him call her, Aunt Lisa, and now she really is his Aunt Lisa."

"I wouldn't mind at all, Steve. I thought, a few times, of suggesting it. Grandma too. But, I didn't know if it was my place. I don't know how Yale would feel about it."

"What does Yale have to do with it, grandpa? He doesn't own the kid. Anyway, if it means enough to Josh, for him to bring it up, it seems like that's what should matter, doesn't it?"

Lisa exchanged glances with her father. "Yale's very close to Josh, Steve. They've bonded. I think Yale should make the final decisions about Josh's guardianship. He's been closer to Josh than the rest of us. And for much longer. I'll mention Josh's feelings about wanting to call grandma and grandpa, as such. That shouldn't be a problem."

"Well, if you ask me, he's too protective, Mom. He stood by the waters edge the entire time we were on the sailboat. He didn't spend five minutes with you. What did he think, that we'd let Josh drown, or something?"

"I didn't ask you, Steve. So, let's drop it, okay? Yale feels a responsibility for Josh you don't understand. He's never been in a parental role before. He's got a lot of transitions to deal with."

"Well, someone should tell him to give the kid room to breathe. He's going to make a pansy out of him otherwise. At least Ronnie let us fall a few times, so we'd learn how to balance."

"Ronnie? Since when do you refer to your father as Ronnie, Steve?"

"Since he stopped acting like a father, Mom. He doesn't have time for us anymore, so we don't make time for him. He's become narcissistic and self-centered. We hardly ever talk to him or see him."

"Well, in front of me, I'd appreciate it if you referred to him as your father, not Ronnie. He raised the two of you, and he is your father, whether you like it or not!"

"Big deal, Mom. If it'll make you happy, I'll call him, Dad. But Frank was more loving than our "father". Are you happy now? What good is a title if it's meaningless, anyway? It's what you feel for someone, and the love you get in return that counts. Dad doesn't give a damn about anyone but himself. Why do you think Josh wants to call our grandparents, grandma and grandpa? It's not for the title. It's because they show they care. He feels loved by them, like Marc and I do."

Yale sAuntered back into the room, sitting down next to Lisa. "How does your back feel, honey?"

"Hot. Very hot. Did Josh wake up at all?"

"Just for a second. But as soon as Buster and Matey took their positions, he went right back to sleep."

"Good. So, shall we turn the movie back on?"

"Not for us, Lisa. Ma and I are going to the Bingo Night at the Temple in a few minutes. They're raising money tonight for the relocation fund, for all the immigrants coming here who need assistance. I bought ten tickets for a thousand dollars already, so I might as well go and play a few games. Anyone else interested in Bingo?"

Marc and Steve looked at each other, before Marc replied, "Sure, grandpa. We'll go with you and grandma. The night's young. Mom, how about coming too?"

"Lisa, are you up to it?"

"That's alright, Yale. I'll stay here with you. I thought the movie was kind of cute."

"Well, I'd like to go, Lisa. Come on. We can see the movie anytime. I heard there are poker tables, roulette, entertainment, and refreshments. It was advertised on the radio all week. Might be fun."

"What about Josh, Yale?"

"Belle's here. I'm sure she won't mind staying a little later tonight."

"Will you be comfortable with that, Yale?"

"We can leave the number if Belle needs to reach us. What do you say? There won't be media to deal with, or busybodies with a lot of questions."

"You're on, Mr. Frye. Give me ten minutes."

Yale only called Belle once, to verify everything was fine, and the evening was more enjoyable than any of them anticipated. Harry and Rose won enough tokens to redeem them for an electronically controlled metal roadster, for Josh. Yale redeemed his winning tokens for a stuffed animal, which he presented to Lisa with a smile. "You used to love Koala bears, Lisa, if I remember correctly. I hope you still find them cute."

She kissed his cheek, her eyes glistening, "Thank you, Yale. It's precious."

They sought out Marc and Steve, near the end of the night, and found them in the big banquet hall where a local four-piece band had been playing all night. The music was lousy, but everyone seemed to be having a good time, nonetheless. Marc and Steve were standing with a few other young people, watching some of the older generation move around the dance floor slowly.

"If they played something with a little tempo, maybe these 'alte cockers' would move a little more. What's the matter with this band? We're not dead, yet!"

"So, tell them, Pa. Put in a request."

"What for, Lisa? They probably only know four numbers. I think this one's been played half a dozen times already. Right, Rose?"

"Yes, Harry. They were playing it when we first got here, too."

Yale heard another woman comment, after the number ended, "For a hundred dollars a ticket they could have hired better musicians, Charlie. These kids stink!"

Yale excused himself as Lisa, Harry and Rose went in Marc and Steve's direction. He approached the quartet, asked if he could play a number and give them a break. They gratefully accepted, and left the podium. Yale sat down at the piano, removed his sunglasses and cap, and began playing. Within minutes a crowd gathered near the stage, clapping to the familiar folk tune, and swaying to the music.

"Look, Lisa. Yale's at the piano. Come on, Harry. Let's move closer."

"Okay, Rose. Stop pulling on my arm. I'm coming."

Lisa stood back, watching and listening.

"Come on, people, you know the words. Help me out. I'm a little rusty."

Soon the room was filled to capacity, as Yale played number after number of Yiddish arias they all knew. His powerful voice led the mob as the hall resounded with rich melodies and wonderful rhythms. "More, More" the crowd echoed after each number ended.

The melodies reverberated, as Yale was spattered with platitudes and requests.

"Okay. This is the last one. And I dedicate this tune..."To Me You Are so Beautiful"— also known as..."Ba Meir Bis Du Shein"—to my beautiful wife. And I need your help. Don't let me down. Let me hear all of you singing this one. Please! A big finish—"

He finally made his way back to Lisa. He was grinning broadly.

"Not bad, Yale. The voice is still there. A little weak, but there."

"What do you mean, weak, Lisa? I thought, I sounded strong—"

"I've heard you sound better. Let's go." She turned, winking at her father, as she headed for the doors.

Once inside the car, Yale asked again, "Did I really sound weak up there, Lisa?"

"Not really weak. Maybe, just rusty, Yale. Just a tad. Nothing a little practice wouldn't cure. You know, there's plenty of room on the property if you ever decide you want to have a studio built. You know, like the one at your place, only a little larger, perhaps."

"Why would I want anything larger, Lisa? Mine was big enough."

"What if I wanted to dance in there, too, Yale? Would it still be big enough?"

"I'll get the original plans from my office next week. If we're going to do it right, we might as well add a screening room, too. That way we can watch the galleys of "Regrets" at home, when we're ready to go ahead with it."

"Whatever you say, Yale. You know much more about the entertainment industry than I do. I just write—a little."

She was receptive to Yale's advances, once they were in their bedroom, after they checked on Josh together. He held her for a long time afterwards. "You know I was never in love with Marissa, don't you,

Lisa? I never wanted to marry her. We were such dumb kids. We were so full of ourselves. We thought being famous was the ultimate. I swear, I wouldn't have even remembered that night, if the cassette didn't jar my memory. You believe me, don't you?"

"I believe you, Yale."

"Can you forgive me, Lisa?"

"For what? For being human, Yale? For a night many years ago? I don't think there's anything you have to be forgiven for."

He was quiet, unable to go on for minutes. She felt the salt of his emotions cascade on to her shoulder. "Do you know how much I love you, Lisa?"

"Yes."

"But it isn't enough, is it Lisa? I can feel it."

"No, Yale."

"What's missing?"

"The trust."

CHAPTER 49

Josh returned from his first day back at school beaming. His cheery voice couldn't relate all the events of the day fast enough. He spoke with so much animation it was like watching a banner on a windy day. He reminded Lisa of Marissa, when she watched Josh's gestures and his sparkling smile. He was speaking in the same fragmented sentences Marissa used to get trapped in whenever she was excited and frantic to state everything before she forgot the slightest detail.

Yale stood there, shrugging his shoulders. "He's been like this since he got in the car," he finally conveyed to Lisa.

Harry and Rose continued to sit at the kitchen table trying to decipher Josh's rhetoric, with seriousness and total concentration.

Amidst the oratory, Josh halted abruptly. "Time out. I have to go to the bathroom. Stay right here, grandma. You too, gramps. I'll be right back."

He didn't wait for a response as he rushed off, barely making it to the toilet in time.

"So, Rose, what was Josh telling us?"

"I'm not sure, Harry. But I think it was all good."

"Let me clarify it for you," Lisa offered. "Josh told us, all his friends were so glad to see him, the teacher let them have a longer morning recess. Then Josh related that he was sad about his Mom going to heaven, but some good stuff just happened, too. He told his classmates he's living with his Uncle Yale and Aunt Lisa, and that he just got new grandparents, and two older brothers, too. He, then, said, "he's got four friends who signed up for the soccer lessons with him, and they'll be having three practices a week."

He indicated his uniform is the neatest; he needs more sweats, and a friend suggested they practice next weekend. He added, that he broke his lunchbox, and it wasn't his fault, exactly, but he still got to eat his fried chicken for lunch. He needs two wide ruled notebooks, and some t-shirts because his sweater made him itch. He also told his friends, we promised to take him to Disney World for Christmas vacation, and his Uncle Yale was going to make a movie soon."

Yale's mouth hung open in amazement. "I can't believe you got all that, Lisa. Do you and Josh have a secret decoding formula I'm not aware of?"

She giggled. "Not exactly. I raised two boys a while back. They were no different. I guess, some things stick. I've been through this type of disclosure with Marissa, too. She used to speak in half sentences with me whenever she was in a hurry to share thoughts she was worried she might forget. Frenzy runs in the family, I guess. You're prone to doing it too, Yale. Only, you get angry when you can't find the right words."

"I do not."

"Yup. You do, Yale. Then you get defensive."

"I do not."

"See?"

"See what, Aunt Lisa? What are you talking about?"

"Talking about you, Josh. I just said, "see, I knew Josh would be happier in school than being tutored, here, by Miss Nelson."

"You got that right, Aunt Lisa! Can we go to the store after dinner to get the stuff I need?"

"Ask Uncle Yale. Maybe, he'll want to take you this time. He's better at picking out sweats. I was planning on going to the salon with grandma Rose. We wanted to get our hair done."

"Will you take me, Uncle Yale?"

"Sure. Maybe, grandpa will come with us. Belle is off today. Why don't we go for dinner too? Make it a boys night out."

"Good idea. How about it, grandpa? We can go to Eddie's Deli. You like it there, gramps. Right?"

"You have a deal, Josh."

"Well, Ma, looks like we're on our own. Maybe, we can even find a store or two to stop in. I need some jeans."

"You need to stop losing weight, Lisa. It's enough already."

While Josh was trying on apparel in the fitting room of the athletic shop, Yale asked Harry, with candor, "Why are you and Rose going back to Florida next week? Lisa's very upset that you're leaving, you know."

"It's time, Yale. We want to go back to our condo, and spend time with our friends there. It's for the best, anyway. You and Lisa have to go on with your own lives. But it's hard. Make no mistake about it. This is the first time Lisa's cried, as she has, at our leaving from a visit."

"Why do you think she's so reluctant to have you and Rose leave? Do you think Lisa's not adjusting to Marissa's death as well as she makes us believe?"

"No. That's not it, Yale. She's scared. Very afraid. It's why she's losing so much weight, too. Lisa's still on the battlefield, Yale. She's terrified of moving, for fear she'll step on a landmine."

"Who's the enemy, Harry? Is it me?"

"Perhaps the enemy has surrendered, Yale. But the area still holds risks. Perhaps, the fear of the unknown dangerous zones is enough to create as much terror as, face to face, combat with the foe."

"How do I provide the safety Lisa needs, Harry?"

"A treaty would help, Yale. A significant, binding guarantee, which states the conditions of maintaining peace. Why don't you resolve that which stands between safety and the battlefield already, Yale? I'm watching my daughter suffer, Yale. And I'm helpless to do anything about it."

"Josh's mental well-being is at risk, Harry. Let's stop fencing. I have to consider the child's best interests before I do anything, Harry. He's fragile."

"And what about your wife's mental state, Yale? She's dropped twenty pounds since Marissa's death. She's fragile, too. Only, my Lisa never learned how to be selfish enough to demand anything of anyone, even when her own well-being is at stake. She proclaims she's not a martyr when I confront her. But all I see is a sacrificial lamb when I watch her deny her suffering."

"I love her, Harry. Lisa's the most important person in my life. She's all I want, Harry. I've never loved a woman as I love Lisa."

"Those are words, Yale. Beautiful words. But, still, just words. Lisa needs your words backed by actions. Perhaps, then, serenity will follow, and the safety she's yearning for as well."

"Did Lisa ever let you hear the cassette Marissa left before she died, Harry?"

"No. And I don't want to hear it, Yale. Not ever. This is between you and your wife, Yale. You have to deal with the situation the way you see fit. It's not anybody elses business."

The conversation terminated as Josh came out of the dressing room in a blue and yellow jogging outfit. "I like this one, too, Uncle Yale. It's got a lot of pockets for stuff. See?"

"The bottoms look a little baggy, Josh."

"They're supposed to be loose, Uncle Yale. You said the same thing about the other ones. I like 'em like this. Anyhow, I can always roll them up at the top, like Aunt Lisa does with all the pants that got loose on her."

"Okay, Josh. Get dressed. If Aunt Lisa doesn't like the way they look, she can bring you back to exchange them." He sounded irritated.

"I like shopping with her better, anyhow, Uncle Yale. Aunt Lisa always helps me pick out neat stuff. She doesn't just stand around like you do!"

Yale was annoyed with himself for being curt with Josh.

"Not easy parenting a child, Yale, is it? Your fortunate Lisa is willing to share such a big responsibility at her age. Not many women would want to go through raising a child, after they've raised their own already. It's work. A lot of work."

"She loves me enough to want to do it, Harry. I'm not forcing her to do anything she doesn't want to. She adores Josh. She's very maternal."

"I know," Harry responded without elaboration.

Both Yale and Josh were crabby by the time they got back home. Lisa and Rose were already there when the guys came in. Josh tossed his package on the library floor. "That's the dumb clothes I got. It doesn't fit so good, but who cares anyway! And I didn't even get the dumb notebooks, either, 'cause Uncle Yale forgot about 'em, too!"

"Oh shit!" was Yale's greeting, standing there; feeling like an idiot.

"Josh, pick up the bag. Let's see what you bought."

"Alright. But I'm not gonna put them on again. The pants are too big. They're dumb!"

Lisa inspected the outfits in the bag, then glanced at her watch. "Come on, Josh. You too, Yale. We have time to get these exchanged. For one thing, the bottoms are not Josh's size. You bought size twelve-L. L—is for long.

Josh wears a regular twelve. And this navy top is defective. One of the elbow patches is missing on the left sleeve. Wasn't anybody helping you?"

"Yeh, Uncle Yale. I told you to get someone to bring us more stuff. But, no—o—o, you said, we could manage just fine. Now we gotta go back to that dumb store again."

"How was I supposed to know—L—was for long? I thought it stood for length. And who examines every little section. It's not my fault the patch is missing. It's the stores fault. They shouldn't have crap on the racks with defects!"

"Why don't you stay here, Uncle Yale. Mom will take me—I mean, Aunt Lisa," he quickly corrected, feeling awkward about the slip of the tongue.

Lisa instantly noticed Josh's discomfort, and how close to tears he was. "Josh, come here and help me put the stuff back in the bag, will you? We have plenty of time to get the right size, and pick up those notebooks."

Without a word, he shoved a top into the bag. His eyes were aimed at the floor as he tried to act nonchalant.

Lisa wrapped her arms around the uncomfortable child. "You know, Josh, your mom knows, up in heaven, that you will always love her, and that she was your one and only mom. I think Marissa is up in heaven laughing right now, Josh. She's probably saying—"Lisa; Lisa; you talk to Josh just like I would. You're acting like such a Mom that Josh is going to call you Mom sometimes." She's probably giggling, just like we used to do on the bed in her bedroom, and saying, "Josh, I love you. It's okay if you call Aunt Lisa Mom by accident. She loves you as much as I do. I understand. Mom is up there, smiling down from heaven, Josh, and she's not upset. And Mom doesn't want you to be upset either. Okay?"

She lifted the small chin until Josh's wet eyes met hers. "Can I hug you tight for a minute, Josh, while your Mom smiles down at us, because she's glad we're doing better than before, even though we still miss her bunches and bunches?"

He wrapped his little arms around Lisa's neck. She held him close. Yale watched the two of them in awe. Lisa knew just what to say and do. She was more of a parental figure to Josh than he was. And he was the boys' biological father. He was Josh's Dad.

"Okay, Josh, do you want to use the bathroom, and then we'll go?" He let go, nodding affirmatively. "Then grab a jacket, too. It's getting chilly."

When they returned the second time, both Josh and Yale were in better spirits. Josh gleefully showed Harry and Rose his new attire, and then carefully selected which outfit he'd wear to school in the morning.

Yale thought he had tucked Josh in bed for the night, when the youngster ran back into the library. "I forgot to hug you goodnight, Aunt Lisa. You were on the phone with Harvey."

"Thanks, Josh. I love your hugs. They're the bestest."

"I know. Mom always said so, too. Don't forget not to pick me up after school tomorrow. I'm going to Billy's house. Remember? His parents will bring me home before dinner."

"I remember. See you in the morning, Josh. I love you."

"Love you, too. Come on, Buster. You too, Matey. You were supposed to stay in the bedroom. Don't you ever listen? Sometimes, they're so dumb."

They all watched, with amusement, as the hounds followed Josh playfully out of the room, oblivious to his admonishing.

Yale slept little that night, and even less the next. Lisa heard him leave the bed early in the morning, two days before her parents were scheduled to leave. She had ignored Yale's restlessness of the past few nights, hoping whatever was troubling him was something he'd voluntarily share with her, when he was ready. She had wanted to make love with him, upon retiring the previous night, but he was unresponsive to her overtures.

He was sitting alone at the kitchen table when she came in.

"Where's Belle, Yale?"

"I gave her the day off."

"Why? Where are the folks?" Her heart started racing.

"The folks went out for a while—at my request. I need to talk to you alone, Lisa. I've turned the phones off, too."

"Whatever it is, Yale, we can work it out." She was going into a panic. His face was so serious. "Yale, I love you—"

"Lisa, sit down. Please."

She was starting to shake inside. Her pulse rate was escalating. She was scared. There was no one around. Josh was in school. Yale had sent the folks away. Belle was given the day off. Belle had never been given the day off by Yale before. This was heavy-duty stuff. Whatever he was going to tell her was major. She didn't want to hear it. She was terrified. He hadn't wanted to make love last night. Unusual too.

"I know this is absurd, Yale, but I have to go back to bed. I feel so lousy; sort of weak—"

"Please, Lisa. Sit down. I need to talk to you, now. This is very important. This is between you and I. I sent everyone away so we could be alone. Please."

She slowly sank into a chair at the kitchen table. She sat on her hands so Yale wouldn't see them tremble. She braced herself, and waited.

He poured her a cup of coffee, and brought it to her at the table. "You know, Lisa, you are incredible."

She couldn't stand it. Her heart was pounding so hard. "Just say it already, Yale! What is it? What am I going to have to handle now?"

"Nothing, compared to everything you've been through, I hope, Lisa. I have been doing some serious thinking, Lisa. I've hardly been able to sleep.

My mind has been in a quandary. But, I've finally made a decision. I hope you'll agree that it's for the best—"

Tears filled her eyes and ran down her cheeks. "I love you, Yale. Do you know how much I love you?"

He pulled his chair directly in front of hers. He brushed her tears away. "It's because I know how much you love me that I can do this, Lisa."

He sat in front of her and put a hand in his bathrobe pocket. "Lisa, this is the cassette and documents from Marissa's safe. The proof that I am Josh's father."

He opened the plastic container and took the cassette out. He grabbed the magnetic tape and started yanking it out, until it was a mass of ruined audio ribbon lying on the table. He took the documents and shredded them into little pieces, then dumped the confetti next to the mangled cassette ribbon on the table.

She was speechless.

"Lisa, I am Uncle Yale. Not Daddy. I only hope, I'll be as special as Uncle Yale, as you are as Aunt Lisa. Do you understand, honey? I finally comprehend what it's all about, Lisa. And as long as I have your love, and Josh's, I don't care what title I wear. I've been selfish, Lisa. Very selfish. I hope you can forgive me."

"Are you sure about this, Yale? This is—"

"I know what this is, Lisa. This is—my gift to you. This is—saying thank you—for not keeping the secret from me. Because you could have. And I never would have known. This is—you loving me enough to take the risk. This is—this is—Oh God, Lisa. This is me, saying I trust you completely, honey. This is me, telling you, that you are the most important person in my life. This is me, saying, that long after Josh is grown and walks away, I will still want you to share the rest of your life with me. This is what I want to do. This is—for all of us."

She touched his face with an angels hand. "Take me to bed, Yale. Please. I can't believe how lucky I am."

Hours later, Lisa came down the staircase with Yale. They found a note from her father, beside five playing cards. There, on the kitchen table, face up, was, the Ace, King, Queen, Jack, and Ten of hearts. The note read: **DEAREST CHILDREN, I knew my day of joy would come! I came upstairs to tell you Ma and I were taking Josh to dinner. But I heard Lisa singing—"I'M IN LOVE...I'M IN LOVE...I'M IN LOVE... WITH A WONDERFUL GUY"—and decided not to enter. Although her voice still stinks, I pray I will hear the sounds of "singing" outside your doors for all the years to come. SINCERELY—I DO!"**

EPILOGUE

It was Marissa's yarzeit. The Hebrew day, commemorating the yearly anniversary date of her death. The day Lisa chose to believe Marissa's soul was closest to earth. It was a traditional time to visit the grave of a loved one.

Lisa and Josh were planting flowers in front of the simple monument of marble Josh had selected, to mark the place where his mother was at rest. It was hard to believe Marissa had been dead for two years. Yale hadn't been able to accompany them on this visit. He was at home itching, and complaining, about the chicken pox he'd contracted from Josh, who still had a few lingering blemishes himself.

"Well, Mariss', we've got a lot to share." She clutched Josh's hand. "Marc and Steve are moving out here permanently. They've decided California is where they'd like to finish their undergraduate studies. I'm delighted, naturally.

Harvey and Michelle's little boy is adorable. I'm his Godmother, you know. I think, I've mentioned that before. But what I forgot to mention is that little Frank is going to have a sister soon. Guess what name Michelle and Harvey love, and have decided to name the new baby? Yup—Regina. Isn't that a great name? Of course, I suggested it, initially.

My parent's are coming out during Josh's winter break from school, Marissa. We're all going to Josh's first competitive soccer tournament in San Francisco. Your kid is a natural, Marissa. You'd be so proud of Josh, Mariss'. He has your wonderful spirit. He's grown so much. I think he's going to be very tall and slender."

She placed a hand on Josh's shoulder.

"I got a lot to tell you, too, Mom. Besides being a great goalie, and getting all A's in school, I'm now studying for my Bar Mitzvah. Grandpa Harry and Grandma Rose said, "I sing like a cantor". I guess, I got my great voice from you.

Aunt Lisa is writing a book about you, Mom. She's calling it—"More Than Friends". She won't let anybody read what she's written so far.

And my big, big, news, Mom, is that Uncle Yale is legally adopting me. I, sort of, brought it up, when we all went to Disney World, again, this past summer. After all, Lisa's last name is Frye now, and we're like a family, Mom." He paused briefly. "Actually, that's not the whole truth, Mom." He looked at Lisa. "The truth is, we are a real family. And I wanted to legally belong. I think of Uncle Yale as my Dad already. After all, he's been around since I was born. My new name is going to be Joshua Myers-Frye. He cried when I asked him to adopt me. So did Aunt Lisa. They love me a lot. I know you're happy that I have a family, Mom. Aunt Lisa said it would be what you'd want for me. I think so too."

"Oh, one more thing, Mom. My Dad has been nominated for an 'Oscar' for his performance in "Regrets". When I come back, next time, I'll let you know if he won. I don't know why, but I got a feeling he's a winner."

"I miss you, Mom. We all do. I hope you're smiling, up in heaven, at how lucky I am to have Dad and Lisa... Bye, Mom... I love you.

THE END